GUTTERED

Red Guitars in Heaven
Hell's Golfer: A Good Walk Spoiled

GUTTERED

Tom Morton

MAINSTREAM
PUBLISHING

EDINBURGH AND LONDON

First published in Great Britain in 1999 by
MAINSTREAM PUBLISHING COMPANY (EDINBURGH) LTD
7 Albany Street
Edinburgh EH1 3UG

ISBN 1 84018 162 1

A catalogue record for this book is available from the British Library

Subsidised by   THE SCOTTISH ARTS COUNCIL

Typeset in Caslon
Printed and bound in Finland by WSOY

Sometimes I have a sherry before dinner.
Charlie Parker, musician

I only take them when I'm feeling low.
Willie Johnston, footballer

They had been lurking in the grim, shopping-trolley shadows behind the supremely naff Mr Whizz nightclub ('Pride of the Cool North') all that day, sweating in the dank cement heat, occasionally sharing a bottle of Diamond White cider or a can of Tennent's Superlager. Frankie had some Golden Virginia and, in a resealable baggie, what he claimed was Dingwall grass, though Karen was sure he'd simply ripped up a couple of Honeyrose herbal cigarettes to impress them. He'd never had dope before, to her recollection. Tosser. Still, you needed a dickhead around, sometimes, she thought. For reference.

Mostly they talked. Coded chat, all ken this? And aye, right! Little asides and laughs and half-jokes to which everyone already knew the fragmented punchline. They'd all been at school together, a mixture of social classes and interests, intelligences, ambitions. Unified by a deliberate, luxurious, almost sensual indolence.

Karen's dad wanted her to go to university, if her highers were good enough. She doubted that, seeing as she'd skipped out of three of the papers early. She'd only stayed to the end of English so she could watch Mr Heard, the new young teacher, play with himself under the desk when he thought no one was looking.

Karen's ghettoblaster, kept low to avoid attracting the cops, played a tape she'd nicked from Fried Records in the Ferry, a C90 of some live trip-hop night at The Heathery down in Kirkcaldy, DJ'd by The Roadwarrior, whoever he was. Another decrepit hippy trying to hang on to youth, and youths of whatever sex. She giggled to herself. It was the summer, a time of waiting, of not caring. Someone handed her a can of Carlsberg Special. Who was it? Bobby, the busker with the old Fender Stratocaster and battered Pignose battery amp. There was a cracking, foamy hiss as he opened the beer, a heavy smell of impending drunkenness. Hey! Magic Juice!

Bobby, fresh from belting out thrash versions of lumpy, lumbering Britpop songs down on Arminius Street, sometimes joined them in this cleft between the hill which crumbled up towards Arkaig Heights, the middle-class part of town where Karen lived in a glum red sandstone fortress, and the main shopping precinct. He was almost a hippy, but not quite. Neither sufficiently old nor desperate enough. He might have been twenty-two. Or so.

The density of darkness in their refuge increased. No one disturbed them. She wrapped the old army issue parka around her, felt Bobby's arm creep round her shoulders. Maybe later, down at one of the bothies on the banks of the Ness, in the leafy depths of Bught Park, she'd let him . . . or not. It was a matter of indifference to her. She smiled, smelt his rank sweatiness, heard, felt change chink in his jeans pockets.

Zippers, the grimly, determinedly fashionable – in a Marks and Spencer's sort of way – bar beneath Mr Whizz was getting busy, and as the noise increased, underpinned by the thud of commercial techno, bass frequencies amplified by the building, thumping through the brickwork, she switched off *her tape machine, lay back against Bobby's Embrace T-shirt, through which she felt the cooled stickiness of his body. She didn't care. She thought of her mum and dad, now resigned to her absence until, oh, later. Much later. And she smiled, secretively. These days, pleasingly, their worry was constant, suppurating.*

She became conscious of a figure standing watching, outlined in the washed-out sodium light behind the big commercial wheelie bins; silent, alien and apart. Not one of them. An adult. Her father? No, too slight, too . . . certain of itself. Himself. Then Bobby was scrambling up, anxious, hurried, not caring about her back bumping onto rough concrete. And he was talking to the shadowy shape. ducking, jerking, shaking hands. Ob . . . sequious. That was the word Mr Heard had used when . . . She couldn't hear what it was about. She didn't care. Though maybe there was a twinge of disappointment. Bobby had always seemed like a free spirit. Unobsequious; decidedly.

When Bobby came back, he touched her face with the rough guitar-hardened fingertips of his left hand. 'Hey, babe,' he whispered. 'Guess what I got for us.'

She gazed at the glimmering blue-black shapes she could just make out in his right palm; neat, precise, friendly, like him. Eager to please. She felt a warm easy laughter starting down in her gut, bubbling up in expectation.

★ One

'Stop fucking drinking. Just cut it out for keeps or you're going to fucking die. I mean it. You . . . you pathetic *bastard.*' The doctor was using his best bedside manner, as usual. Then again, I wasn't in bed. Neither was he.

My doctor. My drinking buddy general practitioner, Cecil 'Hernia' Holdsworth, a refugee from Doncaster addicted to falling off Highland mountains, an obscure malt whisky called Millburn and collecting old *Beano* annuals. Funny he never married. On the other hand, it was understandable. He was a fucking poof, wasn't he? But, then, most mountaineers are. There they go on their madcap stony way, cuddling great soaring lumps of penile rock. Can't get it up any other way. Get it? Up. Oh, never mind. We got on. Without getting it on, so to speak. We were friends. Hetero-homo pals, and never the twain shall meet, willie-and-arsehole-wise. Buddies. No stool-pushing. Clear? All right, then. That's why he was swearing at me. Or maybe he treated all his patients in the same way: obscenity therapy.

'Let's see . . . stop drinking . . . or die,' I pondered aloud. 'Which is to say, logically, if I do not stop drinking, I will live forever. I mean, that's one way of interpreting your . . . injunction, Hernia, no? Correct me if I'm fuckin' . . . awry. Agleft and agley. Aff rational rhetorical course.' I paused to wipe a smidgin of dribble from my chin. 'You say "Stop drinking . . . or I. Will. Die". But let's face it, every poor bastard dies eventually. We are all going to snuff it one way or a-fucking-nother. I mean, here you are, celibate as a eunuch, or so you say, and presumably HIV tested up to your arse . . . if you see what I mean. But you could go out there into Hangman's Row and get run over by a fleet of continental touring tandems tomorrow. Spoked to death by foreigners. So I mean, what I'm saying you mean, is, logically, that you are offering me the chance to live forever through drink.'

I smirked, pulled out a Grants of Dalvey sporran flask from my jacket pocket and unscrewed the top. '*Uisge beatha*, Hernia. The water of life. Here's health! *Slainte!*' I just about managed to find my mouth with the cool stainless steel spout, and felt the prickly liquid heat of sixteen-year-old Lagavulin, neat, catch at my throat and begin its warming, healing descent into the gut, nipping at the ulcerating ache in my gullet, then dulling it. An overwhelming aroma of peat smoke, seaweed and ancient sherry wood engulfed me, or maybe it was just a memory of an ancient description in some crap whisky guide. Relief. Then, without warning or hope of control, I threw up, horribly, smokily, peatily, seaweedily. All over Hernia's rather nice beechwood desk, his Psion Organiser, sphygmometer and leather-bound drug-company-supplied blotting pad.

Lovely.

A cold sweat licked at my shoulders and forehead. I felt shocked more than nauseous. Conscious of a sudden, surprising itching in my shins. They were already scratched raw. I reached for them automatically, let my fingernails do their digging through the soiled linen of my trousers. Exquisite ease, and then pain. But ain't that always the way, boy? Ain't that always the fucking way? Whatever makes you feel good hurts like buggery, or worse. How sore was buggery, anyway? Hernia ought to know. I was appalled at myself, for a moment. It passed. Hernia looked at me like I was some kind of intestinal parasite discovered during a routine examination of someone's shit. I could tell he was struggling to disguise his disgust. And failing. I lifted the flask to my lips again.

'You've got to do it,' he said, pulling tissues from an oversized box with the message: 'Varixamat – defeat the misery of haemorrhoids'. Lick your piles at a price; that would be a better slogan. 'At least for a while. You're running on fucking empty, man. You're going to be like Jim Baxter, a hero with a liver the size of a fucking football. Or Shane McGowan, a pathetic joke.'

Hernia looked as if he might cry. That feminine side coming out. 'I've got stuff that'll help you, Antabuse, makes you sick and collapse if you drink while you're taking it – not that you need much help for that. And we'll bang you on Librium for the first three days to get you through the worst of the DTs. Seriously, I got your liver enzyme tests back, and it is fucked. It feels like an overripe melon in there.' He gestured in the general direction of my torso. 'What do you want? The *grand mal* seizure? The stroke? The heart failure? How many times have you pissed yourself in the past six months, eh? Hepa-fucking-titis? I've seen it happen at least once. Come on, Zander, I like a dram as much as anyone – more than most. But, man, you've been knocking back – how much a day? A bottle? Two? Ever since you got sacked and set up this daft fucking agency, where all you do is sit around pretending to be something out of a Dashiell Hammett novel. I mean, what is this shite, eh? A bottle of whisky in the drawer, a fucking Indiana Jones hat on a wooden stand? Why don't you just wear spats and have done with it? Good for keeping the sick off your socks.'

I'd never seen Hernia this angry. Okay, maybe he wasn't addicted to Millburn. Maybe the bastard had been sneakily putting on that pissed act. Now that I thought about it, I only saw him once a week. God, perhaps he was sober the rest of the time. What a thought. Christ, the way he was reacting, though, you'd have thought all my drinking was self-inflicted or something. Half my drinks I didn't even pour myself.

'Not a bottle,' I said. 'Nothing like. Blackouts? Can't remember.' I waited for the laugh, but it didn't come. 'Maybe a couple of pints at lunchtime, three or four drams at night, couple of nips during the day. This . . .' I shook my head, which was a bad idea. The room followed each movement after a delay of about a heartbeat. A slow swirl began at the edges of my vision. 'This is just . . . och, I met McGrooch in the Albatross this morn . . . just at lunchtime, and we had a few, catching up . . . you know how these things happen . . . Sludge was doing his usual glowering redneck curmudgeon act, and then the White Settler came in . . . I was just kind of hanging on for Celia, but she didn't show . . .'

Excuses. You should never start making them. There's no place to stop.

Hernia looked at me wearily. Suddenly I realised how unhealthy he looked, this so-called superfit mountaineer, free climb expert. Emaciated face, shock of dull red hair, pitted skin, sunken eyes. But climbers are funny buggers, full of strengths you can't imagine, capacities you would never credit them with. Even gay climbers. And as I said, you virtually have to be an arse bandit to take up the sport. All those fucking crampons and clips and chains and harnesses. I mean, do me a favour. S&M or what? Admittedly, Hernia wasn't into all that technical gubbins, and he was a strong bastard. He could handle his drink. Well, better than me, anyway. Obviously. Which was why taking this stuff from him was hard. I mean, he was as much of a drinker as I was. Wasn't he? Just showed it less. A pro. I passed my hand in front of my mouth, caught the rank whiff of my own breath, and was nearly sick again. Fuck me, I'd have to get something to eat. A black-pudding supper to soak up the ethanol, anchor me down, gut-wise. That's what was wrong with me. I was just hungry.

Hernia had wiped up most of the puke, and was waving his Psion about as if wondering whether he should run it under the tap or chuck it in the bin marked 'medical waste'. He gazed at me with a kind of angry sadness. 'Look, Zander. Not only are you not as young as you used to . . . aw, fuck. Forget it.' He turned away, shaking his head and the little digital organiser in a kind of reggae rhythm. I felt awkward now, sad that I had wasted his time, messed up his surgery. I knew it was just lack of food. Everything would be okay once I got some chips down me.

'I'm sorry, Hernia,' I began, swaying earnestly to my feet. 'The fact is . . .'

'The fact is, none of us can sustain that industrial drinking we used to do.' Clipped. His voice was definitely clipped. Almost medical in tone.

'Besides, we used to be able to climb it off, or run it off, or whatever. Not that you ever did much of that. Anyway, what happened to you . . . I know it was a dick-ripper, a real fucking hetero nightmare. But you're just living out some kind of pisshead fantasy. All the redundancy spent, a few poxy jobs, most of them blown out because you were drunk or hungover, and more and more maintenance boozing just to keep you doing whatever it is you think you are doing.' He was shouting now. I wondered what the receptionist was thinking. '*Fuck's sake!* You're sick on my fucking *desk!* You *bastard!* And you smell, too. How long have you had that shirt on? It's reeking, boy.'

I flinched slightly, catching an underarm scent which proved the inadequacy of modern deodorants. Christ, you'd think they'd last more than just a day or two. Then, mustering as much dignity as a man who has flecks of his own vomit on his chin can, I moved backwards with what I considered admirable steadiness. 'I think our consultation is at a . . . finish. An end,' I said, carefully. '*Fin.* And I would remind you of the great example set by Bukowski, Charles, American author and *mal viveur*, who defied medical advice and drank and smoked and shagged and stank his fucking heterosexual way to an unrespectable old age, producing marvellous . . . truly marvellous . . . creative work on the way.' I may have slurred the French bit, but they deserve slurring, the French. Them and their language. Fuck them and their Citroens. The 2CV. I ask you. Call that a car? Call that a country?

Hernia, who was remarkably well read for a doctor, too sussed to suggest stupidities to me like Alcoholics Anonymous, with its religious bullshit and its weak-willed wankers, shook his head sadly. 'Bukowski wrote one good book fourteen times, and each repeat of *Post Office* he did, the old drouth just grew sadder and stupider. People who take refuge in Bukowski's example are, without exception, dickheads.'

'But the French gave him the Légion d'honneur . . .' Oops, a slip-up and no mistake. Quoting *les francophonies* in Charlie's defence? Tactical error, *mon frère*.

Hernia looked at me as if I were a particularly dim child. 'Exactly,' he said.

Outside the surgery, in the brassy northern glare of a summer afternoon in Inverness, Queen of the Highland Fleshpots, capital of the tartanised north, I had that momentary daytime drinker's epiphany, that sudden surge of insight and knowledge only the frequent pre-twilight *habitués* of dim and smoky public houses achieve. My eyes ached with the vibrancy around me. The sky throbbed like neon. Everything seemed bigger, more brashly colourful. The teeming tourists in Hangman's Row, the spine-bowed backpackers and identikit families from Germany, Australia, even

France, so grossly insulted by Hernia. And internally by me. Had I said that stuff about 2CVs out loud, or just thought it? I couldn't remember. But it didn't matter. I knew the secret, I had the magic potion which made the bastarding backpackers of Inverness, Inversneckie, as the unlucky inhabitants called it, or Sneck, almost bearable. The Sneck-gawpers passed, pilgrims bound to their rucksack burdens, seeking salvation through scenery. But I could handle them, render them watchable, could even make them vanish. I shut my eyes. They became crayon ghosts on black paper, then disappeared. I opened my eyes again, and the faces, the clothes had changed, although the shapes remained the same. Large and lumpy, thin and delicate. *Genus Touristicus* in full, hideous flower.

I lurched up the hill from Hernia's surgery entrance, crossed the road before reaching what had once been the site of Inverness's gallows, and was now a youth hostel, and climbed laboriously up to the little park surrounding the statue of Flora Macdonald and her unhistorical dog, who definitely had nothing to do with Bonnie fucking Prince Charlie's escape to venereal disease and liver failure. Some liver, the prince: pretty much like Jim Baxter, Scotland's greatest footballer, the man with the football liver, pumped up with booze until one day, like Peter Percival Patterson's Pet Pig Porky, it popped. Hey, maybe I could retrace his steps! Not Jim's into teetotalism and a boring mineral water life. Charlie's! The Neverking!

I slumped down on the statue's base, and gazed west down the River Ness to the silver shimmer that was Loch Ness, the great Scotland-wide fault called the Glen of Perdition receding before me, a country-wide ravine edged with glowering hills purple in the pre-sunset haze. *Purple Haze is in my fucking mind doo-doo-doo* . . . I reached for the whisky flask, unscrewed the top, and dropped it. What the fuck. I drank, once, twice, until, surprisingly, the flask was empty. This time, the *uisge beatha* stayed down. Water of fucking life, ya bass! Top o' the world, Ma! Funny. I wasn't hungry any more.

I woke up, oh, maybe seconds later, and it was dark. Jesus, I thought, I've had a stroke. What had I been drinking? Meths? No, I'd never plumbed those particular depths. Didn't like the colour. Too much like lager and blackcurrant. Well, not so's I could remember, anyway. No purple lips for old Zander. I looked around wildly, but all I could see was a kind of orangey-brown darkness. I could hear a rustling noise, and what sounded like laughter. Then, some form of sentience returning, I realised I had a bag over my head.

It was a brown paper Safeway bag, the kind you get to carry bottles in. Somebody's idea of an apt joke, maybe. It smelt of shopping, domesticity, memory . . . fuck that. So who was the joker, the insightful paragon of aptness? One of the grinning arseholes facing me, almost certainly, a bunch of acne-ridden students from the youth hostel up the road, jabbering away in French. Two girls, I noted blearily, both beautiful, and half a dozen boys reeking of and erupting with hormone overdoses. '*Bonjour, monsieur,*' said one of them. 'Have a good drink, yes?' And he cracked up in a tinkle of Gallic giggles as I crumpled the bag in my hand, threw it to one side. I could hear the heavy rasp of old booze in my voice, feel it in my head, in the increasing gap between my skull and my shrinking brain. I should have risen, dignified, and ignored them, tiddly as they were on tiny bottles of crap supermarket Kronenbourg, presumably the recent contents of the bag which had crowned me with foolishness. I should have ignored the small wet stain at my crotch, or tried to. But suddenly all the shame hit me; a flood of self-disgust, self-knowledge, washed over me, cold, clammy and pungent like tubercular sweat.

'Fuck *you*, you fucking Citroen-lover!' I began. 'You and your bloody Muraroa Atoll, poison the whole Pacific, kill a few Greenpeace workers, *bastard!* Crap cars, crap . . . pneumatic suspension is fucking *crap*. Total. Total, that's a French petrol, right? Elf – run the Flotta terminal in Orkney, or used to. Snails in the fucking canteen. I mean, French – what have you ever done? Started wars then fucked off or fucked up or both. I mean, World War One, Maginot Line, useless wasters, just ripped off the ordinary Tommy, black market sex and fags and . . . World War Two, you even occupied part of Berlin, you cowardly creeps. Creep *creep* . . . Radiohead creep, only good song they've played in France. You only got to Berlin because the other Allies let you. I mean, when did the French ever conquer anything, recently, by themselves? *J'a*-fucking-*ccuse* ya bass . . . Peugeots – absolute shit cars, so're Renaults. Invented the fucking Espace, so what? A VW bus with a sloping front window . . . Aye, wine – *shite* on your wine, pal. Chilean wine, any fucking wine is better. Better for you too, Chilean has all those flavonoids. Bio-fucking-flavonoids. Good for you. French farmers, setting fire to British lorries, slaughtering unborn calves, eating horses. And Vietnam – you started Vietnam, incompetent arseholes at Dien Bien Phu, morons, ran away, left a colonial mess for others to . . .'

But they had gone, leaving me swaying in passionate Francophobia at the foot of Flora's statue. There was no applause. Sometimes I think Hernia and I are the only two real French-haters in the Highlands. And all because of, in his case, a bad experience with a Citroen XM, and in mine with some vicious policemen in the Basque country, the French side of the border with Spain, back in the 1970s. I reached for the whisky flask. It was empty. There was a chill in the air, and I could tell by the sky's gradual bruising that the late nightfall of the Highland summer was approaching. The neon brilliance of colour had vanished. Now my eyes hurt, a pulse drumming like an impending stroke in my right temple. Fuck. I must have been asleep, dribbling, half-peeing myself, for four hours. Hell's teeth, it was lucky the court, contained in the crenellated pile of Victorian sandstone Sneckites call a castle, hadn't been sitting. Otherwise some police prick would definitely have been lurking, and maybe have lifted me from my stony, pile-inducing seat – perhaps even have woken me up. I was an affront to touristic Inverness, and some concerned copper should really have removed my carcass. Some uniformed officer of the law must have passed, surely?

But, then, they all knew me, probably felt sorry for what had happened to the fine, shining example of citizenship I had once, quite recently, been. Oh my God yes, I had shone, finely, in a citizen-like way. Not.

Most likely, they hadn't noticed. People slept on the grass, on benches, on bits of pavement, even, during the hot days of summer, when Sneck filled with travellers keen to experience the Highland landscape (mountains and midges) and the legendary hospitality (scowling rip-offs involving tartan made in Taiwan, and deep-fried haddock fillets still frozen in the middle). Just like the fucking waitresses.

I wasn't some wino, after all, some tramp. This was a good suit. It was an Emporio Armani linen number. A bit rumpled, yes, a couple of years out in styling. A bit stained. But, hell, I wasn't a down-and-out, not yet. I still had money in my pocket. Enough – I tapped my hip pocket instinctively – to get me through a night at the Albatross. Then tomorrow, Sunday, I'd be hungry by then, hit a fried brunch about noon, and go on the wagon, get straight, get well, hang around a fucking inkwell. If I could think of some reason why. Don't follow leaders, man. Watch parking meters.

I felt light, like I was going to float away, as I clambered unsteadily up the slope to the fake frontage of the castle, then started to cut round behind it to take the shortcut down behind the Town Hall into Arminius Street. I fell over once or twice, just to kind of reacquaint myself with the planet's surface. And it was while levering myself back into mobility from one such meditative moment that I saw it. One of those extraordinary Landseer sunsets was forming behind me, and I paused to gaze out westwards at the burnished coppery clouds, just a few of them, looking so basically unreal in that Richie Blackmore solo of a sky. Florid, overblown, sort of dodgy. There were great views from Sneck, in all sorts of directions. It was a pity the place itself was such a shithole.

Behind the castle, the steep drop to the river below was protected by high metal railings. Which is just as well, otherwise the first forceful shove would have taken me straight down into the River Ness's reasonably clean shallows, there to mash myself on the stony bottom and provide food for the salmon. The limited amount of wind in my body left, hurriedly, as I turned around, only for the iron bars to slam agonisingly into my back. Two large hands gripped my lovely linen lapels, and a curry breath filled my nostrils. Was I hungry, after all?

'Latha math dhut fhein,' said a voice, the Gaelic words full of the irony that worn-out language specialises in. And a good day to you, pal. 'Or perhaps not. Your good days have come to an end, I think, Alexander Flaws. Zander Flaws. Insanity Claus.' Ha ha; never heard that one before, dogbreath. 'Not that they appear to have been so good for a while. Is that not right, mhath?' Sing-song Stornoway Gael-English, deep, measured Presbyterian tones, the fractured pieces of dog-Gaelic an affectation, but one reaching back to the womb, or further. A large man, bigger than me, maybe six foot. And his face wrapped in one of those IRA ski-mask balaclavas, his head cropped with a classic black preacher's homburg. Effect, not disguise. The angel of death, fresh from Calvin's Geneva, and pure fucking mental to boot. There was the unmistakable, silky metallic click of a switchblade opening. Either that or a stonechat was trying to get into a mussel shell somewhere in my immediate vicinity. And that was ornithologically unlikely, to say the least.

Another voice, sickly smiling, heavily accented: 'Move aside.'

Suddenly, I felt like boking again, it was the curry aroma that did it, that unmistakable niff of saag gosht on someone else's breath. I was surprised there was still sufficient liquid in my stomach to emerge at such a velocity. The Large Be-hatted Gael staggered back, choking and muttering indecipherable Gaelicisms, cannoning into the shadowy figure behind him. I caught a glimpse of a baseball hat and one of those Arafat Palestinian I'm-all-for-terrorism-me scarves wrapped around the face beneath, before my liquid legs found enough solidity to jerk me away, running, tumbling down the path towards the lights at the top of the Town Hall steps. My heart was rattling like some kind of bad techno record, blood beating in my head, going STROKE-STROKE-STROKE-STROKE, CORONARY-CORONARY, the queasiness almost crippling. Got to get fit, stop this, lose weight, just the occasional Laphroaig or Port Ellen . . . I am hungry. I could do with a black pudding . . . my mind rapped out the orders to move like some sprinter on steroids, but my body wasn't listening. I knew that Large Be-hatted Gael, ski-mask or not, but from where . . . Another life. Sick. I felt sick. Sick-stroke-coronary, here they come . . .

At the top of the steep flight of steps leading back down to the teeming touristy heart of the Queen of the Highland Fleshpots, the soul of Sneck, I paused, only to feel a massive thump in my back; then I was falling downwards, conscious only of two terrified eyes gazing up at me, eyes like tiny tunnels into which I was trying to dive, like some demented lover whose dodgy erotic metaphor had been brought to optical life. Getting bigger, bigger, bigger. And the sound of screaming. Two lots, actually. Mine and someone else's.

★ Two

Apparently I'd fallen onto Mrs Montellano, a woman from the town of Clearwater, Florida, who was holidaying in bonnie, haggis-eating, hoochter-teuchter Scotland; part – a rather significant part, physically, I gathered – of a Scientologist bus tour which was in the midst of doing its Highland fling thing. I had knocked her backwards onto Arminius Street, but her cranium had been saved from major injury by a beehive hairdo of early Dusty Springfield stature, and her body by rolls of cheeseburgers, converted into fat. Were Scientologists allowed to eat cheeseburgers? Encouraged, even? I cite fat John Travolta, m'lud . . . Well, if it was indeed a dictum of Ronald Lafayette Hubbard, inhabitant of Conman County, Nutville, I had a lot to thank him for, albeit posthumously, because I had been cushioned by Mrs Montellano's love handles, guard rails, safety flesh-bags, call them what you will. Unfortunately I had also bounced off her well-toned obesity and banged my head, which was not surrounded by an extravagant hairstyle, indeed much of a hairstyle period, on a stray stone step.

Hence my arrival at St Buidsear's Hospital, the casualty unit's check call to Hernia, my official GP, after and despite all, and the immediate assumption that alcohol had caused my fall, maybe even some sort of fit before the actual tumble. Jesus, they never let up, do they? A man likes the occasional single malt, and suddenly, every stumbled word's a fucked-up Hemingway paragraph. Every mistake a Robin Friday career: Jim Baxter, only worse, and English. What a concept.

Anyway, after gaining consciousness, proving I could count my fingers (roughly) and feel pain (easily) I was X-rayed, cleaned up, and without further ado, hooked up to a Heminevrin drip, a substance which apparently flushes the booze from your body and prevents reaction, i.e. the DTs. As was carefully, not to say gleefully, explained to me by Hernia in the woozy period between coming out of unconsciousness and the result of something else being pumped into me which left me not asleep, but floating kind of pleasantly on the edge of wakefulness, feeling something, a kind of inner trembling, but not severely. And unable to think of much but a deep Gaelic accent, and where I'd heard it before, and why that bloody hat was so familiar.

18

Actually, Hernia was bending the hospital rules severely in an effort to dry me out without my consent. But, hell, he was a pal, so I forgave him. I later found out they'd been taking a risk with the Hemenevrin, too, which isn't meant to sit that well with head injuries. But according to the good Dr Holdsworth, I was in such a state it had been worth throwing any sort of chemical cocktail at me to see if they could deal with Big Ethyl and her physical withdrawal symptoms before my liver exploded. Or whatever the medical term is: Doing a Baxter. He could have been lying, of course. Doctors do. The other drugs were pretty damn effective at keeping me passive, anyway. If you're going to go cold turkey off The Liquid, where better than a hospital? After four days they took me off the drip, and I was able to sit up in bed. As long as someone arranged my useless limbs for me. I felt, as Michael Stipe from REM once informed his public, like dog. Which, he added, is God backwards.

'And how are you, Mr . . . Flaws?' This doctor was Asian, about twelve, smiling a big toothy grin, his head cocked on one side. I had been trying to drink a cup of tea and spilled most of it over my pristine hospital-issue nightshirt, which immediately dissolved. It seemed to be made from old toilet rolls. 'I am Doctor Azad, registrar. Bad bang on the head, but no cracks in the old eggshell, no? The noggin? How are you feeling?'

I tried to keep my hand steady. And my brain, which flopped about inside my cranium like a mummified cantaloupe melon. I attempted to stop the deep inward shaking which seemed to be affecting my voice, my thinking, the entire ward. I felt as if I was in an everlasting earthquake. One which was personal, designed by God just for me.

'No . . . nothing painful, just . . . bruised and . . . shaky.' My throat was doing that gulpy thing you usually get when you're nervous. I wasn't nervous. I was fucking terrified.

'Ah, yes, the demon drink. Indeed, we checked out your gamma GT levels and frankly, sir, you are in many ways fortunate to be here now, with a little bang on the head and a chance to drink a little H_2O for a change.' The smile fell away like a tropical sunset, and was replaced by a stern professional frown. 'Now, temperature, pulse, blood pressure, please. You have let yourself go, Mr Flaws. Once you would have been a strong man. A fairly fit man, I surmise. And now?' He shrugged. I let my trembling gaze fall over my five and three-quarter foot of bone and wasted flesh. Not big to start with, and getting smaller. No wonder Mrs Montellano hadn't been injured badly. Not even a cracked rib, the nurse had informed me. Mind you, they'd have had trouble finding her ribs.

According to Hernia, they'd wanted to give me an AIDS test immediately, before touching me, but he'd told them I was celibate, not to say impotent, as faithful drunks are, and not to bother. He could vouch for my freedom from The Big Disease With The Little Name. Great.

Now everyone probably thought he'd shagged me. Ah well, it was his name on the medical register, not mine. He didn't have the AIDS test results; he shouldn't have had them, anyway; they were held, supposedly under conditions of strict confidentiality, at this very hospital's genito-urinary disease department, where I had come, guttered and guttering like a crap candle, for an HIV blood test, oh . . . last year? Something like that.

The terror of it had penetrated the alcohol: the smiling, mumsy promise of anonymity, the little numbered plastic disc they used to identify you, once you'd handed over your personal details. The dishes of condoms on the table, like wagging fingers: if only you'd been sensible, son. Two days' hellish wait, mostly smashed, and then the utter joy of being given the all-clear, celebrated with a two-day blind bender. I hadn't told anyone, had I? Had Hernia been there? Fuck.

He was only guessing about the impotence, unless he'd been talking to Celia. That last disastrous clutching of lonely drinking pals, sodden sometime lovers, back in her flat, all flaccid unreaction and excuses I couldn't even be bothered making. A memory of another vomiting, this time on bedclothes, sprang to mind. Shit, it had been all flowery, the bed, like lying on a garden centre display. We'd ended up not caring, just lying in the boke, until the morning, when Celia went into a sort of hypermanic cleaning mode . . . and I didn't even have the grace or the energy to be embarrassed. Fuck it. Or not. Was this what sobriety was going to be like? Remembering the best forgotten?

'You should rest now,' said Dr Azad, smiling again, his teeth and skin so bright it hurt. Did they do neon in white and brown? 'Tomorrow, you must go home, I think. Bed space here is very much at a premium, you know. It is time to make your own way, Mr Flaws.'

'Th-thanks, Doctor. I will s-seek the path of true r-righteousness, all being well.' My throat felt parched, but strangely there was no wrenching desire for alcohol. It was as if that whole range of experiences had been yanked out, like one of those stories about tourists getting mugged, and waking up with a kidney ripped out for transplant surgery. No doubt the sensation of want, love, liquid lust, would return. The drugs don't work. Not like Ethyl.

'We will arrange counselling, or rather your GP, Dr Holdsworth, who seems to be truly and admirably concerned for you, will.'

'Don't w-worry, Doctor. I'll speak to Hern . . . to Dr Holdsworth about that.'

His smile stretched in what I took to be cynicism.

'N-no, I will. Really. Righteousness. Honesty. Truth. These I will . . . pursue.'

'Delusion,' said Dr Azad, looking suddenly older, older than the earth.

.

'Delusion is where the path must begin. But then you must leave it behind. Good luck, Mr Flaws.'

He walked to the next bed, which contained a skeletal, half-human shape, glimpsed beneath a mound of blankets. It had wheezed and rattled wordlessly during my period of blurred consciousness, never showing its face. Now Dr Azad drew the screens around it, and presumably began poking. That would have been my guess, anyway. That patient was ripe for medical pokery, if not jiggery.

With hands that seemed to have some kind of electrical problem, running on alternating, not direct current, I carefully wrapped the hospital radio headphones around my head, just in time to hear a would-be DJ with a Caithness twang introduce 'an oldie but goodie, requested for Zander Flaws by his friends at the Albatross bar, which many of us know rather too well, speaking for myself, listeners, you understand. Here's The Bluebells and *Falling On Down Again . . .*'

Timing. I always had it. Great timing. Secret of good comedy. Even when the joke, and not a very good one at that, was on me. I lay back as Ken McCluskey's plaintive vocal hummed over the top of those chancily chiming guitars. Bobby Bluebell had always looked like a pudgy Ramone, I recalled, and hadn't he gone out with the whole of Bananarama, or was it – no, it was just Siobhan, the one who married Dave Stewart from The Eurythmics. Weird taste in men. Weird taste in women on Bobby's part, for that matter. Eclectic. Bad eyesight, maybe, both of them. Oh, fuck all that useless pop trivia. Maybe that was what started it all. My teemingly trivial mind, so capable of getting wrapped up, obsessed with the ins and outs, the jots and the tittles of worthless hackery. That and sex. The stuff my wife had been getting. But not from me. And I'd been getting, but not from her.

We'd moved from Lucy's beloved Aberdeen, that oil-rich, fish-breathed city a hundred miles south-east of Inverness, for the sake of promotion. My promotion, needless to say, to deputy editor of the *Northern Mail and Courier*'s Highland edition. I'd worked my way up over fifteen years, through the *M&C*'s interminable editorial backwaters, starting as a graduate trainee, the scum of the journalistic earth in that repository of old-fashioned hot-metal values, ending up as chief investigative reporter. On a heavily editionalised regional paper like ours, that meant anything from child abuse by cabals of pagan nuns in children's homes to drug scams and fraud by cabals of pagan nuns in children's homes. Writing about them, not participating. Always on the point of taking the shilling offered by other papers south, in Glasgow, Edinburgh, even London. Never doing it. Fear, mostly. Lots of journalists are cowards, secure only in their clubby little worlds, with its seedy glamour, its daily hit of by-lined fame. And Lucy. Lucy had her family, well-to-do, oil-accountancy-fuelled, big house in Wankery. I mean Banchory. She was a northern girl, she would say, slipping on the Nicole Fahri and heading out into her town, a sleek, sophisticated fish in that small north-eastern pool. But Lucy had hated all the time I spent on, well, research.

Yeah, yeah, research. In bars. Of course in bars. It is the great truth about journalism its practitioners like to keep hidden away. I mean, it was like when my father tried to talk me out of it as a career, after the degree, the months of reading, talking, the time spent learning how to combine all that with beating several kinds of shit out of opposing rugby players, preferably without the referee seeing. The staying strenuously teetotal, like my hideously humanist, sweetly liberal, half-radical, loathsomely loving but innocent parents.

'Don't, son,' he said. 'It may have glamour, it may even have a political pedigree, offer possibilities of societal change. But think of the pressure you will put your own integrity under. Think of . . . of your liver!' It was the kind of thing Dad said. The reason people laughed at him, though usually not his fellow native Shetlanders. He was seen as a principled teacher who had returned home to rear his sons and also to escape the censure his political stance had attracted in the big bad mainland. And so they did not laugh, at least not in public. He was respected. A nice, nice man. *Nice.* That's all I ever got. Nice. And I was nice, for a long time too, unlike my brother. If I was Nicey, he was Smashy. Our nice parents were kind of warily, nicely indifferent to him, maybe unsure, threatened. He was the first, had been the great interrupter of their life together. Sometimes their indifference towards him turned curiously nasty, bitter; and of course I was happy to fuel it. Anyway, he got out of it all early. Wisely.

But of course I did do journalism, hung out in pubs in that gloriously intimate, secret way hacks do, clubbing together, huddling in their insecurity, their pretended importance. But alcohol? Me, no longer playing rugby, but pure of heart, solid of spirit, body a fucking temple? I inhaled a lot of secondary smoke and drank gallons of fucking mineral water, ginger beer, disgusting fake non-alcoholic lager, tomato juice with that Chandler mix (it's in *Farewell My Lovely* – 'that California drink') Angostura Bitters and Tabasco. I know Angostura Bitters is alcoholic, but somehow it didn't seem to count. I know for sure the stuff's fucking proof because I later drank an entire glass of it for a bet. Tasted good, too, if I remember rightly. Which isn't likely.

After five years of non-alcoholic hacking I took a whisky one night, in the little distillery town of Keith, during an investigation into the activities of some seriously pissed-off distillery workers who had been inserting foreign objects into whisky casks: things like, well, dead rats, tins of Nitromors, that kind of thing. The point was, these workers had been annoyed with their employers fifteen years previously, and the results of their spiritous sabotage were only just becoming apparent as the whisky went for bottling. I had found one of the workers, and he informed me that defecation in the cask before sealing was a regular habit at the time. Great story. Of course, I had to have a whisky. My informant recommended a MacDiarmid as free from all possible taint. I bought a twenty-five-year-old, just in case. Before his time.

I remember everything about it, from the swirling oiliness in the glass, above the liquid; the enormous sherry nose of a quarter-century dram, the hint of raw peat, the silky sophistication, the warming, then raging heat of it. It was like Scotland in a glass. Suddenly, life seemed easier.

Not for Lucy. She did PR with one of the big oil supply companies in the Granite City – I'd met her researching a story about desperate alkies on the rigs knocking back drill-bit lubricant and dying, ironically enough – and as I lubricated my life courtesy of Big Ethyl, she made it plain she didn't like being left alone. But, then, she had her parents.

Then her mum and dad decided to move to the little Highland seaside town of Gurn, about fifteen miles from Inverness, retire to a life of golf and sailing. They'd had a holiday home there for two decades. It could all have ended then. I could have stayed while she followed them, and maybe, really, that's what she wanted. Lucy said she'd been in PR long enough, wanted a change, the Highland air; I had hit a plateau of drinking which stayed, I thought, on the right side of heavy. I could have let her go, let myself go, too. And then a desk job came up, number two on the Sneck-based edition covering everywhere from the Western Isles to my old home archipelago of Shetland, from Argyll to Moray's whisky country, and I went for it, got it. We moved together, north-west to a bright new future.

And it was fine, if boring. Lucy didn't have a job, which she said she didn't mind, because there was so much to do on the beautiful converted farmhouse we'd bought out on the Black Isle, twenty minutes across the Whore's Bridge from Inverness, Sneck, as I learned to call it with the right tone of scathing contempt. Because I quickly grew to dislike the town's preening parochialism, its dour hatred of strangers, its garrison mentality, traceable right back to the days when Cromwell forced his troops on the local maidens, and changed the accent forever to its screeching 'raiiiit enaaafff', right enough nasal howl.

'Do you mind, *mo graith*?' The deep voice broke into my memories, dredged up from the tender scar tissue that was my brain. Who was calling me 'darling'? 'Prayer, I believe, thrives on privacy.' Stornoway accent. Ministerial. Christ . . . he was drawing the screens carefully around the bed, the big, black-clad, be-hatted figure with its back to me, in Crombie coat, black leather gloves. My heart began a ragged pitter-patter. How the hell had he got in here?

Then the figure turned, secure now in the screened-off, sacrosanct bed-space. No mask on the face now, just the preternaturally slabbed jaw and cavernous eyes that I had helped put on the front page of the *Northern Mail and Courier*, and, I had hoped, behind bars for a long time. How long ago was it? Two, maybe three years? Fucking hell. That was plenty of time for remission to kick in, for something like video piracy, which was, I remembered, all he'd eventually gone down for. Yeah, that would have him out, right enough. *Raaaiit enaaaaff.* The assault charges hadn't stuck, thanks to wavering witnesses. And who could blame them? The murders he was suspected of were bar-blethering legend, and all involved pre-mortality pain on a massive scale. That was their point. They were markers; warnings. I shivered, and, as was my wont since coming off the sauce, couldn't stop easily. I settled into a light bodily shoogle that might last five minutes, fear permitting.

'So,' said Jeremiah Gideon Smith, 'what are we going to do with you?'

I gazed up at him, with his clerical collar and mountainous, sinister ministerial presence. 'How . . . how did you . . .?'

'Oh, please, Mr Zandy Pandy Flaws. That should be obvious. This hospital is right in the epicentre of Highland religious mania, with death and fear stalking its corridors. St Buidsear's? The very name means "butcher". Seriously. This place reeks with the very intestines of Presbyterianism. This is the happy hunting ground for the black crows of the gospel.' He swept off his Isle of Lewis funeral homburg, revealing a very un-preacherish number-two crop. 'The real question you should be asking is, why?'

'Wh-why, then? Why what?'

'Indeed. Why? Why should I be interested in you, after your minor league persecution, what was it? Three years ago? After your pathetic scribbling of lies and innuendo betrayed me to incarceration? Surely, you think, a man of my stature should be over all that? Perhaps you consider forgiveness a possibility?' He scraped the bedside chair along the shiny rubber floor and sat down, leaning on the back with his hands, like Sally Bowles in *Cabaret*. Well, not really. More like Rocky Marciano in cabaret, dressed as a minister, if you can imagine such a thing. Try.

Jeremiah Smith – no one had ever called him Jerry, at least not more than once – had been born into a viciously religious North Lewis Free Presbyterian family, his father a minister in that extreme fundamentalist offshoot of the Free Church. The Free Presbyterians it was who excommunicated Britain's Lord Chancellor, Lord Mackay, for attending the funeral of a Roman Catholic colleague. Jeremiah didn't stay around to be excommunicated for setting his dad's church on fire at the age of fifteen. His father managed to escape, despite all the doors to the building being barred from the outside. A miracle, some called it. Jumping through a window to severe spinal injury, said others. His son was sent to what was then called a List D School, where he learned everything he needed to know about making a proper professional start to a life of crime. Which he duly did. Long terms of enforced institutional life gave him an Open University degree in theology, and the vocabulary of John Calvin crossed with Mad Frankie Fraser. Something not too unusual in fact amongst certain Gaelic families.

'I get a real . . . *frisson* out of wearing these clothes, you know,' he said, moving the various strata of his face into some semblance of a smile. 'It's like being a kind of transvestite, I suppose. You know it's not real, but it's sort of thrilling, consuming. Consummately so. Maybe I could forgive you . . . but then, that would be a Catholic thing. A heresy.' He smiled. Bits of his face seemed to be splitting. 'True forgiveness comes only from the Lord, unmediated by man.'

The ward, usually so busy with the rubbery snap and click of nurses' footsteps, the murmur of colluding doctors, was unnaturally silent as he reached into his pocket and removed a Swiss Army knife, the really flash kind with the watch in the side and about a hundred useful attachments for removing horses from their hooves. The only one he seemed interested in, though, was the ordinary cutting blade, which he tested against a massive thumb. I heard doom-laden scraping, like the beginning of an avalanche.

'But I am, in fact, taking preventative, rather than punitive, action. For various reasons which, really, sadly, it is just not worth my while explaining to you. Indeed, I may be a little beyond my, ah, remit.' He stood up, smiled. His teeth were dull yellow. 'Call it over and above the call of duty. All of which does not negate one whit the pleasure in this. The personal nature of this . . . encounter. I really thought, in your physically debilitated state, you would not have survived your little tumble. But God works in mysterious ways. Fat, American ways, I hear.'

Slowly, he moved over me, the knife edging towards my throat, the other hand reaching for my mouth. 'Let not your heart be troubled,' he intoned. 'Believe also in me. Especially in me.'

I looked into his eyes, so certain of their prey, and with all the weakling force I could manage, rammed the heel of my hand upwards under his nose, in a move which, I'd read in some lurid martial arts magazine, was supposed to force the broken bits of the nasal bridge into the brain and cause instant death. Sounded good to me. Perpetrated by a cowering, desiccated wreck of an unrecovered alcoholic into a face possibly constructed of titanium and concrete, it didn't raise much of a tickle. But he did jerk back, possibly in nothing more than surprise at the loud screaming I unleashed directly into his fizzog.

'HELP! I'M BEING RAPED! BY A . . . A CLEANING WOMAN!' Don't ask why I said that. It came without prompting, probably some sort of fantasy which had been lurking in my frontal lobes. Healthy, actually, given the lack of sexual reactiveness which had been my fate of late, even after determined foreplay and the desperate application of pornography. 'I MEAN A PRIEST! NO, A MINISTER! FAKE! HE'S A FUCKING FAKE!' Hoarse. I was hoarse and whispering, that nightmare everyone gets, shouting and you can't be heard, longing to run but you can't escape.

The screen around my bed rattled back, revealing Dr Azad. Thank fuck. He must have just been passing. I could hear his pager bleeping, weedily, irrelevant in this situation. Smith whirled round, the knife still in his hand, and for a split second I think he contemplated taking out the diminutive doctor, who was smiling in a toothily uncertain way, as well as me. But he just said, 'Ah, Doctor – I'll leave the tracheotomy to you, then,' and was out of the ward and away. Only his homburg remained, like some kind of felt bomb on the bed; black and monstrous.

'Tracheotomy?' Dr Azad's smile shut down as his teeth vanished. 'I think not. Such shouting would not be indicative. What the fucking please is going on?'

I looked at him. My entire right arm was throbbing, from the heel of the hand to the shoulder. 'I wish to hell I knew,' I said.

★ Three

'I wish to fuck I knew.'

I was not impressing Detective Sergeant Nicholas Shearer and the tame spotty constable with big ears – every DS has to have one – whose name I neither knew nor cared to find out. Dr Azad had called the police, and then openly contemplated referring me to Craig Na Fergusson, for my own safety and to cleanse me of the alcohol he was certain lay at the root of my problems. As if being sober somehow stopped psychopaths from trying to slit your throat. As if Jeremiah Gideon Smith only killed drunk people. I'd heard the dread five syllables muttered to a nurse: 'Craig Na Fer Gu Son.' The psychiatric hospital, which was hidden away in some nearby woods, looked like the Wicked Witch of the North's castle and had a legendary alcohol treatment unit. So legendary, indeed, that Hernia had bent every St Buidsear's rule to keep me away from it.

'I mean, I did the number on Smith when I was through in Aberdeen, but I wasn't the only one. Granted, all his family would have seen the *Mail and Courier*, and we spelled out his background, big time . . . but, from what he said, there's got to be something more to it.'

Nicky Shearer looked at me witheringly, his stupid silk waistcoat glinting in the hospital fluorescence. Too many telly cop shows had made him imagine some touch of sartorial eccentricity was essential to detectivedom. We were in an empty ward, echoing and breeding killer staphylococci, for which purpose it had doubtless been closed by health authorities desperate to get rid of patients, for whose treatment they had no money. Or maybe they were planning to convert it into a private ward, where inveterate snorers could have their nostrils cut open and given a good seeing to for a thousand quid. Amex'll do nicely, sir. Any complications, any risk of trouble, and they'd be whisked next door to a properly equipped NHS ward, one where lives were saved, not tinkered with for consultants' pocket money.

Nicky Shearer was two years off the beat, had spent time hanging around the Albatross, dropping heavy hints to hacks that he could be a useful source. A Freemason from the handshake, which was par for the polis course. I even knew one local hack who'd joined the Sneck lodge in a state of complete cynicism, seeking only better police sources. It had worked, too.

Medium height, fat, balding fair hair, too easy a smile, that slippery, thumb-clutching handshake. Nastily ambitious. I'd disliked him instantly.

'It was definitely him, Zander, old lad? Him and somebody else at the castle, possibly foreign . . .'

'Definitely foreign.'

'. . . And old Jeremiah, without a mask, in the hospital here, dressed as a minister? A bit unlikely, old lad? Even for you.'

Fuck. Old lad? Ah, the familiarity bred by a fall from grace, if you could class newspaperism as in any sense divine. More loathed than social workers, they always said of journalists. Social workers, though: some of the ones I'd met were okay, but my attempts to consider them useful members of society always foundered on a woman I'd once met in a Glasgow casino, on a horrible bender which had ended with temporary membership of the Riverboat Club, betting sixty pounds in chips to win at roulette, always on thirteen. She'd been attractive in a hard-bitten sort of way, I think. I'd slurred my way into a conversation, learned how she came to the casino three times a week, shedding spare cash, sometimes winning, not caring, just glorying in the seedy, tinsel decadence of the experience. 'I spend my days organising gas heaters for people who've torn up their floorboards to burn for heat,' she said. 'This is where I come to spit in their faces.' I don't think I shagged her.

I tried to focus on Nicky's Zapata moustache. 'Yes, son, it was.'

His thin lips disappeared. I was ready to bet he'd had a bad, thin, womanly moustache as a street constable, desperate for the fake authority of age. I had ten bad years on him, so to hell with his sensitivities.

'All the shite was intact. The pseudo-Gaelic culturespeak, the largeness, the general sociopathic aura. All fucking shipshape and Stornoway fashion, boy.'

The constable was goggling. Nicky would be out to impress him, as if he was some sort of job creation cop, shadowing the big tough sergeant, or a work experience sixth year from the IRA. That's Inverness Rechabite Academy, not the other, less dangerous IRA. It is a hotbed of vice and Christianity, the usual Highland mix. I'd once been asked by a Mrs Heard to keep an eye on her husband, a young IRA English teacher whom she suspected of nymphette-shagging. I'd turned the job down. Too tempting.

No, the constable was a properly recruited Agent of Repression, probably equipped with all the necessary idiocies. 'And, besides, Dr Azad saw him, didn't he? It was he who called you, not me.'

Nicky spoke, with all the bigoted, racist, pompous would-be cool of a true dickhead with a warrant card: 'Paki doctors, you know what they're like. Never know what they're on about, what they saw. Could have been something innocent, couldn't it? Anyway,' he cleared his throat self-importantly, 'you can't think what life-or-death case you've been working on that would merit any interest from him and this, ah' – he consulted the cheap little Casio palmtop he was pretentiously taking notes on, the prick. I prayed for a microwave oven to explode and wipe his flashcards. For his hard disks to droop, his floppies to melt. Maybe he couldn't write – 'this foreign gentleman?'

'South American, maybe, or Spanish. I don't know.' The bastard knew that my investment of a year's redundancy money in the formation of Highland Investigative Services, my fantasy of private-eyedom, had not set the northern heather fiscally afire. A contract with two local firms of solicitors taking precognitions from thugs in Alness or the Ferry area of Sneck, with the occasional trip to the likes of Fort William or Thurso, had initially kept me active, but increased drinking had been necessary to make the boredom of those stupid jobs disappear. It had worked, too. And then it made the jobs vanish. Alcohol was magic like that. 'And, no, there's nothing on the books just now which would've provoked any interest in terminating me with extreme fucking prejudice. And knives. Or knife singular, to be accurate.'

'A Swiss Army knife, you say?'

'That's right. The one Smith had here in the hospital. The Spanish guy had a flick knife.'

'Which is of course illegal. Whereas the penknife . . .'

'. . . isn't.' In a flash his lightning mind appraises the fucking situation. 'So what? You got a secret scanner which can tell you that someone's carrying an illegal switchblade beneath their jumper? Do you want to know whether it was a real Victorinox Swiss Army knife or a fake one? If you do, you better ask him. Or ask that famous Russian expert on all things forensic, Fucktivano.'

Nicky looked as if he'd swallowed his lips and he didn't fancy the taste much. Weren't pig lips a delicacy in Spain? I wondered if you sucked or chewed them. 'Listen, Flaws,' he said, 'try taking a more co-operative attitude. This Paki doctor isn't very sure of you, either, but your pal Cecil can-I-put-my-finger-in-here Holdsworth is keen you shouldn't go for a bit of rest and recreation at the Craig. I mean, by rights we should've just ignored this as more ramblings from some sot with a brain gone spongy on cheap vodka . . .'

'Actually, I only drink expensive vodka.'

'Shut up. Anyway, Smith is indeed out and about and hasn't turned up for his mandatory sessions with whatever wank probation officer was assigned to him. So there's a warrant out for the bastard. Thing is, if

Smith really did attempt to murder you, and frankly it seems a bit far-fetched, what possible good are you going to be in defending yourself? You'll need us, and if I were you I'd be nice to us. To me. I'm your fairy godfather, pal. I'm the one who'll come running to stop him mincing your testicles into pâté. Maybe.'

'Fairy godfather? Unfortunate turn of phrase, Nicky, son, don't you think. Never took you as a bent shot.'

He snapped shut the Casio and stood up. 'Come on,' he ordered the spotty constable. 'Let's leave this pisshead to his deluded, snotty –' he narrowed his eyes in concentration '– clever clever wanderings.' Coo, hot rhetoric babe!

Why was I feeling better? Christ, I was hungry. A black pudding supper would go down a treat. He looked at me, his lips appearing, magically, all red and wet and regurgitated. What a gift the man had! He was the lipsucking king of Sneck. And possibly other kinds of sucking, too.

'You know what I think?' he said. 'I think you were hallucinating. I think maybe some big innocent minister blundered into your little hidey-hole, or mistook you for someone else, and –'

'What about the castle?'

'– and you were seeing some pink elephant, did that DT thing, thought the gay Jumbo was Jeremiah Gideon Smith, come to kill you, make you important for once in your slimy little life.'

Charming. He hadn't said that when I was deputy editor of the *Northern M&C*, northern edition. When I was a man to be reckoned with. Within the portals of the Albatross bar.

'But . . . Dr Azad . . . what about him?'

'I told you, what does he know, in a strange country, strange habits. So he saw a penknife. Maybe this minister fellow was peeling an apple. Or picking his nails. A Swiss Army knife, for God's sake. Hardly a machete. And if not, I mean, if Jeremiah is on a mission from God to remove you from us, well, who's going to miss you, laddie? Apart from your poofy doctor pal and a host of pathetic drouths? Not me. Not your good lady wife, I hear, down there in Edinburgh.' He smiled triumphantly at me, then at the pluke-ridden constable bumboy companion. I had nothing to say. He was probably right.

Later that day I was told my bed was needed. There was whispered nursy talk about some kind of emergency, something really nasty involving youngsters. Once I would have been the curious sniffing hack, all bloodlust and notebook. But fuck that. That was history.

Dr Azad was nowhere to be seen, and when Hernia arrived to get me, complete with an ill-matched set of clothes he'd collected from my sumptuous bachelor abode, also known as The Tub, I was already an ex-patient, signed out, with instructions to see my GP as soon as was convenient. Which was immediately, as he was the one holding my elbow as I faltered along the squeaky, balefully clean hospital lino. I could walk with reasonable steadiness by this time, and my hands only shook when I tried to hold something. A messy inconvenience, but a wanker's delight. Potentially. I hadn't tried it. I still wasn't conscious of any craving for alcohol, but I could feel this strange sensation, like having a large piece of machinery lying dormant inside my body, just waiting to be switched on. A cement mixer, with a giant greedy maw, ready for the sand and gravel to be thrown in. Or maybe it was a fire, glimmering at the ashes and embers stage, waiting for the petrol to come showering down. Or the cask-strength Springbank.

'How do you feel?' Ah, yes, the great medical and journalistic question, refuge of the unimaginative, the nervous, and, when push came to verbal shove, everyone.

'Twitchy. Shaky. Anything ending in "y". Crappy.'

'Thirsty?'

'Well, come to mention it . . . no. I mean, it's amazing how much of our drinking isn't anything to do with thirst quenching, isn't it? It's a drug delivery system. Like cigarettes are supposed to be the most efficient method of introducing nicotine into the body, with infinite gradations of control available. Big blast or little tipple, all available to you, easy as breathing. Drinking's the same, only all these fucking socialising aspects to it have evolved, different tastes, different strengths, different rituals – drinks to go with food, drinks for men to knock back together, to compete with each other in speed of consumption . . .'

I could hear myself wittering. Alcotalk: My name is Zander Flaws and I am a weak-willed tosspot. Fuck that.

We walked totteringly; we must have looked like two ancient crones, clutching each other for reassurance that we were still alive, Hernia with his kind of half-withered, half-honed body, me just a kind of worn-out husk.

'Everybody talks about it when they stop,' said Hernia in Dr Holdsworth mode. 'It's one of the reasons AA works so well. You can go and talk to other alcoholics about drink, about how it functions, what it did to you. You said AA was religious. It is. Drink is the religion. And they're escaping from it. They're like satanists are to Christianity. Can't leave it alone, so they turn on it, sort of worshipping it in reverse. It helps.'

'Some people, some of the time.' Jesus, satanism as a model for the sober life.

'All kinds of shit is going down in casualty at the moment. Azad's involved, otherwise he'd have seen you off the premises. Whole bunch of kids, some overdose thing . . . usual shit, except one of them's in a coma, and her parents are upmarket Sneck, big time. He's Director of Development at Highland Capital Investments.'

'Philip McVeigh?'

'Yeah. A bastard. It's his daughter, I think.'

My journalistic memory banks seized up when faced with demands for a name. 'Kate? Carol?'

'Karen. Don't know much else.' He spoke shruggingly, like doctors do. Tragedy, death, disablement? Somebody else's patient, thank God. Not my pager that's bleeping.

Philip McVeigh, eh? The papers would be all over him. I felt a momentary twinge of regret that I wouldn't be doorstepping the prick, followed by a stab of guilt. Just another wee girl pushing at the barriers of adolescence. What was wrong with plain old booze, eh? That, after all, was harmless.

Hernia was pointing one of those infra-red key things at his car. There was a blip, then a clunk. Ah, technology! He was driving a docmobile, one of those Land Rover Discoveries which have an aura of cross-swamp capability but are in reality pale imitations of the hideously expensive, much smoother and more rugged Range Rover proper. He helped me in, or up. I was never a fan of four-wheel drives. Short men's cars. Perhaps because I wasn't that tall myself, I was hyper-conscious of such Freudian compensations. The diesel rattled like an extended death. I hate diesels. All that carcinogenic crap they push out, pretending to be environmentally friendly just because they do a few more miles per gallon. Spill it on your hands and you get dermatitis. The diesel engine was invented for developing countries, a foolproof, simple motor for pumps and tractors. Now you find it in gigantic toys like luxury off-roaders, because it sounds chunky. It sounds macho, like Schwarzenegger's name pronounced by Tom Waits. Bullshit.

'What about you, Cecil, old chum? All that jarring it back, all the mountaineer pisshead bravura shit? When underneath it all, you're as camp as a tentpeg? Substitution? Displacement? Transference? Is that it?'

I remembered Hernia telling me he was gay, which of course I'd already guessed, both of us rolling down the High Street, cannoning off walls. As long as you don't fucking fancy me, I'd said. He was celibate, he muttered. Fuck fucking. Spartan friendship was the thing. I wasn't sure I liked the sound of that. I had a book-memory of Spartan warriors having to sleep together to guard each other in battle. But we never did.

'Once a week, a bit of a blow-out,' he said. 'And not as much as maybe you thought. Actually, I feel pretty guilty, now, because I always really enjoyed drinking with you. You were good value. A happy drunk, mostly, except over the past few months. Then it started to show. Whisky roses on the face, that and the memory losses. Same jokes told twice every hour, all night.'

'So, how about you tell me how little you drink, I'll drink less, and then I'll be okay. You know what they say about doctors . . .'

'Yeah. Well, listen, I don't mind not drinking that much. It's just not that much of an issue. But . . .'

'No, fuck it, I'm not going to make you suffer on my behalf. Be responsible for my thoughts and decisions. You've done enough. And there is such a thing as freedom of choice. You know that trick question existentialists ask? Is weakness of will possible? It's up to you, mate. Or, rather, it's up to me.'

Whisky roses? I felt my face for the tell-tale warmth of broken veins and lost looks. I just seemed very cold. My skin was plasticky, fake.

'What about some kind of counselling, psychiatric help, or . . . I mean, there's guys up at Craig Na Fergusson . . .'

I winced. 'Fuck's sake, Hernia. I thought the idea of moving heaven, earth and the NHS to get me sorted at St Buidsear's was to avoid having to head for loony tune central. The alcohol unit up there'd drive the Pope to smack. Just leave me to my own devices. One way or another. You've assuaged any guilt for enjoying watching me get pissed.'

It was his turn to wince. And mine to feel guilty.

We scrunched off the tree-lined road which led to Loch Ness and all points west, down into the hamlet of Disruption, towards the white splash of pleasure boats moored on the Caledonian Canal. The great eighteenth-century engineer Thomas Telford's watery masterwork, linking four lochs and splitting Scotland along the Glen of Perdition. It was one of the best things about Inverness. The Discovery halted at The Tub, and I realised it was almost ten days since I'd been home, for want of a better word.

'I'll see you in,' said Hernia, eyeing the murky waters of the canal in which the tall car's reflection shimmered greenly. 'It's a mystery to me how you haven't killed yourself here already.'

'Drowning your sorrows is the best defence against a watery death,' I replied. 'Liquids repel each other.'

Besides, the gangplank leading aboard the good ship *Gerda* – she'd always been The Tub to me, initially The Fucking Tub, as this was how my aghast drinking pals had reacted when I had taken them to see my new home – was firm, wide and had secure handrails preventing anything but the most strenuous attempt at total immersion. Come to think of it, if Smith and his unknown Latin crony had wanted to kill me, they'd have been much better doing it here. No one would even have thought twice about the accidental drowning of a known toper. But, then, they hadn't thought that much about it anyway, and I'd managed to convince the dodgy detective sergeant to bin any possible investigation into the whereabouts and motives of Jeremiah Gideon Smith. What a damned clever guy I was. I shoogled the handrail. It was solid. I held up my hand to Hernia. 'See that, mate? Steady as a very steady thing.' Old joke. Then the left one, which was flapping about wildly. 'But I shoot with this hand, unfortunately.'

Hernia looked at me, not smiling, his emaciated, hatchet face, not unhealthy, I realised, just thin and fit. Unless he had AIDS, and wasn't telling. Doctors rarely did, understandably. But just because someone got thin didn't mean they had the slimming sickness. These days, tubbiness was next to godliness.

'Uh huh,' he said. 'Now stop it shaking.'

I did. Eventually. It's harder when you have to think about it.

The Tub, *Gerda*, was originally a Dutch river barge, built in the 1930s, sixty feet long, decommissioned from life on the Rhine as a kind of primitive floating hotel a decade previously and converted, professionally and at considerable expense, into a kind of rough-hewn motor yacht. The old Saab diesel, smelly and ferociously noisy, still worked. It was one of the reasons I hated diesel engines, though I only ever ran it to charge up the batteries. Which was rarely, because I had a mains connection, as well as a telephone, thanks to the nice British Waterways people. No plumbing, though. That was why the interior of The Tub smelled like shit. I should have used more of that horrible blue Elsan liquid in the Porta-Potti.

'Well,' I said to Hernia as he slumped into the built-in sofa-cum-spare-bed-cum-storage-chest. 'Fancy a drink?'

They washed down the pills with Special Brew, the five of them. Bobby and Karen had two each, the others just the one. 'You and me, babe, we'll fly higher than starlight tonight. Higher than the planets and the stars, we are.' She'd found that very funny. Guys who thought they were poets. Could there be anything more hilarious? But Bobby hadn't liked her laughing, she could tell. That was the problem with sensitive guys. They were so . . . sensitive.

She hadn't asked what exactly she was taking, assuming it was some kind of E, which she'd had before and enjoyed for the sense of affection, of community. She had problems with that . . . belonging thing, normally. Touching, shagging, that was fine, but inside she always felt, maintained, a distance. Felt smarter, stronger. Superior bitch, she thought. E had melted her into the mass of dancers out at the village hall raves in the Black Isle, expanded the laughter in her.

At first, this felt the same, with something of the world-shifting edge of acid. The talk with the others was initially wild, then grew hysterically funny, like dope, only with more behind it. Everyone was a genius, everyone totally brilliant. She didn't feel that frustration you sometimes got when you smoked a joint, when someone else wouldn't stop talking, and inside you felt the rage, the fury at their stupidity and boringness, but you were too stoned to care, really, to do anything about it. Then she felt every nerve in her body tense and flutter. The darkness warped slightly, shifted around her like cloth, thick and coarse. She reached for Bobby, felt his chest rising and falling, and pulled the night around them, trying to stop the trembling which was affecting every centimetre of skin, her bones, her core. She was conscious, in touch. Not stoned or spacy, but sparkling, brilliant and clear, but the shakiness was growing, becoming like . . . what was it? Like Simon the epileptic boy who'd forgotten his medication in second year, who'd fitted, they said, shaken like he was being electrocuted on the history classroom floor. She reached through a tear in the coarse blackness for something big and bright, cratered and ghostly glowing. An orb of heat, but it wasn't hot, it was icy, sent out rays of cold, deep into her being. She felt Bobby's lips touching her throat, her face, her eyes. Then abruptly she was being sucked at by some huge, stinking animal, a hippopotamus, a crocodile, bitten, consumed. A huge vomit of panic gripped her, and as the shaking took control of her, the cold became numbness, creeping, then surging through her body from her feet to her neck, where it seemed to hesitate. Then there was nothing.

★ Four

We had coffee. Nescafé, no milk, no sugar, though both of us normally took both. I thought, Jesus, if I'm going to drink The Unalcohol, I'm going to have to get some effect from it, some taste. I resolved to invest in some serious bean action at the first opportunity. Assuming I didn't just head straight down the Albatross and hit the twelve-year-old Glen Grant as a light starter for the main course of old Islay peat bog specials: Port Ellen, and oh God, the beloved Ardbeg. Could I actually face life without ever again tasting a 1973 Ardbeg? I sipped the weak coffee and wondered.

When Hernia left, promising to keep in touch, clearly concerned but convinced I wasn't quite ready to top myself, I checked the answering machine. Celia had called, pissed, wondering where I was. Good news travels fast, girl. Thanks for the fucking flowers. Four hang-ups in a row. And that was it. Popular guy. No threats from Smith, no offers of a ten-grand contract to investigate the sex life of Bonnie Prince Charlie for a telly programme, no frantic calls from Camelot, asking when I was going to claim my fifteen-mill win on the lottery. Life.

I sat down to open the mail, which was bills, circulars and a card from Lucy, postmarked Edinburgh. 'Having a lovely time, wish you were him.' It didn't say that. Nor did it say, 'Hi Zander − it's great fucking your erstwhile boss, who knows how to treat a woman, not like you, you bastard. Think yourself lucky you're not in jail after what you did to us both.' That could be taken as read.

What it actually said was, 'Have a drink on me.' Brief and to the point. Fuck off and die, basically. She must have heard about my fine state of physical well-being. Jesus. A woman scorned. Well, slightly worse than that, actually. Though she started it. The scorning.

Actually, that's not true. I began it, back in Aberdeen, the slip-sliding away into the golden glow of liquid comfort, felt the first pull of otherness, of strange new flesh. There are times in a marriage, every marriage, when you can resist. It helps to be sober.

Life in Aberdeen was okay, though no one who hasn't lived there will believe that. It's a small city, but it is the only conurbation in Britain with a serious beach. I mean a proper, gosh-darn two-mile stretch of silver sand, and what's more it's clean. Of course, the city's masonic uncles have fucked it up big time by selling off the common grassland behind it, the linksland supposedly owned by the people, left for the people. Now it's all grotesque industrial and leisure developments made of spit and cement. But there is also a totally sinister fairground, and occasionally, in places like the Venice Café, situated right on Beach Parade, aptly enough, you get to meet the truly weird. And sometimes I took the truly weird there to interview them, just to see what happened. Whether some spark would fly, some magic take us to an unknown destination.

Did I mention I was serially unfaithful to Lucy during my late nights at the print face? Well, once the first flush of faithfulness wore off. A woman scorned. I didn't feel scornful, selfish, nasty at the time. It just seemed natural. A progression.

Anyway, one day I set myself up to interview the actress-writer-performance-poseuse who had brought, amid much controversy, her one-woman show called, succinctly, *Clitoris*, to the Sands Ballroom. Despite Aberdeen's oil-driven, unwilling cosmopolitan side, its one or two groovy bars and occasional wonderful restaurant, underneath it is a repository of pure kailyard Calvinism. The Church of Scotland Women's Guilds went utterly fucking ballistic. What was a clitoris, anyway? Clearly I had to talk to the woman responsible, who was American and around fifty, but still – let's not pussyfoot around here – shaggable. I was up for it, to start with, and then, well, not. I closed my eyes and tried to remember the conversation: an icy winter rain battering the Venice, hot cappuccino, fried egg on toast, with the yolk suggestively trickling down my chin. Deliberately, of course. And me looking as tough, journalistic and doubtless pathetic to Belinda Sheringham as all the other two-bit regional hacks who'd tried to shag her. Just to be able to say 'I was there . . .' Too.

So what you're saying is that you slept with Frank Sinatra?

'LISTEN! Honey, lemme tellya, there wasn't much SLEEPING goin' on, ya know what I'm sayin', Zander baby? Gggarooovvvy name, boy . . . I mean, do I havta SPELL IT OUT FOR YA?'

No no . . . we're talking sexual intercourse here, then? Are we?

'Aw, come AWNN! Whaddaya think? I mean, this was the '60s, honey, no worries, no AIDS, no condoms, no comebacks. Ya took the pill, no one said anything about strokes and high blood pressure back then, son. I mean, there was SUCH A THING as sexual intercourse back then. Not like nowadays.'

No, I'm sorry, it's just . . . this man was by then possibly the biggest singing superstar the world had ever seen, with the possible exception of Elvis Presley, and . . . how did you meet him?

'I was a dancer.'

What sort of a dancer?

'A dancer. A NEW YORK STRUGGLING ACTRESS sorta dancer. A DO WHADEVAHYAHAVTA sorta dancer. A CLOTHES-OFF BUTT-NAKED sorta dancer. Clear enough? It was a long time ago. I was a different shape.'

And how was he?

'PARDON ME?'

How was he? How was Francis Albert Sinatra, crooner and on-screen smoulderer, lust object of millions, in bed? What was his sexual performance like?

'I don't talk about that.'

Why not? You have had an experience half the world's female population of a certain age would love to have shared. You have been there and, to put it one way, swung upon a star. I mean, did he sing to you? Did you ask him to hum *Three Coins in the Fountain*? Was this during one of his fat stages? Did he take his wig off during, before or after? You are the only woman I've ever met who has claimed a sexual experience with Frank Sinatra and I think I should be informed as to what the goddamn thing was like. Frankly. How was it for you?

'You know, I thought we were here to talk about the weather.'

Yes, well, it's just that this thing came up and you can hardly blame me . . .

'Well, I'm not going to say anything more. We dated once or twice, and, okay, I will say it was great. Got it, babe? GREAT! But then so was I . . . anyway, after being a dancer, which I only was in for the money, doin' that audition thing all the time, I got into the movies. Change the subject, okay?'

So what kind of movies?

'Horror porn.'

What?

'Ya know, horror, porn, *Rosemary's Baby* remakes on a budget of three pizzas and ripped-off truckload of cigarettes. Cheapo sexploitation shit for college frat house showings out in the Midwest. Crap. But, hey, it was work. What can I tell ya?'

Did you . . .

'Christ, you gotta one-track mind, Zandy. No. I was demure in those days. DEEE-MOOR! Did you know that's how Demi Moore got her name? They went to a movie psychologist – it's true, they got those things in Hollywood – and said we want a name that gives good audience insertion potential. And he goes, demure. We're in a demure phase, people want demure. Guys want demure. And small, demi, half in French, exotic. Demi. Demi Ure. Demi . . . Moore. And, amazingly, Moore was her real name anyway.'

But you just said you were a stripper. That isn't demure, surely?

'*Dancer*, babe, *dancer*. But not in my soul. Not in my heart. Anyway the answer to your question is that I did not have sex. However, I did once have to give birth to Satan.'

I see.

'Well, the spawn of Satan, actually. I'm not talking method acting, here. This was no Lee Strasberg, get-down-the-local-voodoo-church-and-learn-how-to-do-it-for-real schtick. I mean, all I had to do was get a load of slaughterhouse stuff, offal, and hide it in a plastic sack in my dress. Then they had defrosted a frozen chicken, large family size, and I just had to sorta splurge the whole damn thing out when the director shouted action. With a bit of preliminary gruntin'n'groanin and flashes of thigh and tit and stuff.'

What was the film called?

'Oh, God knows. All that's behind me now. I don't remember the details. I was drinkin' a lot then, Zanny, loads. It was a drinkin' kinda time. I mean, how could you get through somethin' like that without being stoned or smashed? Impossible. Forget it.'

What happened to the chicken?

'I took it home and had it with some saffron. I do remember that. Cooked it in Californian chardonnay and saffron and spring onions. And it was just after that that I became Mary Tyler Moore's personal assistant. It was her who told me about Demi's experience, 'cause we keep in touch. I mean, she obviously keeps up with Demi, being her mother.'

Of course.

I woke up, cramped and sweating, in the lapping darkness of The Tub's saloon, panicking: what time . . . where . . . Lucy . . . For a few blind, fearful moments I was back in those scorning, unfaithful days, waking up in some godless hotel room or bedsit or student flat, wherever drink and the lustful search for soft skin and odd perfumes had taken me, certain, guiltily convinced that Lucy had found me out. And, of course, she did eventually. Which is what you want, really, when you're doing that deliberate drifting thing – dawns beneath weird duvets, lost in the tides of unfamiliar lusts.

Then, with relief, I realised that it was all right: that it was all in the past. Now I was just a fucked-up alcoholic (yeah, use the word, go on, why don't you, you weakling) newly out of hospital, possibly with some psychopath trying to kill me for no good reason I could fathom, and that Lucy had pissed off to points south with a superior little shit who had a prick like a pencil and an accent like Michael Heseltine's farts. And I was living on a boat in a canal right on the edge of Britain's most beautiful, most inspiring collection of landscapes and seascapes. Right on the edge, yeah, but still with what remained of my life centred on the most soulless, mentally and emotionally crippled town in Christendom. Oh, Inversneckie, how do I love thee? Let me count the ways! There, that didn't take long.

Belinda – self-proclaimed 'Cuntess of Clit' – had come back to me so clearly in that dream. I remembered reading somewhere that when you're drunk, you remember things you learned when you were drunk; presumably, now that I was sober, things that happened when I was off the sauce would also come back, either consciously or in the guise of dreams. But, Belinda . . . The curious thing was, we never fucked. But then, maybe it wasn't so curious. I thought I was the king of Aberdonian hackdom, a kind of MacWoodwardstein-meets-Wolfe'n'Thompson in Hemingway's Pamplona hotel room. Wearing Maggie O'Kane's knickers. Only in a granite-hearted oil and fishing port, north-east of almost everywhere except Sneck. She thought I was an arse-wipe scribbler who preferred sheep to women. And, besides, we were both absolutely sober. If you don't count the hangover.

Seduction and journalism both require drink to make them fly, to make them sing, get erect, get wet, get down and dirty and do the two-backed dance, between the sheets or on the page. Sobriety and reporting do not go hand in hand. Drink is a journalist's comfort, escape, caressing confidant in times of editorial trouble. But it is also a serious weapon. Unless a journalist knows not so much how to drink, but that he or she will have to drink, and how to cope, work with that, problems will ensue.

There is trust, for one thing. Myself and the Woman Who Gave Birth To A Chicken – as Belinda was ever afterwards known, at least within the confines of the Zander Flaws in-head pornography broadcasting company – were in a state of distrust, and possibly dislike. Don't get me wrong, I'd still have fucked her, or been fucked by her. But the blurring of awareness, of conscience, which alcohol – more than any other drug – brings, was absent. Besides, we were in a beachfront café in Aberdeen at eleven o'clock in the morning. Notsexiness was rampant.

She was almost certainly telling one or two porkie pies – make that four-course dinners featuring pastry-encased pigs – to impress, and I was meant to know that. Or was I? I played the game, sort of, maybe asking too many questions, but had I been drunk I would have thrown myself wholeheartedly into the Sinatra story with boozy belief. I would have given that chicken-is-the-Devil business the applause it after all deserved. Instead, we played oral tennis with tendentious tales. It was very unsatisfactory. After all, Mary Tyler Moore is not Demi Moore's mother. I mean, how could she possibly have met Patrick Moore, who's well known to be Demi's pater? The resemblance is striking.

The reporter meeting a source, or grooming a contact towards sourcedom, or even pretending to socialise with someone in the hope of provoking them into glorious indiscretion, cannot hope to get away with matching their mineral water to the target's whisky, gin or beer. They have to prove their own susceptibility, give away their own secrets, open up, get stupid too. And drink does that beautifully. Local politicians are the boys (and it's nearly always boys) for this.

I have spent far too much of my life in conversation with these creatures, many of whom are, by necessity, drunks. After all, who can cope with the interminable boredom of the average planning meeting without reaching for the cyanide or the flask of Stolichnaya? Very few. Sadly, of course, this liquefying of the local politician's brain can result in embarrassing, not to say highly amusing, public spectacles. Who can forget the eminent Central Tayside councillor who rose to his feet one day, the fumes from his rumpled clothes and even more rumpled face rising like dangerous flammable gases in the already-foetid air? His object was to attack a long-haired Puce Party representative, called Autumn Breeze Ghost of Sitting Bull (he was a convert to Native American religion), an admittedly eccentric chap who once appeared wearing military dress and an Iron Cross with oak leaves to make some obscure point about the behaviour of the leisure and recreation committee. He was last heard of begging on the streets of southern Spanish villages, having left various aggrieved creditors, not to say members of the Puce Party, barking angrily at his hard-to-follow trail.

Remember the Puce Party? It put the environment on every mainstream politician's temporary agenda before disintegrating in one leader's push for Christ-dom and every other vegan origami-brained member wanting to lead the organisation in a wholefoody sort of a way towards a daft permaculture jungle.

Anyway. The rumpled representative, Councillor Moan, began making very loud but indecipherable noises, some of which eventually reconciled themselves into the words 'fucking' and 'bastard'. This was illustrated by much body language which was just as out of control as his speech. If a body could be slurred, this one was. Gavels were banged, voices as reasonable as you ever get in a local authority were raised, and Councillor Moan was removed. Later, there was a small scuffle featuring Moan and Autumn Breeze Ghost of Sitting Bull, settled by some relatively sober journalists who were hanging around watching other journalists trying to provoke the pair into fully fledged fisticuffs. Afterwards, all the hacks settled on the exact events, complete with pooled quotes, because, after all, that is what journalism is, mostly. A collective effort, where the blind, halt and lame through drink, are catered for by the sober or almost so.

Councillors long for importance. They have ambitions to be powerful people, but probably lack the intelligence, stamina or cunning necessary for proper politics. If merely stupid and relatively incorrupt, they love, just *love* the press, because being in the papers not only impresses the electorate and their various mistresses or other sexual partners, but at a senior level can be important in upper-echelon negotiations with government and its faceless minions. And even those on the take like to hang out with hacks, partly to try and buy them off with booze, sex or cash, partly to show their shadowy, corrupting cash-cows how important the corrupted really are. What value for dirty money. Plus they get some weird *frisson* from the sophomoric, sulphuric repartee journalists think they have evolved to convince themselves they are the scathing inheritors of Johnsonian wit and rhetoric, defenders of democracy. In fact, this drunken mumbling is usually scabrous gossip, and everyone wants a piece of that. Especially when you might be the subject.

So, let's say . . . you find yourself one day in a bar somewhere in the Teuchterlands, surrounded by various councillors on an overnight visit to . . . I don't know. Perhaps the opening of the first legal marijuana processing plant in Scotland (a crucial supplier of employment for the local area, currently suffering severe unemployment in the wake of the cocaine smuggling downturn) and suddenly one of the top councillors, no longer young but still, so to speak, thrusting, grips you masonically by the hand and elbow. Reflexively, you give him back the Royal Arch third-dan Kobe-Osaka thigh-stroking identification sign you were taught during an entire day's imbibing at the Jinglin' Geordie in Edinburgh, sent down to cover the General Assembly of the Church of Scotland and mingling with masonic ministers for fun and frolics. You both slink off to the corner, where he, fuelled by expensive claret, brandy and now some let's-slum-it-with-the-boys beer, begins to tell you about the secret discussions which have taken place between the operators of the Braveheart nuclear plant and certain councillors regarding the possible use of Wick in its entirety as a nuclear waste dump.

'But it is already. I mean, let's face it, the sand on the beaches up there glows in the dark. All those surfers from Cornwall go up to try and catch a wave and when they fly back south they keep setting off the airport security alarms.'

'No, no, Zander, I mean, seriously, off the record, deep background only –' (these guys have seen *All the President's Men* at least a dozen times and have based their entire political lives, not to mention their views of the press, on ideas of being Deep MacThroat) '– the place is depopulating anyway at a rate of knots, what with the leukaemia and everything, so the Braveheart folk thought, what the hell, and you know, I mean, Wick? Give us a break. Now this is just between us, okay? Diary piece, maybe. Have another Laphroaig. It's all coming off the council tax, anyway . . .'

How to react? He thinks I'm drunk, but is playing some sort of mini MacMachiavelli-type game: probably he's got some grudge against the Wick councillor and wants some daft garbled, half-recollected-in-sobriety story to appear which will cause the poor soul embarrassment and a brief flash of local anguish before smiling denials are issued from Teuchterland HQ. Or, he wants to punish me for some imagined or genuine hurt by planting an entirely fictitious story. Or else he's more drunk than I am and it's true.

What he wants is power, remember, and power over the hack, even the power of ostensible friendship, floated on a sea of freebie alcohol, might be useful.

I want power too, though. I want a source. I want exclusivity. And next day, in virtual sobriety or at least the throes of hangoveritis, trying to sift through all the various options and traps set the night before, can be tricky. The best way – you remember? That's right! Get drunk again, recreating in your brain the sozzled conditions of recollection.

That way liver-related, pancreatic or marital disaster lies, though. A Baxter. Which is why, in the not-quite-end, I moved to Inverness with the aim of becoming a newspaper executive, a man in an unstained tie, someone who went home at night. Leaving the eternally blootered and violent industrial correspondents and unutterably pompous parliamentary specialists to their assignments, or rather issuing them with those tasks, and then reading the crap they came up with.

These dickheads who think they control the country's future with their mottled complexions and tight-arsed tedious prosody, their brown-nosed sucking at the orifices of politicians in a search for the gamey taste of self-importance. These insufferably self-sanctified priests of radio, print and television, unfit to tie the patent plastic shoes of Bruce Forsyth, the tiny plimsolls of Ronnie Corbett, or shine the polished leatherette of Bob Monkhouse's face – those three gods among light entertainers, for whom I have rather a soft spot. Because that, in the end, is what journalism is. Light entertainment with, occasionally, facts. Or farts. Or both.

I left the pack, I suppose. And hacks love to hunt in packs, and the man or woman who secretes a mineral water in their round instead of a gin and tonic will be found out and regarded with suspicion. You must share the drooling, dribbling oblivion to be One of Us. Being in the Masons does help (obviously, not for women, and the Order of the Eastern Star just doesn't pack the same twisty-fingered punch) not just within the journalistic community, but in relations with police, kirk ministers, Labour and Tory politicians and, of course, criminals and builders. But a collective rolling in the gutter does wonders for the credibility. Because, hey, aren't we all just looking at the Wildean stars together? Bottom of the world, Ma.

Thing is, you grow, inevitably, less and less able to cope physically with drink. While mentally, the experience and knowledge is there about cause, effect and strategy in the War of the Next Round, those liver enzymes can let you down. There are few sadder sights than the aftermath of editorial Christmas or retirement parties – and indeed office events in general; men and women of middle age, with families, responsibilities, position – even, in a few cases, respect – drooling and gabbling and cackling and falling rubber-legged into bushes, the glorious gutter, or ill-advised arms. Once they were able to cope with the incessant attempts to kill off every last liver enzyme, every functioning braincell. Now – well, now the body betrays them, giving the illusion of hard-quaffing drink-you-under-the-table-son solidity until suddenly, one glass tips the scales and turns them into gibbering, soiled wrecks. Or they go the whole way, abandon amateur status and turn pro. Like I did.

It begins, I think, with the promise of comfort, of oblivion, an illusion of brilliance. At the end of the day, or the week, there was always deliverance available for the price of a bottle. Reward. Hope. And wrapped up in that was the possibility of new encounters, of strangeness and consequently fresh, glistening sex. Because drink broke down barriers, provided friends, a community, a shifting cast of stars to share a mind-movie which could be anything you wanted it to be – hard-edged noir, soft-focus romantic, surrealist vision of hell or heaven, or sometimes just a seedy documentary about lost hopes and abandoned dreams. Drink smoothed the wrinkled complexion, rendered the bore witty, the fat thin, the bad breath sweet. It provided a myth of obtainable happiness.

Christ, I needed a fucking dram.

★ Five

Instead, I popped a couple of the Librium Hernia had given me and slumped into the cave-like built-in bunk which always reminded me of the double-decker beds my brother and I had slept in, back home. Home. Shetland had always been, would always be, home. That's why I never went back there. I hated home. Home had never hated me. That just made it worse.

Alcohol stops you dreaming. That had been one of the best things about being a drunk. Librium, fortunately, has the same effect. I woke up with a dull, throbbing chemical hangover, ravenously hungry at two in the afternoon. It was time to think about living again, and what that involved. Like eating. God, I could have murdered a black-pudding supper. It would have to wait. I'd missed the lunchtime frying session in the Sneck chip shops.

I did the things I had for the past year or so been increasingly neglecting – shaving, washing – with the result that my face was a bloody, tissue-daubed mess, unused to the kiss of a new double-blade Gillette Sensor. Razor sharp. At St Buidsear's I'd used the dodgy plastic disposables they had for shaving body hair prior to operations. They inflicted pain, but tended to bruise rather than wound. The Tub had, ironically, no bath, just a little electric shower which could barely take my none-too-enormous carcass. A carcass I examined curiously, as if I hadn't seen it in a long, long time. It was not just thin, but blotchy, itchy and flaccid, like a body which had been under water for days. Pickled. I poached myself in boiling water and felt a little better.

I called a taxi and had it drop me at the central Safeway, built on the site of what was once Inverness's greatest heavy-industrial complex, a railway machinery construction plant, long gone. Only a tiled mural above the nearby Albatross bar indicated the pride and power which had once bred here. The Albatross was open, of course. Like some black hole, ready to suck me into its maw, it stood there, malevolent, mysterious and familiar, just another old pub, the bottom floor of a Victorian tenement which had been converted into unlet offices. A friend waiting to betray me.

I headed for the supermarket and suffered stale cappuccino, heavily flavoured with rubber, for some reason, as if the beans had been packed in

condoms, and the full, all-day five items of your choice megabreakfast. I
wondered about taking another couple of reality-blurring pills, but decided
against it. Instead, I shopped, wandering the aisles, still woozy, picking up
milk, and butter and bread and ham and chicken soup, and other instant
comfort food staples. Porage. Scott's Porage Oats, the only ones that had
ever tasted right. The ultimate gut-cuddler, day or night, and good at
putting you to sleep, too. Bananas, another natural anaesthetic. Berocca
effervescent multi-vitamins, designed for women having their periods, but
ideal for men with partially wrecked livers. Baxtered bastards like myself. I
paid by Switch, got fifty quid cash back at the checkout till and hitched my
couple of carrier bags like a seasoned bachelor shopper. Then I went to the
Albatross. Temptation? Give me some.

I walked in, and immediately they all went into their act. Which
involved an initial collective pretence that they hadn't seen me.

Sludge, mine host, rubbed his enormous, callused hands on an old
copy of the *War Cry* and spat in the pint of dubious brown beer before
him on the counter.

'Here, that's no' very healthy,' said McGrooch. 'What poor soul is going
to have to drink that? If it's for you, you'll end up poisoning yourself.'

'No, no,' murmured Sludge, his voice reverberating through the pub
like a faulty set of plumbing. 'It's not for me. It's for one of those
Campaign for Real Ale people in the lounge. It's more of a symbol, like,
no' an attempt to infect him with my multitudinous pulmonary
infections. Anyway, I'm going to stick it in the microwave for half a
minute; that'll kill all the germs. It's my special Old Flatulence real ale
stuff, anyhow. Needs to be warm to be real, or so all they so-called experts
say.' He shot a glance at the only other figure in the bar, a slight, denim-
clad man with a grey ponytail, wearing small round John Lennon glasses
and nursing a half pint of something pale yellow. 'You've gave it up now,
Settler, that no' right? For the good of your health?'

The man who had been dubbed White Settler from the moment he
entered the Albatross, two years previously, looked at Sludge. His accent
was a flat, nasal Yorkshire bark. 'Force of circumstance, mate. Soon
realised the only thing that was drinkable here was the lager. I think I got
the message when I found that dead mouse in my pint of whatever the
Ale of the Month was back in 1994.'

'Royal Cream of Wartsqueeze,' said McGrooch, nodding his head,
which bore a crumpled and one-size-too-small grey homburg hat. This
item of headgear was never removed, leading to strong rumours that
McGrooch, a retired suppository salesman, slept in it, and that it had
become permanently attached to his scalp by a mixture of dirt and
crushed, liquefied lice. 'Still the same guest ale, Sludge, if I'm not
mistaken. Never changed the barrel.'

'The brewery,' sighed Sludge – a noise which caused every glass in the place to rattle – 'insisted on it. Trendy, they said. Got to keep up with modern shifts in the *Zeitgeist*. I mean, what's wrong with a pub specialising, I say. If somebody wants to specialise in stupid dirty beers that you serve at the temperature of Horlicks, look like liquefied manure and have names like Ancient Scrotum or Filthguzzler, fair play to them. The Albatross has always had a name for fizzy brown beer and fizzy yellow beer. Heavy and lager. Consistent, we are. Then the brewery comes along and says, get in some real ale, do a guest ale, different every week. I told them it wouldnae work.'

'What do you expect when you keep on the one barrel of – what was it? – Royal Cream of Pimple-Pus for three years, and dump vermin in customers' glasses?' The White Settler pulled out a package from his pocket. 'Anyway, here's that old video of Sarah Dunant interviewing Gore Vidal on *The Late Show* you wanted. Collector's item, man. There might be a bit of *Jules et Jim* at the end, too. I recorded over it.'

'Seen it a dozen times,' grumbled Sludge. 'Always fancied that Dunant, though. Ken this, she writes detective thrillers, too, ironic feminist takes on the hard-boiled genre.'

'Really,' said the White Settler, 'are they any good?'

'Naw,' said Sludge. 'Crime fiction is a male hegemonic construct, if you ask me.'

'What about that woman who does all the, you know, cutting up dead folk on slabs?' demanded McGrooch. 'Got into a bit o' bother wi' some FBI agent and her man, having an affair wi' one or the other, or maybe both, I cannae mind.'

'Patricia Cornwell,' said the White Settler. 'Barely literate.'

'And Sarah Paretsky's even worse,' rumbled Sludge. 'Barbara Cartland crossed wi' Ed McBain and Enid Blyton. And that's no' a bedtime combination I even like to think about, eh, McGrooch?'

'You're right there, Sludge. An unshaggable trinity. Anyway, what about that pint for your CAMRA man through in the lounge? Think he'll give the place a really bad write-up, save us from hairy bearded men in fishing smocks? And what is that Old Diarrhoea stuff, anyway? You've never had it in before? I don't believe these ironic names they're giving drinks now, by the way. Damn disgrace. We should get copyright money. Wasn't it you who first started calling that bottled gin-and-tonic stuff Dog's Breath, Sludge? Next minute, it's on the fucking label.'

Sludge shook his massive head, the shiny scalp and greasy, ever more isolated central quiff gleaming in the glare of the Albatross's bare lightbulbs. 'This isn't the true Old Fartulence. This is just a mixture of what was left in the glasses when I cleared up last night, plus a bit of cigarette ash and pakora sauce I found in a dish outside the door this morning on the pavement.'

Funny guy, Sludge. With him, you always knew where you weren't.

'Sounds great,' said the White Settler. 'I'll have a pint when I've finished this. It'll go well with that tape of Melvyn Bragg interviewing himself you keep showing.'

'Aye,' said Sludge. 'It'll taste the same coming back up as it did going down. Now, sir,' he turned to me, fixing me with his red-rimmed eyes, then encompassed the others in his gaze. 'The bastard will have an orange juice, methinks.'

'And fucking like it,' muttered McGrooch.

'Yeah, get it down you, ya poof,' said Settler, whose real name, fancifully enough, was Hamish MacTavish, the result of two East Anglian parents lit by a Celtic twilight they had gleaned from coach tours to Callander and the Trossachs, during one of which he had been conceived. Or so he claimed. These days, if you called him Hamish, he thought you were taking the piss.

'Britvic, then,' I said, noticing that my hands were shaking. 'No ice. Shaken not stirred. All that shite.'

'Take a stool and it'll be right up,' said Sludge. That was meant to be his real name. His first was allegedly Justin, though he had never confirmed that personally, except through gratuitous violence to one individual who had muttered the name in the last stages of being thrown out, two hours after closing time. 'That's no' a fuckin' name,' Sludge had muttered, 'it's a fucking disease.' So maybe it was his name. Who knew? And where the clan Sludge hailed from nobody had ever asked.

'Heard you assaulted some American tourist,' said McGrooch, his overgrown moustache, more of a mouth-curtain, flickering with foam. It resembled the jungle growth covering some secret cavern in a Tarzan film. Behind it were nameless horrors which smelt of bad curry and carried awful illnesses. 'Had to take her to St Buidsear's and pump her up. Heard she was shipped back to the States, at grave risk of permanent hairstyle damage. Presumably her insurance covered the whole deal.'

'I heard you were nearly dead and gone, mate, assaulted with a deadly bottle . . . I mean weapon.' Settler laughed a great snorting guffaw. 'All right?'

The others went silent. Sludge was pouring two small bottles of orange into a half-pint glass. I realised that Hernia must have been in, and threatened all sorts of godless revenge if I received a proper drink. Probably had a Millburn or two while he was at it, the prick. Maybe he said he would sing some of his fucking favourite show tunes. A Barbra Streisand medley. Or give them a reading from a 1954 *Beano* annual.

'Seen Celia?' The words just slipped out, like a reaction to the orange juice, so metallic and acidic, so empty of promise or relief. There was no reply. Then I felt a sharp pain in my left buttock. I was wearing a pair of old Levis and an even more venerable Incredible String Band T-shirt, from the group's latter days, when they were a bunch of raggle-taggle gypsies who made The Waterboys look like Pringle-sweatered golf club members. I'd been pinched, hard. Very hard indeed to get past the sagging denim and into my desiccated flesh.

'Saw her just an hour ago,' came a voice, liquid over slow stones, cigarette-roughened without being harsh, that lovely Bristol burr, a sort of urbanised ooh-arr Wurzel tone, with a touch of Cromwellian Highland twang from the years in Sneck. 'Not too pleasant a sight, but at least the mirror stayed in one piece.' Two cool, small hands slipped over my eyes and a warm tongue flicked pleasantly into my right ear. 'How does it feel to be sober, then, big man?'

'Hard, Celia, hard.' I shifted on my stool. Sobriety wasn't the only thing I was talking about. Then, lightly: 'So, no visits, eh? Thought I'd died and gone to hospital heaven, such was the lack of you guys. Heard the dedication, though. Thoughtful.'

This time the silence was awkward, not piss-taking.

Celia slipped onto the stool next to mine in that loose-limbed way she had, drunk or nearly sober, and started struggling with the old Eddie Bauer rucksack she used as a substitute handbag. Taking out a pack of Silk Cut, she ripped the filter off one and lit it, sucking at the cigarette with the casual hunger I'd always found attractive in her. The short, bleached-blond hair needed another dose of dye, and her eyes were more deeply shadowed than usual, courtesy of nothing more cosmetic than drink and fatigue. 'Taken up smoking then, Zander? Transference and all that?' She flicked her head to one side and blew lungfuls of blue smoke towards the gantry.

'No, I don't think so. Bad for my clean-living image.' The Librium was wearing off, but I still felt hollow and slow. 'Besides, I prefer inhaling yours second-hand.'

She grimaced, and demanded a glass of the Albatross's dubious house red, a Chilean Cab Sauv of dodgy provenance: Château Pinochet.

'One glass of Blood of the Revolutionary Martyrs, coming right up!' Sludge was suddenly all efficiency. 'Clean or dirty glass, madam?'

'Oh, dirty, I think, Sludge,' said Celia. 'I wouldn't want any special favours I might have to repay.' She turned to me. A hiss of clothes, nyloned thighs. My hearing was suddenly preternaturally acute. I could hear her heart beating, her lungs wheezing, lightly. 'Hernia was in, just after you did your tourist-squashing thing. Immediately after, in fact, trying to get Clingfilm McCorquodale to put a block on the story.' Clingfilm owned one of the main press agencies in Sneck, the avenue south for dirt, sleaze and quirky tales of mad Highlanders. Crushed tourists would certainly qualify. I had glanced at few papers over the past ten days, but hadn't noticed anything about me and deflating Americans. Nobody had mentioned any such notoriety.

'So . . . what happened? Did Clingfilm send anything south?'

She stubbed her fag out, angrily, thoroughly, until there was a round patch of black ash surrounding the half-inch of unsmoked cigarette. 'What do you think? Clingfilm's a greedy, ruthless son of a horse fucker. You were just lucky. Two pars in *The Sun* and *The Mirror*. There was a bank robbery in Fort Hanover the same day. A teller was killed. Two Highland stories was one too many.'

'What about Radio Fuckwank?'

Celia worked, off and on, mostly on, for both Clingfilm and a local commercial radio station, Northlands, hacking in a freelance fashion as a news reporter, sometime producer and general dogsbody. She'd blown into Inverness about five years previously, halfway to being a new-age traveller, but not quite so acid-frazzled as the majority of them. No dog on a string. No underarm lice. A bit of cash from somewhere. Maybe family. She never talked about them. Clingfilm had picked her up in a pub one night, shagged her, and she'd insisted on something in return. What the disreputable old shite considered a training in journalism followed, during which he dropped her for a travelling taxidermist, up in the Highlands for the shooting season. Stuffing interested him. But for whatever reason, Celia stayed, picking up work here and there. Doing okay, but drinking enough to calcify the liver of a buffalo.

'The Fuckwankers had to carry it, I'm afraid. It was running on the police wire. But it was swamped by the Fort Hanover stuff. Mind you,' she permitted herself an arch grin; her face suddenly crinkled and then opened up, like sun on an autumn afternoon, 'I doubt if you'll be back as The Private Eye of the Airwaves for a while. Not that you hadn't blotted your copybook sufficiently,' pronounced *soofishently*. 'But, then again, if they get desperate . . . and you're all clean and sober . . .'

That *soofishently* sent a shiver down the spine. But clammy memory intruded. Oh yes. When I first set up my fantasy investigations business, the whole idea was so novel in the Calvinist climes of Sneck that I'd appeared on Radio Northlands' *Round the Houses* afternoon show, being interviewed about the rough-and-tumble world of big-time detection. A subject I knew loads about. From books.

'No risk of you carrying a gun, then, Zander?' the presenter, Fergus Evelyn, had one of those deep, mellifluous and utterly fake voices which usually match up, in radio, with smelly, ugly, diseased individuals dressed in Bri-Nylon and corduroy. He was no exception. I assured him there wasn't, and soon was on the show regularly, doing a phone-in spot called, you guessed it, Private Eye of the Airwaves. Remember Eddie Shoestring? You don't? Anyway, I would advise callers on how not to take the law into their own hands, how to check up on partners they thought might be cheating on them. I even got a couple of crap divorce cases out of it. Up trees with a telephoto lens. People like poor, uncertain Mrs Heard, wondering about their husbands. No husbands concerned about their wives, funnily enough.

It all went horribly wrong one afternoon, when, after a moderate lunchtime of whisky tasting at the Albatross, I told Fergus Evelyn, on air, that I would have to leave the studio, as I was about to be sick due to the aroma his armpits were giving out. I believe my final words were 'See that brown stuff you rub under your arms in the mornings, Ferg?' and then the engineer, overreacting in my opinion, hauled the fader down on my broadcasting career.

'I suppose Hernia also put the fear of God into you all about letting me drink anything other than this pish?'

Silence. I felt the overwhelming presence of the bar, smelt the wood, soaked in beer for decade upon decade, the sour overlay of fag reek, the sharp tang of whisky as it was poured, watched motes of dust spin and flicker in sunbeams brave enough to penetrate the murk, heard the low rumble of inconsequential talk, the gradual softening of reality, the illusions of brilliance, the truth of oblivion. A great, crying, unbearably sad thirst erupted, deep in my gut, and I could feel myself shaking, a huge trembling which began in my dried-out soul and spread to the tips of my fingers. Then I started crying. Fuck. Fuck fuck fuck fuck fuck. The embarrassment.

'Come on, Zander,' Celia had her hand on mine, gently kneading. 'Whatever's in those bags is melting. Want a run home?'

I nodded, girnily, breath snuffling like a wean. The rest of them turned away. Sludge came out from behind the bar and fiddled with the ancient jukebox, stocked with the favourites of his regular customers. The sound of Linda Ronstadt came on: *Poor, Poor Pitiful Me*. The censored version of a Warren Zevon song. Nice one, Sludge. Tasteful as ever.

Celia helped me gather up the proud signs of my sober need for sustenance and we left in a fug of embarrassment.

'See you soon, Zander,' said Sludge, as forthright and normal as I'd ever heard him. 'Come back but . . .'

I didn't like to think what the 'but . . .' meant. Don't ruin our little world with your tears, perhaps. With your shitty real life.

Celia's car was in the Safeway carpark, behind the pub. Like a married couple, we arrived at the dirty, heavily restored but still rusty Alfasud she loved, had inveigled from years of beloved storage in the garage of an old ex-RAF pilot she'd gone to interview. I slung the meagre shopping in the boot, and climbed in after she'd unlocked the passenger door, leaning over, exposing one black bra strap in the wide, scalloped neck of her midnight-blue satin top. She was wearing a long, half-hippy blue cotton skirt and looked, as ever, smokily sexy. Not beautiful, not even pretty, unless you looked hard, and then you glimpsed a great vulnerability amid the late-twenties, self-consciously mysterious Bristolian bravado. She was Lauren Bacall on a mid-period Bergman body. I'd love to have loved her. Instead, we just had sex. And more often than not in the past few months, tried woozily to have sex, but didn't; ended up in the drunken comfort zone of cuddled, resigned frustration. Hernia had told Dr Azad I was impotent. Maybe he had been talking to Celia. Or, more likely, she had been talking, garrulous and unguarded with booze.

'Look, I'm sorry for not visiting or getting in touch, but it's just . . . Hernia thought it was . . . said we'd better stay away. He said you were out for the count mostly, anyway.' She shrugged. There was a casualness about Celia I'd never come to terms with, a deliberate lack of concern, a vague distance. Maybe it was a protective device, or perhaps she was truly what she sometimes appeared: the zipless lust child of Erica Jong and R.D. Laing. The background? Bristol? She'd let slip something about art school, but that was the lot. Even juiced up, she protected herself from revealing certain things. Maybe not about my flaccidity, though. It rankled, Hernia's comment in the hospital. Accusations of impotence often annoy, even if true. Especially if true.

'Well, that's right enough.' *Raaaiiiat enaaaafff.* I wiped my face. It felt that diminished, playground way, when you failed to stop yourself greeting at school. As if everyone would know immediately you'd been crying. Would remember forever. 'Sorry about that. In there, I mean, it was . . .'

'You know what they say about strong men,' she interrupted, smiling that cloud-ripping smile again. 'Unafraid to weep.' She leaned over and her lips, familiar and yet strange in their cracked softness, met my sticky, swollen eyes, then my mouth. I reached for her hair, like some strange fungus, dry where the chemical dye had sucked out the life, felt the lumpy scalp beneath. 'Inertia reel,' she said, when our mouths parted in inelegant strings of saliva which tasted of smoke and oranges. I loved kissing a smoker. It was like drinking Laphroaig. Shit. Did being sober mean you had to stop even that? Stop kissing drinkers and smokers, in case you remembered too much, and the memory sucked you in, down into the drowning depths of a golden glass?

'What?'

'Inertia reel. Your seatbelt. Automatically adjusts in the event of an accident. Still restrictive, though.' That smile. I looked out of the car windows. We were in one of the darkest recesses of the multi-storey; the other vehicles looked long-term. Besides, the old Alfa had tinted windows. I snapped the buckle on the seatbelt and reached for her.

★ Six

If you thought, really thought objectively about sex, about the actual idiotic interlacings and curious couplings, the smells and stretchings, sounds and physical ungainliness, the sheer fucking hydraulics of it all, no one would ever shag, except from dire reproductive necessity, in a grim spirit of squelching, progeny-producing duty. Add to that a requirement of performing all the bits and bobs of bonking in-car, even an Italian car presumably designed for such eventualities, and the distanced, analytical, balanced, sensitive observer will find himself or herself overwhelmed by the utter silliness, the farcical ugliness of it all.

Which is why we have hormones, great, storming surges of bio-chemicals which take the shyest, the most self-analytical, the most cynical, and transform them into raging animal acrobats behind steamed-up windows, shamelessly, obediently enacting that physical imperative, human lust.

Of course, it's all a lot easier to lose yourself on the roller-coaster, the veritable Alton Towers of coitus if you're a fucked-up, unfucked alcoholic (I was getting used to the word; there was a nice self-lacerating slash of abuse, a shiver of self-hatred, every time I deployed it) who hasn't had successful sex in months, and whose body is just beginning to recover from the deliberate application of toxic anaesthetic in vast quantities, not to mention falling down some stone steps onto a lardy Yank. In a purely platonic way, of course. Thing is, in sexual terms, things happen or they don't. But control is not an issue. When those secretions kick in, the wasted muscles reach for memories of youth and tone, oxygen pounds through lungs and the heart hammers like a redundant riveter brought out of retirement for one final big job, one last liner. That intellectual part of your humanity just shuts down: animal instincts take over, in a frenzy of licking, sucking, tasting, of substances and places that would normally – whatever 'normally' is – appal. Unwashed, sweaty, fag-reeking, shitty, rank, greasy, twisted, hairy, unshaven, knobbly, infected, diseased – all these cease to matter, cease to be even remote considerations. It's like fighting, getting ready to die in some kind of battle. Or that moment when Harrison Ford sends the ship into warp speed in *Star Wars*. Reality just whooshes away behind you and you enter some kind of high-speed space-flume.

Oh yes, tumbling down the tunnel of cosmic luuurrrvv we go, skooshing along, out of control, sperm-swimmers together or in the case of Celia and me, a kind of damp, snarling, scratchy wrestle of clothes and flesh and sweat, fingers and lips and pricks and fannies – one prick, one fanny – as the windows of the car became almost instantly opaque and condensation formed on the plastic roof lining. Jesus, it was like a sober drunk, or a coke rush. Not that I had much experience with cocaine, save the supremely confident, temple-pounding, blood-rush-jabbering conversations I'd had once or twice under its expensive influence. No. The sensation was more like the one time I'd taken opium, accidentally smoked it mixed with some hash in a car outside a village hall deep in the Grampians, all on top of about six pints of heavy beer. I'd felt, then seen my stomach erupting, pleasantly at first, in a fiery rage of ash and molten lava, up, up into the night sky. Unstoppable, wondrous. I threw up soon after.

The bra under Celia's blue satin shirt was, thank St Michael, not one of those underwired, spring-loaded, push-up-and-out affairs, things that could trap a man's finger and lead to embarrassing scenes involving the fire brigade. Her breasts were never, short of suckling an entire football team of hungry children, going to be pendulous but they weren't by any means small, either. The nipples hardened instantly at the clumsiness of my hands, and then I was reaching, scratchily, along her legs, snagging the rough skin of my fingers on black nylon tights, pushing at the soft dampness, hearing Celia groan, then feeling her hands leave my own body as she lifted herself and smoothly pulled them down, complete with knickers. Just as well, because unlike in books and movies, Marks and Spencer's cotton knickers are not designed with little perforations of passion which just zip away when some stray man decides to do a bit of genital exploration.

A scent of musky warmth rose, mixing with the Arctic Tree air freshener and her own Armani Giò perfume, and I was pushing gently at moist flesh. I could feel her nails raking my chest, cold and sharp at my nipples, scratching, not lightly, then struggling with my belt, pulling it out of its loops in one sudden whiplash movement.

Put it this way, we helped each other, and bit and rubbed and tongued until there was an overwhelming mutual need to connect utterly, completely, handbrake levers notwithstanding. Condoms? Is sex meant to be safe? I can't think of anything more innately dangerous, more designed to be risky. Seats can recline very quickly when you want them to. I prayed the brakes would hold, and that this great outpouring of lust would not turn into a *Carry On* sketch, a Sid James and Barbara Windsor special with a runaway Alfa banging into some shopper's beloved Vauxhall Nova while uninhibited body-bouncing continued within a steamed-up Alfa Romeo-stroke-Fiat. The anti-roll bar squeaked, but fortunately the old rustbucket's springs were relatively hard. There didn't seem to be too much suspicious, untoward rolling. But, for all I knew, a crowd had gathered outside, and were watching in expectant delight. I couldn't have cared less.

Romeo, Romeo, wherefore art thou, Alfa. I could feel myself coming like the long, microsecond fall from a diving board, all expectation and fear, and then the trembling, crying, choking urgency of Celia's orgasm as my entire body shook with the moment. It was like getting slapped about by God, crashing through rapids in an ill-equipped boat, halfway between terror and delight. Unlike any sex before; scarily abnormal. I climaxed ferociously yet without the same choked pleasure, somehow. I probably hadn't had an alcohol-free fuck in twenty-odd years of shagging. From first fumbled gropings on peat banks in the *simmer dim*, the endless midsummer daylight of home, fuelled by Snakebite, cheap cider mixed with Special Brew, onwards and upwards to the whisky-splashed shores of Lucy and Celia and all the others. And now this, curiously empty conclusion to the surging lust. Holding, clutching, grabbling each other, trying to meld two bodies into one, lost in a wash of cum and spittle and sweat and tears.

At least I was. But, then, the mutuality of a successful fuck is largely guesswork and lies, isn't it? In the hiddenness of sex's aftermath lies the truth about you, me, her, him, us. Or am I being cynical? Does my technique need adjustment? Celia was always cool afterwards, whimpering in the lostness of orgasm. Never screaming or yelling. Wouldn't talk about it afterwards, either, not in specifics. Once, early on, I'd whispered, 'Did you . . .?' She had laughed that chesty, pre-emphysemic laugh and replied in her West Country burr: 'There are some things you never ask a woman.' In my experience, that hadn't been one of them, but you were always learning. Whatever, she seemed to need me as much as I needed her, when I needed her. If.

And after the coming, the coming to, the ebbing hormones' betrayal as recognition hit of where we were, the state we were in, what anyone would say or think if they saw us; the sheer loss of control which we'd both encountered.

'Missed you,' she said, her breath shuddering out, her heartbeat ticking somewhere deep down in those ash-strewn airways. 'Christ, I need a fag.' And with the kind of easy grace she'd always had, she separated herself from me, accompanied by a soundtrack of unsticking skin, a damp Velcro tearing. I withdrew, but she was instantly withdrawn, other. Unashamed, but somehow strangely modest in this near-nakedness. But, then, this was her car; for her, this was almost like being at home. Maybe she did this kind of thing a lot. If so, it had never been with me.

'I . . . I wasn't really capable of missing . . .' I began, stumbling stupidly into honesty. 'What I mean is, I'm sorry, but I was so fucking wrapped up, so . . . I don't know, Celia. I was drowning in it, I suppose. Drowning in the big thirst.' I had pulled on my trousers, never a moment conducive to important, insightful conversation. In that competent, controlled, efficient way she and many other women had, gracefulness under pressure, she was very nearly the civilised working woman again. I examined her neck for lovebites. None. She was always careful with me. She'd had to be back when . . .

'How long is it since you had a sober fuck, then, Zander?' She was frowning, squinting through the smoke of fresh Silk Cut. 'I tell you, I think it's a while for me. Not that I've always been rat-arsed for it, but the bright edge of it's always been dulled. Long as I can remember. Had to be, really. Had to be that way, to take away the sort of . . . worry of it all. Know what I mean?'

I smelt my fingers, licked the taste of her, already fading. 'I know, yeah. You can't be sure the other person wants what you do, and the last thing you need is rejection. So the drink breaks down the fear, and any barriers. Fuck, I don't know. It's a long time since I even had sex in the daytime, let alone without distilled help.'

'It's good though?' Was there uncertainty there? From the woman who never talked about it afterwards? Or maybe she had, and I'd never noticed, so asleep, worn out with the effort of delivering some sort of facsimile of orgasm through the mists of inebriation. Even with Lucy it had always been a drink thing. A bottle of wine, couple of G-and-Ts, coffee, whisky, a glow on, recognising definite signs, confidently making old moves, receiving expected responses. *Yeah, yeah, let's . . .* but not having to say. And eventually, when ease became monotony, resorting to drink to get through the tedium of it, to kindle the fantasies, dull the reality of boredom and betrayal.

'This? This was great,' I said, maybe some false note of eagerness there, I don't know. Yes. Detectable. 'It was like –'

She reached a finger, smoke-tasting, and placed it against my lips. 'Don't. You don't have to. Don't say anything. You have a habit of ruining things with words. Save the metaphors for some gullible girl.'

'You sound like a sub-editor. A subber of sex. Cut to the meat, to the bones, to basics. Put the whole lot in the first paragraph.'

'Yes. Well, I always thought too much emphasis was put on foreplay,' she said. 'Sometimes. If the story calls for . . . plunging straight in . . .'

We both laughed. She inhaled, opened the quarterlight – Italian cars still have them – and flicked ash expertly out. She always made a solid *thwick!* noise when she flicked a fag. A determined, convinced, from-the-gut smoker. 'Remember what you said, the first time we had sex? The first time we made love?'

I shook my head, but I knew what she was going to say.

'You said: "Don't worry, I'll never leave my wife for you." Don't worry. Fuck, that was perfect post-coital conversation, that was. Just what I wanted to hear.'

'I thought . . . anyway I was drunk . . .'

'That going to be your excuse for everything that's happened, is it? Everything you said? You were pissed, now you're not. Thank the good Lord above, I'm free at last? *In vino* fucking *veritas*, sunshine. Anyway, I didn't want you to leave your wife for me. That wasn't what I was after at all. Bad fucking bargain, mate. That's what you were. Damaged fucking goods.'

'Worse now.'

She half-giggled, a little snort, derisive.

'I was just trying to . . .'

'And then you leave her anyway, and all that shite flying around. Turns out she's been shagging your boss ever since you moved to Inverness, and you, you're basically up to old tricks, because from what I hear from the granite-hearted city you were up every set of female journalistic drawers like a ferret up a particularly tasty drainpipe.'

'Rat. And how can you have a tasty drainpipe?'

'Yeah, rat. That's you. But I still like you. Liked you. Of course drainpipes can be tasty. Treacle down a drainpipe. Golden syrup, dripping, down that pipe, bit by bit, slowly . . .' she grinned and reached for my groin. 'Yum, yum! Anyway.' She ground the fag out on the yellow-stained glass of the quarterlight, then flicked it out into the carpark. No spilled fuel. No explosions. Presumably no spectators. 'What is this, then? What was that? Who are you not going to leave for me this time?'

I took her hand while it was fag-free. 'Listen, Celia. Weird things are happening. Have been happening. I think, I honestly think, someone's trying to kill me.' She tried to control the flash of amusement; failed. I ploughed on anyway. 'A guy called Jeremiah Smith, who . . .' As soon as I began saying it, I sounded ridiculous to myself. Well, maybe not ridiculous, considering I was a paranoid drunk on a temporary sober kick. Who knew?

She looked away, withdrew her hand, and began laughing a mirthless, inner set of demi-giggles. 'Yeah, yeah.' Another fag was being knocked out of the purple and white packet. 'Tell me, would you have killed Lucy and that prick Charleson?'

Ah, Celia, you really choose your fucking moments, don't you? Frederick Charleson. A name to conjure older nightmares with. Different from Jeremiah Gideon Smith, but in their own way as bad. Or worse.

The number one at the Sneck office of the *Northern Mail and Courier* was a fast-track whizz kid from one of the English papers in the Courier

Group, a product of Cambridge and the company's own super-selective training course. Two years younger than me, earmarked for something on one of what they called the nationals, the English papers, the London fucking locals. As the months passed, he left me more and more to wrap up the edition's make-up on screen, liaising with the printers in Aberdeen as he went drinking in the hacks' pub, the Vintners, waiting for the call that would take him south to some warehouse out in Docklands, the centre of the bloody newsprint universe, the barbed wire repaired from the last strike . . .

I remembered the moment, the returning home from some godless function at the Caledonian Hotel, something to do with farmers, Highland Beef Will Not Make You Mad, the launch of some backs-to-the-wall, BSE-is-good-for-you campaign. More than half drunk, as per normal; throwing open the door to the bedroom and there it was: Cuckold City. Or rather, way out in the Black Isle sticks as we were, Cuckold Country. Hey, mate! Here's a set of horns for you, put them on, there's a good chap and run around outside while a hundred hidden loudspeakers blare out Billy Paul's *Me and Mrs Jones*. We got a thing goin' on. Too fucking right.

'No, I wouldn't have killed them. Yes, I felt like it. Anyway, I was pissed . . .' *Anyway I was pissed*. The old excuse. She leaned back against the car door, as if I was some monster about to snatch away her virginity. Which was, on the face of it, unfair. What we had been mutually snatching at was certainly not virgin territory. 'I admit, tying them together and then dumping them naked in the garden was a bit extreme.'

'It was winter.'

'I know goddamn well it was winter. That was the point. Make them contemplate their sin for a while.'

'Oh, come on. You and I were fucking then as well. What about that for sin?'

I looked at her. 'Don't you imagine for a minute that I hadn't been contemplating that every time . . . oh Christ, Celia, I don't know. Maybe it was a guy thing.' How feeble can you get. 'It was . . . in my bed.' It sounded crap as soon as I said it.

'Oh, yeah, thank fuck for feminism. The marital bed. *Your* bed. What is this crap? You live away out in the country, the nearest neighbour is what, a mile away? Two? And you call it a guy thing? You went to sleep. On the couch. You lay down on the sofa and went to self-satisfied sleep. You fucking idiot. The police had to wake you up with the two of them almost hypothermic in the back of their squad car, which just happened to be passing when a stark-naked Frederick Charleson, newspaper executive, and Lucy Flaws, freelance PR consultant, ran out in front of them, his bollocks doubtless solidifying before their very eyes. But then, they were more probably looking at her tits. She had good tits, didn't she, Zander?'

'Not bad.' I didn't want to dwell on those particular aspects of my ex-wife. 'But look, I made my point, didn't I? And I wasn't arrested. Not . . . officially.' I hadn't actually meant to fall alseep. The drink.

'Oh, yeah, you made your point. Writing "I AM A TARTCUNT", which isn't even grammatical, on the back of your wife in lipstick –'

'No matter how attractive a two-syllable epithet it may be.'

'– and painting Charleson's cock with black Hammerite. Jesus.'

'Don't forget writing "DON'T TOUCH AIDS RISK" on his gut, which was, I may add, hairless in the extreme. Plus everything was spelt right. So I couldn't have been that pissed. Mind you, it took a bit out of me, holding them down. The poker helped. To be honest, I still can't believe I had it in me.' That at least was true. It had been like another person taking over. A much stronger, unamused, ruthless, less dithery person. But when I fell asleep, he went away, and then the police were there.

'You're a maniac.'

'What can I say? I am a different person now since Jesus changed my life and I forswore strong drink? I don't think what I did was anything to do with drink, actually. I think it was there, lurking. Possibly it still is. Maybe that's the real me. I tell you, sometimes I think that fucker Charleson was lucky I didn't cut his balls off and stuff them down his throat.'

Big talk. But to tell the truth, I had considered it, albeit briefly. Falling asleep had been a mistake. I had intended to put them out in the back garden for ten minutes or so, tied together, get their teeth chattering as they considered the errors of their various ways. But what can I tell you? I had locked the doors, sat down, satisfied, the calm demon in me feeling angrily, eerily at peace; I put my head back and the Land of Nod had me in its pleasant grip immediately. They panicked, understandably, after fifteen minutes, and hopped into the front garden like entrants in a nudist three-legged race – they were tied together hand and foot, amazingly secure considering my condition and the slippiness of plastic-coated clothesline – shame fleeing as the goosepimples gathered, and started screaming for help. Which, from the fascinated neighbours, a herd of shivering cows, they did not get. So they ran sobbing down to the road, along to the crossroads, where, by some accident of fate, a police car was cruising, probably looking for parked adulterers they could harass. When into their mainbeams runs the stuff of constabulary fantasy.

Somehow, the *Mail and Courier*, using its not inconsiderable media muscle, hushed the thing up, though God only knows what they say about that prick Charleson behind his back down in Edinburgh. Well, actually I know, because Jimbo Clark, one of the few still working at the *M&C* who speaks to me on occasion, told me. Among other things, they call him Turps, short for Turpentine Balls. Hammerite is the very devil to get off. What amazed me was that Lucy and he had, ahem, stuck together after the shame and embarrassment of it all. But then, they had probably established a real bond out there in the cold and dark. Besides, the bitch turned out to be pregnant.

'She was pregnant, too.' God almighty, Celia wasn't letting up.

'I didn't know that. Do you think if I'd known that I'd have . . .' I opened the passenger door, letting a burst of warm air into the already saunaesque car. They'd lost the child. My fault. My fucking fault. Sometimes I wondered if it had been my baby, if Lucy had just said it was Charleson's to snare him. But he – it had been a boy – was lost now. Gone. Maybe Lucy knew. She would tell me whatever she thought would hurt most.

Outside, the carpark was still quiet. Our encounter had created little interest. Despite the heat and the sweat, the dry dustiness of Inverness in high summer, the Sneckie drought season, I shivered. Celia had taken our brief warm spurt of passion and chilled it in the memory of a past winter's evening I had drunk a great deal of money to try and forget.

'Let's get out of here, Celia,' I said. 'I'm cold.' Just then her pager went off. Christ, everyone was in demand, everybody was needed. Except me.

Maudlin bastard.

Radio Northlands News, I'm Trevor Allcock. One local youngster is dead, two are recovering and one girl is in a coma at St Buidsear's Hospital in Inverness, after what police are describing as a drugs experiment which went tragically wrong.

The dead boy, sixteen-year-old Frankie McCormack of Picardy Place, in the Ferry, suffered heart failure after being unconscious for two days. His parents, Jimmy and Marjorie McCormack, are devastated:

CUE MINIDISC INSERT 1 (ONE):

JIMMY: Ah . . . he wis a . . . good boy, like. Always quiet and . . . kind. He was goin' to college next year to do hairdressing. He always fancied bein' a barber, ken? I don't think he ever took drugs afore, to be honest wi' you. Ah'm jist . . . he wis wir only . . .

MARJORIE: Ah'm devastatit. Absolutely devastatit. Ah don't know whit we're gonnae do, now. He wis hangin' oot wi' his pals, ken, jist a crew o' young folk, ah wouldnae hae said they wir bad. Mah boy never took drugs, never. Not till this. Ah cannae bear it.

END INSERT

A hospital spokesperson said that two other youngsters, believed to be male and also in their teens, were making a good recovery after treatment for shock and the effects of narcotics. The fourth person involved, a girl, is still seriously ill and her condition is described as giving cause for concern. She is understood to be sixteen and from a well-known Inverness family. Neither she nor the other two can be named for legal reasons. All are thought to have been pupils at the IRA.

Detective Sergeant Nicholas Shearer of Highland Constabulary had this to say:

CUE MINIDISC INSERT 2 (TWO)

DET SGT SHEARER: We in the umm, Highland Constabulary are concerned not only about the ah, dreadful personal impact of this tragic, uh, tragedy, but its, emm, wider imprecations. Implications. So far, the drug which these young people took has been identified only as having been . . . intaken in, so to speak, tabular, tablet form. I am informed that it is a form of narcotic hitherto unknown here in the Highlands, and possibly in the rest of Britain's eh, the British Isles. I would urge young folk to be cautious and emm, just say no. Also to contact us if they have any information about the supply of this substance. We are particularly anxious to speak to a Mr Robert Lacey, known as Bobby the Busker, in connection with this tragic . . . incident. I would urge him to contact us urgently so he can be eliminated from our inquiries.

END INSERT

And more on that story as it comes in. Meanwhile, a school of dolphins attacked two canoeists off Kessock today in what naturalists say was a sexual frenzy. This from Dominic Idaho . . .

★ Seven

It was around six by the time Celia dropped me back at The Tub, and I was feeling, to tell the truth, more than slightly knackered. Having one's libido reawakened in a public carpark fairly takes it out of a recovering drouth. And reawakened was the word. For the last two embarrassing months of my headlong dive into the Big Bottle, I'd been as limp as an unstuffed sausage skin during my infrequent sheet-bound adventures, despite Celia's occasional presence and the desperate ministrations of the one or two other ill-advised women who had passed my way. If by 'ministrations' you mean increasingly frenetic pumping by drunken, dodgy females with the sensitivity and sexual technique of a chicken-skinner. *Please, please, let me just have a wank*, I'd cried during one such onslaught. It didn't go down well. Not that I was in any condition to care. Celia hadn't been like that, in our one or two sexual collisions, prior to my bounce down from the Castle, and all the consequences of that tumble. She'd simply given up and gone to sleep. On the other hand, maybe I had, and she hadn't minded. Or I just hadn't noticed.

'I'll see you, then?' I didn't look at her. Suddenly, losing her seemed unbearable, yet asking her in was a step too far, too soon. Or maybe too late.

'Yup.' She gunned the engine, as if anxious to be on her way. Or giving me an excuse to get out of the car. I did.

The telephone was ringing as I crossed the gangway with my two bags of sustenance balanced like swag in each hand. I reached the phone just as a male American was speaking onto the tape. Breathlessly, I snatched the receiver and yelled '*What?*' into it. Good telephone technique had never been my strong point.

'Mr Flaws?' The voice was deep, educated southern states, and speaking into a mobile phone. It came and went in bursts of static. I guessed the Great North Road, the A9, also know as the Killer Motor-way, north or south of Sneck. Good cellular reception was still a problem in the Highlands. I would argue that was why I'd got rid of my Nokia, but the truth was I had fallen on it one drunken slither down the banks of the Ness, then submerged it, and the lower half of my body, in the river itself. Mobile telephones dislike that kind of treatment. So do trousers. My testicles weren't too chuffed either. It had been in my back pocket, and the phone-shaped bruising on my buttock from the slide down the riverside had faded eventually. The Nokia had never recovered. I know it shouldn't have been in my hip pocket, but I was expressing my contempt for the thing, to be honest. I hated it so much. And so it died, with no great grieving on my part. Aside from the fact I still had six months of an airtime contract to go.

'Zander Flaws speaking. Can I help you?'

'Uh . . . yes. I hope so. I understand you are an . . . investigator, sir? Is that the, uh, career situation with you?'

Weird syntax, Americans. And weirder timing. But, hell, a man had to live. Unless this was some pitch for double glazing. It seemed unlikely. There was little call for replacement windows on a barge. Or that the pitchee would know or care about my occupation.

Seeing as I was alive, just, I might as well set about making some cash to let life, such as it was, continue. 'That's correct, sir. Highland Investigative Services. At your . . . service.' Was I fit for investigations of marital misdemeanours, petty in-store thievery, even the taking of boring precognitions from dangerous little neds in Dingwall? There was only one way to find out.

'Uh . . . right. I and my, myself and my wife . . . we would like to meet with you. We are currently *en route* for, aahhmm, Inverness from Glasgow' (pronounced Glass-gow, the last syllable rhyming with cow. So that was the Killer Motorway, right enough. Please, God, keep them alive) 'and I would anticipate . . .' – heavy burst of static – 'bein' in your city later this evening. Can we buy you dinner, sir? I'm afraid it will have to be fairly late, but uh . . .'

'Yes, eh, oh sure, yes, certainly.' My eagerness was pitiful. 'I should be . . . let me just check . . .' I made a brief pretence of scuffling through an address book, too late. But there's a dignity in fakery, sometimes. 'Yes. Where exactly are you at the moment, sir?'

(Muffled shouting) 'WHERE ARE WE? . . . Sorry, Mr, uh, Flaws, my wife is driving because I . . . well, never mind that right now. She says we're near . . . is it Dunk-elld?'

'Dunkeld, yes . . . you're at least two hours away. Where are you staying? I'll meet you.' I could sense the conversation sliding from mobility into stasis.

'Okay, now let's see . . . yeah, the Cluthaaaah House Hotel. You know it?'

'The Clutha, yes. Shall we say 9 p.m., give you time to get settled?'

'Nine it is, then, Mr Flaws. We'll look forward to it.'

'Wait . . . what name is it? I'll have to ask . . .'

'Hey, sure, nearly forgot to say that, and that's the whole . . . point, too, the name . . . it's Thiebault, pronounced *Tee-bo*, but maybe you remember . . . listen I'd better spell it . . .'

But he didn't have to. I knew very well how to spell it.

I put the phone down and slumped squeaking back into the neat built-in vinyl settee which was quite the most loathsome form of seat I'd ever come across. It was possessed, that sofa, and would deposit the unsuspecting on the floor with its carefully designed sloping cushions and general slippiness. Despite that, I occasionally fell asleep on it. Waking up was like being on a kids' bouncy castle. I wedged my backside in firmly and remembered the Roger Thiebault story.

It had to be Roger. It was all of three years ago now, but at the time it had occupied the *Mail and Courier*'s front page for a full week, and then off and on for a good summer. He had arrived in Aberdeen at the tail end, it seemed, of a trek through Europe, courtesy of a rich daddy and mummy from – where was it? – New Orleans, that was right. The South. Yes, and the French name, Acadian. Cajun. Rockin' Dopsie and his Zydeco shit-kickers, Christ, I hated accordions. Over-exposure when I was a kid. My brother had played an old Hohner with the local fiddle and accordion club, and it had been a really big thing for him, something my parents were happy for him to be keen on. Native proletarian culture. Mama's got a squeezebox, she wears on her chest. Something like that. I'd had it day in, day out, until one day I ripped the bellows of the thing with a knife. My brother's much-prized penknife, just to make matters worse. A Swiss Army knife, funnily enough. Not that Jeremiah Gideon Smith could be expected to know about that little incident. Mum and Dad had half-heartedly scolded me, but my brother had been almost mad with anger. The accordion had been repaired, but it was never quite the same again. Like an emphysemic miner, it wheezed and spluttered, its lungs fucked. The knife had been symbolically thrown in the sea, as if it was all its fault.

Anyway, Roger. He'd been everywhere – Scandinavia, Russia, France, Spain, Greece. All, it seemed, alone. Somehow, after a visit to London and a trawl through the Lake District, he'd ended up in Aberdeen.

Ended up. Vanished. Disappeared. Backpack, all his belongings, a few souvenirs, a Sony digital camera, a Toshiba laptop, left neatly in a bed-and-breakfast room in John Knox Street. Nothing, no programs, no files, on the computer or camera. All seemingly wiped deliberately. No trace of drugs, not even any hash residue. The landlady had taken cash in advance from him for a two-night stay, and after he'd unpacked the first night, he'd told her he was going out to get something to eat. Which he didn't. Or if he did, no restaurant in the city could remember serving him, and no credit card transaction took place. Sure, there were a lot of Yanks in what was, after all, a major oil town, but he was young and tall with curly, longish, darkish hair. Smiling, remembered the landlady. 'A right bonny loon.' He just walked out of the little guest house, remembered as tall, sunburned, confident, handsome, polite, neat and, well, American, into thin air. Or, as the cops suspected, deep water.

Well, that wasn't quite true. Or it might be true, it might not. There was the small matter of a vagrant wino called Edward MacHaffie.

Eddie was a well-known character along Union Street and its winding granite tributaries, a hustler, panhandler and occasional seller of *The Big Issue*, when he could steal a few copies. One of his favourite tricks was to stand with a single copy of the magazine, shouting '*Issue! Issue!*' in the requisite homeless manner. Then, when some sucker handed over the pound coin, he would take the money, hold tight to his single, fingered, stained copy of the magazine, and say something along the slurred lines of 'Eh, mister, eh, ken, this is my last copy, like. Any chance I can keep it and sell it again, pal?' And as most people buy *The Big Issue* out of guilt and for charity, they nearly always let him.

Truth is, there wasn't a hope in hell of Eddie ever being a registered seller of the magazine. You had to be sober on the street and trustworthy for that, or relatively. Eddie most certainly was not. He was an ex-fisherman and deep-sea merchant seaman, fallen on hard times and one step away from the methylated spirits, the milk-and-hairspray cocktails. His big thing was to shout stuff at you in Spanish, really complicated things like '*hola*' and '*buenos dias*'. It was a hangover from his seagoing days, time in South America or something. He was always turning up at the *Courier*'s offices, trying to claim a tip-off fee for something he'd seen, or imagined. It was impossible to tell the difference. A local hero thicko footballer screwing some big-haired woman? In a black BMW at Footdee? 'Aye, ken, that's richt, m'loon. Naw, no name, pal, couldnae tell you his name. Dinnae ken it. But a footballer. Had the look, ken. And a real doll . . .' Perhaps he had seen something. But it was all too much trouble, usually, to check.

So when he turned up, out of his head on hairspray, and told the porter he'd seen 'that American loon, ken', it was hardly surprising. I had talked to him, anyway, as I was working the story and stumbled across Eddie as I came into the building. The gist of his tale was that he had met a young American down at the docks, and . . . that was it. Basically, he'd tried to blag some cash off him, and the young man had walked off. Understandably. But there had been some conversation, now I thought of it, between the pair, or so Eddie had claimed. What was it? I had written it up, partly as a sort of tongue-in-cheek piece, partly because we were so desperate by that stage for any sort of new line on the saga. It had been something to do with Eddie's much-vaunted ability to speak three words of Spanish . . . but it had gone. The alcohol had probably burnt out those particular braincells. Suddenly an internal rumble of hunger hit me, and, like a telly banged by a frustrated fist, my memory flickered and cleared: Meat. Mutton. Lamb. *Chuleta de cordero*, that was what Eddie had said. I'd looked it up. Lamb chop. Big fucking deal then, enough now only to get my digestive juices flowing prematurely. The old bastard had probably remembered it from some long-lost menu in a Cadiz dive.

Aberdeen could be a seriously rough town. There was a major drug industry building up in those years, mainly heroin, and the fact that the place was a port meant that supply lines were almost unbreakable. Add to that some dockside pubs and clubs which dealt in almost every form of flesh you could think of, and there was plenty of scope for an innocent young lad to get himself in trouble of the wet, permanent variety.

But it didn't figure. Roger had been all over Europe, and had handled himself well enough. Or, at least, he'd made it to the granite-hearted city without any recorded incident. He didn't seem to be a drinker, and if he had a habit, no one was saying. His parents – curiously vague, difficult to contact, who had never appeared in Aberdeen – hadn't thought so. The police had relayed that. I'd never got to speak to them. The words Eddie had spoken, or been told, floated at the edge of my memory again. What were they? Fuck it.

Aberdeen didn't just lose tourists. People walked out of Inverness into the hills and were found the following summer in a block of ice floating down some trout stream. But Aberdeen? No one was entirely sure why he'd gone there in the first place, though there had been some talk of a possible trip to Orkney or Shetland. I'd drawn a blank with P&O, the ferry company, on that one. I'd eyed the towering bulk of the *St Sunniva*, readying herself for the nightly fourteen-hour wallow to Lerwick, Shetland's capital, after I'd finished quizzing the bookings manager, and felt a brief, quickly smothered pang. But you can't go home again. I would, some day, but not, brutally and realistically, until one or other of my parents died. It had left me, my home. And nothing had been right about the distant relationship, between myself and my mum and dad. Long before the leaving of Lucy, that whole fucking mess. Or, as Dad had tersely put it, 'Your bad faith.' Not the first time he'd said that. Christ, for an atheist, a materialist and a self-appointed rural rationalist, he had such a, well, *holy* attitude towards matrimony. Childbirth. Lucy losing the baby, that had shocked them. Another lost child, like Victor, like me, only full of hope and innocence. Victor and I had been spoilt – ruined, really – before we vanished from their orbit. And then of course there was the sordid little affair of me and Ruth, just another teenage abortion. My fault. My fault, my fault, my fault . . . it was all my fault.

By the time Lucy came in from the cold, and I began my descent towards having a Safeway bag put over my drunken head as I slumbered at Flora Macdonald's feet, I'd long since ceased to be the golden boy. And that was self-inflicted, too. I'd not so much rebelled as dispensed with my upbringing. Shut it down.

I had never met the Thiebaults, that was certain, and something was ticking away in the mush that was left of my mind . . . that they'd been ill, or old, or at any rate unable to travel. I'd made numerous attempts to call them in New Orleans, to track down some of Roger's pals. But they'd just moved to the town, or something, and it all got mangled in the hum and expense of transatlantic telephone calls. The Aberdeen police, incompetent and occasionally corrupt, typically weren't that interested after the first week or so, though they kept up a pretence of looking for him. Basically, a file was left open. The press furore over his disappearance came and went depending on how quiet a day it was, but ebbed on into the autumn before fading away, becoming a minor-league mystery which popped up once, badly handled, on television's *Crimewatch*, provoked a few phone calls from the usual attention-seeking maniacs, and was then forgotten. I'd moved from the granite-hearted hole, stopped being an on-the-road hack, and put it out of my mind, too, along with a lot of other things. Until now. Here were the parents, risen from their sickbeds, at long last, looking for Roger. Odd, to say the least. Especially here. Why Inverness? What was the Sneck connection, apart from me?

I showered and changed, thankful that I'd be able to blag some dinner from the Thiebaults, thus avoiding any need to learn to cook again. If you could call making toast cooking. I ate a banana to keep me going, and pondered a tranquilliser. No. The taxi number was engaged. Fuck. My mind went to the locked shed down by the British Waterways workshops along the towpath towards Lurchend and what was inside it. Not tonight, Mr Mansell. By some miracle, I hadn't lost my licence during the Great Binge, but returning to the road of an evening just as darkness was falling was asking for trouble. Assuming the old hulk started. Crash courses are not the thing when it comes to cars.

So I tried the Golden Plaid mini-cab service, always a dodgy option, and was picked up within ten minutes by a man old enough to be my grandfather, driving a Ford Granada Ghia with so many cigarette burns on its dashboard it looked like a Greenpeace member who'd been in the hands of the French police for a night. Thank God it wasn't a Citroen or I'd have felt the need to do a bit of surreptitious damage to the thing myself. On principle.

I slid into the front seat, which had one of those covers made from knobbly wooden balls that are supposed to do wonders for your back. It was like sitting on a stony beach, but with the disconcerting thought that in the event of an accident, some of these wooden spheres could lodge themselves with terrific force in various anatomical orifices. I reflexively clenched my buttocks. *He died as a result of a car accident during which he was raped by a seat cover. Nasty business. Cue newsdesk hilarity.*

'Clutha House, please.'

'Aye.'

Thank God, a quiet mini-cab driver. Most of these veterans were pensioners supplementing their meagre incomes with private-hire work, and they considered incessant gabbing a perk of the job.

'Clutha, eh? The Clutha?'

'That's right. Quick as you can, please.'

'The Clutha House Hotel. What a travesty it is. What a fucking travesty, son.' Aw, shit. '"Scuse mah French. Ken this? Ah was a wean, coming here from Glasgow on my holidays, Clutha House was a fucking legend. Ah mean . . .'

'This is a bad exit, here, by the way.' He was barrelling along towards the junction with the A82, blithely unconcerned about the risk of colliding with the cars on the main road.

'Never spoke a truer word, son, never did. But aye, you were asking about the Clutha . . . I'm happy to tell you whit ah ken. The old man who lived there when ah was a lad – old Bailey, Jonathan Kettering Bailey, he wis called – what a fucking benefactor to the young! Tell ye, he would have the wee toerags from aw aboot in there for sweeties and lemonade, any time o' the day or night, nae bother. Ah mean, I was frae Baillieston – ken it?'

I shook my head.

'Anyway, east o' Glasgow, but in the city tae, ken. And such kindness. It would bring tears tae yer eyes, pal.'

He went on. And on. He had been given a glimpse of the good life, of human kindness and generosity and it had taught him a lesson he would never forget. Blah, blah blah. It was barely a ten-minute ride to the Clutha, which was in the Arkaig Heights area of Sneck, a leafy refuge for the settled and secure with money to invest in Edwardian and Victorian sandstone villas. Phil McVeigh lived there. I wondered how his daughter was getting on. Poor sod. I half-caught a radio news bulletin which seemed to indicate a major new drug problem in Inversneckie, some new substance nobody knew how to handle. The tabloids would be heading north at a great rate, hustling for headlines. Celia would be involved, too, almost certainly. I waited for the pang of jealousy, of loss. It wasn't as bad as it might have been.

The Clutha was one of several massive edifices in the area, set in their small wooded parks, which were either hotels or obscenely profitable old people's homes full of abandoned, living corpses.

As the Granada, its power steering howling, turned onto the crunchy gravel drive, a connection clicked into place in my memory.

'The Clutha,' I blurted without thinking. 'Jonathan Kettering Bailey. There was some scandal.'

'Aye, that's typical, that is. It's all anyone remembers, nowadays. You can be a fucking millionaire, pillar of the community, benefactor o' dozens o' innocent weans, and they were a' still innocent efter, ken what I mean? But anyway, what happens? You shag wan sheep . . . ah mean, who among us havnae been tempted, eh? That'll be six quid, by the way, seven if you need a receipt. I believe it was a particularly unusual sheep, by the way. A really gorgeous Suffolk cross . . .'

I paid him the six and opened the door to get out. Christ, that was it. Kettering Bailey had kept a flock of prime ewes in an outhouse for purposes of personal, well, relief. And some scurrilous scandal sheet had found out, coyly hinted at his 'deep affection for beasts of the field' in unmistakably arch terms. The wooden seat cover moved sickeningly underneath me with an oily rattle.

'There's plenty of famous folk have shagged sheeep and got aff wi' it, ken,' the driver shouted after me. 'Why d'ye think they prime ministers all have country mansions, eh?'

I slammed the door shut and turned to look at the astonished faces of a young, clearly post-golfing couple in matching Pringle sweaters and nasty trousers, leaving the Clutha after a few 19th-hole gins.

'Mini-cabs,' I said. They nodded sympathetically.

The Clutha's lobby was like the interior of some great 1920s ocean liner. No coincidence, because that's exactly what it was. The first-class lounge of the SS *Clutha*, scrapped in 1928, had been dismantled and painstakingly rebuilt inside this enormous house, which had been owned by the same family as the shipping line. Hence the hotel's name. The Kettering Baileys had been seriously rich buggers until the scandal which shipwrecked the family reputation. I seemed to recall a suicide. The only decent thing to do, if you were a convicted fondler. Not from the point of view of an aged mini-cab driver, it seemed. Poor old sod. I wondered what direction his life had taken after his brush with Kettering Bailey, what had happened between then and his used-up Granada Ghia life now? I'd never be making a trip with him far enough to find out, I hoped.

The girl behind the reception desk was a middle-aged woman in disguise. I recognised her, vaguely. Which probably meant she knew me, and had been an audience at one or other of the emotional displays I had put on over the past year. The Great Gantry Destruction which got me barred from the Spanish Galleon, a pub which, in my opinion, had always smelt of urine. It was in protesting this fact that the destruction began. Through my decision to add to the aroma personally. The

Television Smashing Incident at the Dolphin. Buck nakedness at Mr Whizz, an appalling nightclub. And more. And worse.

She stiffened, marginally, then forced a smile, her make-up shimmering under the stress, but holding steady. High silicon content. She was around forty-five, a smoker, with that crackle-finish skin heavy users get, but effectively filled in with expensive make-up. A Jennifer Anniston Mark One haircut. Bad, bad mistake with the see-through satin blouse and a figure not so much hourglass as pint mug. The kind with dimples. I smiled, and tried to exude sobriety.

'Can I help you, sir?' Bad false teeth. Always a major kissing problem unless you were really drunk. What happened if they slipped out, if the Dentifix gave way under some serious tonguing? *Man chokes to death after dentures come adrift? It's the tooth, claims gummy girlfriend!* Christ, had I kissed her? Mhairi, said her nametag. There had been a Mhairi or two. There were always Mhairis about in Sneck.

'Zander Flaws for Mr and Mrs Thiebault.' I gave her my best sunburst smile, and felt my skin stretching painfully. For a second I wondered if my eyes and mouth would split at the corners like rotten rubber. But everything held. 'They're expecting me, and I'm sober, not to mention relatively clean, so don't look at me like I was some form of centipede, dear.'

'The last time we . . . met, emm, sir, you were crawling around the floor of the Albatross trying to look up my skirt, *sir* . . . so the centipede comparison is particularly apt.' She curled her lip, revealing a bad case of gingivitis.

'Yeah, well, this may be foreplay to you, but it's just tiring banter to me, honey. Are the Thiebaults in? I suppose a shag's out of the question?' I kept the smile in searchlight mode, my voice absolutely neutral.

She flinched, to my satisfaction. 'Yes they are. And yes it is.' Cold and angry, but seeing it through with a good old corporate grin. That's the service industries for you. Slavery with a smile. 'Please wait in the Prebble Lounge, and I'll buzz their room.'

The Prebble Lounge was one of those misconceptions the half-educated tourist developer thinks up, presumably under the influence of hallucinogenic drugs issued by the Scottish Tourist Board. A Royal Stewart tartan carpet was hideously offset by Buchanan plaid curtains. On the walls, some of the great paintings of the Highland Clearances were reproduced in bad facsimile, framed in fake gilt and spotlit: *The People of Drumgairm Watch the Firing*, a crude work by a painter sympathetic to the dispossessed, F. Ronald Unwin, made worse in the flat colour print. The reds and browns of John Pettie's *The Chieftain's Candlestick*, and a photograph of the names scratched in the glass of Croik Church, where an entire glen was supposed to have been imprisoned before being sent into exile or brutal hardship at home. I'd been to Croik, and a spookily moving place it was, too, even though the scratched glass was supposed to be fake.

A Runrig album was playing, and high on one wall was the head of a Highland cow. Above the bar was a set of antlers from a venerable and now headless stag. The venison it had provided was probably still in the Clutha's freezer. As was the mutton from the stuffed Cheviot ram which formed the base of each glass-topped table in the lounge. To my horror, when I leaned closer to the tabletops, I noticed that the scratched names from the Croik Church windows had been reproduced on the tabletops. Even worse, I found the effect quite attractive.

'I'll have a pint, please.' It was out without thought. I could actually feel my brain catching up with my body. My mouth. 'Fresh orange and lemonade . . .'

'Certainly, sir. Sit down and I'll bring it over,' said the acned youth behind the dark oak bar. His Ancient Douglas tartan waistcoat was too big and his Adam's apple seemed set to pop out of his mouth at any moment, like a half-sucked gobstopper. I retreated before it did.

I was halfway through the icy, acidic pint of yellow gunge when the Thiebaults arrived. They were not what I had expected. He was in his mid-fifties, heavy but seriously cool, dressed in a black silk shirt, not tucked in, which flattered his waistline. The face was bulbous, but hard, as if he never stopped chewing and the muscles had developed accordingly. The blue eyes were harder still. Too much hair for a man of his age, at least for my liking. I felt my thinning, ragged locks automatically.

She was slightly over half his age, and dressed to wound. Black hair, Uma Thurman in *Pulp Fiction*, but with a kind of rampant, self-conscious sensuality in her undershot jaw, her amused eyes. To say nothing of her figure.

'Mr Flaws?' he said. I stood, shook both their hands, hers barely brushing my grip, his surrounding my hand like a mould, the skin jelly soft. 'We are so pleased to make your acquaintance. This is my wife, Melanie-Joanne. I'm Gareth Thiebault.' That southern twang. Faulkner and all that sinister politeness, that evil charm. 'Will you permit me to buy you a drink?'

I gestured at the horribly fluorescent yellow semi-liquid in my glass. 'Same again, only a half pint. Fresh orange and lemonade. Not diet, sugared.'

'Well, honey . . .' Her accent was southern but overdone, fake. There was an urban edge to the way she talked. 'On the wagon. I don't know if I can trust a Scawt who won't drink whisky . . .'

'Not won't,' I said, feeling a cold sweat break out on every square inch of skin. 'Just not at the moment, thanks.'

'Hey,' he was leaning in, reassuring, his hand on my arm. 'Don't let Meljo make you feel bad, sir. It's just her little testin' way. Why don't we all have somethin' soft, make Mr Flaws feel at ease, Meljo? A soda?'

Her playful smile snapped off, and her lips lost their blowfish pout. 'Jack Daniels on ice, and I mean on ice, not with one rock floating in it. Plenty soft enough for me.' She was all northern hustle now, assurance and snarl. Not New York, though. 'Like Lake Superior in winter, babe, with that warm undertow. *Laaahk mahself!*'

'Uh, sure, Meljo. Waiter!'

They sat down as Mr Adolescent Hormone Eruption shambled towards us to take the order. I wondered if Meljo's Calvin Klein jeans were subtly laced with lycra to stop them splitting. No seams tore as she sank into the imitation leather seat. I was astonished when she rummaged in a little kind of clutch bag she was carrying, a kind of half handbag in black suede, and pulled out one of those expensive crystal glass aerosols of perfume.

"Scuse me, boys,' she said, and puffed a hefty shot of whatever it was over her hair, which looked like it would fracture in a frost. 'Got to create my own little atmosphere, if you don't mind. This place smells of . . . of rancid animals. I like my little touch of "Mystère". It's by Ivana, you know.'

I tried not to breathe.

When the drinks came, I poured my half-pint into the pint glass, while Meljo sipped suspiciously at her whiskey, and lit a Kent 100 with a Varga Girl Zippo. Very stylish. And, given the amount of vaporised alcohol which had doubtless condensed in her hair from the puffs of Mystère, dangerous. A flammable woman. She would bear watching. Especially near open log fires liable to sparking. She had something, though. Enough of whatever it was to make a susceptible man fall hopelessly in lust. I was too busy trying to keep my eyes off her Black Jack. I could smell its dark pungency surrounding me, merging with her aromatic stink like some spell, drawing me in.

'So,' I said, 'what can I do for you folks?'

'Well, Mr, uh, Flaws, it's about Roger, as you may have . . . well perhaps you didn't. I mean, I have cuttings here –' he tapped a leather file case he was carrying '– which you, I think, wrote two years ago when he, uh, disappeared in Aberdeen.'

'I remember Roger well . . . or rather . . .' Fuck, what was I saying? 'I remember his . . . disappearance. Very well.'

'If you do, you'll know there were all *kaahnds* of theories.' He was businesslike, now, almost curt. Like the words annoyed him. 'He'd fallen into the harbour, been mugged, murdered. Hell, his mother was . . . distraught.' He looked down into the Diet Coke he'd bought, swirled the ice and lemon around in the glass. His firm, bulging face seemed suddenly older, vulnerable. 'I'm certain that, uh, it all contributed to her death. She could have fought it, but she . . .'

'Now, Gareth,' Meljo was rubbing his hand with one of hers, being careful not to strip any of the flesh off with her varicose-vein-blue nails, and tapping her cigarette out with the other. 'Best not to dwell on it. Deborah made you so happy for those precious, precious years. Now we gotta work together, to set your mind at rest.' She fired a piteous grin at me, a bolt of southern-fried sentiment. 'I nursed her, you know.' Anyone less like a nurse I have never seen outside of *The Rocky Horror Picture Show.* 'Afterwards, Gareth and I . . . well.' She gripped his hands. I could see the nails jabbing into the flesh. 'Suchlike things happen. Don't they?'

I nodded. Not normally they didn't. Not in Inver-fucking-ness. Not in Sneckie, Sneck, the Sneckopolis. Hereabouts we simply tied our wives to their adulterous lovers and threw them out in the cold. Then went to sleep.

Thiebault cleared his throat. Fuck me, emotion. Americans didn't so much wear it on their sleeves as dress in it, head to toe. Wash in it. Then skoosh it at you. 'Mr Flaws.'

'Call me Zander.' Americans would like that. Expect it.

'Zander. Meljo and myself are united in this, and I don't suppose but there's any question that it's selfish. And perhaps you think a bit late. All I can say is that Roger's mother was so unwell, and I couldn't keep the whole, awful thing from her. It was a dreadful strain, and it took its toll on me. Now I'm recoverin' from that, in recovery, so to speak. And we . . . I need to know what happened. Your police force in Aberdeen have been . . . well, let's say they've done what they think they can, all they think they can, but . . . I think it's time to try one last . . . tilt at the thing, see if we cain't come up with . . . something final. And I would like you to be our man on this.'

'Me? Well, I . . .'

'I have some information, sir, new information, somethin' which could narrow the search down. Takes us right into the Highlands, this glorious geography . . . and you come recommended, sir, by the local police force here. I spoke to a sergeant – what was the name . . . Shearer?'

Oh yeah. It wasn't just that I was the only private investigator in Inverness listed in the Yellow Pages, and had a personal involvement in the Thiebault thing through my evil past as a hack, but Nicky had decided to offload the case onto my sweet self as a kind of joke, and also because he probably reckoned I would just fuck it up and drown it in a sea of malt whisky. Or it would die with my liver. Fuck him.

'And, of course, there is your prior knowledge of the case. The fact that you . . . met him. Met Roger.' His voice caught.

I began to say something, protest. Say that he was wrong, that I'd never met their precious son, for God's sake. I'd have remembered, written it up, been some kind of superhack if I had. *Please God let it be on my shift.* But I hadn't. How the hell had the Thiebaults got that idea? But then I looked at them, sensed something odd, almost unhinged in the father's eyes, and realised that he was obsessed, driven, either heading for madness or maybe just prone to using metaphor in a rather bizarre way. What was this so-called new information, anyway? As for meeting Roger – sure, I'd *met* him, known Roger through my work, through following his tracks, his ghost for all those weeks back in the grey, hard city of the east coast. I cleared my throat. They were both gazing at me. Suddenly I felt hungry, and remembered we hadn't eaten.

'I'd be proud. Proud and . . . privileged to take on the case, Mr Thiebault, Mrs Thiebault.' What else could I say? For my own self-respect I had to do it. And if I did stay alive in the undertaking of it, I would seriously piss Nicky off, the bastard. The self-important prick, probably all wrapped up with this fucking Phil McVeigh business, pontificating about drugs, when the only dope he knew anything about was himself. Plus it was true anyway: I had worked the Thiebault thing before, had met Roger, if only in spirit. Sniffed his spoor. Unfinished business. Something nagged away at me, like a toothache, though. I shook it away. Fuck it, I was hungry. I wondered if the Clutha did black-pudding suppers.

'Well, look.' Thiebault had become suddenly upright. Energised. 'Let's go eat and we'll talk turkey. Or eat turkey and talk business.' A sense of humour. How I liked that in a chap. If only Gareth Thiebault had one. Mad or metaphorical? Maybe this hitherto undiscovered Highland aspect to Roger Thiebault's vanishing act would tell me. And the colour of his father's traveller's cheques.

★ Eight

By the time I left the Clutha, my guts uneasily inflated with badly reheated frozen steak pie, mushy peas, crinkle-cut wet-sawdust chips and about a gallon of fizzy orange mush, I was working on A Case, and feeling . . . sick. Again.

I regained some measure of intestinal composure by walking the twenty-minute route down the hill into town, and picked up a cab from the rank in front of the station, thinking about the Bank of America traveller's cheques in my wallet – three thousand dollars up front, definitely not allegorical. Metaphorical in a sense – yes, symbolic of a relationship in which I was bought-up servant. Thiebault was master. Around about £2,000 in real money; it would cover a week's expenses and wages. It wouldn't meet the months of unearned expenses and wages, or suck back the pissed-away cash, but it was something. A result.

Basically, the Thiebaults knew little more than I did, or rather I would by the time I'd restored my memory by taking a look at my old cuttings. There had been no communication, and until his disappearance, no indication from Roger that anything was wrong. So far, so same old same. But there had, they said, been one lead. An unexplained e-mail which had been dug out of a long-unused Internet mailbox at the University of Southern Louisiana, when the systems people there were doing some housekeeping on their students' computer access. There was no return e-mail address on it, no name, and the servers used to route it indicated a Compuserve account, one of the biggest service providers in the world. There had been no success in tracing the precise origin of the message, which had been filed during Roger's trip abroad.

'He could access all his messages from that little Apple thing he carried,' Gareth had said. 'But this one had a one-digit mistake in the address.' He'd written it all out so I would understand. I did. Barely. 'Instead of going to Roj@physchem.unisla//fiz/com, the physical science department, it went to Roj@physchem.unisla//biz/com. Business studies. And it's a big college, so there was a Roger studying there, and he used Roj in his e-mail address too.'

He'd had a print-out of the message, which was short and to the point:

'Och aye the noo! Highland (and Island) :) welcome awaits. Try the lamb chop when you get here.'

New information, eh? The little smiley signs were Internet-speak for a private joke of some sort. Someone on an island? Northern Scotland was replete with islands. Someone with ready access to lamb chops? There were more sheep than people. No wonder the police hadn't been interested. No wonder Nicky fuckface Shearer had palmed them off on me.

A name kept echoing through my less-than-unfuddled brain, although the words he'd spoken, that I'd written and had printed, remained annoyingly opaque. Eddie MacFuckingHaffie. A couple of Librium wiped him out for the night, though. And me. And the thirst for something other than orange juice or lemonade.

Towards the morning, in the twilight of pre-dawn, I woke, groggy and furred of mouth and mind. There was a momentary physical surge of desire for something enlivening, a Bloody Mary heavy on Tabasco and Virgin Vodka. I had always enjoyed some pseudo-Soviet spirit in the mornings. But I made do with water. My gut felt swollen and somehow alive. It was like being pregnant with an alien being, and I suddenly thought of John Hurt in *Alien*, his stomach exploding in a welter of slaughterhouse waste and a plasticine model of ET's nasty uncle. Lamb chops, mutton chops – I felt like I'd eaten a freezerful, unthawed, uncooked. Fuck. Eddie MacHaffie. What had he said? *Chuleta de cordero*. Lamb chop. Mutton chop. Christ, which was it? Did it matter? The pain in my gut took precedence. Thought could wait. Should've had the black pudding.

I went back to bed with a couple of Zantac, that wonderdrug for hungover guts, and now just sober stomach pains, and I dreamt. It was becoming a habit. As I said before, alcohol – and, indeed, the previous night's little chemical helper – kills dreams, stops your brain dealing with all the shit of the day, processing it, sifting it like a neural sewage farm. Leaves you stuffed with crap and poisoned every which way. Opiates are good at bunging up the cortex, probably better than booze. More sort of directional. Alcohol does all sorts of other fucking-up type things, too. Now it was as if parts of me were coming back to life. I dreamt not of lamb, mutton or sheep, but of cats.

Bad news. The cat dream was an old, recurring one, going back to a schoolboy Christmas job I'd had back in Shetland, working at the post office. They'd given me a shoulder badge with 'GPO' on it, made me sign the Official Secrets Act, for some bizarre reason, in case any military missive should burst open in my hands and I couldn't help but notice instructions to the Lerwick branch of MI5 telling them to immediately murder the Lord Lieutenant for suspected liberalism. Most of the time, I helped sort Christmas cards, piled up parcels, tried to decipher smudged or inadequate addresses. 'Jim McGuire, North of Scotland' was one. Someone in Wick had written 'TRY SHETLAND' on it. I wrote 'TRIED' on it and sent it back south.

Two days before Christmas there was a lull, and one of the rural delivery drivers picking up his mail from the office in a bitter dark fake northern morning, collared me to help him with his run, hauling brown-wrapped boxes over gates and through fields to crofts and oil-funded bungalows out past Tingwall, site of the islands' ancient parliament.

It was at the second house that it happened; a grey croft with a flaking felt roof, peat reek choking from the two-chimney, ben-end and but-end. As I reached the door, bearing several packets, a box from South Africa and cards from, among other places, Sydney, Australia – another sign of the Shetland marine diaspora – an old woman, dressed in heavy wool *ganzie*, or sweater, black wellington boots and a waxed cotton jacket so stained it was like rotting flesh, opened the door, and thrust a fertiliser sack into my hands.

'Here du is,' she said. 'Aye, dey need seein' tae afore New Yule. Twa days is enocht.' And the door was slammed shut. The inside of the house was opaque and swirling with peat reek. You could have preserved salmon in there. The bag in my hand was moving.

Back in the little red van, the postman, whose name was Magnie, saw the squirming bag in my hand and grinned. 'Kitlings,' he said. 'Pairt of the job, du kens. Dealing wi' da kitlings.' Innocent, living in a pet-free house (my father had strong feelings about animals: they were for eating and working with, but not petting, licking you or blocking access to Rayburn stoves or armchairs), I had never considered the fate of unwanted kittens.

I was soon given a crash course. Magnie stopped the van at Hennie's Blade, a small, gritty beach with a plastic-cluttered brown burn running down its centre. There was twine twisted around the neck of the bag keeping it shut, and Magnie cut this with his old Cold Finger penknife, peered inside. He looked at me, all acne-faced and curious, in the passenger seat surrounded with cards and parcels, *National Geographic* magazines in holly-emblazoned gift subscriptions. 'Want a look?' I didn't, shook my head. But I followed him down to the water's edge. The tide was almost fully in, right up to the line of wrack and sea debris. Magnie picked up several lumps of pink granite, dropped them carelessly inside the wriggling sack, then took his knife, and sliced four or five incisions in the hessian. 'Let da watter in quicker,' he explained, his voice muffled by a thin Old Holburn roll-up. He heaved the sack around his head, birled it around his pinched shoulders and let it fly out into the sea. It went a surprising distance.

It was a relatively calm day, and there was little swell. The sack, for some reason, didn't sink immediately, but settled gradually in the water. Spellbound, I heard a tinny, tiny yowling, and, as the kittyshroud disappeared, saw a tiny white paw emerge from one of the cuts Magnie had made. Then a whole, brown-mottled head, followed by an entire kitten.

'Christ,' I said, maybe the first time I'd blasphemed without being self-conscious about it. 'That kitling's geen ta soom for it.'

Magnie was drawing fiercely on his roll-up. 'Na, na, never fear, boy,' he said. 'Kitlings canna soom. Maybe doon, but that's a'.'

He was wrong. The tiny creature, paddling desperately, in absolute silence, made sure progress towards us. Magnie looked nonplussed. 'Well, I'll be fuckit,' he said, flicking his fag towards the approaching cat. 'Thrawn peerie sod.' He made no move, and neither did I. The creature finally arrived on the shingled shore and dragged itself from the water, for the first time unleashing a mournful set of miaows which would have turned even the most virulent of cat-haters into T.S. Eliot crossed with Brigitte Bardot. An interesting shag. I should take it home, I thought, but no sooner was that idea followed by an appreciation of the contempt and horror my parents would display than Magnie had picked the thing up by its neck, looked it directly in the eye, then brought it down onto the beach stones again, where he methodically beat its brains out with a rock. It didn't stop moving until well after its head had been turned to a bloody mush, seeping red into the white tide-foam. 'Dere du is,' muttered Magnie. 'Noo du willna float.' And he threw the small carcass into the water.

The cat dreams had started that pre-Christmas teenage night. It was always me smashing the creature's head, feeling the sickening, squelching impact, but oddly, the same kind of terrifying, awful thrill I'd felt watching Magnie. Go on, give us a go. Let me. I can do that. That looks like fun. No, no, it's not, it's bad, it's evil . . . and I'd wake up, convinced of my own utter moral nastiness.

This time the dream was different. It began earlier, too, with me, alone on a beach, watching the cat swim towards me, through big waves, tumbling over in the swell, but always surfacing, its mouth opening and shutting, no sound coming out. Then reaching me, washed up at my feet, only for me to pick it up, hold it down and slowly, methodically, hit it, feeling the body move under my fingers, soft, wet and warm. All the time a 'NO!' bursting painfully from my lungs, one for each blow. And when I finally finished, when I stood up and flung the bloodied body into the sea again, the whole process began once more, with the mashed head bobbing up in the breakers, and the little dead legs swimming, paddling towards me. Doggy style.

Groggy in the morning, I showered and poured a vicious brew of coffee down. No beans. Just Taylor of Harrogate's Hot Java Lava, double caffeine brew, specially made for recovering drouths. There was a trick to getting the best hit: pour the black coffee, load it with sugar – four, five spoonfuls, then let it cool. Finally, knock it back in a oner. There was a tremor in my hands, the usual, but I felt focused, energised. Something to do other than not drink, nurse regrets and dream of fucking. Some direction to pursue.

But first there was a mountain to climb, or at least the small slope to negotiate which led to an old workshop two hundred metres along the towpath. It was another parched, dusty morning, and the gravel felt as fragile as burnt cornflakes beneath my feet. At the big sliding doors, I hesitated for a moment. Was I ready for this? Then I wrestled with the stiff lock and pushed the squealing slabs of wood back on their runners.

Six months it had sat there, gathering dust, put away after one near-miss too many, driven down here after being extricated from a ditch over on the the other side of Loch Ness at Beast Bay, by the White Settler and his Series One Land Rover. It had been a drunken drive after closing time at the Albatross, the aim to annoy Celia, who was ostensibly having some kind of girls' night out, a hen night, staying over at the Beast Hotel. I'd put us into the ditch and we'd made it to the hotel, dirty, dishevelled and well after everyone had crawled into bed. The owner had not been pleased to see us, but eventually let us in when I brandished a hundred-pound note at him. It's what hundred-pound notes are for. Brandishing. And then . . . the usual dive towards liquid darkness.

Oh, well; that was then. The old Mercedes 280 E, pillar headlight model, known to me, indefensibly, as Riefenstahl, was sitting pretty much as the Settler had reversed it in. He'd disconnected the battery – partly to discourage me from driving, partly to save it discharging, but the pair of pliers he'd used were lying inside the engine compartment. I put the terminal back on, certain there wouldn't be enough juice to turn over the massive six-cylinder engine. Amazingly enough, though, there was, just about. It was like that scene in *Sleeper*, where Woody Allen starts a thousand-year-old VW Beetle. Only a Mercedes engine sounds much nicer. I sat in the driver's seat, inhaling the aroma of old leather and exhaust fumes, revving Riefenstahl lightly, wondering if I should just shut the doors of the garage and breathe in that sickly, sweet pungency. But fuck it, I hadn't got this far to do something so tacky. So naff. So weak. I shoved the automatic gearbox into D for Drive and nosed the car out onto the towpath.

It felt like being seventeen again, nervous at the wheel of Dad's horrible Morris 1800, the landcrab shape which was like a genetically mutated Mini. The power steering brought the big Merc around, and I went back to shut the workshop doors. Now to see if I could still handle a car.

Riefenstahl was a twenty-year-old ex-wedding limousine, and bits of confetti still turned up occasionally in the orifices of its interior. Despite the name, I couldn't call a car 'her'. In Shetland, objects, even boats, were often referred to using the male pronoun, a Norse hangover. But then sometimes old Leni had appeared more macho than most of her Nazi pals.

Okay, so it wasn't a politically correct name for a car. Naming a car at all was fairly dodgy. But Riefenstahl he, it was, and would stay until the final MOT failure came calling. Worn, slightly shabby but not rusty, Riefenstahl had been my treat to myself when the redundancy came through, along with the miserable ten grand which was all the lawyers had left me from the sale of the marital home, most of it now gone on renting The Tub and . . . stuff. 'Who do you think you are,' McGrooch had said, 'some sort of South American dictator?' It had presence, at least in the Highlands. And in Glasgow I'd been stopped twice at traffic lights by raps on the window from passing Asian men who'd offered to buy it. I suppose I liked the way the big lump of Stuttgart tin looked simultaneously impressive and slightly pathetic, as if the driver was trying to reassure himself of his own worth, yet couldn't afford anything newer. Which was accurate enough.

I'd always loved the kickdown facility on the three-speed gearbox, the way you could slam the accelerator to the floor and shunt the car into second gear, sending the hugely heavy machine thundering forward, and petrol consumption into single figures. Gradually gaining confidence, I did it on the way past the alcohol unit at Craig Na Fergusson, a salutary reminder of my reprieved state. Then I was in Inverness proper, and it was time to recall all those close manoeuvring skills.

There were restrictions on my ability to penetrate the realm of my former employers, that great and worthy newspaper the *Northern Mail and Courier*. I was *persona non grata* in both the Sneck and Aberdeen offices, and while there remained one or two staff like Jimbo Clark who would take a risk for me and check the archives, it could take time, someone else's fax machine, and explanations I did not feel like giving. So I parked Riefenstahl in the Safeway carpark of recent body-trembling memory, and headed for the library, a kind of Graeco-Roman edifice fronting onto the diesel-soaked bus station.

All the editions of the *M&C* were kept on disk and were accessible via computer. I could probably have got into them from The Tub using my own PC, if I hadn't let the Internet subscription lapse months ago. I'd had to stop using it anyway, having spent too many nights staring at a prompt screen, unable to remember my e-mail password, then waking up next morning with an irradiated head and a phone bill to shit hedgehogs over. I'd have to speak to my brother, though the thought did not delight me. He was the technical whizz of the Flaws family; an estranged technical whizz, though I occasionally went to fight with him in person, in his high-tech den over on the west coast. Keep up that bitter sense of family. Listen to some fucking accordion music.

It was the early-day Highland editions which had been scanned and archived, so some of the reporting on Roger Thiebault's disappearance wasn't as full as in the local Aberdeen finals. I scanned through my own old copy, automatically subbing as I went, cutting back, searching for the kernel, recognising space-filling and fluff, feeling the loss of a career which I only realised I'd loved when it was over. The Eddie MacHaffie stuff was as vague as I remembered it, only turned into something much more precise than it actually deserved:

> Mr MacHaffie, a well-known city character, believes the man he met was undoubtedly Mr Thiebault. 'I'm certain it was him,' he told the *Mail and Courier*. 'He was tall and spoke with an American accent. He was smiling and friendly and took the time to say hello – or *buenas noches*, as they say in *Espagne*!'

That had been my little joke, my little clue to the readers that they should not take Eddie's rambling seriously. Hey, it said, we had to include this, but you know Eddie, always rambling in dog Spanish down the Bon Accord Centre. This is just shite.

Or maybe not. Spanish. Where had I heard Spanish recently? *Spanish is the loving tongue, She Always Spoke Spanish to me . . .* Joe Ely? Bob Dylan? *Spanish Eeeyyyyess . . .* suddenly I felt the lack of music, another passion all burnt out by Big Ethyl. Were there tapes still in the car? In the glove compartment? Christ, it was like a hunger, a thirst. But everything was a thirst these days. Everything except what I really wanted. And the Albatross was just around the corner.

The Inverness library archiving system was okay, but there was no word search facility, and you wouldn't have expected that some poor sod of a librarian would have to read every story in every copy of the paper just to give an occasional nosy parker researcher an easier job. Dates had been enough to take me back to my days on the Thiebault case, but now I needed more pixellation, more digitisation. I needed to get onto the Net. Which, at the library, was simply a matter of paying a fiver for an hour, launching Bill Gates's attempt at browser monopoly, Internet Explorer, and finding *www.normail&c.com*.

A doddle. If I was going to take this staying alive shit seriously, I would have to get back on-line. A new mobile. Maybe even an office. But no. One day at a time, Sweet Jesus. Lena Martell. Hadn't helped her. Give me them ole twelve-step programme blues . . . aw, fuck it, maybe I should enrol with the Autonomous Alkies, see what they had to offer. But then I'd have to tell them all sorts of skin-crawling things, confess to shagging sheep while under the influence, like poor Kettering Bailey. I hadn't, though. I just woke up in a field once with my trousers round my ankles, thinking I had.

Hello, hello, here we were in the archive search section of the *Mail and Courier* website, designed by my good friend Wes Furnigarth, and bearing occasional signs of Wes's hash habit. We'd had to remove the tiny cannabis leaves, hidden in the coloured buttons you clicked on to get to Features, News and all those other boring newspapery things. And the *M&C* wasn't quite ready to have its weekly round-up of top stories described as Cool Clips. Here in the newspaper graveyard, though, traces of dope smoke could be hazily sniffed: 'Press hash to continue', indeed. A mouse click would have sufficed.

Search for: MacHaffie; period: 1995 onwards, see what we get. Blink, blink, blink. I half closed my eyes and the screen seemed to flicker and curve away . . . blue hypertext links appeared: found seven matches. An obituary for an Old Shaftings farmer. Three letters of appreciation for the same good man, suddenly at home, tragic; mention of modern agriculture's stresses and strains. Nowhere saying what had happened. I was betting on a shotgun and a toe curled through the trigger guard, barrel in the mouth. Messy. Aha, there was Eddie, in court for disturbing the police, three months before the Thiebault business. My story about him and the alleged sighting. *Buenas noches*, my arse. And a story from last week, scrolling up through cyberspace like a chunk of electronic doom:

WITNESSES SOUGHT TO BRUTAL KILLING

Police are treating as suspicious the death yesterday of a well-known city man. *[Yep, that classic single-sentence intro, less than twenty words, says it all really. I found it suddenly difficult to swallow.]*

The body of kenspeckle Aberdeen character and former seaman Edward Forbes MacHaffie was found on the old north pier in the early hours of yesterday morning, during a routine police patrol. A post-mortem examination was carried out, which revealed that Mr MacHaffie had been, according to a police spokesman, 'severely beaten'.

There was a little more, not much. Mr MacHaffie, originally from Footdee, the clutter of crammed cottages at the harbour mouth, once a fishertown, now a groovy ghetto for bourgeois bohemians. Occasional resident of the hostel at Ford Street, no known relatives. Once employed as a fisherman, served on the Murmansk convoys during the war, went deep sea. Stuff from Eddie's own self-proclaimed tap-room legend, and maybe what the Seamen's Mission knew. Sometimes he accepted their charity. Used to. Had done. Europe and South America . . . then home, and whatever happened, had happened, whatever shite. And he was a well-kent character, joking his way around the hairspray and the meths, the booze and that stolen copy of *The Big Issue*, in the end pulped by somebody's feet and hands; normal folk: brutal and unforgiving. I searched the day's paper, but nothing else matched MacHaffie. A week.

They wouldn't pursue Eddie's killer long. Some drunken brawl. He had annoyed a sailor too much with his Spanish shite. *I was deep sea once . . .*

Fuck me. A clammy sweat was licking at my back, my head and hands. I had a few minutes left on-line, and I shifted to the Search By Issue facility Wes had included in the archiving section of the *M&C* site. Back to the day after Roger's disappearance, an unseasonably cool summer Wednesday. Find: ship movements. I hoped the team of secretaries had left the links in, but I could find it anyway. It was always on page eight, along with the fish prices. It had to be there, because this was part of the grey city's history, its salt lifeblood. And there it was.

Oil support vessels, coming in and going out, *Oceanic Conqueror*, *Stormrider Three*, a few yachts with crap names – *Bellyflop*, what the hell was that? *Quoyle*, some asshole reading that Newfoundland book, what was it called? *The Fishing News*. And fishing boats, twenty or so, most ABDN or WK registered, one or two Buckie, a Lerwick and a Stornoway, way off course. But not as off course as the *Chuleta de Cordero*, registered in Vigo, Galicia. Which is in Spain, though some Galicians might not appreciate being reminded of the fact. Unusual, but not unheard of for Spanish fishing boats – unpopular because they were often accused of raiding Scottish fishing stocks – to come into Aberdeen for water, stores, whatever. Even to land fish, though the prices elsewhere were higher. *Spanish Is the Loving Tongue.* Christ almighty, Eddie and his Spanish. Mutton or lamb, which was it? Mutton was old lamb, much preferred in my native islands. *Chuleta de Cordero.* Jesus.

I flicked forward, my on-line period running out, to the following day's paper. The *Chuleta de Cordero* had left with the tide, heading for Salvation, a little west coast port on, funnily enough, Loch Salvation, now mostly a whitewashed centre for tourism, uneasily unsettled white settlers and a rampant rump of Gaelic-speaking church fanatics. Not far from my brother's retreat, actually. Assuming the *Chuleta* was small enough, she would have gone through the Caledonian Canal, her wash lapping at the hull of The Tub after the sail north from Aberdeen, then into the deep gouge of the Moray Firth, and the most magical bit of the canal, for my money. Not the four lochs, the mighty mountains. No, the best was the cautious crawl up the five locks called Neptune's Staircase, a wonder of nineteenth-century engineering.

My on-line time was up. I logged off, gathered the notes I'd scribbled together and got ready to leave. On my way out, I detoured into a glass-walled room, home to those redundant objects, reference books. A heavy Spanish-English, English-Spanish dictionary, stiff and smelling of old churches, revealed that *chuleta de cordero* translated as 'lamb chop'. So, not mutton. *Try the lamb chop when you get here . . .* Och aye the noo. Whatever, it was a stupid name for a boat, even in Spanish.

She lay like something less life-like than a corpse, he thought, a horizontal shop-dummy, in a gauzy white paper robe, blue-clear tubes poking from nose and mouth, drip into the arm which lay naked and outstretched, as if pleading.

Monitors flicked in green, regular waves, saying, hey, Mr McVeigh, your daughter's functioning, bodily. Something's still happening here, so wait, don't despair. We have the technology. We are the bloody technology.

He'd sent his wife home to her anti-depressants and Bombay gin. His arse felt serrated, crushed by the rubber webbing of the supposedly comfortable chair they'd fussed over giving him. He rubbed the unshaven mass of his chin and wondered about the extent of his failure with Karen. Theirs. No. His.

That teacher had come by, a couple of hours ago, left some flowers. What was his name? Karen had mentioned him. What was it she had called him? Seen And Not. That was it. Seen And Not. Heard, that was him, Mr Seen And Not Heard. He'd not stayed, just mumbled something about sorrow, regret, concern. He'd looked terrible, ravaged. As if it was somehow his fault.

The doctors had made reassuring rumbling noises, but they still couldn't say what the stuff was she'd taken. The stupid bitch, after all they'd said, all he'd told her about. Sure, try some weed, he had, though don't tell anyone, not the big-noise COSLA councillors and MPs who sometimes came round to see his collection of single malts, taste his Longrow 1973, make lip-smacking noises of ignorant appreciation. Because he knew it was actually just bog standard Bell's eight-year-old, decanted. The fuckwits. His little joke. He'd told Karen that, and she'd laughed that curious, inward laugh of hers. Unified. He'd felt one with her, for a few seconds.

Now? Well, now, what the hell? What the fuck? All that career stuff was up the proverbial anyway, and it didn't matter, he knew that now. Christ, it was a bit late to realise. If only he'd . . . if only. If only. If only.

There was a discreet cough behind him. He turned, creaking in the uncomfortable chair, smelt his body odour mingling with the Daniel Hechter deodorant he favoured, duty-free on the flights to and from Brussels. That doctor, he was a local GP . . . what was his name? Holdsworth? What had he been doing here, flitting in and out, nervously, like an emaciated ghost? A man and woman, both young, smartly dressed. The woman was tall, red hair tightly pulled back, formal, tough. Official, not medical. And dangerous, potentially. He could tell, had had plenty of opportunity over the years to get to know the type. Oh, for fuck's sake, he thought to himself.

'Mr McVeigh?' Her voice, drawling privilege etched in crystal. He just gazed at them, his eyes nipping with tiredness, regret, bad hospital germs. 'Could we have a word?'

★ Nine

I had a car. I even, it seemed, retained some remnant of my driving ability. It was time to move, get on the road, start doing something other than thinking about drinking, playing with computers, doing that web-wank thing. And yet the aloneness of the whole procedure, the exposed nature of the job, suddenly hit me, and my mouth went dry. Pre-beer dry. I wondered if Celia was persuadable into a trip west. An existentialist moment shared is always better than . . . whatever.

First things first. I wandered into the centre of Sneck, discovered at the bank that Gareth Thiebault's Bank of America traveller's cheques were apparently the real thing, and found a franchised money pit called a Vocalafone Shop, where a heavily razor-burned young man tried to flog me business tariff low-user shitephone cellular systems that cost ten quid to start off with, but tied you to punitive monthly payments for an eternity. Worse, they made you fill in forms and looked for references before they would connect you up. Fuck that for a game of sojers. I bought a pre-pay handset, a badged-up Ericsson, for the not-inconsiderable sum of £199, which gave me instant connection, half an hour of free calls and more air time whenever I wanted, by calling in a credit card number. And doubtless paying through the nose for the call. There was an optional voicemail system you could have for an extra fiver a month. I allowed myself to be talked into it.

Visa? Yep, that'll do, I suppose. Just enough leeway on the scored and folded card to handle the damage. Funny, I had no recollection of paying the monthly bills . . . ah yes. Direct debits. The Drunkard's Rescue from Credit Blacklisting. Click-whirr-beep, I was contactable and accessible, had anyone known my number. I called Celia at home, only to have the divert put me through to the lower-than-low freelance media-whore-desk at Radio Fuckwank, where I found her in a state of what could only be described as frantic frigidity.

'Hi,' I began, imaginatively. 'It's Zander. Got a new mobile . . .'
'Number?'
Oops. That kind of to-the-point response had always indicated crises in the past.
'0421 077307. What's biting you, anyway?'

85

'Not you.'

'Lovely, and I was just going to ask if you fancied a weekend in Loch Salvation, fresh prawns and oysters at the Chalmers Hotel, build up the zinc levels for . . .'

'What, in the middle of the Free Presbyterian State of New Geneva? Where they spy on you on a Sunday to see you're not doing anything carnal? No way. Anyway, forget it two times, babe. I'm up to my ears in this drug scandal thing. The kids are all out of hospital now, and they've fucking disappeared, along with their parents, haven't they? No names allowed anyway, but the nationals are climbing all over the story, looking for anonymous whatever, and the houses are deserted. Nothing from the police, less from St Buidsear's. What the fuck is going on?'

I sympathised, slightly. It was odd, my creaky old journalistic self told me. 'What about the McVeigh girl? Is it her? Cora?'

'Karen. St Buidsear's say she is, quote, "no longer a patient, and has been transferred to a specialist unit elsewhere". Jesus! The McVeigh mansion is empty, Highland Capital say Big Phil's taken leave of absence. What fucking specialist unit? Where? No one's saying.'

'Wasn't there a name in the frame, someone Nicky Shearer was looking for –'

'Bobby the Busker. Yeah, you know that noisy grunge merchant down on Justice Street every lunchtime. Checked out his usual haunts, too. Nothing. And I'm going to be covering this all weekend for Clingfilm. The arsehole slimeball bastard has swanned off to Dounreay to have his lobotomy re-done, or get his gonads zapped with extra radioactivity. Call it a press conference, whatever, and the little fuck says he might as well make a weekend of it. In bastarding Thurso.'

'Must have a woman up there.'

'Yeah, well. Who would have McCorquodale? Maybe a nice-looking sheep. If he could find one he could reach the arse of.' Oh dear. Celia was not a happy camper. Her West Country accent had assumed a growling, bear-like quality. 'And to make matters worse, they've got me fixing for *The Digestive*, the lunchtime show, total fucking emergency. The main guest has just pulled out . . .' She trailed off. Thinking trickled down the line. Dangerous.

'Who was it?'

'Oh, that white witch from Cairnmore, Madame Frogspawn. You know, the one that claims to be able to find missing persons, lost dogs, car keys . . .'

'Madame Olagon? She's just a highly imaginative single mother who worked out a good way of supporting herself and her kids and has the pick of suggestible young women for a bit of lesbo recreation.'

A complete charlatan. Charlataness. There were people in the Highlands who did possess what for thousands of years had been called the second sight, who were both excessively strange and oddly normal. Madame Olagon – Jean Barrington, originally from Yorkshire – had come north with her boyfriend when he worked at the Nigg oil yard, was abandoned for a female apprentice welder, and proceeded to read every library book she could find on divination and palmistry. She even applied for a Small Business Grant to set up a consulting room in Carrbridge. She had been turned down, but then she must have seen that coming . . .

'Yeah, the very one. Listen . . .' Uh-oh. 'You don't fancy popping up for a favour, please please, oral sex, shag city, drinks . . . except not, not now, you don't . . . anyway. Highland's only private dick, I mean detective, talk about searching for missing – I mean, I know you haven't, don't . . . not for . . .'

Articulate, Celia? A fucking pro, mate! 'Try English, why don't you. Christ, are you serious? What about that *Round the Houses* débâcle? What about Fergus Evelyn? The Private Eye of the Airwaves asking him if he'd rubbed shite . . .'

'Well, not in so many words . . . fuck, I forgot that . . . ah, but Fergus won't be in, and anyway you're sober now. Aren't you?'

'I thought I was on a life ban. Didn't the Independent Broadcasting Authority . . . ?'

'Doubt it. Only if they get complaints. So few people listen at that time in the afternoon they probably didn't get any. And life bans in commercial radio only last until there's a need to fill up some dead air. Which there is.' Flattery. I'm such a sucker for it.

'Actually, I'm on a case, a task, paid employment. A job. Actual. Actually.'

'What? Since when?'

'Since yesterday. So, if I do this show, will you come to Loch Salvation with me? I need some moral support.'

She was beginning to thaw, to sound genuinely annoyed. Upset.

'Listen, Zander, I just can't. I just cannot do it. But will you? Please. I'll make it up to you. I promise.'

The Northlands studios were located in an anonymous industrial unit on the Highland landfill industrial estate, between a chainsaw service engineer and a banana ripeners. It is a little known fact that bananas need a place to ripen, and this was the location where all the tropical bent-penis fruit for the Highlands and Islands was taken to turn from green to yellow. I knew because I had once subbed a hilarious story about tarantula infestation there. The spiders had run amok and two had managed to infiltrate Radio Fuckwank, causing on-air horrors during the late-night phone-in on 'marital problems' which had run for a month before being cancelled due to lack of interest. But, then, it had been broadcast in Gaelic.

I parked the car and walked into the foyer, where giant photographs of the main presenters were displayed. There was my near-nemesis, Fergus Evelyn, looking like a ballet dancer run to vast amounts of seed. Seed potatoes, to be exact. Valentine Crawford, my host on the quaintly named *The Digestive*, and a host of others, among them a Tammy Wynette lookalike from whom you could almost smell the Nuits de Paris. This was Margharetina Molly MacSween, the Gaelic Goddess of Cookery, a woman who could make mince and tatties swell with the erotic impact of . . . haggis and cabbage. Her catchphrase, 'C*han eil sinn ag ithe an seo*' (We're not eating here!), was sometimes to be overheard in Inverness restaurants as a not very funny joke between uneasy Hebridean couples with lawnmower haircuts. And more commonly as a genuine reaction to the pseudo-food served throughout the Queen of the Highland Fleshpots. Then there was an impossibly battered face, peeking from behind a 1970s footballer fringe. Dennis The Bicycle was the English translation of his name, one of those Gaelic nicknames traceable back to schooldays and based on something really fascinating, like the fact that Dennis Macleod once had a bicycle. He was Gaeldom's Howard Stern, only the naughtiest he ever got was to make jokes about Free Kirk ministers' housekeepers. Extreme stuff, considering he was once cursed from a pulpit, to no obvious effect. Maybe God was busy that day.

Radio Fuckwank broadcast a full Gaelic service which was listened to by about two thousand people deliberately throughout the Highlands and Islands, and five thousand by accident. The whole thing was only possible because of government subsidies, all part of an effort to support Gaelic language and culture – best summarised in the poem by an eminent bard, much quoted by McGrooch, the Albatross bar's resident would-be Gael. Who could forget the genius of the man McGrooch claimed was called Mordecai Macblubbergreet:

Oh, and how the Gaels weep
now that they are all dead
Or nearly all
Well, quite a lot, anyway
Though a rump remains
Yes a rump
A rump, a rump, a rump
A tumpity, tumpity tump
Rump

Wailing in the language they no longer speak
And not just because they are dead
Because they are the rump
After all
The silent rump
I-ti-tump
Only not quite silent
Silent in the pure speech of the Gael
Imprisoned within the foul consonants
Of brute English
The language of candlemakers and craft shop owners
Who eat their own children, frequently
Unlike the rump
Who do not do so quite so often

Oh, how the Gaels weep . . . etc etc

Anyway. As a non-Gael and a barely adequate English speaker, I was here only to secure future relations with Celia and because for once I was not blurred and slurred by the effects of hangovers or their cure. I was to be interviewed by Valentine Crawford, The Only Official Homosexual In Inverness, or one of the very few prepared not just to admit the fact, but celebrate it elsewhere than the bus station toilets. A gigantic, bearded, frequently be-kilted personage of fragrant late-middle age and fruitily upmarket tones, Val was one of the few honest men in broad-casting, having entered it, he once told me, 'in search of as much youthful arse as the BBC could provide'. This he had pursued without apparent fear of infection or scandal, and had somehow avoided both. 'I have a dick like old leather, darling,' he said. 'Pickled in meths when I was a tootsie, chafed and hardened up nicely at fucking boarding school. Or, to be precise, buggering boarding school.' He lived, these days, in a small cottage out towards Aich, high in the wooded escarpment which looks over the Beauly Firth to the Black Isle. There he entertained suspecting and unsuspecting prey, charming them into his mouth and arsehole ('Care for a little oral pleasure, darling? On the house!'), or sending them screaming into the night, trainee reporters, flattered interviewees, supermarket stackers and visiting executives alike. He had been badly beaten up once, by an unlikely assailant. One of Channel Four's senior commissioning editors had been on a prowl through Scotland looking for potential network cannon fodder, using up the slack in his expense account, when he lurched into Sneck off the London sleeper and entertained a selection of local hacks and media tarts to lunch. After a lengthy drinking session and a consequent attempted grope by the redoubtable Val, he had kicked The Only Official Homosexual In Inverness into a bruised insensibility, and then panicked, incoherently phoning the Northlands newsroom for help. Fortunately for him, Celia had been doing a shift, and somehow managed to get Val medical treatment and the Channel Four commissioning editor on the sleeper to London, all the while keeping the hacks away from the affair. The quality of mercy. If I'd picked up that phone I guarantee mine would have been a bit more strained. I suspected a similar campaign of damage limitation had been waged by her on my behalf, after the Lucy'n'Fred chilled Hammerite testicles débâcle.

Val had regaled every journalist in town with the tale afterwards – he hadn't been badly hurt, just bruising to the gonads which had put him out of cock action for a while – but nothing had appeared in print or on air. Lucky old sodomite.

Celia grabbed my hand, dragged me into the tiny smoking-room and, slamming the door shut, grabbed me by the neck and kissed me with a kind of distracted fervour. Tobacco tongue: a nice chemical tingle.

'Thanks, Zander. I really, really appreciate this. I've got clearance from the managing editor for you to come in from the cold, make your glorious return. Well, a sort of shrug. That's good enough. Just don't say "shit" on air.'

'I didn't say it anyway . . . so you'll come to Loch Salvation with me? I wouldn't ask, it's just that . . . well, it's a . . . long way, and . . .' The fact was I hadn't been out of Sneck on my own, sober, for over a year. Or longer.

She shook her head. Her regret seemed genuine. 'Look. You know I would if I could.'

I was seized with the desire to run a finger over the pulsing blue vein on her temple. So I did. To little effect.

'There's nothing I'd like better but . . . it's just not a good time. The McVeigh story is major. Like . . . poised. Newsdesks everywhere waiting for several varieties of shit to hit a whole bunch of fans.' She flicked my finger away from her head. 'You know how things are. I've got to work. I have rent to pay, and if I cross that bastard McCorquodale . . .'

I sighed, spread my palms in supplication and acceptance of defeat. She was right about Clingfilm, he was a vindictive prick. 'Okay. Let's do this, then.'

'When you come back from Loch Salvation, you insatiable stud.' A clinically affectionate squeeze of the gonads. 'Meanwhile, you've got a radio show to do.'

Oh, well.

She shepherded me down a set of stairs and three soundproof doors, into a space which had been acoustically treated so that it sucked all the echoes out of the air, and the spirit out of all but the most extremely over-projected voice. A figure sat at what looked like a large, green-baize covered card table in the middle of the room.

'Zandy! Love! How are you, you old reprobate?'

Jesus. A mincing James Robertson Justice.

Val had coiffed his thick white hair into one of those ridiculous menopausal Melvyn Bragg quiffs, but managed to look remarkably well preserved for his fifty all-singing, all-dancing, all-buggering years. He was off-air in the studio, a record playing, Celtic but funky. Caperclannad or something.

'Fine, Val. Keeping on the straight and narrow these days.'

'So I hear. I went on the wagon once, for three solid weeks. Ended up eating fags just to keep sane.'

'Cigarettes or willing male flesh, Val?'

A great roaring cackle burst forth from the huge frame. He was wearing one of those Highland dancer's shirts with puff sleeves and a lace-up collar, and a worn, maybe moth-eaten kilt in the Buchanan tartan, as favoured by that arbiter of good taste, the Clutha Hotel. 'Both, you dirty-minded prick. Listen, do you like my latest?' He stood and did an overstated camp twirl. The kilt was massive. It must have been cut for an obese giant. It almost fitted him. 'Got it in Oxfam. Not my tartan, but what the fuck? Buchanan is for colour-blind clansmen to fire their muskets at, they say, but I like it.'

'Lovely, Val.' I could sense that the record was building to a crescendo. He might not be nervous, but I was. 'What are we talking about?'

'Oh, the usual shit, don't worry. Life as a private dick, keep it in your trousers, ha ha, investigations, working on anything interesting at the moment, that sort of stuff. Okay?'

The record was finishing. I could see the engineer gesturing through in the control room. I settled down at the felt-covered table opposite Val, who adjusted a foam-covered microphone, played with a sheaf of typewritten notes, and, as the music faded away, began to speak as if he was addressing the clans at Culloden.

'Welcome back! That was the lovely Karen Matheson and Capercaillie with their new single, *Gaelic Mafia* – a wee joke there, I'm sure. I'm Valentine Crawford, and with me on *The Digestive* this lunchtime is a man who gave up the secure life of journalism for something a touch more exciting. From mild-mannered reporter to Maltese Falcon-seeking gumshoe, he is the Highlands' only private detective. Zander Flaws. Zander, good afternoon.'

'Valentine, how's it hanging?'

A microsecond of silence. Had I gone too far? Then the geniality of the broadcaster, unfazable, unshockable. 'Fine and dandy, Zander, fine and dandy. Good to have you back on air, after a little *frisson* of rudeness with the great and the good Fergus Evelyn . . . But enough of the man who must try and follow this show' – there was no love lost between the two – 'Now, moving into the exciting, nay thrilling world of detection from being – what was it – editor of that esteemed organ the *Northern Mail and Courier?*' Flattering bastard. 'Why?'

Christ. 'Well, Val – I may call you Val? – just the need to . . . move from a sort of . . . observational role in the world of . . . events, to something more . . .' I could feel my brain seizing up as my mouth made nonsensical word-noises and my hands moved about with a will of their own. It was like being suddenly divided into three lumps of existence.

'Participatory?'

'Sorry?'

'Something more participatory. Than journalism. Moving into.'

'Ah . . .yes.'

'So, here you are, over a year now, working in the murky world of investigation, doubtless divorces, that kind of thing?'

'A bit.' Suddenly I wasn't interested. A cold indifference settled over me. Indifference to Celia, to whoever was listening, and to Val and his soft, all-enveloping ego, his need to do this useless, parasitic thing, this broadcasting of the self: Lookatmelookatmelookatme . . . Listen.

'A bit what?' There was an edge there now, something I hadn't noticed before in Val. 'I would have thought divorces would make up the vast majority of your work?' Surely he knew? Surely he realised that divorce, separation, annulment, all these words still left me chilled to the heart, a belated empathy with Lucy and the bastard Charleson's icy predicament.

'No.'

'No?'

'No. Mostly boring precognitions for solicitors, doing the interviewing they're too important or busy or fed up to do. Tracking down runaway witnesses, or scared clients facing debt-collection proceedings.' Suddenly I felt reckless. 'I have done a divorce, though.'

'And how was that?'

'Tedious. Walked in, found the wife in bed with the boss. Tied them up, threw them in the garden, forgot about them. They nearly froze to death.'

'Ah . . . you're joking, Zander, of course.'

'Ah . . . I'm joking, Valentine. Sometimes the police use me in cottaging investigations, you know, get me to proposition men in toilets while they observe from the comfort of unmarked Austin Maestros.'

'Thank you, Zander, your sense of humour is on . . . ripping form this afternoon. You can quiz our tame dick' – he used the *double entendre* with a degree of malevolence, I thought – 'free, on the usual number. Ask him anything you want, anything decent, honest and, of course, it doesn't have to be truthful. Call now. Meanwhile, here's a wee accordion track from the Muff MacTaggart Ensemble, *Rory's Reel.*'

The red light on the desk went off. The sound of flailing squeezeboxes filled the studio, momentarily taking me right back to my brother's incessant practising, that nagging, honking, grating melodicism, as Val ripped off his headphones and turned to me.

'What are you trying to do, you shit? This is a game which may appear crapulent to your booze-burned braincells, but it's how I make my living and there are rules. One is you don't try and be a cynical smartass or you appear totally hateful to the listeners, and the other is you don't make stupidly snide comments about the kind of holes I like to place my podger in. Jesus.'

Suddenly, I felt mildly ashamed. Just mildly. 'Sorry, Val. I'll behave, honest.'

'Good.' He smiled, an avalanche of gums, bad teeth and flesh beneath the beard. 'Listen, great story. There was a wee newsroom party the other night in here, and you know Tony the Tadger?'

I did. The famously promiscuous senior reporter, forty-five going on fifteen, who was reputed to have successfully shagged Stornoway's only prostitute in an effort to discover if a certain royal schoolboy had really had it off with her during a school sailing trip. And then tried to claim the price on expenses as 'four packed-lunches for school party'. 'Yep, I sure do. How is the old bastard? Still taking the antibiotics?'

'Oh, sure, that and everything else he can cram into whatever orifices he hasn't already blocked up forever. Anyway, here's Tony, doing his I'm-pretending-not-to-drink thing as usual, bottle of tonic water spiked with a quarter-bottle of gin, swigging it like he's some kind of marathon runner, which in a sense he is, I suppose. News trainee, a Gaelette, fresh from Eriskay, school hostel, university – in other words, systematic shagging experience. Fantastically good-looking twenty-two, completely shit-faced, giving it that Gaelic shouting thing all over the place, screeching laughter heederum hoderum, *tha ah–uile duine air mhisg* – everybody's pissed. So she and Tony get in a clinch and then disappear. People are coming and going, off to the smoking-room for a joint or some speed, whatever. The usual. So nobody notices anything until someone flicks on the newsroom radio monitor to get the news, check if anything's been missed. Anyway, it's switchable from the mixing desk in the control room, right, and suddenly it's *je t'aime* in Gaelic, what is it – *tha gaol agam ort* – complete with scraping noises, bonking, scratching, howling, all coming, if you like, and going up and down in volume.'

'Yeah, sure. That old shagging on the mixing desk thing again . . .'

'No, I'm serious! They were doing it right on the faders, and there everybody was, rapt audience, silent in the newsroom, and it's *I love you, Mo Graidh* and *Can sin a-rithist sa' mhadainn. Oof oof oof* . . . found a used condom in there next morning, according to the cleaner, who wasn't amused . . . Jim, the engineer reckoned her arse needed a few decibels' tweaking. Too fuzzy, he said . . .'

The record faded, a red light came on, a green light flashed.

'. . . and that was Muff MacTaggart, the inimitable sound of, emm, Muff there, and *Rory's Reel*. I'm Valentine Crawford, this is *The Digestive*, a chance to let your lunch go down with me, and taking the biscuit today is Zander Flaws, the Highlands' only private detective. Calling in from Dingwall we have a . . . Reverend . . . Smith? What's your question, Mr Smith, you footloose man of God, you?'

Shit shit shit shit *shit*.

'Hello, Valentine.' Oh my God. 'And hello, Zander. I just wondered if you had counted the cost of your calling, so to speak. I mean, it is obviously a pathway fraught with potential danger, is it not? Angry husbands, debtors who don't intend to pay . . . and presumably, if you get involved in anything more serious, the consequences likewise would be more serious, too. I presume, Zander, that you have weighed things up, and placed them before the Lord, asking for His guidance?'

'Sure,' I said. 'And how is the Lord these days? I believe that the God of love and justice has a few questions to ask you, too, Jeremiah Gideon. You are, after all, a prisoner not set free from sin, but only on parole.'

Val looked at me, utterly confused.

'Questions, is it? Not as many as the Lord will be demanding of you when He meets you, and that could be very soon, you cunt,' said Jeremiah. No time-delay on the Northlands transmitter, but I already knew that.

Valentine turned white as a sheet. I'd never seen him so discombobulated. 'Strong . . . language there from a man of the . . . supposed cloth,' he gasped. 'My heartfelt apologies, ladies and gentlemen.'

I could see the engineer slumped over his console, head in his hands. No producer to take the rap, just Val and, unfortunately, Celia, pressganged researcher. Oh dear. All my fault, no doubt. Again. Flaws does it again. 'Now some more music. Some nice cunt . . . country stylings from Big Tam and the Mainliners, with *Your Cheatin' Heart*.'

The music boomed over the monitors, country'n'Irish with a hideous, rough-hewn rural bog-edge, like peat-flavoured burger, and Val ripped off his headphones and lunged for me. He was not acting on an erotic impulse, either. I leaned out of his reach. 'You FUCK!' he screamed. 'You SCUMFUCK SHITDICK! Aw, Christ I said cunt as well, I was so upset. Cunt . . . country. Oh, for fuck's sake. You set this up, you drunken asshole, didn't you? Didn't you? You and that tart of yours!'

'Nothing to do with me, Val. Or Celia. Well, I mean, I didn't expect him to phone in.'

'But you knew him?' He was calming down, seemed less prone to country-soundtracked violence.

'Yep. That was Jeremiah Gideon Smith, violator of parole, convicted criminal, attacker of yours truly and all-round not-nice guy. The police are after him for trying to kill me in the hospital. Not to mention pushing me down the Castle Street steps, though the officers of the law are not so sure I didn't push myself. With a bottle.'

'I can understand how they might think that. Another of your DT delusions. Get the fuck out of here. I should never have agreed to have you on the show. Desperation. Celia should have known better, the drunken slut. The two of you are a perfect pair. Fuckin' perfect.'

It was a time of changes, a day for decisions. I wasn't drinking. I could be gallant. I leaned over the table and its cluster of microphones, and belted Val on the side of his nose with the heel of my right hand, a variation of the move which hadn't worked on Jeremiah back at St Buidsear's. I put a twist in my body as I did so. There was a satisfying crack, and blood spurted from his flared patrician nostril on to the baize cloth.

'There you are, Val. Blood in here on the table, sperm through there on the mixing desk. This is the Bodily Fluids Broadcasting Corporation. The BFBC.'

I opened the heavy studio door, and pushed through the small crowd of murmuring, excited media serfs who had gathered, exultant in an on-air scandal. Celia was there, grim-faced. My hand throbbed, but not badly. I kissed her forehead as I passed. 'See you when I come back, love,' I said. 'Sorry about this, but I didn't say anything.'

'Zander.' Something in her voice made me stop. I was feeling good, buzzing with adrenaline, enjoying having hit somebody, even a defenceless old queen like Valentine. I examined my hand. Bruising, but no cut. 'Zander. What is going on?' Bless her, she sounded concerned. Immediately and perversely, I felt like sex, but it seemed there was hardly a surface in the radio station which hadn't recently been used for illicit couplings. Some other time, some softer, cleaner place. What was wrong with me, though? Why did I feel energised by hitting someone?

'You coming?'

She shook her head, tiredly. I could see the rage in her eyes, the betrayals, the disappointments, the sheer fucking hassle of men like me. Life.

'Then I'll see you afterwards. That call that came in? Let's just say that someone seems keen that the lost shall remain unfound, and someone else thinks I'm the man to do the finding.' Oh yeah. Jeremiah and the Thiebaults were opposite sides in some game, and I was along on the centre spot, blinded by the floodlights. But which sport, what rules? They knew, and I didn't. It felt . . . it felt . . . good. Yes. Good.

I left her amid the clucking wash of thrilled media outrage, went through reception where every telephone in the world, or at least this corner of Inverness, Media Acres, appeared to be ringing, and out into the sweet air of approximate reality. I was flying. And for the first time since waking up in hospital, I didn't feel like a drink. I'd discovered a new therapy: hitting radio broadcasters. Being at the centre of a mystery. Fear and violence: the solution to everything.

★ Ten

Glendruin. I'd been going there from the start, I suppose. From the moment I'd stumbled out of the hospital on Hernia's arm, the past had begun throbbing away like an ulcer, the booze which had kept it anaesthetised absent. Mum. Dad. Home. Brotherly hatred. The nearest of the four was the brotherly hatred.

There was more than one way to get to Loch Salvation, and for reasons selfish, emotional and spiritual, or what passed for spiritual in my arid little life, I wanted to misuse the Thiebaults' money and refresh myself with some serious scenery. And, yes, catch up with the past, with the bits of myself which were held in other people's memories. Or to begin with, one other person's.

Not before time. If I could face it. I suppose I'd never really wanted Celia to come with me. Or maybe I'd been looking for an excuse to avoid Glendruin, because I couldn't, wouldn't take her there. If so, why was I going by way of that hidden enclave? Partly because I couldn't really help myself; partly for the groovy views, sure, and partly because I was half-worried about pursuit. Stupid. Or maybe not. I phoned the number, left a voicemail message. What was the difference between voicemail and an answering machine? Leave your reply after the beep . . .

Riefenstahl thrummed as soulfully as Stuttgart's engineers had deemed permissible as I twitched the power steering through the sweeping bends beside Loch Ness, heading west. Between me and the more northern direct route to Loch Salvation were mountains, deer, bogs, lochs, trees, sheep and one or two people. This was going to be a convoluted journey. But there was a prickly feeling in my gut, a kind of breathless indigestion of excitement. *Oh–oh oh Thunder Road* . . . Except at that moment I was in a riot, a white riot, a riot of my own. It was 1978 and I was *White Man in Hammersmith Palais*, cutting peats in a brutally hot Shetland day, a pimply boy resentful of too much fresh air, wishing for urban dirt. And then it was now, I had the sunroof open and The Clash on the stereo, an old compilation picked with a clutch of other tapes at random from the sea-chest which held my music collection back at The Tub. In the back was an Adidas bag casually stuffed with clothes, toothbrush, condoms, Librium and Antabuse. Beside me, an old Aero leather jacket and the mobile phone. In my pocket was money. Things could be worse. I could have picked up my (single, unwisely, almost unforgivably purchased) Saw Doctors tape by mistake.

But things were by no means perfect, either. In that Mr and Mrs Thiebault had vanished from the Clutha, bound for destinations unknown, despite saying that I could contact them there for a week at least. I'd phoned just before leaving Sneck, and the receptionist had been frostily co-operative. She clearly didn't remember me. I was just another shooshing, whistling mobile-phone voice, some other dickhead getting cancer of the brain from digital radio waves. A headache arrived, on cue. They had stayed for one night, and then announced that they were planning to do some sightseeing 'up north'. Christ. Where was 'up north' when you were in Inverness. Wick? That would be sightseeing for the blind. Shetland? I didn't like to think about it too much. I sometimes caught some film on telly of my erstwhile home and found myself thinking how stunning, how beautiful, how strange it was. Barrenness made gorgeous. And then I recognised it and lost the vision. True love gone bad. It happens.

It seemed fairly clear that the Thiebaults had heard something which had provoked that stampede away from the Clutha. Like on the radio? Or maybe the food had just become too much, the awful décor of the Prebble Lounge too overwhelming. Still, I had the money, and they had my number at The Tub, which I had, guided by a helpful BT contract employee working from an open prison in Surrey, diverted to the Ericsson. And the mobile had its voicemail, featuring an anonymous English female asking for messages to be left, as I was probably out of range, batteries or patience. Only she didn't say patience. On the whole I was technologied-up, as contactable as anyone could be who was heading for the remote west Highlands, looking for a fishing boat in the most convoluted coastline in Europe, an area so commonly used for smuggling that the average beachcomber was as likely to find cocaine as driftwood. Well, not quite, but there was lots of cannabis resin in bales floating around. So they say.

The Customs and Excise, cut down to a rump by financial constraints, announced roughly one major bust a year, which meant that around fifty major landings took place without them knowing anything about it. Or perhaps they knew, but were either unwilling or unable to interfere. Their only hope was informants, and the busts they did get were usually on the basis of yachts or fishing boats tracked all the way from Morocco to somewhere like Inverbervie, way north of Loch Salvation. The serious pros – the local fishing skippers who rendezvoused with oil supply vessels out in the Atlantic, who towed submersibles packed with heroin from long cables, all armed to detonate and sink if trouble arose – didn't get caught. They threw the weak, the desperate and the amateurs to the excisemen every so often to keep them quiet. Drug-smuggling was a major part of the west Highland economy.

And there remained the nagging possibility that I was being played for an idiot by Gareth Thiebault and his tarnished trophy wife over this whole business of finding Roger. I was not unaware that the whole thing stank, positively reeked, of illegal substances. And fish. A combination Loch Salvation had once, briefly, been famous for in the 1980s, when a yacht was stopped offshore and found to be packed with prime Afghan Black. Maybe they were involved themselves, or knew Roger had been. Perhaps Roger had seen something that night in Aberdeen, and he had been taken on board the *Chuleta de Cordero* and – but no. That e-mail. He knew about the boat. He'd been looking for it. *Police and Thieves*, stuttered Joe Strummer.

I stop-started my way through quaintly named Drumnadrochit, with its competing Loch Ness Monster visitor centres, its great walls of parked buses, its ugly scattering of tartanry, swathes of Nessie-hunters. A deeply unpleasant place.

Buggart castle, where St Columba apparently saw the monster, passed on the left, the carpark heaving with bus parties and car loads of the curious. I slowed down to weave through the traffic waiting to get in. It was another boiling hot day, and I thanked God I wasn't a tourist. Lucy and I had spent a winter afternoon here, alone apart from an icy wind, clambering over the rocks and mistaking diving cormorants for monster sightings. A brief pang. Both of us had been shagging other people at the time, but the illusion of closeness had been nice. Funny how winter was a time of romance. Cold, cuddling, warming each other up, log fires and whisky.

Whisky. I swallowed the thought, tasting it, feeling the heat from my throat to my gut. An emptiness spread from my chest to my arms and fingers, leaving me weak and shaking, then suddenly nauseous. And just then there was a shriek of metal and a huge, squealing impact from behind me. My neck snapped back, but the headrest stopped whiplash turning my vertebrae to matchwood and sending me inexorably to the land of permanent nod. Automatically, I stabbed the accelerator, and the big six-cylinder engine howled as the kickdown engaged. With a tearing of metal, the Merc leaped forward. So much for my immaculate usable classic, one bibulous owner.

I checked the mirror. Bearing down on me was a silver Toyota Landcruiser, all bullbars, broken spotlights and smears of green Mercedes paint. Difficult to match Mercedes paint. The windows were illegally tinted, so the driver's face was invisible. Funny, I wouldn't have put Jeremiah Gideon down as a Toyota man. More of a Roverista. But, then, thieves and parole-breakers couldn't be choosers, let alone attempted murderers. Unless someone else wanted a piece of my battered body, not to mention Riefenstahl's.

The A82 Loch Ness-side road is a murderous piece of engineering, originally laid out by General Wade as part of his attempt, post-Culloden, to subdue the nasty Jacobite clans. This main route through the geological fault of the Glen of Perdition, alongside the canal-connected four lochs, mountain and forest, joins west and east coasts, and features, typically, great juggernauts, laden with trees or fish, thundering back and forth. Foreign tourists trundle along in hired cars forgetfully driving on the right, while cyclists lay themselves open to carbon monoxide poisoning and flattening, and motorcyclists flirt with evisceration, all half-hoping, half-fearing they catch a glimpse of Nessie. To cap it all, most of the locals using the route are pissed as the proverbial farts. I rather like it, actually.

But not when some psychopath in an oversized four-wheel-drive was attempting, in broad daylight, to damage my rear bumper, and me, beyond repair. This, when I was basically a returnee to driving, somewhat shaky at the old handbrake-turn avoidance manoeuvres.

Things were happening fast. At seventy miles per hour on a twisty road, they do tend to.

Except in my befuddled brain, but then that was par for the course. Films flickered through my mind, or frames from them: *Bullitt*, with Steve McQueen and the streets of San Francisco, still the best ever car chase; *Mad Max One*, easily the finest thing Mel Gibson was ever involved with. Well, no, I would make an allowance for *The Year of Living Dangerously*, because it had Sigourney Weaver in it: World's Most Shaggable Tall Old American Bluestocking. No car chases, though. *Two Lane Blacktop*, now there was a film. Broooooooocie, baby, sing it for me: summer's here and the time is right, for racing in the . . . crunch. *Vanishing Point*.

The Landcruiser hit me again, this time going at a considerably increased lick, and Riefenstahl swayed wildly, almost putting me directly into the path of a truck loaded with stripped fir, and heading for the chipboard factories of the east coast. A blare of bull horns faded as we continued to surge westwards. Would anyone contact the police with their mobile phone? Mobile semaphore kit? Not me, I didn't have a hands-free model of either system. And, hey, I was safety conscious! But, anyway, this was mountainous terrain, and I could see the phone's No Signal indicator flashing on the passenger seat.

James Dean in *Rebel Without a Cause*, playing chicken . . . without thinking, I swung the Merc into the opposite lane and slammed on the brakes. Thank God there was nothing coming in the opposite direction.

It took the Toyota driver by surprise long enough for him to come storming past me on the inside. I swerved back left, hit kickdown and sent Riefenstahl barrelling into the big off-roader's ample backside.

I have no idea what I intended, but the effect was gratifying, terrifying and surprising. The inherent instability of large, high four-wheel-drive vehicles was revealed as the ungainly vehicle swerved to the right, into the path of an approaching camper van.

Terror. I could see it on the faces of the tourists, an elderly couple, perched high on their velour seats, one moment Nessie-spotting and the next facing the monstrous prospect of being mashed into handily canned meat by a giant Japanese executive truck, with leather seats and enough solidity to pulverise a bulldozer. A frozen millisecond. I braked, and the weaving Toyota spun suddenly away from the camper, which never wavered for a moment from its onward track, and down the bushy, fern-grown bank on the left which led to the loch.

Fuck it. It was an off-roader, after all. On its wheels or on its roof, who gave a shit? Jeremiah Gideon Smith, you bastard, may you be eaten by Loch Ness's famous nematode worms. At least *they* exist, unlike the bloody monster. I hit the accelerator and left Smith, assuming that's who it was, to rallycross, drown or burn. Tell the truth, I didn't care. In the excitement, the raging fear of it all, came that coldness again. Ice-cream of the soul. It was new. I liked the feeling.

I hoped the motor-caravanners didn't die of Toyota-induced coronaries. If they'd had faster reactions, they'd have crashed themselves. Fuck them. They came here to see a monster, didn't they? One thrill was as good as another. Plesiosaur, Megasaur. Very sore. I hoped Smith was, or worse.

Ten miles later I took the junction which led across country through Glenarrant. I'd made this journey once, in winter with Lucy, and it had been almost unbearably beautiful, strange and Narnia-like. The White Witch era, of course. No Aslans in this universe.

Still following the line of General Wade's military road, the original of which wove in and out of the new carriageway like an old ghost. I took Riefenstahl up the side of Loch Revell, then stopped at the Revellers, that great old hotel and pub which is enough to turn the most hardened slob into a gay mountaineer or at least a bisexual hillwalker. Roaring fires, good brown beer, crinkle-cut chips just the way everyone secretly likes them, straight from the freezer to the deep-fat fryer. And on their way they go, shining of face, keen of mind, heading for the high tops of Creag nan Damh or Sgurr Beag, some destined to die through carelessness, freak weather or sometimes deliberate policy. Not for nothing did the Highlands have the highest suicide rate in Britain. People came here to snuff it staring at a good view.

I locked the car, its hissingly bizarre pneumatic central locking system apparently still working, and examined the damage. Stuttgart steel, even underlaid with corrosion, was robust stuff, and though Riefenstahl was unlikely to win any classic car competition, it was all repairable, doubtless at vast cost. I went into the hotel bar for a pint.

A pint. I deserved one. A pint of what? Lemonade? Coke? No fucking way. I deserved a pint of alcohol, or if that was not readily available, beer. Maybe with a wee dram on the side just to nip the throat, anchor the soul down, grease the fear a wee bit. I walked up to the worn mahogany bar, conscious of my feet clacking on the flagstones, hypersensitive to the place, the murmur of voices, the few early-evening faces, all seeming to belong through locality or purpose: climbing trousers or the flushed faces and broken veins of habitual refreshment. The fire sparked and ticked, and I felt its heat hit my face. If ever there was a pub to relish a drink in, this was it. It was for real.

I was away from Inverness, out from under the droopy wing of those who knew my drouthful past, and I was ready to take a dive into a fresh new glittering sea of moderate drinking, of controlled alcohol-enjoyment. I leant on the bar and looked at the gantry, at Scotland in spirit: Bladnoch, Bunnahabhainn, Bowmore, Littlemill, Old Pulteney, Talisker, Glen Scotia, Highland Park, Balblair, Glenmorangie . . . The roll-call of amber wonder went on and on. I felt my throat constrict with longing. The beers – brown smelly real ale was not to my taste anyway, but the attitude was important. A place which looked after its beers usually looked after its staff and its guests.

'Yes, sir. What can I get for you today?' An Australian voice. Dirty blond dreadlocks swam into view, surfer biceps and a neck which looked capable of holding up a scrum on its own. An international mountain bum. Oh well. I breathed in, still not knowing what I was going to say. And then, for the first time in my drinking career, I was able to foresee the future. Feel it. The dram's burn, the cool foamy flood of beer, repeated and repeated, the opening up of confidence and conversation. Stop there? Too pissed to drive, driving anyway, then fuck knows, crashing, burning, maybe making it through . . . but no, I wouldn't stop. No beer, straight whisky, spirits, anything, by the neck, by the bottle, book a room if I was sensible, I mean still in possession of any sense; if not, keep on drinking until the sickness and attempted violence and the falling over sent me out the door to slump beside or, if I was lucky, inside Riefenstahl. And who was to say who or what might be pursuing me, ready in the course of the evening to drag me out and beat me to a pulp? Or wait until I went into my alcoholic coma, spoon-feed some spare vomit – there would be plenty around, there always was – down my throat, close off my airways and wait . . .

'Coffee,' I said.

'Sure.'

Men could drink coffee at the Revellers, thank Christ, without being accused of homosexual prostitution. And, as you know, most climbers are into that anyway. I took the cup of stewed Cona over to the table near the entrance, with a window looking out over the carpark. No one had driven up. Outside the evening was closing in, not with darkness, which was hours away yet, but a kind of thickening of the mountain air. Midges flickered in clouds. I shovelled six spoonfuls of sugar into the congealed black coffee, then stirred it for five minutes, blanking my mind to the chink of glasses, the stuttering murmur of conversation. Then I drank it down in one. The caffeine and sugar jag kicked in, a weird, zingy but oddly Presbyterian version of a whisky hit. Another three, a piss and I was ready to go.

At Hell Bridge, the gloaming was turning Loch Druichan into a science fiction orange lava, and it caught at my throat with its sheer, effortless beauty. I turned west into the deepening shadow cast by the mountain called Drum Sgurr nan Caar, and began to climb the corkscrewing Alpine track which leads, eventually, to the hidden, magical valley of Varshtar, a fertile tract of land low down on the shores facing Skye, and one of the most peculiarly atmospheric places on God's earth, with, near by, mysterious brochs and the burnt-out wilderness at Sandaig which was once Gavin Maxwell's Corryvraig. Now burnt out and impossibly spooky, the place where all the strange and occasionally perverse acts which gave rise to *Ring of Bright Water* and its sequels is still a pilgrimage destination for otter lovers.

Maybe in some other lifetime. As the road breached the escarpment and the awesome sight of Skye's Cuillins, starting to be silhouetted by the slowly dying sun, met me, I hauled the old Merc, which had protested not a whit at the brutal climb, into an unmetalled track leading south, into a dense patch of planned forest, mostly Norwegian spruce. Christmas trees. My heart was banging painfully, loudly, like it had for Santa's presumed arrival on Christmas Eve, choking in under the eaves of the old croft house, unable to sleep, screamingly fearful that if I didn't, he wouldn't come. Just inside the patch of trees, an aluminium farm gate, topped with an extra layer of razor wire, blocked the track. I got out to open it, but I could see that a heavy, dull grey electronic lock with an infra-red sensor on each side had been fitted. Through the trees and difficult to spot, an electric fence the height of an average man stretched away. To keep out deer. To keep out everything unwished for.

The first bullet – a large-calibre high-velocity round by the sound of it, the kind salmon farmers use on seals – howled off the steel gatepost like a grumpy firework. The second ploughed into the stony dust at my feet with a dry cluck, spouting dirt over my battered commando-soled brogues. I stood still, then putting both hands to my mouth, bellowed into the strange, absorbent darkness of the trees, the woodland he'd had planted to provide the swishing, soothing sound of the sea, and maybe to deny its omnipresence in his early life too: 'DU'S A FUCKIN' NYAAF, VICTOR. DU COULDNA HIT A GRICE FA TWA FIT. IT'S ZANDER.'

There was a rustling, woody silence, and then with a buzz followed by a rasping clunk, the electronic latch was opened remotely. It seemed my brother was in residence.

★ Eleven

The track wove for about a mile through the mass of conifer, and then suddenly opened out into what seemed like an eternity of gloaming. Where the artificial forest ended, the ground fell away into a kind of shallow gorge, the geographical feature known as Glendruin, which itself dropped gradually as a kind of side-channel to the floor of Varshtar proper, the last lick of land between the Sound of Sleat and Skye. In the gathering gloom, it was still possible to sense the epic grandeur of this location. Beyond the pale, narrow glimmer of water, the Cuillins snarled, jagged black against purple, like some Dungeons and Dragons fantasy landscape.

The house came as a contrast. A low clutter of wood and glass, it was based on the Scandinavian kits which offered dwellers in cold northern climes triple glazing, mega-insulation, a buried heat-exchanger supplying hot water and warmth, and the necessity of painting their exterior walls every five years. Somehow, it seemed inappropriate in this setting. A hulking, brutish Scots baronial tower in twisted stone and slate would have suited the place, would have stated superiority, warning, possession. But then that had never been the intention. Victor had wanted to wear his proprietorship lightly. Or so he claimed.

The tall figure in a camouflage Ventile jacket stood in front of a dark-green Mitsubishi Shogun (suddenly, four-wheel-drives were breeding like rabbits) cradling a rifle equipped with high-intensity telescopic sights. The face, the family resemblance, crinkled pine bark to my battered elm, etched with eight years' more experience than my fizzog, but less diminished, shadowed – less pickled, basically – and attached to a taller, rangier body than my own. Victor cracked his features into a broken grin as I climbed out of Riefenstahl.

'Well, boy. How's du?'

'Fine dat,' I replied. And thus was the ice, the eternal, initial awkwardness fissured. It would never be entirely broken, or melted; the uneasiness would remain, but I was relatively pleased. Victor could, after all, have shot me. He had done it before.

Not that my esteemed elder bother made a habit of it. And he had been provoked by my accordion-slashing activities. It happened not long

105

after that, when I was seven, he was fifteen, and he had been shooting rabbits with a .22 bolt-action rifle on the croftland of our neighbour, Minty Ball. His real name was Walter Peterson, but he had been Minty Ball to the entire community ever since his schooldays. Something to do with the theft of a bag of sweeties, my father had told us, one day, after hours of incessant prompting. The name was never used to his face or in his hearing, but at all other times and in other company, there was no such person as Walter Peterson. He was Minty Ball or, if you were young and rude and did not know him well, Ballsie.

Anyway, I was picking up the rabbits my brother had shot, and cutting their tails off for the fifty-pence bounty the council was then offering, in an effort to get rid of the animals and the plague of stoats their vast numbers had caused. Victor shot me, quite deliberately, in the left hand, because, as he put it, 'Du's no moving fast enyuch.' He seemed to find my agonised howling quite funny, and was, as far as I could tell, pleased with his marksmanship. My hands were, after all, small at the time. I had never known there could be a pain so bad. Or so much blood.

Why? Why did he do it? Without compunction or apparent regret? I had often wondered if he was some kind of psychopath, devoid of any feelings but his sense of himself, his utter completeness and importance. But no. There was resentment, too. Of me, my parents. A kind of cool contempt for us.

He had always been into guns, though the .22 had been the maximum firepower Dad would allow. 'Dis shite is no guid,' I remember Victor saying savagely, while poring over a gun catalogue with increasing frustration. 'A Ruger .357, like the salmon farmers use for pittin awa' da selkies. Dat's da fellow.' We both knew the sullen bark of those big weapons, had seen the bloody bodies of seals washed ashore. It was that kind of rifle he'd fired at me as I approached the Glendruin gate.

Once the blood had been washed off, that long-ago .22 bullet had left a neat crucifixion hole, surrounded with bruising, which, after some agonising stitching at Gilbert Bain Hospital in Lerwick, healed quickly; my father's palely, quietly furious words left wounds which gaped for a lot longer. He didn't hit Victor. Neither of us were ever beaten. Maybe we should have been. I never found out exactly what was said, but a week later Victor turned sixteen and left home, surfacing, after an initially miserable two-year period of frantic searching by my parents, and then a kind of negation of his existence, in the Parachute Regiment, eighteen and beyond parental reach. In the two years before he was old enough to join the army, he had travelled, spent time in Amsterdam, Morocco, the hippy trail to Afghanistan, which even then was dangerous. Anyone less like a hippy than my brother I've never met, and maybe that's why he survived, intact enough to become a squaddie. He never talked about those travelling days much. It was a great deal later that I wondered how many years of resentment at his young, soft brother's appropriation of parental affection resulted in that bullet through the hand. Anyway, he left me with my mum and dad: I got it all and then chucked it back in their faces.

'I knew you'd be coming,' said Victor, turning from the Shetland dialect neither of us felt entirely comfortable with any more.

'I should hope so,' I said. 'I mean, I presume you check your innumerable voicemail services. Anyway, what's the fucking use in being a professional clairvoyant if you can't predict your own family's movements?'

Victor looked at me oddly. His hair had turned patchily grey, but remained relatively thick, unlike my own thinning locks. I took after Dad's hormonal make-up, clearly. 'Clairvoyance,' he mused. 'If only. Facts, figures and logic plus some inspired guesswork, Zander. And the facts about you have been coming thick and fast lately.'

'Intelligence, eh?'

'No. More like stupidity. In large doses. Come and have a coffee.' He looked critically at the back of Riefenstahl. 'Bit of a bash, eh?'

'Aye,' I said. 'Some arse in a Toyota came off second best.'

'Greased your Panzer tracks with his guts, did you?'

I shrugged. We both half-laughed. God knows why.

Victor always claimed not to care what I was up to, and admitting that I had penetrated his rarefied world of on-line upmarket credit checks and silky industrial blackmail – all legal, he said – was unusual. But he could follow my spoor without me knowing it most of the time. Because Victor's speciality was intelligence. Or rather he specialised in knowing things. About people. And especially companies. Knowledge had paid for Glendruin, and what he'd built there. And of course, my own move into pseudo private investigating had not been in the slightest influenced by his quiet success in the abstruse areas of information demand and supply he worked in. Rarely did I ask him for help. Never did he offer. We were, after all, brothers, and the baggage we carried, mutually, had never even been opened properly. Sometimes my hand throbbed. The scar still itched. Maybe occasionally he looked at me, or thought of me, and still wished I had never been born, like I'd once, as a barely sentient child, overheard him telling my mother. Me, I looked at that pink scar on my palm and wished I knew him better, that he'd never left, that he hadn't shot me. That everything was all right again.

'What kind of rifle is that, Victor?'

'A Ruger .357.'

Uh-huh.

In the vast dining-kitchen, with its combination of restaurant stainless steel, polished Skye stone and blunt pine, Victor switched on his professional Gaggia, a vintage 1950s one straight out of *Espresso Bongo*, with shallow Duralex cups piled along its top to warm, and burnished lettering which vibrated in the fluorescent light like bad skiffle. 'Half an hour,' he said, 'and the macchiato will be available to taste.' We slumped into two battered maroon leather club chairs and eyed each other. As ever, he made me feel gawky, nervous.

'So,' I began, as the coffee machine burbled in the background. 'Why the hell should you be picking up static about me and my actions, when you have for a long time evinced hardly one iota of interest in me and mine?'

'So,' he replied, 'why should you leave some garbled message and then arrive forthbloodywith on my rather nicely camouflaged doorstep, shouting in rusty Shetlandic, barging in to see me after all this time of separation and sorrow? Should you apologise?' He looked up at the arched wooden ceiling, into the muffled glow of expensive pencil spotlights. 'Should he say sorry?'

'What for?' the voice was amused, very English, very expensive, very female and not in the least bit soft. Like broken ice floes rubbing together. Framed suddenly, almost magically in the double doorway which led to a lounge of tennis-court proportions was a tall, loose-limbed woman with a blaze of red hair flickering around a narrow, strong-featured face. She was dressed in a Timberland shirt and jeans which were too well cut to be anything available from the average main street Millets. Caterpillar boots, well worn but clean. She was about thirty and exuded an extravagant healthiness. Tough, though. And unpredictable. Dangerous.

'This is Zander, or Alexander if we're being formal,' said Victor, half turning to her with a face carefully stiff and expressionless. 'My little brother, come to attempt a family reconciliation. He thinks.'

'Oh, really?' The woman rippled into the room, bringing a slight scent of elderflower with her. Either she bathed in Body Shop accoutrements or she was a heavy closet Aqua Libra drinker. An Aquaholic. 'I love reconciliations. Emotion in the raw, tears in the whisky.'

'Not for Zander,' said Victor. 'Not unless you want to see broken glass and blood in the booze. Last time I saw him he had one drink and then tried to kill me.'

'It had been a bad day, Victor,' I said, attempting a smile of dazzling power at this hugely attractive newcomer. 'And, besides, you'd already shot me once. I was just trying to get some retaliation in.'

'A bit late.' He allowed himself a small grimace. 'Nursing your revenge for a quarter of a century. Pathetic. Zander, this is Rosie.'

'*Companion of the Rosy Hours*,' I joked. Nobody laughed, but then Buchan's *Greenmantle* was hardly cool and cultivated reading.

'Huh,' snorted the woman, which could have meant anything, offering an unexpectedly rough hand to shake. 'Rosemary Whittingham-Webster.'

'Or Hyphen for short,' said Victor, openly grinning now. 'She's a toff of the deepest dye, Zander, a genuine lairdess, holder of the land in the face of popular resentment, exploiter of the masses, that sort of thing.'

Rosie walked over to him and grabbed a lump of the greying hair, pulled hard. Victor didn't flinch. 'Fuck you, you millionaire gossip trader.' Then she turned to me and frowned. 'Apologies. Actually, I'm here partly to give up being a lairdess, as Victor puts it. I am dispensing with land and largesse which was forced upon me by . . . circumstances. I may even become a gypsy. Your brother claims he was one, once.'

'He's good at lying,' I said, 'though I believe he has travelled occasionally; as far as Milton Keynes. Time to grind some beans, Victor. I think this reconciliation demands liquid. And for your obviously not entirely complete information, I am on the wagon. See?' I held up my right hand. I was getting good at this. I was even fairly sure I could keep my hand from shaking about this time. 'Steady as a rock.'

Victor and I both held up our left hands at the same time, and in unison said: 'Yeah, but I shoot with this hand.' Suddenly we were back five hundred miles to the north, kids watching the video of *Blazing Saddles* for the eleventh time, before he'd shot me and gone away and stupid adulthood had intervened between us.

'I'll make the coffee,' said Rosie. 'You two clearly have a lot to talk about.'

But we didn't. I was pretty sure I knew everything I needed to know about Victor, except the exact nature of his relationship with Rosie. Apart from that I needed, *wanted* his help. While I was waiting, wondering if I could bear to ask him, I was happy to share memories of Mel Brooks movies, to gloss over with nostalgia the moments of division back in our Shetland youth, to ask, emptily, how Mum and Dad were. Because after all the crap, he had been the one to get back in touch with them and gradually effect some kind of relationship there, with his eternally dependable sobriety, his fucking e-mail and video-phones, his technological bent. Methods of distancing while maintaining an informed, supposed closeness. And they were fine, and he'd know that I wasn't okay, not at all. But he hadn't done anything, or moved to get in touch. Instead he'd listened and watched, as he did. It was, after all, his life.

What had happened was this: Victor had enlisted in the Paras, done well, played the psychopathic hoodlum card with skill and objectivity. Native cunning came out, was spotted, educated, honed. Spent his allotted time in the SAS, done stuff here, there and you didn't ask where.

He was an NCO, but fell in with the new generation of technocrat hooligan officers straight out of university, and, in and out of uniform, advised shithead oil-company-funded dictators, protected government-bankrolled wheeler-dealers in chunks of the old Soviet Union, got into electronics in a big way, surveillance, remote taps, information hacking, all that computer shite. Then he'd taken his lump sum, the legal bit, and added a much bigger piece of cash action from God knew where, little freelance jobs he wouldn't talk about, not that he talked about any of it much. Bought a lump of commercial forestry land in and around Glendruin, built his Norwegian kit house with assorted knobs on, installed satellite and digital phone lines, ran with the technology as it changed, updated as soon as the latest whizz-bang gadget was on the market, or before. And became a one-man consultancy service for people you didn't really want to know about, who wanted to know the things nobody wanted to talk about. He had, he claimed, renounced violence, but there was something almost like rape in his approach to other people's information. Straightforward hacks into restricted databases were his stock-in-trade, but he also had the hard- and software to get stuff which was publicly available but difficult to find. Let's say you needed to know all about a couple called Thiebault, a fishing boat called the *Chuleta de Cordero*, a man called Roger Thiebault. Not the paltry stuff I'd been able to access in the Sneck library, but dirt on a major-league scale, half-whispered pieces of gossip somebody had once e-mailed to somebody else. Victor was your man. And my brother. Handy. If I could bring myself to ask him.

'So will you do it?' We were sipping the second macchiato Rosie had brought us, double espresso with just the merest blob of foamed milk on the top. The coffee was Thomson's Seattle Blend, and I could feel the hit, the sugar and caffeine surge in my veins. A Gold Label Mezcal on the side would have made it perfect. Victor peered through half-shut eyelids at me, a trick I remembered from my first consciousness of him, or at least my first consciousness of him after he'd seen *A Fistful of Dollars*. Always an Eastwood man, Victor.

'You're getting screwed here, Zander. I'd picked up a sort of story from the police in Inverness that you were under possible threat from some two-bit hoodlum who'd just got out of jail, some moronic religious nut or something, but none of the signals . . . none of the stuff I came across seemed to evince much concern, I have to say. And as you know, I don't intervene . . .'

'Yeah, you only watch and listen and report. I know.'

Once or twice I'd tried to tap into my brother's range of expertise for the sake of some story or other, after his resurfacing into the family consciousness as some sort of ex-army nutter with long hair; always the stumbling block had been what lay unspoken between the two of us. The fact that we were, perchance, related.

'Look,' I said, 'I'll be honest. I'm in a hole of my own fucking digging, scrabbling about and possibly making it deeper all the time. I mean, if I'd still been on the sauce, then maybe this would all have made perfect sense. But to come out of hospital, getting progressively straighter only to run slap bang into people who want to give me cash money to disinter an old story, plus another old story who wants to kill me . . . why now? Why should all this happen right at this particular juncture in my sorry and unsuccessful life? I mean, it's not as if my career as the Highlands' private dick had been underscored with major success. We are not talking *Two Jakes* here.'

'We are not talking even *Dead Men Don't Wear Plaid*,' said Victor. 'We are not even in the generally decadent and diseased realm of Altman's remake of *The Long Goodbye* –'

And just then my mobile rang. I had been sure there was no digital cellular signal until Kyle of Morinachal or Loch Salvation at a pinch. I'd simply forgotten to switch the infernal thing off. Or indeed how to.

'Got a relay reflector out at Haggernish,' said Victor. 'Ran a landline to the house, put in a central aerial. You're probably getting cancer from it right now.'

'Probably,' I grunted, digging the handset from a pocket and shoving it against my ear. 'Zander Flaws.'

'Flawed by name and flawed by nature,' came a well-kent voice. 'Surprised this thing still works. Celia said you were headed for points west.' The voice was reassuring, recognisable and just slightly slurred.

'Yeah, well, Hernia, true enough. Just had a family call to make first, but west is the right general direction.'

'No problems, then?'

'Well, you could say that. Just a Toyota Landcruiser which tried to run me off the road into the lair of the Nessiething, plus two clients who seem to have disappeared and who want me to revive the hunt for a lesser-spotted great disappearing student. Missing American werewolf in Aberdeen. But maybe as you say, it all points west.'

'Really.' Hernia sounded that hyper way you get with not enough drink. 'I was wondering more about your own sweet self, Zander, and let's face it, liquid intake.'

The words made my throat dry, conjured up images I couldn't control. I wondered how many Librium were left. I hadn't taken one for ages, but suddenly I needed something.

'Well I, uh . . .' I swallowed hard. 'Just hitting some serious espresso, Dr Holdsworth . . .'

'Macchiato, you cretin,' murmured Victor. Rosie was leafing through a copy of *Handgun World*, which I thought a trifle odd, but perhaps she was simply a congenital leafer. Many aristocrats are. She was drinking water like it was the most erotic action in the universe. Or maybe that was my perception, and my problem. I did have a problem, I admitted to myself, with Rosie the remote goddess-lairdette. Or maybe not. My brother, after all, was her keeper; or vice versa. It was hard to tell.

'Fine, Hernia, fine. Haven't touched a drop since hospital.'

'Really? That's great, Zander. Really great. Christ, I wish I was the same, but actually I've just nipped out from the Albatross to ring you. A bit pissed myself, that way, you know, just the start of the evening, a couple of beers, mapping out the time. Celia's here, and Sludge obviously, and the Settler.'

What was this about? There was something odd about having your saviour from alcohol phone you a wee bit pished. 'I thought you were taking it easy,' I told him.

'Ah, you've only got a problem if you think you have, Zander.' Jesus, he was rambling. 'Only if you think you have, that's the ticket. Me, I've got . . . problems. This McVeigh thing . . . it's all out of hand. That stuff she took . . . Tune, they're calling it. Helps you breathe more fucking easily . . . I don't think . . .' he laughed mirthlessly. Drunk as a skunk. 'The drugs don't work, Zander.' He began singing, a one-man Verve. 'How is your brother, anyway? How is Mr fucking Whizz?'

What the fuck was he on about? My brother. I looked at Victor. An echoing, fizzy silence filled the airwaves in my ear. Mr *Whizz*? 'He's fine, Hernia. Listen, I better go. Save my batteries, and yours. Have a good time, now.'

'Yes, I will, listen, Zander . . .' There was a suddenly clear sound picture of Hernia's surroundings. I could hear street noises, the whoosh of night-time cars, the hot shouts of summer Sneck, all tourist bare-bum jollity and local slurping. It hit me like a train: Christ, I wished I was there, getting guttered with the rest of them, comfortable in that communion with wasters and meaningless time, waiting for a tired, half-cut fuck and maybe the same again the next day . . .

'Yes, darling Cecil?'

'Don't worry. It'll all work out fine. Give my compliments to the chef . . . I mean, give my regards to . . . to Victor. Tell him . . .'

'I will.' But I didn't. I pressed the 'no' button and laid the handset down.

'Hernia? That's an interesting term of endearment.' Victor's face was completely unreadable.

'Nobody,' I said, 'just an old drouth trying to make me jealous.' I was trying to remember if I'd ever mentioned Victor to Hernia. Probably I had, his existence at least. Maybe even a hint of what he did for a dubious living. Wee brother boasting. But the fact that I was on my way to see him? I didn't think so. The decision had been taken within the parameters of sobriety, after I'd left Celia. One quick call to the unlisted number I had for Victor, doubtless one of several he possessed, and all I'd done was leave a message on the inevitable voicemail, saying that I noted he was in, or at least said he was, and maybe I'd see him later. I shook the nagging worry down into a corner of my mind, where the lump of wormy concern lay and wriggled nastily, not quite ignorable. I'd certainly never told Victor about Hernia. But, then again, could I be sure? Mr Whizz?

'Mr Whizz,' I said, neutrally.

'That's an old one,' said Victor. 'Remember you used to call me that, way back. Before . . . It was quite . . . cute.'

'I don't remember,' I said. 'Did you know there's a disco in Inverness called Mr Whizz?'

'Really?' Victor's face was still utterly blank. 'Some coincidence, eh?' We held each other's gaze for a second. Remembering, or just wondering. 'Anyway, to business: I'll have a crack at it, your little . . . conundrum. Give me a couple of hours. You're staying?'

I nodded.

'Okay. I'll need what you've got – the boat, the boy, this pair of Americans.'

'No problem. I've got a file in Rief . . . the Merc.'

'And in the meantime Rosie can take you to see her family seat. That's the reason she's here, after all. To sell up her lady lairdness and magically transform herself into a member of the hoi polloi.'

'Actually, that's a wrong usage,' I said. '*Hoi polloi* was the French revolutionary term for the useless artistocracy.'

'Then it's not wrong usage at all,' came Rosie's melodic tones from the midst of *Handgun World*. 'Is it?'

'And by the way,' said my brother, aiming a metaphorical .22 at my metaphorical hand and letting fly. 'She and I are friends and colleagues, nothing more.'

'Which means that you can try and shag me with a clear conscience,' said Rosie, fixing me with eyes which were shameless, innocently beyond guilt and an oddly opaque shade of china blue. 'Not that you should assume I'll let you.'

I was nonplussed. Fucking aristos.

★ Twelve

The caffeine had set my heart to a Keith Moon gallop as Rosie climbed into Riefenstahl, having taken a critical and disapproving eyeful of the rear-end damage – which, frankly, I thought wasn't too bad, considering the mechanical mayhem a Toyota Landcruiser driven by a homicidal maniac with a full-blown Presbyterian complex of Calvinist predestination-mania could have caused.

'What happened to it?'

'Oh, nothing much,' I replied, airily. 'Tailgated by a tourist in a hurry. I . . . lost him.'

'Hmmm . . . I suppose I'm safe enough with you.' It wasn't a question. She seemed to have reached some sort of decision; assessed my suitability for the post of chauffeur, with other duties possibly thrown in. Maybe I imagined it. Fantasised it. Relaxing, she turned to me and fired one of those devastating power smiles the ruling classes use to charm servants into licking their verrucas. 'Out of the gate and left down the hill. It's only a mile or so to the drive.' She pulled a small electronic handset from the battered Barbour she was wearing. 'Victor has given me the keys to his kingdom.'

I clunked the Merc into D1, and we crunched off, up towards the looming entrance of the tree-tunnel.

'So how do you know Victor, then?' Always the subtle questioner, me. *Are you sleeping with him? And even so, any chance of a quick fraternal-competition fuck?* Shut yo' mouth, you stupid bastard. All that stuff inside the house had been a sly joke, I was sure. But what was the punchline?

'Oh, he's done a little work for my firm, you know. Remotely. I've been his sort of company minder for a couple of years now. Never met, though. E-mails, telephone calls . . . always got on well. Bit of banter. Loved his accent, of course. Obviously I knew his, ah, locality, and when I found out I was going to have to come up and settle my uncles' estate, I thought I'd tap him for a bed.'

'So you've never been up here before?'

'Oh yes. When I was a kid, Ma and Pa used to bring us up every summer, a month in one of the cottages next to the big hoose, doncherkneeeow?' She smiled at me. 'You really don't like me, do you?'

I was ready to bet that was a ploy she used on all men with downmarket or interestingly regional accents: *Despisemefearmefuckme*. Before I could reply, she raised the black beeper and pointed it at the gates, revealed by my headlights and looking like the entrance to some kind of treeless Valhalla. Out there, beyond the fake forest, a sky of an almost impossibly deep azure soared into eternity, with the solid broken-tooth shadows of the Cuillins to the west.

'Into the unknown, then,' she said. There was a whirring clunk, audible above the engine, and the massive steel gate swung inwards. Driving out of the pines was like being launched into space.

The road fell steeply away towards the valley floor and the sea, but after about a mile of twists and turns west, a plateau had been formed by the retreating glaciation. The entrance we were looking for had been designed to be noticed. The gates this time were gigantic, piss-off-proles stately home efforts, rusting now but obviously well maintained until maybe around a winter ago. But it was the gatehouse which caught the eye and then rammed itself down your gaping throat. In daylight it must have been even more astounding. But the headlights' glare made it dramatic enough.

It was Little Red Riding Hood's granny's cottage, or the woodcutter's home from *Hansel and Gretel*, only transformed into a stern granite model, as if the White Witch had waved her wand and frozen it in punishment for frivolity. The half-timbered beams of the front were rendered in brutally carved stone, while the rounded, fake-thatch roof, what I could see of it, had been done in complex roundels of slate. Tiny windows attempted a kind of Alpine cosiness, but had ended up black and sightless, at least in the car's white tungsten assault. It squinted, that cottage, mean and dangerous and somehow disturbing.

'Never liked the gatehouse,' said Rosie, shivering theatrically, but not entirely without genuine dislike, I thought. 'Despite the accent, we weren't wealthy, you see. Dad and Mum were both teachers, and it was the nuncs who put me through Roedean, paid for everything, set up a trust fund, the lot. They had a truly horrid estate manager, retainer person who stayed in the gatehouse, kept everyone out, fetched and carried for them. You see, the main house isn't that grand, really . . . it's . . . oh, you'll see in a minute anyway.' She jumped out of the car, this time taking out a gigantic and decidedly non-electronic key. 'No beepers for this kingdom,' she laughed, grimly. I doubted she would be able to open the gates, but with surprisingly little hassle, she pushed them back, one after the other. I nosed the car inside.

There must have been a control panel for the lights at the gate, because as we rounded a bend in the rhododendroned drive, the glow was like some *Lord of the Rings* fairy gathering taking place just beyond your vision. Then we were there, and outlined in the yellow-and-violet aura of not-yet-warmed-up floodlights, was the house. If you could call it a house.

'Welcome to Bartholomew Lodge,' said Rosie, getting out of the Merc and standing at the door like Minnie Mouse in front of the Magic Castle. I just stared. It was not, as she'd said, that big a place. Compared to the real thing, it was tiny. What I was looking at was a miniature Edinburgh Castle. Obviously without the later additions of Auld Reekie's monster pile, the visitor centres and galleries, but complete with a section of fake Edinburgh Castle rock, for God's sake, on which had been built an esplanade, probably for use as a kind of dancefloor-cum-patio. It had battlements, a soaring tower at one end, and was as camp as a tentpeg. Bells began ringing in my head.

'This is . . . your uncles are . . . were the Bartholomew brothers?'
She nodded.

'Christ, yes, this place is famous, or infamous. I remember reading a big *Express* exposé on some of the parties that were held here in the '70s. Victor never told me it was near him. Or maybe he did . . . it never clicked, anyway.'

'Well,' she took out her keys and began fiddling with the front door, which was suitably studded and massively baronial, 'I rather gather Victor and yourself have not been tremendously good communicators over the past ten years or so, have you?' The door opened with barely a creak. 'At least, not to each other.'

'What is it your firm actually does, Rosie?'

Unseen but echoing, she was flicking lights on. The hall was a bizarre cross between Brideshead and a twentieth-century sculpture park retrospective. The great stone-flagged space was full of Henry Moore-ish sculptures, all lumpily massive enough to be genuine; but what did I know? Big and bent, anyway.

'Oh . . . this and that,' she said. 'Oil industry this and that, mostly in what people used to call the Third World. Actually, Victor did some pretty useful physical stuff for us in the old days.'

I looked at her. What age was she? Suddenly I could see tiny lines and wrinkles I hadn't noticed before. Maybe she was in her late thirties, or older. She moved like a ballerina. Or a thin kickboxer.

'Victor and I, and an old woman from down the glen who used to clean here, we've managed to sort through most of it. Just a question of waiting for the chap from Christie's, and he's due tomorrow. Be here for three days, I reckon. The last insurance valuation was ten years ago, and the nuncs did a great deal of purchasing before they died. Trying to stave off the inevitable fading of the great and glorious light.'

A news clipping popped up in the mangled circuitry of my brain. 'They died . . . close to each other, didn't they? In time that is.'

Rosie was gazing critically up at a piece of polished granite which resembled a cross between a rhinoceros and a tank trap. Possibly it was an intentional similarity. 'Yes they did. Nuncie Ranald fell and broke his hip horribly at the bottom of these very stairs' – she pointed at a sweeping Hollywood stairway to castellated heaven – 'and at eighty-two, unless you're the Queen Mother, that's a baddie. They flew him by helicopter to Raigmore, but there was a haemorrhage they just couldn't stop. Nuncie Jonathan was here, with his . . . companion, Vasco, when the news came through. They must have arranged it all in advance.'

'Shotgun, wasn't it?'

'Yep. No mess. Plastic sheeting, towels around the heads. Up in the tower, a winter sunset, they estimated, gazing out over the Cuillins. Vasco blew Nunc's head off, then his own. Nuncie Jonnie was younger, you know.' She clenched her fists and pushed against the statue's surface as if she could move it with her arms alone. It would have taken a JCB at full stretch to do that. I wondered how the hell they'd got it in in the first place. 'He was fit and well. Just seventy-nine. I mean, clearly he made Vasco do it. He was younger, about fifty-odd, still trying to be beautiful for the old tart.' She relaxed suddenly, and let out a long breath, then reached into the capacious pockets of the old Barbour. The packet of Dunhill glinted glamorously red. The click of a small brass Zippo, the ignition of petrol, the rank whiff of burning tobacco . . . combined, they made me long for the comfort of a fag, but I hadn't come this far to get hooked on some foul and expensive carcinogen. It always struck me as weird, alcoholics turning to tobacco in a completely obsessive way. Same problem. The big thirst. Only instead of destroying themselves and the rest of the world, or what they could reach of it while pissed, it was just goodnight Vienna to their own health and strength.

'Want one?'

'No thanks.' Too quick. Too anxious. A drink would be nice. Course it would. I was ready to bet there was a very discriminating selection of malt whiskies somewhere in this house. 'So . . .' Businesslike. 'What do we have to do?'

'Well, we've checked out the pictures against the last inventory, and Victor and I stacked the ones we couldn't find listed in Nuncie Jonnie's boudoir. I'd like to shift them out. I don't necessarily want the Christie's chap seeing all their secrets.'

'But you don't mind me? I'm an ex-journalist, you know, trained to be curious. And now a . . . well . . . a kind of private . . . detective, for want of a better word.'

A brief, enigmatic grin flitted over her face. 'Yes, I know. Victor told me.' Stopping on the stairs, she whirled to gaze down at me, cigarette smoke swirling in the concealed lighting, her face shadowed like a film noir anti-heroine. 'So maybe I can be one of your clients. Maybe I could make it worth your while. My very own private dick.' And with a great peal of mildly bronchial laughter, she skipped up the steps, leaving me wondering what the hell was going on. As usual.

The boudoir was actually a dressing-room, a kind of large corridor between an ornate, Taj Mahal of a bathroom and a bedroom which had clearly been on the grandest and campest scale – the round, enormous bed, stripped of its covers, was located under a mirrored ceiling and seemed to be made of carved ebony. The room was fitted with wardrobes and chests of drawers calculated to give the term 'built-in' a whole new level of grandeur. The bow-fronted mahogany was a couple of rainforests away from Ikea. Piled against one wardrobe were paintings, dozens of them, framed in a mixture of traditional gilt and contemporary aluminium, and all sizes from human-height downwards.

'Okay,' said Rosie. 'Grab an armful and follow me.' She picked up a pile of the smaller ones. I followed suit. We put them in the hall outside, a strange mixture of styles. There was what looked very like a late Picasso print, a couple of smallish Howsons, a Wiszniewski, a Hockney, and others I didn't recognise. One or two older things, a lovely pastel signed James Kay, and a huge Hornel. It went on and on, until my arms ached with art. At last we had finished, and as I stood puffing in the dressing-room, Rosie puffed on a Dunhill.

'Shouldn't you watch where you're dropping your ash?' I coughed. 'This place could go up like the Reichstag.'

'Maybe the best thing. All this stuff – and there's loads more, furniture, those bloody statues . . . it'll just draw the gawkers and the voyeurs.' She tapped the battered Barbour. 'Got a pocket within a pocket just for secret ash, you know. We aristos get all the best gear.' She half-turned to the wardrobe the paintings had been piled against, ran her free hand over the dusty wood. It shone where her fingers had been. 'Know where those pictures were? Know where me and Vic found them? Under Nuncie Jonnie's bed. Stored away for gloating over, the old prick. Except I doubt he even did that.'

'What about Nuncie . . . I mean your Uncle Ranald?'

'Oh, he was always a true romantic. His bed had a box under it, and in it was a watch, a gold Cartier Tank watch, from 1938. Unworn, it looked to me.' She held up her wrist. I'd noticed that dully expensive glow earlier. 'It is now. You know that Rannie was celibate, all his life? Supposed to be, anyway. Made a thing of it. I wonder what the story of this watch is? He was in Paris in 1938, you know. And most of 1939.'

'Yes . . . yes, come to think of it, I know the story. *Boy's Own* stuff. Some sort of SIS hero, imprisoned by the Gestapo, managed to break out . . .'

'Bought his way out, he told me once, when I was a little girl. Gave me some cash, twenty quid, a fortune at the time, at least to me, and said to me, "Money will do what love and guns can't, dearie." Then he told me. But nothing about the watch, whose it was.'

'It's a woman's model.'

She gazed at it as if seeing it for the first time, mysteriously attached to her wrist. 'Yes. But who knows if it was a woman's watch? Maybe just a boy with a slim wrist. Nuncie Ranald wasn't screamingly effeminate like Jonnie. But who's to say? He kept his secrets . . . just like . . . anyway. Look at this.' She opened the wardrobe doors, and a light came on inside what was revealed as yet another room, but one which gushed with strident femininity. It was a cave of dresses, in lilacs and china blues, in pinks and emeralds, in chiffons and silks and satins and lace. Suddenly the silence of the house overwhelmed me, broken only by our breathing, the rustle of cloth.

Rosie stubbed her fag out in the depths of her jacket pocket, and I wondered if waxed cotton wasn't in itself a fire risk. Otherwise people would make portable ashtrays out of it, wouldn't they?

'Come on, Zander,' she said. 'Let's go to Narnia.' And she ducked into the tunnel of dresses, the perverse adornments of an old, rich, dead man. What could I do? I followed.

Inside, everything smelled of mothballs, but none crunched under our feet, or became snow the further in we ventured. A good ten feet past the rows of clothing hanging on either side, we emerged as if into a forest glade, an oval, mirrored changing-room with a bench running around it, and a carpet so thick and fine it could only have been silk.

'Shut your eyes,' she said.

I sat down on the bench, and played the game, hearing my heart bang away, sending shockwaves up into my throat, knowing what this was about, at least on the hormonal level, but wondering why, why me, why now, why not Victor? Looking for meaning. I could hear the sound of clothes moving, being taken off their hangers, of aged waxed cotton being shed, shoes kicked off clunkingly. Then her bitter, smoky lips were on mine, and Dunhill spittle was in my mouth, an ash-anointed tongue momentarily probing my fillings.

'Open your eyes, Zander,' she murmured, the same tongue flicking into my ear. I kept still. There's nothing worse for the confidence of an ear-licker than missing. I could already feel the spittle drying on my lobe. 'I'll be your client if you show me exactly how private your dick is.' Then that great gust of smoky laughter.

She was almost wearing a short green dress, which is like saying that George Best could almost play football. Bad comparison. It was a creation in silk and tulle, transparent to below her none-too-small breasts, which was probably what made the overwhelming green of the outfit so short, and the whole so tight. That guffaw again.

'Nuncie was smaller than me, and thinner, believe it or not. Well, certainly in some places.' She ran a hand over her left breast, pinching the nipple and breathing in sharply as she did so. 'Why don't you try one on, too, Zander?' She reached between my legs, where my jeans were having some trouble containing an erection capable of hammering in fence posts, and then took my left hand, guided it gently to her knee, and slowly drew it upwards. She was wearing nothing under the tiny dress, and her inner thigh felt cool, smooth and slightly trembling to my touch. She smelt of Anais Anais and fresh moss. As my fingers, by this time of their own accord, at least I think so, stroked the warmth and wetness beyond, I suddenly thought of Theakston's Old Peculiar on draught. As one does. I'm sure Rosie would have been delighted, had she been a mindreader. A glass of that deep, wine-red, almost flat brew, delicate and hoppy, but tasting of ages past, of mystery and magic. And capable of putting you onto your back within three pints, if you weren't prepared. An erotic image? I don't think so.

'Cheers,' I found myself saying distractedly, one hand halfway up a strange woman's fanny, my dick now being strangled by a bare female thigh. It was at this point that I realised for the first time what alcoholism means. Even in the throes of fantasy foreplay, you still crave a drink.

The foreplay did not last long, and I'm afraid the sex didn't either. Someone of stern moral fibre would probably have resisted altogether, because ticking away at the back of my mind was the growing certainty that this was all part of a game being played by people other than myself. I was the little metal motorbike on the Monopoly board, and for the moment I was being ridden into the ground, or at any rate the carpet.

Don't get me wrong, it was fine. Let's face it, for men, sex is always good, even when it's with a sock and a dodgy petrol station video. But sometimes it's fantastic, fuelled by either rampant mutual lust or that weird rarity, love, and, very occasionally, both. I wondered what motivated Celia and me, and the answer came thumping in just as my head cannoned off the bench behind me, my body being pummelled by the highly energetic Rosie: loneliness.

Rosie was athletic, and, once, so to speak, docked securely, entirely selfish, or rather self-absorbed. It was one of those couplings where, once in, you feel, well, a bit left out, and you become conscious of all the stupidities of sex. How heavy women are, for one thing. For years, right through my untouched and untouching adolescence, I thought women weighed mere ounces compared to men. I mean, you saw them, all kind of feminine and, if fanciable, thin, and you were sure you could pick them up with one hand. Then one night, in a jammed car coming back from the pub, I had a fanciable girl from a local fish factory sit on my lap. Astonishingly, the Apollo Launcher of all hard-ons did not, as I'd expected, lift her bodily through the roof of the car. Her entirely moderate weight, however, made me feel as though my bowels were being ironed.

And then I was back with Rosie, to put it brutally, relieving herself on me, and belatedly I realised that we weren't using a condom; for some reason I couldn't dismiss that absence as I usually did. Somewhere in this fuck there was fear. I tried to block it out as I came, but it was too late. Allow fear, and then guilt and regret will come juddering in immediately afterwards. The usual cocktail of remorse.

Cold and stupid, too. Lying there all spent, dribbly and damp, sober. Shit. Seeing it all, being seen too, watched coolly by Rosie as she leaned back against the bowed wall, the tight dress, pulled roughly back in place, a Dunhill already lit. No hatred, though, that nasty little demon which sometimes popped into the post-coital mind. Just a kind of watchful, worried indifference on my part. So that when Rosie suddenly said, 'Fancy a drink? There's a stock of whisky in this house that would keep the Ritz going for a decade,' I just shook my head. That Theakston's would do me. 'Oh, sorry. I forgot, you're TT, aren't you?' A smile which could have meant anything, from 'just testing your resolve' to 'poor sod', to 'let's do the mindfuck again, baby'.

'Don't you think we'd . . . better get back?' I sounded hoarse. All that second-hand fag smoke.

She just grinned and exhaled, copiously.

I did all that embarrassing stuff, the pulling on of knickers, the buttoning of jeans, the waiting for stains to appear. Yuk. When I reached for her, she was cold; icy. She looked at me with those weird blue eyes.

'You should go home, Zander.' Her voice was vibrating, and I could feel a minute, fine-tuned trembling in her body. 'Wherever the hell home is you must go. You're not part of . . . just get out. Don't say anything to Victor.'

What about? Our fuck? Or her warning me about going home, wherever that was? She looked for the Barbour jacket to stub out her fag, couldn't find it, and instead disentangled herself from me, and nipped the glowing end between two fingers. I noticed, belatedly, that her hands were workwomanlike: no nail varnish, strong and mildly battered. No rings. They hadn't felt like that on the various bits of my body she'd been poking, fondling, squeezing and rubbing. Modestly, I pushed my way out through the brushwood shrubbery of cloth, and waited for her to get dressed. When she came out, she was wearing the old Barbour, and I suspected the green dress was in one of those poacher's pockets.

'What do you mean?' We were walking down the huge staircase, and I said the words quietly as I reached one arm companionably around her waist. She shrugged me off, but not before I had felt the hard metallic lump in her jacket's right-hand recesses. Something small, heavy and solid. No ashtray, and not the controller for the Glendruin gates. Just displeased still to see me, or a gun in her pocket? She said nothing.

We locked up, switched off the lights, drove down the drive as the glow of the illuminated façade behind us faded. Rosie cut it off finally back at the gate, and we drove back to Glendruin in absolute silence. Except for her asking if she could smoke in the car. What could I say? She was my client, after all. She'd paid, or so she had stated, with her body.

I said no. I mean, what the hell was she going to do, anyway? Shoot me?

★ Thirteen

Victor had been cooking. Or somebody had. Savoury smells wafted out of the kitchen as we entered the house, and we were ordered to take a seat at the blockwood table in a candle-lit alcove.

'I see all this isolation has turned you into a cordon-bleu chef,' I observed, perhaps a tad acidly, as a defrosted, microwaved lasagne made out of something chewily mince-like was placed before me. Close to, the aroma became more industrial, like a slaughterhouse mixed with a tannery.

'Yes, well,' Victor shrugged, 'what's the point of technology if you can't use it to save time? Come on, it'll get cold. And speaking of time, what took you two so long? I thought you were only going to move some of those pictures?'

'Broke the glass in one of the frames,' said Rosie. 'Had to find a brush, sweep it up, that kind of thing.'

'That kind of thing, eh?' grinned Victor.

'Yes,' I said. 'That kind of thing.' For a man with underwear which was rapidly growing crusty, I thought I sounded placid and unconcerned. As if Victor didn't know, the would-be magus that he was.

'Finding a brush,' my brother mused. 'Such potent erotic imagery.'

I almost decked him. Or thought about trying to. Nearly.

The wine was a rather good Australian Shiraz. I was sure I'd had a bottle or two one evening. I'd had something similar, at any rate. Something red. I had to stop Victor pouring me a glass. It was surprisingly easy to keep my hand in place, even when he let some of the wine spill over it. I wondered if you could absorb alcohol through the skin. I breathed in, hoping for some kind of inhalatory high.

'No thanks. My liver is under repair. I thought I'd mentioned it.'

Victor did a neat imitation of shock and surprise. He knew all right. What was this fucking game about? 'Sorry. Want some Aqua Libra?'

'I'd rather shit razorblades.' Which may or may not, depending on one's definition of political correctness, have been rather indelicate considering the presence of Rosie, but what the hell. What was the point of all those years of feminism if you ended up not being able to swear in front of women? 'Water's fine.'

After an extraordinary sweet of Fruit Corner yoghurt, which Rosie gobbled up like a Girl Guide at camp, she suddenly got up from the table and announced that she was off to bed. 'I'm sure you two boys have lots to talk about,' she yawned, and kissed us both with a matter-of-fact mumsiness which left me wondering if the weird fuck down the road in Castle Camp had ever happened. But I could still feel the carpet burns. Good-quality carpet burns, courtesy of the silk pile, but burns nevertheless. Now that was fucking feminism: women on top and a whole new experience of back pain for men.

'Coffee?'

I was drooping, so to speak, with tiredness, but more caffeine would leave me heart-palpitatingly wakeful later, so I declined.

'Wimp.' Victor fetched himself an espresso, and when he came back he was carrying a single sheet of paper. 'Made a few notes. Better not to download anything. Anyway, most of it was on the phone, in the end. Technology will only take you so far.' He sipped his coffee. 'Now. Where did you say this fishing boat, the what was it? *Chuleta de Cordero* – that's lamb chop, isn't it? – was going from Aberdeen?'

'Loch Salvation.'

'Yeah, you told me that. But it could have gone lots of other places first. I mean, it went through the canal, and it could have stopped anywhere along the way, you realise. You could have the whole of the Glen of Perdition to deal with, peerie bridder.'

I knew that. It was one of the reasons I'd driven part of the way along the glen before branching off north-west. Just to get a feel for what might have been going on. But, then, I wasn't big on feels, these days, as my sexual encounter with Rosie had shown. My nerve ends were numb.

'Suppose they killed him, for whatever reason. I suppose you're thinking, Spain, Galicia especially, some sort of drug thing? Maybe he saw too much, was hit on the head, spirited away?'

I nodded. 'Or something.'

He took a sip of espresso, grimaced. 'Did you fuck her, then?'

I looked into his eyes. It was impossible to read anything there. That part of his face was a dark mirror of mine.

'Don't be ridiculous.'

He grinned. 'Seen Mum and Dad?' I hadn't, of course. Not for more than two years now. There had been telephone calls, but when they had been on the mainland, I had made sure I was out of town, or uncontactable. And I never went home, couldn't handle the familiarity I knew would envelop me. Despite everything. The way Shetland simply took back those who had been exiled, no matter how long away they'd been. And no matter what they'd done. Almost. I'd heard of one seaman who'd returned after thirty years, walked off the P&O ferry *St Clair* and bumped into an old schoolfriend on the Victoria Pier in Lerwick. 'Aye, Sandy,' the friend had said. 'Has du been awa' sooth?'

I needed the tattered remnants of a life I'd built up unaided; needed, wanted to hoard that little pile of rubbish for myself. It was my rubbish, after all. I hadn't made my Shetland life. It had been created for me by circumstance, birth, geography, family. And I'd wanted my own stuff, my own existence. My own, as it had turned out, considerable mess. There was a great lump of experience left on the islands I would go back to some day, but not yet.

'No. Du has? I mean . . . och, have you?'

'Six months ago, I went up for a trip, for Up Helly Aa. Just for a spree, to see it again. Du kens, da . . . the galley, the crowds, that paraffin smell . . .'

'And?'

'Cold night, a good burning. The Jarl Squad had real raven's wings on their helmets. I didna ging ta a hall. Just watched the burning. Felt less than I towt I wid.'

'See anyone you kent?'

'Aye, Christ, aye. Just slid through them, maistly. But I saw Ruth. Remember? Ruth Burgess? She's affy blyth . . .'

For a moment all I could hear was my own breathing. That was a name from the past, from the drunken car rides across the island, the illicit tokes on badly rolled joints, the fumbled gropings outside halls throbbing with bad rock music. 'Cut the accent,' I said. 'It's making me get cramp in my lips. You saw Ruth? So what.'

'Just thought you'd be interested. First ever, wasn't she? No little twinge of nostalgia?'

After the first flash of memory, there wasn't, not really. 'Well?'

'What do you want to know? She's a Harrelson, now, married to a shareholder crewman on the *Berserker*, a Whalsayman. Three kids. She didn't ask for you. I could tell that she wanted to, but she didn't. I just met her after the procession. She was going to a hall, dressed up to the nines out of the Next catalogue. I didna ha . . . *have* much time. She seemed happy. Looked well. Put on a lot of weight.' He smiled, the same cruel smile I remembered from our youth, from the rabbit killing. Games. Fucking hook-operator games. My hand throbbed. 'You wouldn't fancy her now, Zander. She's not in Rosie's class.'

I put all I could into the punch, but he was faster than me, dodging his head to one side, grabbing my hand as his coffee went flying, slamming it down on the table, twisting it as he did so, painfully.

'You stupid fuck. I could kill you with one fucking finger.'

'What?' I was breathing heavily. You do when your arm is being torn off. 'A guest in your own house? Where's your sense of hospitality?'

He released me, but he wasn't finished. 'The thing with Ruth . . . I know about that. I know about the abortion. I know how you feel you fucked it up, want to just get rid of all that Shetland shit. But it's over. She's happy, she was over it long before you were. And then there's Lucy, and all the crap around that little situation. I mean . . . I know this sounds like bullshit, but none of it represents the end of the world, Zander. You should let it go. All the guilt and shit. Go back and see Mum and Dad. It's over. Gone.'

'But not forgotten.'

'Maybe not, but you know how things work.'

I did. In a small island certain events were accepted or buried, for the sake of mutual survival. Feuds were few and far between, although when they happened they could be bitter, not to say fatal. Like me and Victor. Although so far we were just talking twisted arm and holed palm. Sometimes I looked at the little scar left by the .22 shell and felt like it was a kind of miniature, one-armed crucifixion. But only when I was feeling really sorry for myself.

'Anyway, the *Chuleta* . . . the *Boat of the Chopped Lamb* probably dropped your man into Loch Ness, or put him ashore at Fort Mountbatten or Fort William. I've got a log-out by some vessel entered as the *Coleta de Corduroy* at the Fort William end of the canal, which sounds like your lump of mutton. Close enough for rock'n'roll, anyway. One thing seems certain, though. He didn't get off at Loch Salvation.'

'Really? How do you know?'

'Because according to the harbourmaster there, who happens to owe me one or two small favours and thus saw fit to check all his logs, there is no record of a vessel called anything remotely like *Chuleta de Cordero* ever docking there. Not ever. And he would have known, because he's extremely efficient. He has . . . tracks to cover, some of them his own. Okay, they could have anchored off at night, and then put someone ashore secretly. But what was the point of putting Loch Salvation on the manifest back at Aberdeen? They must have changed their minds, or never intended going there in the first place. Anyway, they watch out all along the west coast at these wee ports. Because of the drugs. A Spanish fishing boat? Dodgy in almost every respect. Suspicious at the very least.'

'So where did it go?'

'Ah, well.' Victor permitted himself a small smile of satisfaction, as he perused his piece of paper, which it was clear he did not require. 'This is where the mighty PC proves its digital worth. I happen to have full remote on-line access to the port control system at Ullapool, and I thought, seeing as I did, I'd give it a wee check, just to avoid telephoning all my friends and acquaintances on the west coast. I mean, *El Lamb*

Choppo could have gone south, too, you realise?'

'Well?'

'Anyway, he didn't. He went north all right, and, hey presto, two days after being logged out of the Caledonian Canal at Corpach, he asked for berthing facilities in Loch Broom, a spit off Ullapool, right in the middle of a mackerel-seeking klondiker mini-boom, which these days means three ships.'

'I suppose you know which ships, too?'

'You betcha. One Estonian, probably Russian-mafia-owned. One Nigerian, infested with rats and moored out in the loch under arrest, for health reasons. Everybody loves that in the tourist office, you can imagine. A floating consignment of vermin just off the pier. I don't know. All ships have rats, anyway. Just some of them wear uniforms.' That was rich, coming from someone whose career was based on the skills acquired and the loot purloined while wearing khaki, at least some of the time.

'But most relevant to your inquiry, little brother, is probably a klondiker called the *Margarita*, registered in Santiago de Compostela, Galicia, Spain.' He looked pleased with himself.

'Bingo,' I said because he seemed to expect some praise.

He leaned back, folding the paper as he did so. 'Well, not quite. I took the liberty of checking up on your clients, the – what was it? Thiebaults? Let's see, their travel arrangements – Christ, airlines and car hire computers are just wide open – open return to Boston via Glasgow, hire car still out and about, already extended once by telephone, no indication where from. Now two days overdue, no further word. I did a search for any credit card usage in those names, and after paying the bill at the Clutha – disgustingly expensive, by the way – I'm afraid I came up with nothing at all.'

I didn't query the ins and outs of gaining access to information like that. My own searching through old newspaper files on-line seemed suddenly ham-fisted and amateurish. I felt that old stirring of jealousy, of weakness in the face of brotherly superiority.

Victor shrugged. 'They seem to have vanished, and probably with a load of cash they're using to pay for everything. Or they could be staying with friends.'

'Or they could be dead,' I sighed. 'Perhaps I'm just being melo-dramatic. Thing is, they gave me traveller's cheques. Did you check that?' I felt the reassuring lump of notes that was left in my back pocket. Undamaged by my recent exertions, though there could be some bruising.

'Nope,' said Victor, 'but I'm glad you've got something for your efforts. It's always nice to get money from people who don't exist. It sort of removes any sense of responsibility.'

I could feel my jaw dropping open slightly. I shut it with a firm and audible click.

He consulted his sheet of paper casually. 'There is undoubtedly a Mr Gareth Thiebault in New Orleans, Tennessee, and he is married.'

'So?'

'So they're both in residence at New Orleans, home of Zydeco, the Neville Brothers and indeed Domino, Fats, right now, and have been for the last two years. He's a paraplegic, in constant nursing care since a car accident, and his wife is at home, watching TV and no doubt giving the nurse hell. Helped, it seems, by a considerable insurance settlement. Neither of them have ever been to Scotland, nor do they have any interest in doing so.' He crumpled up the paper and rolled it between his palms. 'I know all this because I spent twenty minutes talking to Mrs Thiebault not long ago. She was quite delightful. We chatted for a time, I asked after her family, and she ah, vouchsafed the sad fact that she and Mr Thiebault – pronounced, incidentally, *Thee Bolt*, according to her – had never been able to have children. Not ever. At all. So no Roger. And if I were you, I'd take your cash and head back to Sneck, tell the police everything, then go on holiday for a while. Maybe go home. See the folks.' He smiled, almost sincerely.

He opened a new bottle of Springbank twenty-five-year-old, one of my all-time favourite whiskies, and I took refuge in the dose of Antabuse I'd taken that morning, at last. I'd begun to feel under a sort of weird pressure to drink, not from myself, or my own desires – though God knows they were there – but from the situation I was in, the people around me. Antabuse makes you throw up, Hernia had said, if you take alcohol. It makes you sicker than you could believe. More than anything, it gave me some sort of psychological fall-back. That and a kind of weary, hollow acceptance of sobriety. According to Hernia, the worst moment was when you felt that one drink wouldn't do you any harm; when you considered yourself beyond temptation, toughened, normal. In a strange way, I could sense that looming.

We talked a little of casual, irrelevant, unimportant things, like politics, work, my first wife, other snippets about Ruth, all evoking those choking twinges of regret and recollection. Some wounds go too deep, maybe, or come too early. They become part of you, like scar tissue, leaving the slice-and-throb of the cleaver imprinted deep down, sore when remembered. Lucy, on the other hand, grew more and more separate, seemed more and more a part of someone else's past. And I talked about drink, in a torrent, a stream, a river of sodden words. What it had been like. What had happened. What it was like trying to stop.

'I'm sorry,' said Victor, sipping thoughtfully at his Campbeltown malt. 'You should have said outright, and I wouldn't have . . . I mean, put you in temptation's way. I feel bad about it.' Then he brightened. He was slightly flushed on that high-cheekboned, hard-bitten face. 'But, then, you at least had a taste of Rosie. Some sort of compensation.'

I couldn't stop myself. 'Have you . . .'

'Have I? Oh, sure, quite a lot at one time. We're kind of . . . business associates. No longer, emm, what's the word? Fuckees? She's an old pal, and she just didn't fancy staying on her own down in that godless perverted house. Who can blame her?' He grinned. 'I do some work for her people, sometimes, and we communicate. She came straight out, though, when she came up here last week. Kissed me and said she wouldn't fuck me.'

I didn't believe him. 'So what made her . . . take any interest in me? Assuming she did.'

He placed both hands behind his neck, leaned back and put both feet on his pristine pine table. Caterpillar boots, I noted. Steel toes. 'Curiosity? Hormones? Ask her. She's an independent woman.'

I did ask her, when she opened the door of my room much later, after Victor had gone to bed, and slipped, smelling of burnt Dunhill and Anais Anais, naked into my ample double bed. But all she did was take my right nipple between her teeth and bite, hard. It was not unpleasant.

Bobby had always loved the sight of the Moray Firth's bottle-nosed dolphins, leaping and, it seemed, dancing for the delight of human onlookers. He had entertained big, booming thoughts, especially when stoned, that these creatures were truly God's chosen inhabitants of earth, and that they were laughing at the binocular-festooned tourists crammed into their wobbling boats. He could remember the amazing, leathery, rubbery smoothness of the skin on a dolphin which had been stranded, alive, at the Hameferry slip last winter. Pulsing, breathing, but alien and unearthly, fishy, but in an animal sort of way. A fish-dog. Maybe dolphins were angels, he thought. And that triggered some strange memories from his childhood, Sunday-school stuff, pictures in washed-out colours of winged creatures with faces of sickening sweetness, golden curls and white, bunched and folded robes. How he'd longed to be one, to fly away from that cramped council house, his father's swings between beer-stinking, drunken cuddles and savage beatings, the slavering concern of Mrs Avery, his Sunday-school teacher, for his soul. Suddenly he could smell the mixture of mothballs and pungent, powdery perfume which had been her spoor, left on seats, on him when she slobberingly kissed him goodbye each Sunday afternoon. And a queer, piss-flavoured aroma, too. He shook his head, trying to shake off the old smell which had surrounded him, seemed to fill his body with a choking sense of the past. He thought of fairgrounds, and immediately the acrid taint of bad hamburger and burnt onion surrounded him. Oh, Christ, he thought, hopelessly. Oh, fuck.

They'd told him to expect some effects, asked him to try and remember as much as he could about them, and tell them. Remember? They had to be fucking joking. Remembering had become a movie for him; no – more than a film. A kind of virtual-reality life, in perfect detail, filled with sounds but oh, God, in particular smells. It worked both ways. An unexpected perfume or stink would send him tumbling back in time to an exact event from a past he had hardly imagined existed. Or he would think back and suddenly be overwhelmed with odours: the ashtray sourness of his dad's old Austin; wet wool on a rainy day in a primary classroom. Even breast milk, he'd thought, on one occasion. They'd loved that.

He'd told them it all and more, making up some bits, yeah, but truly, not much, and they'd seemed impressed, even excited. Then that stuff with Karen, and he'd just known it was time to light out, to run. They were serious people. He'd seen the look in that red-haired woman's eyes. Christ, if only he'd chosen a different doctor . . .

'Hey, Bobby?'

He turned. It was the guy, the English one with the Paul Newman eyes, the one who hung about with the woman. He smelled of wank, probably wiped himself on his underpants. It took him back to a disastrous school camp, simultaneous scrabbling and tugging under thin bedsheets. A laugh. He wasn't laughing now.

'Dolphins are jumping well tonight, Bobby, eh?'

He had been standing on Arrigus Point, where the Black Isle thrust itself out into the Moray Firth like, well, a dick, basically. Trying to shag Inverness. It was a secluded spot. He had been dossing in a deserted salmon-fishermen's bothy now overgrown with ivy and gorse. It smelled of golf courses, had wrenched him into teenage golfball thieving episodes, grimy sex with a fifteen-year-old classmate, Fiona, by a bunker at midnight. The sand had got everywhere.

It was still light enough to catch the leaping shapes of the dolphins, closer inshore than they ever came in daytime. The fluorescence bubbled green-white, while over on the other shore Inverness's lights glinted and glittered. Noises floated over – car horns, sirens, a dull thudding which might have been music. He felt the touch on his shoulder, becoming a hard, merciless grip, then a crushing blow at his neck which took him swirling into . . . nothing.

Out in the firth, the dolphins jumped, twisted, and crashed upside down into the calm water.

★ Fourteen

The intention, to tell the dishonest truth, had been to drop in on my brother, effect a reconciliation, embrace, swear eternal allegiance and fraternal support, pick his brains and his databases, then set off for Loch Salvation. There to at least faff around a bit in search of the *Chuleta* before heading home, armed with enough knowledge to bluff Mr and Mrs so-called Thiebault into thinking I'd given them value for money. Or, perhaps, having found something, because essentially I don't think of myself as a cynical bastard, provide them with comfort, a chance to grieve, even a body. Some fucking hope. If Roger, whoever he was, had been on that boat – and it seemed at least possible – and had proved surplus to requirements, Victor was right. He could have been dumped anywhere along the aptly named Glen of Perdition, in lochs deeper than the North Sea itself, and not be found in an eternity. Unless they'd been stupid enough to choose Loch Ness, which was infested with midget submarines, Japanese TV crews and BBC newsreaders who called themselves crypto-zoologists and were wired, secretly, to an undiscovered energy source on the Planet Tharg-Paxman.

But what the hell. It was a long drive to Glanachan, along a winding, snaking, sheep-infested, partially single-track route, either looping with the railway around Loch Salvation, the loch, but avoiding Loch Salvation, the fishing village inconveniently named after said loch, and the centre of rampant Free Kirk breast beating on many a desecrated sabbath. Not far from Victor's den of iniquity and inquiry, really. Then heading most of the way back east towards Inverness before striking out north-west again for Ullapool. The for-fuck's-sake alternative was the tourist route involving a wonderfully scenic set of double-backs along the sea lochs of the west coast: Loch Salvation-the-village, Kismul the abandoned oil platform site (a seriously creepy place, crying out to be a nuclear waste repository) then up to Sgurriach and Alt-na-Criche's stunning lava escarpments. Out past Loch Cullen, the amazing gardens at Sellartoon, made from savagely cleared crofters' smallholdings, then past Gruinard and its supposedly anthrax-free earth, cleaned up by Doomwatch scientists after the insane germ warfare experiments of the 1950s. Circle the view of An Dhur, and then zoom along Loch Broom to

Ullapool. I was tempted. But despite the frustration of doubling back, the inland route had it. It would end up much quicker and, besides, I liked the idea of busy roads full of witnesses to any attempts on my life. Not that traffic had stopped that fucking ministerial moron the last time.

I was looking forward to the dulling thrum of the drive, though. I needed it. I needed to get Rosie out of my head, mouth, and indeed other orifices. And the weird sense that everything was out of my control, that I was playing someone else's game.

When I woke, gritty with the tiredness born of long-drawn-out sex, she had gone. Her body had become half-familiar, after the strangeness, the newness and comparisons of that weird encounter at Bartholomew House. Who was she more familiar than? Whose contours had she replaced? Lucy's? Her form had grown blurred and indistinct in my memory map. I remembered a gym-muscled torso, breasts that could give you severe conjunctivitis with an unexpected swing. How her whole lower body trembled and fluttered after orgasm. It was pointless her trying to fake it, towards the end. I knew. The aroma of lapsang souchong tea from her armpits. Fine golden hairs on her inner arms, and those amazing female elbows, bent backwards for better baby-holding. I wondered how she was. Briefly. But not keenly. Like I said: indistinct.

Celia's body was less defined too, thin, essentially, but blunted by years of dangerous living, drinking, inhaling, taking; slightly creased at the edges. Beautiful, though, and voluptuous in a way which stemmed from her movements, the way sex infused everything she did, once it was on the agenda. And how effortless that became, how at ease she was with her body, what she did with it, had others do to it. But her lovemaking was never contrived, didn't feel rehearsed, practised. Always, she was new and tidal when she came, like great breakers on a beach. Not that she allowed herself to let go, all the time. Celia was very into control, herself and the men she slept with. That last time, though, in the car, had been deranged; dangerous. I'd felt as if I was going to merge, physically, with her. Fuse, utterly, in every surface, orifice, lumpy bit of our bodies. But possibly that was the drink, or the lack of it; my body, my mind, both screaming for any kind of narcotic.

Rosie's body was with me now, in the stiffening friction burns, the pleasurable throb of a bruised nipple, the tired pelvic muscles. She was a possessor of men, a taker whose own abandonment to pleasure took precedence, and who could hurt you with that hard, not young, unsculpted, very fit form. She just didn't seem to care, until afterwards, when she would idly pick fluff out of your belly button and whisper compliments into a wet ear, her breath like ice.

Other women's bodies passed through my mind, as I scrabbled one-handed for tapes in Riefenstahl's glove compartment, trying to find some music to match my mood. And my age. I mean, if you listen to pop, you want to feel you can buy stuff which is actually still popular. You don't want to be one of those sad gits who still plays *Tales from Topographic Oceans* or *Harvest* all the time. Sure, pop is memory, moments, but who wants to recollect twenty-minute wank-guitar solos or, worse, keyboard doodling from tossers in capes?

I had made an effort. Drink had maybe helped me to an affection for some of these lumbering young haircuts in their flares and anoraks. That's right, blame the fucking drink. I was trying hard not to. I hated all that fucking dour Calvinist booze-guilt, the way the tabloids picked on Jim Baxter when he got his liver transplant, because he was supposed to have started drinking again. Fuck them. That was so Scottish. Or that school of literature where hard-nosed Hemingway heroes strode through a grim Glaswegian twilight, fighting with maudlin, pathetic nobility and angst the temptation to fall once more into the glorious gutter.

Drink has its advantages. You don't need to search out public toilets. You can just crap yourself, piss your pants, and it's okay, it's fine because you're a pisshead. Hey, make some allowances, people! Can't you see the boy's blootered? And you get to watch kids' Saturday telly programmes in the only state they can possibly be dealt with, that is comprehensively brain-deadened.

Sometimes I would catch late-Saturday-morning Radio One, then blunder into Our Price later in the day, like some hopeless, befuddled, trying-desperately-to-be-hip uncle, asking for The Blurred or Supertramp. Sorry, Supercar. Oh, Supergrass? Yeah, right, man. I had those two albums the over-forties buy to convince their children that they're hey, really umm, cool, daddy-o: Radiohead's *OK Computer*, with its scratchy digital Pink Floydisms, and The Verve's lumberingly melodic *Urban Hymns*, which wasn't a patch on their earlier work, like the cracked, Zeppelinish *Northern Soul*.

Bitter at the way my musical past had been raided by young upstarts with no shame and less talent, I eventually unearthed three tapes to last me the drive: John Prine, unashamed throwback nostalgia, but those songs: *Speed of the Sound of Loneliness*. I hit Achnashellach to that one, the remote railhead high in the middle of Scotland, looking like it sounded: a phlegm-laden cough on the landscape. Ach! Na! Schell! Ach! At the little garage next to the station and the attached hotel, I spent a mind-numbing fifty quid on petrol for the old Nazi tank, and had a superb cordon-bleu lunch of cheese-and-onion Quavers and two King Size Mars Bars, washed down by a full-sugar Coke. Afterwards, I felt as if my gut had been impregnated with Polyfilla. It was Elvis food, Scottish style. I was willing to bet that if Presley had heard about the

Scottish habit of deep-frying Mars Bars, he would have fuelled up his private jet, the *Lisa Marie,* and set the controls for Glasgow.

Along Strath Dram's beautiful, dangerous single-track I drove with Faithless booming out, the acceptable face of techno, hip-hop, jungle, drum and bass, whatever you called it. Songs. They had songs, anyway, and the beats were good to drive to. Frightened the sheep from the passing places, too, if you opened the windows. Up past Stearbhe, one of a number of places in the Highlands where the Devil's footprints were supposed to have been left, seared in stone. I knew one location, further south, where they had taken the form of eternally burnt pieces of grass, that would never grow back. But some arsehole had dug the square of turf out, presumably to use as some kind of satanic centrepiece for his garden. A talking point during church barbecues. Nobody, as far as I could tell, followed me. Or at least tried to put me off the road.

By the time I reached Ullapool, having almost ignored some of Europe's best scenery, albeit dulled by a day of thunderous dreichness, so grey it made your eyes mist over, I was grooving to *Astral Weeks* and, aptly enough for that most sensual of records, had worked myself up into a bout of in-car sexual frenzy, one not allayed by the fact that I didn't even have Rosie's telephone number.

She hadn't appeared at breakfast – Pop Tarts, for God's sake, those jam-filled microwaveable slabs of toasted board, not even any bread – and there was no excuse to stick around. Well, there was. I could have said, I'll just wait for Rosie so I can say cheerio and we can have one last shag. But this was my brother I was dealing with. His sheets too. For the sake of politeness and discretion, I'd bundled them up and shoved them in his gigantic German ASKO washing-machine. Biological Persil for those embarrassing tell-tale stains. Not that it mattered, as he was bound to know. That was what Victor was about: knowing.

I shook his hand and left. No embraces. Mild, dislocated, vague chat about mobile phones, computers, Mercedes cars. Then nothing. I thanked him, not specifying what for. He said not to mention it. He seemed on the point of saying something, but didn't.

As I turned onto the road and headed back east, I thought I glimpsed a long-haired, possibly female figure in a tracksuit coming round the bend to my left. I checked the mirror. Stopped, even. But there was no one there.

The Ceilidh Place, Ullapool's famous bohemian hotel, restaurant, art gallery, theatre, bookshop, pub and general hangout for holidaymakers with pretensions and locals with brains, was full, so I got the tourist office to find me a bed-and-breakfast along the front, north a bit from the pier, looking out at the several rusty hulks anchored in Loch Broom.

Once this port had depended utterly on the dozens of klondikers which came each year from the Soviet Union to buy and process fish from the Scottish fleet. The same big, badly maintained hulks began their transhipping off Shetland, followed the fish south to Peterhead, Ullapool, then over to Ireland. In the old days, when I was a boy, the crews – rumpled men smelling of tarry cigarettes, and gigantic women, refugee weightlifters from old Olympic newsreels – would swarm ashore in Lerwick, stripping the town dump of anything recyclable, buying old Ladas and strapping them in their dozens to the decks, for shipment home. Crap in, crap out.

Now those days were gone, along with most of the mackerel. If Eastern European klondikers came in, they were operated by strange firms with money behind them, sometimes dodgy in the extreme. And the cars they shipped back to Russia or other states ending in -*ia* were likely to be Audis, Mercs or Volvos. Once they had fed the masses; now they comforted the few.

Anyway it was summer, and Ullapool, an ordered, pretty, sterile kind of village, originally thrown up as a fishing settlement in the nineteenth century, was swarming with tourists. The log-jam of cars on the very front was the queue for the final ferry to Stornoway, capital of the Western Isles, for which Ullapool was the busy wee mainland terminal. I wondered if Roger had perhaps gone there, to atone for his sins in the islands' atmosphere of ravaged protestant guilt. It was possible. Christ, anything was. I was fooling myself if I thought I could find the bastard, whoever he was, but I'd taken the money from his so-called parents, and now my brother's thinly disguised contempt was driving me, too. Mr Whizz, Hernia had said. What the fuck was that all about? There was the nightclub, of course, but what the hell would Victor's association with that be? He was hardly Mr Ebenezer Fucking Good, was he? The Slipperene king of the dancefloor? I wondered if he still had the accordion. No sign of it at Glendruin. Maybe he'd hidden it away, in case I felt the overwhelming urge to slash the thing open again. But why should I? We were self-controlled now, the two of us. He hadn't shot me, after all.

At least I could try to do what the Thiebaults had paid me for, and calm the convulsive twitches my long-stunned conscience was now, most uncomfortably, performing. Another advantage of drink: guiltlessness.

After throwing my bags onto the bed of the double room I'd secured at the Bon Sejours Guest House – at an exorbitant, high-summer, two-person rate – and bid the lightly mustachioed English landlady a less than cheerful farewell, I'd gone down to the harbour office to ask private detective-type questions. It was, predictably, shut. But a man in a uniform of sorts was standing outside, watching the antics of a long-haired, bearded preacher with a large and floppy bible, who was shouting at the fish-and-chip shop queue about Romans 10 and 9, and the need to confess Christ as Lord, if grace divine was to save them. As I passed, I noticed the bible was upside down, a mere prop. It didn't matter. He had the imagery off by heart. The fiery lake, needless to say, awaited, hotter than the bubbling fat in that there chip shop. People were tolerant and did not throw him in the harbour – which he would doubtless have seen as a watery martyrdom, or baptism, or both. Wet, anyway. I sniffed. The smell of hot fat, newsprint and vinegar took me back to Lerwick Saturdays, fish teas in the Fort café. It was amazing how smell could evoke the past.

'Shut till the morning,' said the half-uniformed man, a grimy peaked white cap failing to disguise a case of dandruff so bad I wondered the seagulls didn't come and peck at his shoulders for sustenance. His blue, brass-buttoned jacket looked like it had been caught in a snowfall.

'Shut then?' I said.

'Till the morning,' he agreed, equably.

'You the harbourmaster?'

'For my sins, no.' He wiped some snot from his nose in a most unharbourmasterlike way. 'He'll be at home for his tea the noo.' His accent was Scottified Yorkshire English; a particularly ugly brew. A settler. A New Highlander, as the politically correct term had it. My mind went back to the Albatross and the White Settler himself, progenitor of the race, sitting there letting beer hurtle down his throat without touching the sides. A man who had negated the need to swallow. Who refused to allow the term New Highlander to be mentioned in his hearing, on pain of assault with bad breath. 'I have a little wee tour boat down there, the *Merry Jean*. Always in and out with old Captain Bob, though. What you wanting, matey?'

I shrugged. 'Och, nothing much. Just wondered if I could have a look at the berthing records for a couple of years ago or so, find out about a boat might have been in around then?'

'Oh?' His eyes narrowed. 'What, you Excise or something? Customs? 'Cause if you are, you'd better not ask too many questions around here, matey. Doesn't pay to be too curious hereabouts.' He sounded like some saloon-keeper warning off a gunslinger in a cardboard western town – which in a manner of speaking he was. These were, for all the couthy vibe, the tartan souvenirs and great big heathery hills, the drug badlands of Scotland when it came to smuggling. The west coast was where all the hard and indeed soft stuff came in, dumped out at sea attached to mooring buoys, landed on deserted beaches, and many of the bigger, modern houses around Ullapool were reputed to have been built on Colombian cash. This was the Costa Cocaine.

'Nah, nah, not at all,' I replied, grinning my most reassuring grimace. I decided to be straightforward, sort of. In a deceptive kind of way. 'I'm a journalist with the *Northern Mail and Courier*, just trying to get a lead on a missing person case. Don't suppose you remember the boat, do you? It was a trawler, Spanish? Stupid name, like: *Chuleta de Cordero?'*

There was a fractional narrowing of his eyelids before he vigorously shook his head, scattering dandruff like confetti – some of it was that size – everywhere. 'Nope. Don't get many Spaniards in here, not nowadays, matey. All stick down to Cornwall and Ireland.' Which was a blatant lie.

'Ach, well, never mind. I'll pop back in the morning and get the boss man to run the computer files past me, if he can be bothered.'

The peaked cap and its attached face relaxed, smiled, giggled even. The air was full of gently settling dandruff. One shake of the head too severe or too many and he'd be needing skin grafts. If he scratched beneath that cap there was a risk he would penetrate his brain. Maybe that's why he wore the hat. It could be full of leaked brain fluid, for all I knew. 'Not much chance of that,' he said. 'The only computer they have in there's for writing letters. Nobody knows how to work it yet, Captain Bob was telling me just the other day. All the records are kept on good old paper, matey. Just like they've always been. Best way. Fancy a drink?'

Of course I did. I was amazed now at my brother's computing ability. He was truly a genius among hackers, if he had managed to penetrate a non-existent database of ship movements. But, then again, he'd said he'd made a few phone calls. Maybe that was it. Maybe. Mr Whizz.

The Dandruff King's name was Jonathan and he had moved up to Ullapool seven years ago, armed with the proceeds from selling a house in Northampton at the peak of the property boom, pursued by a wife he'd been forced to pay off ('Last I heard, she was in fuckin' Lanzarote, shafting time-share salesmen. Hope she gets fucking AIDS') before investing the rest in a pleasure cruiser and a peaked cap.

'I'd done a bit of sailing, you know, ye ken, Norfolk Broads 'n' that. Got my boatman's ticket easy enough, insurance, shit, and now I just get them gogglers around to the reefs, see the seals, back in port. Not much of a living, but it's fresh air, innit? And one or two extras, sometimes, evenin' cruises, fishing, you know. Things needing picked up.' He winked at me.

He had a couple of pints in the Ceilidh Place while I thanked God for an establishment capable of serving decent coffee. Some whiskies I'd never tasted glinted golden on the gantry behind the bar. It was no longer an issue, I told myself. No longer an issue. No longer an issue. I remembered the Antabuse with relief. Maybe I should take some more. I'd been neglecting it, because, hey, I was tough, strong and, weirdly, I'd forgotten all about it. About Big Ethyl's importance to me. Maybe we were falling out of love. Maybe the passion was shrivelling.

On a trip to the toilet, I took a look at an exhibition of extremely disturbing paintings, like heavy metal album covers done by Charles Manson. They turned out to be the work of a local man who'd been jailed for his part in the biggest ever seizure of Ecstasy by Customs and Excise officials, from a yacht boarded just off Lochinver, some way north. The captain had said not a word, apparently, either before or during his trial. Or the whole time – five years, so far – he'd been in prison. They thought, I seemed to remember, that he was Spanish. Must've been that healthy smell of paella.

By the time Jonathan got on to the problems with Asians in the inner cities, and how it was a relief to move to a place where – and I quote – 'the blacks weren't smelling everything out with fuckin' garama fuckin' masala' – and the subsequent don't-get-me-wrong-mate-I'm-not-a-racist-I-like-lamb-biriyani statements, I thought it was time to make my excuses and leave. There's nothing worse than bigots whose views you don't share. If he'd been anti-French and was suspicious of rock climbers' sexuality, maybe we could have been friends. So I went to the toilet, and this time I didn't come back. I'd just bought Jonathan his third pint – urine-coloured lager, made in Scotland secretly in huge underground breweries beneath public conveniences – and it looked as if his oil-soaked pants had stuck securely to the bar stool. If he needed to pee, maybe they'd take him an empty pint tumbler, a tube and a funnel, position it carefully, and let seepage do the rest. Then they could serve it to him when he asked for another pint.

Back at the B&B, I opened the window and watched the last ferry of the day slip out of Loch Broom for Stornoway. The heavy cloud had gone and the evening was fine and warm, just blue-blackening down into the gloaming; perfect midge weather. They were humming in clouds capable of driving a man to madness. I shut the window again, and lay down on my much-shagged bed, watching the few insects that had managed to gain entry to this anonymous room, with its boxed-off 'en-suite facilities', comprising the smallest shower in the world and a toilet which, with an electrical howl, churned your shit into lump-free gravy before firing it down a microbore pipe to some sewer deep in the bowels of the house.

I suddenly felt homesick for The Tub, and its simple if smelly chemical toilets. At least there you knew where everything was going. You had strong chemicals which simply did for the germs, or most of them, in your poo, your number twos, your personal ordure of the day. There was something about this churning business which made me uneasy. It was as if the house's plumbing was now some kind of digitised electronic extension of your digestive system.

I lay down on top of the thin duvet, with its faded coverlet, and pointed the remote control at a fourteen-inch telly which was mounted – welded, it looked like – to a bracket high up near the ceiling. A programme came on about antiques, with a man who looked as if he used to be Michael Parkinson doing a fair imitation of one. I began to feel that comfortable, fearful, slipping-away which is either death or dozing, or both, and which you really feel you ought to resist, but never do. Unless you're driving a car, of course.

I woke up in the dark, ravenous. It was nine o'clock, just early enough to still obtain food of a fried, greasy and generally horrid nature in the average Highland settlement. Unless you were somewhere like Thurso, far, far up in Caithness, where eating out is considered a great blasphemy against God and microwave ovens. Bleary and stumbling, I made it down the narrow staircase and out of the front door, to find, out of the lightbulb illumination, that it was still twilight this far north, of course, with a creamy pink scar across the western horizon. The coolness of the air had rid this part of the western Highlands, all too briefly, of *Culicoides impunctatus*, the common stinging midge. Female, of course. The males don't hurt you. Ain't that just like life, babe?

I warily checked the Ceilidh Place's bar for my erstwhile drinking partner Jonathan, who had, despite his sticky trousers, clearly managed to unpeel himself from his stool. The restaurant was, inevitably, fully booked for dinner, and the slew of tourist pubs in the centre of town had long given up serving what they claimed was food for the day. It was fish and chips or nothing, and there was still a queue outside the main outlet for superheated cod and flashpoint haddock. At least the fishmarket's proximity spelt possible freshness though sometimes you couldn't count on it in Scotland, where there is a tradition of serving deep-frozen, ready-breaded white flaked fish anything-but-fresh from New Zealand just to save actually buying something scaly, with eyes, from local fishermen. The smell of hot vinegared newspaper and frying convinced me, though, that this was approximately the real thing. I joined the line behind an elderly couple dressed in matching safari suits and hats with full mosquito nets. They were German. They'd probably been told the midges carried cholera. Or mad sheep disease.

The preacher I'd seen earlier had returned, with a small battery-operated amplifier, and was singing tuneless and incredibly melancholy songs to a battered, out of tune, but loud guitar. The words related to being left behind on earth while all the Christians lived it up big time in paradise, having been hoiked heavenwards via some sort of divine levitation. The Germans ignored him. They were lucky not to know what he was going on about, but they still had to put up with a style of guitar playing which made Bob Dylan at Live Aid sound like Paco Pena.

'No fuss,' said a voice I reluctantly recognised, hissing fruitily into my ear. A small, hard object was jabbing painfully into my back. 'The Lord sees all and delivers all, and behold, mine enemy is become my prisoner.'

'Fuck you, you piece of fake Godrot,' I muttered. 'I thought you might be dead.'

'Hoped, and indeed, we all live in hope of that trip way beyond the blue, for it is a far, far better thing to be with our Father in heaven than labouring within this mortal coil. But off-road vehicles made by our Shinto brethren do, oddly enough, manage to shield those contained therein from most hazards liable to be encountered, as they say, off road. Save, perhaps, water. But the loch, praise God, was shallow. And the hiring of a crane within our permitted budget. Now, move your arse down to the shore, and then go right . . .'

Nobody seemed to notice anything untoward. The ghostly gauze masks of the two Germans in front did not turn in our direction. It was dark, and my only hope was the preacher, who was gazing straight at us.

'Don't turn around,' said Jeremiah Gideon Smith, for it was undoubtedly he, though I was in no position to check out whether or not he was wearing his tell-tale Presbyterian headgear. 'Do not attempt any shouting. The gun I have, in the pocket of my inexpensive but generally practical Dickie canvas jacket, is not silenced. But it is among the smallest handguns ever made, a North American Arms Guardian automatic. Named after that voice of left-wing evil, the Manchester *Guardian*, no doubt. I'm sure dying by a gun with the name of a newspaper will appeal to you, you muck-raking filthprick. The sound it makes is akin to a small sharp cough, say on a sabbath morning during divine worship. And, anyway, who would expect gunfire on a quiet Ullapool street smelling of fried fish? Want to know something else about my beautiful little weapon?'

'Talking about your penis again, fuckbrain?'

'Judge not others as you would yourself, my brother.' The whisper retained the rolling, preacherish quality of his ordinary speech. Ian Paisley talking to the ghost of John Calvin, with swearie words. 'The Guardian, despite being so small, is a .32 calibre pistol, with a muzzle velocity of 1,000 feet per second. In other words, just where it's pointed, it will tear your liver right out of your body. And my Dickie jacket's capacious pockets, which incidentally disguise my weapon, will permit my escape, shouting for a telephone and a doctor, after allowing you to slump to the ground with apparent heart failure. Or hunger. Albeit smoking almost indetectably and with generally rearranged internal organs. Bleeding will follow, of course, but by that time I will have departed.' He laughed, a snuffling sound through his nose.

I turned to the man with the guitar, whose eyes seemed like welcoming pools of salvation, and wondered if he had seen anything suspicious. Surely he must have noticed my sudden change in body language, from starvation to imminent death?

'Ah, what a fine witness good brother Ethan is providing,' murmured Smith, digging what I had to believe really was a gun deeper into the lower part of my back. 'Poor Ethan, or Blind Boy Redemption as I believe the local folk call him. Poor soul lived in a religious commune hereabouts for a while. All the others left him behind, I think for a suicide pact in Switzerland or something. The social workers found him a place to stay, on account of his disablement. Kind folks. The Lord will bless them.

'Blind Boy Redemption,' I said. 'That'll be because he's . . . blind, then?'

'You see,' said Smith. 'You see?' That hideous snuffling giggle again. 'That's a wee joke, my son. Now let's get going before I ram the poor bastard's god-fucking-forsaken guitar up your arse. For Christ's sake.'

'What,' I said, 'not even a chip?' Although my hunger had vanished, quite accountably.

'You, prickscumshit, antichrist shithead, have had your chips,' he replied, in a quiet, reasonable tone, still reminiscent of North Antrim's most infamous ministerial son. Paisley Pattern. 'This is the final takeaway. Prayer is advised. Now walk.'

So I did. You can pray while walking, I found.

★ Fifteen

Between the harbour and the empty waste which was Ullapool's golf course was a stretch of common land backing steeply down into the sea by way of a stony beach. At night it was a kind of murky pool between the dull orange-curtained glow of massed guest-houses, and the shifting blackness of the sea.

Suspended in the summer darkness were the riding lights of several ships, and above them the twinkling lights of Alltnaharrie, on the other side of Loch Broom and the site of a famed restaurant, accessible only by boat and those rich enough to walk there on water. I was suddenly overtaken by the hallucination that I was being kidnapped by its owners, in the mistaken belief that I was still a journalist, and would write wonderful things about their food. But reality intruded. I was no longer a hack, the Altnaharrie Inn was booked up months in advance, and I was being pushed down the shifting, invisible pebbles by a deranged religious maniac with a foul mouth, a diseased mind and a gun. And despite the fear, my appetite had returned with a vengeance. It didn't seem fair. God, a black pudding supper would hit the spot. Even the blood would be apt.

'Don't suppose we're heading for the Altnaharrie, then, for a bite of the famous langoustines *en choux* with Beluga on the side? And chips?' Chirpy. I felt unaccountably buoyant. Just as well if I was going into the sea.

'For you, I think some food for the soul will be more rewarding,' said Smith, clipping me heftily on the ear with his handgun. Despite its small size, this hurt. The darkness went blacker than it already was and I fell forward, landing in the water, which was icy despite the summer. Chill out in Scotland. Something warm trickled down from my bruised lobe.

'Luco Brazzi, he sleeps with the fishes,' came the mocking voice, all Hebridean threat and Celtic sneering. People like Smith could put you off Gaels for life.

'Not yet, you pissbrain,' I spluttered. An arm grabbed my sodden Polartec Fleecelite body-warmer, or in this damp case, skin refrigerator. A torch flicked on briefly, and I glimpsed the outline of a semi-rigid inflatable a metre to my left.

'Put the fucking light out!' came a voice, whispering thickly and in excellent colloquial English, but with a marked Spanish accent. Why had the Costas lost their touristic appeal for me, all of a sudden? A dim red lamp came on, guiding us towards the boat, and with a heavy shove I was lolling about in the hard glassfibre bottom of it, as Spanish curses hissed above me. Then came the quiet, liquid whirr of a four-stroke outboard starting, and we were moving, out towards the lights floating in the middle of Loch Broom.

I knew it was a klondiker by the smell. Dead fish, rotting fish, burnt fish. It was a converted whaling factory-ship, from the stern cavity and the steep sloping ladder I was forced to climb. I could have jumped for it, I suppose, and tried to swim ashore, but they took the precaution of looping a rope under my neck and keeping it tight from above all the time I was climbing. Hang the consequences? I didn't think so.

The deck was slippery with fishscales, and the muttered language spoken by shadows was something guttural and latin. Smith, puffing a little, had put away his gun in order to climb on board, but the rope lead was kept around my neck. Holding the other end was a man I recognised, in the dim deck lighting, from the last drunken moments before my tumble down the Castle Street steps.

'*Hola!*' he said. '*Buenas noches.* Welcome to the *Margarita.*' He bowed, a trifle ironically. No, very ironically. He sounded like Manuel from *Fawlty Towers*, lowered about five octaves. Looked like him too, only three foot taller and with muscles in places where most people didn't even have ideas that there might be places. In fact, come to think of it, he didn't look like Manuel at all.

'I am from Barcelona,' I said, before could stop myself. 'I know nothing. *Nuuuu-theeeeng!*'

There was a ferocious tug on the rope around my neck, and then a forearm smashed into my face. I woke up a second or two later, on my knees, staring at the scrubbed but still fishy deck.

'That will teach you, my son,' intoned Smith. 'For lo, such imitations are not popular among Spaniards of any variety. The *Fawlty Towers* producers changed the nationality of Manuel to Belgian for the Iberian market, you know. Anyway, this man is a Galician, and they don't much like the Catalans.'

There was a sweet taste of blood in my mouth, but it did nothing to satisfy my nagging hunger. That's the problem with giving in to a major set of physical desires, like in my case oblivion and brilliance via sex and alcohol. When you deny yourself your hit, your body cries out for something. I could have murdered a fish supper and a black pudding. Or just murdered.

In fact, all of a sudden my chirpiness had vanished. I was becoming quite bad-tempered.

'What is going on? Smith . . . Jeremiah . . . there's no need for any of this. There was no call for the Inverness business, the hospital or that insane shit on the road. I mean, what's the fucking point? I know you're completely out of what passes in your case for a mind, but . . .' I was paralysed by the kind of pain which can come only from being kicked forcibly in the balls. In this case, from behind, where I was open and exposed to the ministrations of the Hebridean psycho.

'I am sensitive to assertions about my mental state,' he whispered into the flare of agony which was burning deep in my body. 'I'd advise you to speak when you're spoken to, and give the right answers, too. And the Lord will bless thee for thy obedient spirit. Take him down to the fish hold, Manuel.'

Christ. His name really was Manuel. Through the choking pain I wondered if they would feed me. Prisoners often are fed, after all. But then I reconsidered. This was one prisoner whose unassuaged appetite wasn't going anywhere in the medium to long term. And maybe sooner. I was being held, it seemed to me, on a purely temporary basis, but the permanence of my prospects seemed undeniable. Why? Put it down to a personality clash. I know I did.

I was taken through a watertight door and down two sets of rusting stairs to what was obviously a canning line. A thick, oily, fishy smell, mackerel most likely, filled my nostrils, seeped into my sweat. Everything was quiet. I imagined the crew were sleeping or trying to ignore whatever strange sounds they overheard, odd visitors glimpsed with blood streaming down their face, trying to walk while a vicious pain made them retch in the overwhelming fishiness.

'Nobody to hear you scream, my son,' said Smith in a great, booming preacher's voice. 'Welcome to the ship of the damned! Although the final word on that matter is of course in His hands. The processing staff have finished their work for the moment, just a few odds and ends to be cleared up, and they're in their quarters watching pirated videos the content of which would not be of interest to a man of culture like yourself. And the transfer crew is trusted, blind, perchance wilfully, to such untoward eventualities as yourself, and ready to take the *Margarita* away from here in approximately one week's time. For lo, the nets have been cast, and her holds are full. The canners and gutters and general fishpersons are being pornographically stunned by some whore of the devil's visual antics, and the cargo of low-cholesterol, Omega-three fatty-acid-laden protein is heading for . . .'

'*Basta*,' said Manuel the Mountain Man Mountain. Which means 'enough', I think, and gave me for the first time a small flicker of hope. If they were going to kill me, why worry about telling me where they were bound? But I was feeling reckless.

'Let me guess,' I spat through wobbly, jellied gums, my damaged ear forgotten. 'Somewhere in desperate need of food, prepared to pay, partly in cash and partly in something grown locally. Not South America, no, but North Africa's not very far away. How about Algeria? International pariah, dangerous but possibly lucrative. And they grow all kinds of opiates there, don't they? Jesus, I would have thought the customs would have sussed this out long ago, though.'

'Ah,' Smith sighed. 'But the essential corruptibility of man remains a factor. Plus patrols are meagre due to financial cutbacks. Not only that, but the excisemen only catch the scraps thrown to them, put them off the scent. You know that. You used to be slagfuck writer, didn't you? A dragger through the dirt, an unearther of unpalatable and untrue slanders. And endlessly inaccurate, as indeed you are now.'

'Libels,' I said. 'Slanders would be spoken or broadcast. And in your case, every word I wrote was true, you wanker.'

Manuel laughed. It was not a pleasant sound.

We had gone down another set of rusty stairs, deep into the anal passage of the ship, well below the waterline. The oiliness in the fetid air had been replaced by an atmosphere thick with dampness and diesel. We stopped in front of another watertight door. Smith took out his gun. I could see it was truly tiny, more than concealable in the palm of his hand. It didn't look capable of inflicting more than a tickle.

'Don't be tempted,' he warned. 'It might not take your head right off, but it will put a large hole through it. Several times. Six in the magazine, one in the breech. This is serious shit, this thing. Had to get it smuggled in from the States.'

'Wow. Smuggling. Isn't that illegal?'

'The only legality and justice you need worry about, my friend, is that of the Lord, and me. And this. An instrument of justice. Indeed, even with just the one bullet. As you will see.'

Suddenly I stopped being hungry. My guts trembled, and I felt my buttock automatically clench in order to avoid the sudden wash of fear staining my trousers embarrassingly brown. Not that anyone would have noticed the colour. And the smell might have been an improvement. But no shot came. Instead, the door was unlocked and I was pushed inside.

'I'LL BE BAAAACK!' shouted Manuel in a hideous Spanish imitation of a Schwarzenegger accent.

'God bless you. And remember: no one expects the Spanish Inquisition!' said Smith, slamming the door. He was obviously a man with something *Python*esque in his past. What a splendid range of influences: fundamentalist religion, surrealist comedy, bad Lewis weather and psychopathy. Lovely chap to be stuck on a boat with.

A caged, 40-watt bulb allowed me to look around my new

accommodation. There were no bunks, and no toilet. The floor, flaking, rusty steel, was wet. And on it were Mr and Mrs Gareth Thiebault, or whatever their real names were, assuming what Victor had told me was true. Not that it mattered to them any more. Both were clearly as dead as the single visible bullet wounds in each of their foreheads could make them. Mrs Thiebault still had her little suede cut-down bag wrapped around her wrist. It had been roughly torn open, and whatever contents not of interest to her murderer scattered around her. That bizarre half-decanter of perfume lay unbroken by her waxy wrist. In death, Melanie-Joanne did not smell nice. She reeked only of her dismal surroundings.

There wasn't much blood, but there were strange marks on their ears, and then I noticed – always Mr Observant – that the Thiebaults' eyes had simply disappeared. Torture. All thoughts of black pudding fled. Christ. I vomited. Strange, considering my stomach was so empty. This was one way to cure an appetite. Then I heard a sort of scratching, scuffling sound, and as I turned to look for its source, a movement in the corner of the room at floor level caught my eye. Bending down, I could see that rust had eaten a hole through the metal of the cabin wall, and then I was face to face with the thing that had gobbled up the Thiebaults' eyes, and had a go at their ears too. *Rattus Rattus* was here.

I could have panicked. I did panic. I banged at the door in a good approximation of all the great prisoners. Of Zenda. Of the Iron Mask. I was briefly Alexander Solzhenitsyn pleading for a chance to become a communist propagandist. And when I turned round the rat – brown and very large – was munching Mrs Thiebault's ear, carefully avoiding the expensive earring attached to it. A rat with taste. It really was rather a naff bauble, and not the kind of thing the tasteful rodent likes to find in its digestive tract. I decided to make the best of the situation. I sat down on my hunkers and watched. And tried to think.

The Thiebaults, as I knew them at least: the Thiebaults and me. Who had the capacity to find out where they had been and where they were going – indeed who they were? Who knew most of my likely movements? Who had, it seemed, baited a trap and led me straight into it, and looked responsible not only for the deaths of this delightful couple – delightful enough to give me several thousand quid, anyway – but for my current predicament? Victor, what did I ever do to you? It was what you did to me, you bastard. It couldn't be him, though. Why should it be? Putting a bullet through my hand a long time ago was no excuse for setting the religious Rottweiler Smith on me. Okay, so I ripped his accordion, displaced him in the old parental affection stakes. But, hey, that's what younger brothers are for.

I sat there for two hours, according to my watch. It was a vintage

Rolex Submariner, Navy issue, which Lucy had bought for me second-hand at a car-boot sale from an obvious resetter of stolen property. Both of us got a weak thrill from that. It still had the MoD issue arrow sign on the back, and originally came with a faded green canvas strap. I'd replaced that with an imitation Rolex metal bracelet from a backstreet Aberdeen jeweller's.

They'd want to talk to me, obviously, and this was all meant to scare the living spiritual shit out of my churning soul. Which it was. Would they kill me? If Victor was involved, surely not. But, then again, I had a feeling that Smith was, if he had ever been under anyone else's authority, now dealing with God and the Devil direct. And me.

There was Manuel, but he seemed happy to back Smith up. Maybe he'd been converted.

I looked at the woman who had called herself Meljo Thiebault, sickeningly frail and fragile in death, the blueness of her skin seeming to spread outwards from the mashed hole in her head. Black around the edges. Powder burns. Smallish calibre, or it would have taken her head right off. Very small gun. Shit.

I looked at her earrings, then at the rat – Roland, I decided, or perhaps Rupert. Definitely Rupert. Supposedly, you were never less than a metre away from a rat, wherever you were. I was a damn sight closer now. The tacky earrings, real gold, too much of it, dragging down with riches what was left of the lobe. They hadn't taken them. Not motivated by greed. At least not petty greed. And then I remembered something.

I scrabbled along the floor picking up the female paraphernalia which had been contained in the little suede bag, and had been deemed innocent: make-up, tissues, lipstick, safety pins and a comb. I could always pin my captors to death, or shock them with an attempted transvestitism before they shot me: if I am to die, let me be true to myself. Kent 100s, that ornate Varga Girl lighter, and the atomiser of that hideous perfume which had left my eyes watering during our meeting at the Prebble Lounge. Ah, the Clutha! Nope, the appeal of its stodge was still absent. Eyeless, rat-eaten bodies put you off your dinner. What was it called, that perfume? Les Misanthropes? Mystère? Mystery was about right. Apt.

I decided to do that French Foreign Legion firing squad thing, and have a final fag, my first for a decade. Why not? If there had been booze there I'd've had some of that too. Might as well die inebriated. Maybe I could drink the perfume. But no, another possible use had occurred to me.

Strangely enough, the Kent felt good, easy to inhale, smooth. And then a sort of tarry tingle started in the depths of my chest and became a gut-wrenching cough by the time it reached my throat in a gigantic wave of nausea. I tried again, and this time felt the top of my head lifting off, spaces opening up behind my eyes. Nicotine. What a drug. After this cigarette, if I lived, the effect would decrease quickly until there was no hit to speak of, until I was smoking just to keep the withdrawal agonies away. It was like drinking, really, only without the social implications. Maybe alcoholics in recovery smoked to remind them how addicted they really were.

I stubbed out the fag and made my desperate preparations. With the distraction of impending activity, my appetite had returned, so I smoked another cigarette, this time without the massive biochemical impact. An hour later, by my watch, I heard the sounds of approaching feet, and with some scratching and rattling the door opened. I wasn't there.

Well, not at first sight. And as Manuel walked in, looking like a cross between Sylvester Stallone and a railway sleeper, a momentarily confused expression on what passed for a face, I stepped from behind the door and sprayed him with some of Mrs Thiebault's Mystère. Rather a lot, actually. And Manuel's head went on fire.

He did smell nice, if you liked a combination of Mystère and burnt flesh. But the Varga Girl lighter I was holding, with its large, ragged flame, just in front of the perfume spray, had transformed the fragrance into the world's smallest and most expensively fuelled flamethrower. Manuel shook his head violently from side to side, but he could see nothing. He was blind very quickly, his eyes milky and opaque. In the frenzy of adrenaline, I felt nothing but curiosity. It was a bit like cooking a fish, the way a mackerel's eyes turned white under the gas. He fell over, clutching at his face. There was a meaty aroma, and I felt mildly hungry. Then sick. I flicked the lighter off.

He was screaming. The screaming had begun when I started pumping perfume at him, and was metallically amplified by the enclosed space. Everything in the world was screaming. The world was a scream, The Scream. And Jeremiah Gideon Smith came through the door, his untoasted eyes on Manuel, shock on his normally superior, ministerial, smirking features. His mouth was open. I could see his teeth, bad teeth. He probably had bad breath. A blast of Mystère might improve things. I held the aerosol steady, trained on his face, finger poised on the valve.

He wasn't looking at anything except the huge figure on the floor, rolling in his own piss, mumbling in Spanish, smelling gorgeous, like a high-society barbecue. I flipped the lighter's switch again. The flame was steady and yellow. Held close to Smith's face, it singed his hair. I couldn't smell it.

'Take the gun out of your pocket, Jeremiah, if you still have it. Crouch down and put it on the floor,' I said. 'Make sure it doesn't go off. I might take fright. I'm right on the edge of it, I would say.'

He reached into his jacket, a natty dark-green Berghaus, and pulled out his much-prized, tiny gun. He placed it carefully on the floor. Slowly, he began to lower himself to the ground. I went with him, the lighter beginning to blister his skin. He was trembling, but whether it was with pain or fear I couldn't tell. Both, I hoped. I slid the gun well out of his reach.

'They . . . the crew will hear the screaming,' he stuttered, sounding most unpreacherlike. God, it would seem, had deserted him.

'I doubt it. We're in the bowels, the fucking entrails, the asshole of this excuse for a ship, and isn't that what they'd expect to hear? You killed these two, didn't you? I ought to singe your fucking balls for you.'

'No!' His voice was high, shaky.

'What's the matter? Afraid of the fires of hell? Strange to see the Lord taking His fiery vengeance here on earth, not giving you time to plead forgiveness, eh?' I grabbed the gun and stood up, then kicked Smith in the head with all my strength. The Reeboks made little impression. At least it felt like nothing bony, skull-like, had caved in. He fell down. I aimed the gun at the back of his knee. Then I pulled the trigger. Nothing happened. The safety catch, I supposed, was the little lever which came naturally to my thumb. Flick. And then the gun worked. Impressive. Very little kick. A flat, coughing crack, metallically echoing in the enclosed space. A thousand feet per second, Smith had said. See how it feels to stop it. Ye ken noo, pal. Aye, ye ken noo . . . A new screaming began. Different register. Different accent. If screaming had an accent.

I waited for it to subside. It was like being in some sort of medieval illustration, all blood, death, blindness and retribution. The curious thing was how calm I felt. In fact I was mildly worried to find myself feeling rather good about the mayhem I'd engineered.

Manuel showed signs of causing some undirected, unsighted trouble, so I shot him in the knee, too, only this time from the front. He fell like a chainsawed tree, and this time said nothing. I guessed he'd passed out. Jeremiah Gideon Smith, my would-be nemesis, was now whimpering, praying to God to have mercy on him. I kicked him again, this time from the front, on the collar-bone. There was a crack, like dried pasta shattering. The whimpering grew louder.

'Listen,' I said, trying to suppress the strange delight which was rising in me. 'Listen, you shite. What the fuck is going on? What is this about? What was all that crap in Inverness?'

The moaning continued unabated.

'How about the other shoulder? Fancy evening things up a bit? Or perhaps the knee? It could be God's will, you know. Why don't we ask Him? Together. Get up on your knees, you bastard.'

He showed no signs of moving.

'Get up on your fucking knees!'

There was a flimsy attempt to move, and then he fell flat on his face again. But he turned his burnt – well, slightly – and bloody face to me after a bit and said, faintly: 'Fu . . . fuck you. God is with me and will welcome me to His right hand on high. You cannot . . . hurt me.'

'I *have* fucking hurt you,' I said, resting one foot heavily on a shattered knee.

Smith moaned. 'He said . . . to scare you, but I knew you deserved . . . judgement. Manuel was happy to go . . . along. What does he care? Scared you in Inverness, right enough, and then I felt called to . . . deal with you once and for all. He said you were easy, weak. He said . . .'

'Who said? Who? *Who?*' I kicked him again, on the already broken collar-bone. There was a fierce intake of breath and then Smith too lapsed into unconsciousness. I was doing well. My Interrogator of the Year award was in the bag.

Anyway, it didn't matter. I thought I knew who. Someone whose intelligence should have been considerably better, considering the business he was in. But I was no longer sure what that was.

I locked and bolted the door, still running on some weird, naturally secreted compound which was keeping me calm and clear and somehow . . . exultant. Was this what being a psychopath was like? Acting without regret? But at least this cruelty had meaning. Some kind of morality. They had fucked with me, and I was fucking with them. It was functional. It seemed necessary to stop them. To stop them killing me. Justifiable.

I remembered that cat, back in Shetland, and how it had swum and swum, fought for its life, survived. The cat had met with the brutality necessary to destroy it, once it reached the shore. Magnie had tried to distance himself from the killing, sent the bagged cat into the sea. But when push came to shove, when he had to engage personally with the thing, he'd just got on and done it. I remembered the taxi driver who had taken me to the Clutha, who had rationalised his own childhood abuse into something valuable, helpful. And maybe I would look back on this and think, hey, those were happy, happy days. Something to tell the grandchildren. Or perhaps not.

I had done what I thought was necessary. It was time to get away. Let Rupert the rat wake them up, or better still, bite off some essential components before they stirred. And then let the rats of fear take them, as Alexander Trocchi would have put it. Everyone gets what they choose.

There were five shots left in the Guardian, assuming Smith had reloaded after sending the Thiebaults to a premature holiday in the eternal sun. Would it be enough to see me past the crew? How about stealing the inflatable for a trip back to shore? God, I wasn't sure now if I could get down the ladder to it, untie its mooring or start its engine.

I reached the canning area without seeing a soul. My watch showed eleven o'clock, so maybe they were all in bed, tucked up with their teddy bears or wanking their way to bitter Iberian dreams. More likely they were all still holed up in a cabin watching dirty videos and drinking.

The canning line was deserted, strangely calm, like a church of processed mackerel. At one end was a huge open-topped tank of vegetable oil, marked ACEITE in flaking paint, and half full. I hoped it was olive, healthy, full of monosaturates, but I doubted it. This looked like a cheapskate operation. There were probably one or two rats lurking dead and sated at the bottom of that tank. Boxes and boxes of tinned fish were packed high against the walls, all bearing a picture of a smiling herring in a kilt, and the easily understood Spanish word '*Escocia*'. There and then I vowed never to touch a tinned mackerel again.

It took very little time and less thought to tear open one of the boxes, dump the cans inside, flatten the cardboard and soak it in the tank of vegetable oil. It caught fire slowly but surely, like diesel. When I picked it up and threw it into the tank of oil, there was no *whump!* of exploding hydrocarbons, just a lick of yellow flame and an aroma of fish-and-chip shops. I felt hungry again.

On the deck, I finally came across one of the crew, walking directly towards me as I emerged from a doorway. He stopped short and opened his mouth to take in a shouting breath just as I fired the tiny gun at him. No messing around with legs and knees this time, I just pointed it at the mass of his torso. The .32 slug took him in the right shoulder, which was no tribute to my marksmanship, but certainly made him shout louder than he would have done otherwise. They probably heard him at the Alltnaharrie Inn. Though not the gunfire – the tiny weapon made only a loud click, not even a crack, in the open air. It had been much louder below. Clangier. More impressive.

I didn't wait around. I shoved the gun in a trouser pocket and jumped over the side of the boat, feet first, hoping there was nothing moored beneath me and that the water wouldn't be too cold. There wasn't. It was. When I surfaced, I could see lights, orange and regularly spaced, flickering in the distance. The Alltnaharrie side of Loch Broom had no streetlights; it had to be Ullapool. As the summer iciness of the water seeped into my bones, I struggled to pull off my trainers, slipping down, and down before managing to lever them off. Tired before I properly started, the salt water making my wounded face nip badly, I began to swim towards the fuzzy balls of light, wondering what the survival time in west-coast waters was at this time of year. It was ten minutes in winter. I hoped I had a bit longer. But the drink had not gone into reserves of fat with me. It had been the perfect slimmer's diet, and I was ill-equipped for long-distance swimming.

I tried to put out of my mind the thought of bullets whizzing towards me, searchlights, pursuit. There was a degree of shouting, but it was drowned by the loud bang and flash which erupted into the soft summer Loch Broom air like God taking His vengeance on Stornoway for its fleshliness and degradation. An overwhelming aroma of cooked fish surrounded me, but I was too concerned with not drowning to feel hungry. Who would have thought vegetable oil would burn so effectively? Who could have imagined tinned fish had the capacity to explode? The mackerel bomb. Maybe it would become the terrorist weapon of choice in future. Mackerel on the streets of Belfast . . . I turned back to my leaden breaststroke as the sound of thin, solo screaming reached me, echoing over the water.

★ Sixteen

I'd stopped being cold. A warm, seductive, comfortable feeling was creeping up from where my feet had once been; voluptuous, almost sexual. My head was bobbing more and more beneath the small surge of a light swell, but the lights of Ullapool seemed no nearer. Behind me, there had been a muffled bang, followed by a low glow, reflected on the water in front of me, which had faded to nothing hours, minutes, weeks ago. It passed through my mind, calmly, that I might drown. Salt water periodically filled my mouth. It became more and more of an effort to spit it out.

My mind detached itself from my increasingly soggy body, and I was suddenly having oral sex with Belinda Sheringham, the Cuntess of Clit, something which never happened and the desire for which must have been buried deep, deep down in an unhealthy corner of my subconscious, to surface at this near-death moment:

Oh, Zandy, baby, did I tellya about the time Sting went down on me? Yeah, oh yeah, baby that's . . . anyway, ya know he's into all that tantric sex stuff, deep exchange of bodily fluids, seven hours' foreplay, all that jazz? Well, fuck me with a fence post but he came after just a coupla minutes of doing all that genital mouthwash thing, and I'm not joshing . . . guess he just got sorta carried away down there in the Cuntess's cunt . . .

And then I was back in the waters of Aithsting Voe, one summer's afternoon, aged five . . . no, six . . . in the aftermath of a quaint social occasion my parents favoured every year. The MacTavish family's annual water rocket competition was attended only by the would-be bohemians, the former hippies and cut-above professionals of Lerwick. My parents went because they were, I think, flattered to be asked, and because they could proudly parade their genuine, at least in their own eyes, radicalism. Hadn't Dad been sacked from three teaching posts on the mainland for his membership of something called the Revolutionary Fabian Brotherhood? That's what he said. But the Revolutionary Fabian Brotherhood was hardly a revolutionary movement, spied upon by MI5, a danger to the state. Mum and Dad were the only members, a matter which caused my mother, eventually, great distress when feminism entered her consciousness and she began questioning her brotherly status. Personally

154

I think the afternoons off for direct action against exploitative supermarkets (pouring paraffin over South African and Israeli oranges, that sort of thing), and the subsequent court action, might have had something to do with it. And Mum, being a good RFB wife, indeed the only one, went where Dad did.

Water rockets. You made them out of old lemonade bottles, fitted them with rubber stoppers which had been bored out, and had the valves used to inflate footballs inserted. Mounted on a variety of launching pads, pumped furiously with everything from plastic bike pumps to electric compressors, they could go surprising distances. Out in the voe, old man MacTavish waited in a rowing boat, to judge the winner. Different family entries sported varying designs of fins, colours, aerodynamic noses and the like. Ours was, that year, a particularly fine piece of work, I recalled. A large Irn Bru bottle, painted dark green and with the words Come Let Us Throw Ourselves Beneath The Juggernaut Of Capitalism painted on the side. I had it all spelt out to me, the Hindu myth, what it meant, something called irony. At six it was hard to take in. But it stayed with me. The irony.

Anyway, that day the competition, which always involved loads of drink for the adults, cakes and fizz for the children, was long over, and we had not won. Victor and I had been left on the beach, while the adults and the other kids partied, bawled, fought and flirted up in the old stone croft house which the oil-rich MacTavishes, who owned a massive bungalow outside Lerwick, used as a holiday home.

Not only had we lost, but Come Let Us Throw Ourselves Beneath The Juggernaut Of Capitalism had been lost, too. And I was keen to find it. So I waded out to sea, which, at the age of six, soon became rather too deep for me to remain standing. I spluttered, I bobbed, I tried to wave and not drown. And Victor stood on the shore, his arms folded, and laughed.

A stray adult, reeling to the beach for an outdoor beer-pressurised pee, noticed, in a befuddled way, that something was wrong, and managed to nearly drown himself rescuing me. Victor, wide-eyed, told my drunkenly sentimental, frantic parents that I had just that moment run into the sea, laughing. My mother, almost hysterical, hit him.

Now something was hitting me, someone was dragging at my arms, and pain was penetrating the warm glow of this west-coast water. Bright lights glared down on my face, and suddenly everything rushed back. Christ, the crew of the *Margarita* had found me, were dragging me back to face the music of Manuel and Jeremiah Gideon Smith.

'Aye aye, pal, let's get you up, *mhath*. By Christ, he's almost dead, Donald. Give him some of that black rum, for God's sake. Don't keep it all for yourself.'

I was on the bottom of a boat, surrounded by creels and bits of broken green crab. A large and woolly fisherman, a man with a nose redder than Rudolph's, was leaning over me, outlined by the open deck's arc lights. He had a bottle in his hand, was pushing it towards my lips. I could feel salt water in my mouth, and, peculiarly, an aftertaste of cigarettes. Suddenly, that was what I wanted more than anything. A fag, Christ. I was addicted.

'No . . . no . . .' I gasped, gagged out some bile and brine. At length I managed to speak: 'I don't . . . drink.'

'Fuck's sake!' said the west-coast voice. 'Developed a taste for salt water, though.'

When we reached the harbour, it was in a state of some turmoil. Police cars, ambulances and fire engines were jumbled uselessly around, their lights flashing. Fire engines? Fat lot of good, half a mile across Loch Broom from the *Margarita*. Now the loch had extinguished any blaze, swallowed the ship whole like a fire-eater.

'All that fish, I suppose. But you wouldn't have thought she'd tear herself apart like that,' mused one of my rescuers, whose name, apparently, was Big Donnie. 'Like she was packed wi' ammunition or something. Last time I saw a ship go down like that was the Murmansk run during the war. Fucking Liberty ship, spot-welded together by some amateurs in America. Split apart like a cardboard box. You some sort of agent?'

I was sitting up by this time, nursing a cup of tea so strong it would have dissolved steel. I could feel it diminishing my teeth.

'An agent?'

'Yes, a fish agent. On to check the state of their mackerel, you know, a buyer? You're no' one of the crew, anyway. They're all Spics.'

'Ah, yes. That's right. An agent.'

'Fucking mackerel. Don't know how they can eat it. Dirty fish.'

'Good for you, though. All that oil. And what about crabs?'

'Aye, whit aboot crabs? It's the Spanish take them, run lorries right in here to pick them up. Norwegians like the mackerel. Grind down everything, bones, eyes and shite, make it into a powder for arthritis. I wouldnae take it, though. In case of getting mad fish disease. Do the same thing wi' bloody salmon. Mad Norskies. Drink like fish, too.' Something crossed his face. It might have been a smile.

'What about the crew,' I asked, slurping the concentrated tannin infusion, 'any sign of them?'

'Aye, well,' Donnie looked completely immune to emotion. Craggy wasn't the word for him. He had a face like Abe Lincoln on Mount Rushmore after a landslide. 'Not so good, I think. One or two of them maybe, made it out in an inflatable, I heard on the radio. The police will want to talk to you. They're waiting for us at the pier. Look.'

'Fine,' I said. The little lump of the Guardian suddenly appeared, magically, against my thigh. I was reluctant to throw it away. I'd never had a handgun before. It made me feel like a real private investigator, the kind I'd longed to be, thought I could become. Now here I was, a probable killer, fingering a gun with stupid relish. And I hurt. Where I'd been hit, yes, but the pain seemed to have spread through every fibre, soaked in with the salt water. Still, I was very nearly alive.

The tide was high, so we sailed right into the harbour's inner basin, and tied up alongside a rusty and weed-encrusted ladder. But just as I was wearily wondering about climbing up, clad anonymously in an old orange oilskin and the scaly seaboots Donnie and his mate, Padraig, had lent me and wondering what I was going to tell the local bobbies, the lifeboat came into view, all floodlight-blaring marine importance, and towing the rigid inflatable I had grown to know and love so well and so intimately earlier on. It was empty. I paused, pulled the oilskin hood over my head, and set off up the ladder, my skin shrieking with the effort. When I reached the tar of the pier, no arms helped me up; I wasn't recognised as a refugee from the sunken klondiker. I managed to get through the small crowd with a few murmurs of 'Fine, thanks,' and 'Yes, it's awfy saft oot there, *mhath*,' in my best teuchterspeak. The sea, I averred, was indeed unusually wet at this time of year, or words to that effect, before I found a pool of shadow behind a towering corrugated-iron ice factory. You're never yourself in an orange oilskin with the hood up. I even felt like a crab fisherman. And smelt like one: of fish. Fish and other things. There was, to my olfactory organ, still a whiff of Meljo Thiebault's mysterious but highly effective perfume about me.

Amazingly, buried in the pocket of my sodden fleece, I still had a key for the Bon Sejours Guest House, which was in darkness. I let myself in as quietly as possible. All the lights went on just as I was unlocking the door to my room. The landlady, her moustache bristling, emerged from her own subterranean quarters wearing a winceyette dressing-gown and a blue hairnet. I was as frightened as I'd been all night. She looked like Eddie Izzard in old age.

'Late, then?' What a question. Her eyes darted over my oilskin jacket, the pool of water gathering around the ancient, scarred, and far too large boots, and my damaged, but seawater-sealed face. There was also the interesting mixture of aromas I carried. Mackerel, cordite, smoke, seawater, Meljo's eau-de-whatever. Quite a recipe. The boots were leaking some form of foot gas, too. In point of fact, I was irresistible.

'Well, yes. Or early. Actually, I'm checking out, Mrs . . . Mrs, ah . . . Mrs Landlady. Unexpected crisis. Medical matter. I'm a . . . a doctor.'

'You registered as *Mr* Flaws.'

'A surgeon. Have to rush, there's been an accident out at sea.' Her eyes began to sparkle with gossipy delight and curiosity. Or perhaps sexual attraction, heaven forfend. But I didn't wait to see some fire of lust kindled by the thought of death and destruction. I slammed the door behind me, stripped off the mess of apparel, and, without washing, changed as quickly as I could into old jeans and a T-shirt and a fleece, my reserve one. Then I squashed my discarded clothes into a ball, and shoved them into my Adidas bag, with the exception of the orange oilskin and the boots. Honest, that's me. Neither a borrower nor a lender be.

I headed down the stairs, trying not to creak. She was there ahead of me. 'That'll be twenty-five pounds, Mr Flaws . . . Doctor,' she said. 'And you'll no doubt be wanting a receipt. I often have medical men here, you know. Now this accident . . .'

I plucked a twenty from my wallet and handed it to her.

'The bed's not been slept in, Mrs . . . Madam. Let's call it quits at this, eh? I'll pass your name on to some of my colleagues. I was most impressed by the . . . décor.' And the smell of stale fat, I almost said. She was in front of the door, and showed no signs of moving.

'Another five pounds, if you please, Doctor. There is a rate, and an empty bed is an empty bed. This is high season. I could have filled your room three times over. I expected better. From a doctor.'

I stood and looked at her, while cogs clicked into place, shards of rust and rot fell away from the shaking, shoogling pile of crap which was my brain, and another piece of the whole fucking puzzle fell into place. Yeah, I'd expect better from a doctor, too. Simultaneously I was filled with huge depression, a vast, crashing blackness. And I realised I was still starvingly, ravenously hungry. The words 'black' and 'pudding' crept unbidden into my head.

'All right,' I caved in. 'I tell you what. Here's another ten pounds, Mrs . . .'

'Farthingham. And it's Miss.'

Jesus. 'Miss . . . Farthingham. How about a couple of sandwiches to see me on my way?'

She snatched the tenner like it was the secret of life itself, which in a way I suppose it was. Her face shut like a trap. 'The kitchen is closed,' she enunciated coldly. 'And I've no change.'

It was that great Highland welcome, or in this case, farewell. Fare badly. See hospitality? Ye cannae whack it in Scotland, ah tell ye. And it wasn't just because she was English. If anything, native-born Scots are worse. She was just absorbing the local vibe. Surfing the fucking Mac*Zeitgeist*. She had moved aside from the door. I opened it and went outside. Cool air hit me like a wall.

'Hope to see you again, Doctor,' she said, brightly, the old bitch.

'Yes, indeed,' I sang back. 'In hell, you bum-faced old toerag.' I smiled sweetly at her, and then threw the old oilskin at her pursed, nippy face. Yes, she was an incomer, but she had learned all too quickly the attitude and expressions it had taken Highland Scots thousands of years to develop: survive through implacable rudeness. *Oh, so it's Bonnie Prince Charlie, is it? And you're wanting a bed for the night? Well, it's double rates for fugitives, I'm afraid . . . and you cannae sleep with that bint Flora, neither . . .*

I walked towards Riefenstahl, and then stopped to look back. She was still standing there, folding up the orange jacket, no doubt as a preliminary to selling it. Padraig's old spare boots were still in the hallway. 'FUCK YOU! I work for the Michelin Guide!'

In retrospect, it would have been wiser to keep quiet, but I was feeling a trifle disconcerted by the events of the evening. Maybe I'd send Padraig and Big Donnie a nice pair of new Hunter wellies in the post, by way of thanks. And then again, maybe I wouldn't.

I was fiddling with the Merc's grumpy central locking when two figures emerged from the shadowed alley on the other side of the road, and walked jerkily towards me. They were by no means secure on their feet, and one of them was Jonathan of the Dandruff, who'd warned me off and swallowed beer at my expense in the Ceilidh Place, in another lifetime. With him was a large young man. Very large indeed.

'Ah, there he is . . . there you are,' slurred my erstwhile drinking companion. 'Asking all those . . . too many questions. Fucking snoop. Some fucking Inland Revenue, muck-raking reporter, fucking . . . this is him, Angus. This is him!'

The younger man was every bit as unsober. He tried to focus on me, his ball-shaped face attempting an Eastwood hardness. But he wasn't in Victor's league when it came to *Pale Rider* imitations. Still, this was confrontation time. He had come to warn me off his territory. Too late.

'Too many questions,' he began. 'Too . . . too many fucking questions get you intae trouble in this town . . .' He took a pace towards me, but stopped when I pulled out the little gun and held it against his ear. It dripped. But then guns are not electrical. I presumed it still functioned.

'Look,' I implored him. 'I'm tired. I'm all . . . stressed out, and I want to go home. Have you and Mr Liver Disease here been waiting for me all night? And by the way, this may not look like much of a weapon, but I can assure you, it's a' – I racked my brain for the numbers – 'a .32 automatic, which pumps out bullets at a thousand feet a second, even when wet. Which is sore.'

'We've not been . . . not all night,' said Jonathan. 'I mean, we just had a few drinks, and I told Angus here you'd been snooping around, like, and he thought, better give you a wee bit of a sorting out, in case you . . . you know. It's business here, you know, the waccy baccy, like lobsters, and waccy baccy, and the Colombian liver salts sometimes. No offence, eh, sir.'

'No. No offence,' said Angus.

'Look, you two wankers,' I was amazed to feel that same absolute, uncaring anger that had risen within me, all scouringly clean, back on the *Margarita*. I flicked off the safety catch. But this was Ullapool. There were people behind these walls. 'Look, rest assured that I have no interest in you or your fucking waccy baccy. Just get the fuck out of my life before I give you a tattoo you won't be able to get surgically removed.'

They both backed away slowly, then turned stumblingly and ran. Angus fell over once, but I've never seen anyone get up so quickly. No one that drunk, anyway.

When I got in the car I realised the phone was still lying there, ignored and unloved. Shame. I switched it on, and it rang immediately. 'You have two new messages,' said the most soulless voice in the universe. The first one was from Hernia. Dr Cecil Holdsworth, king of the Hippocratics. 'Hi, Zander,' said the well-known tones, metallic and slightly faltering, maybe. 'Just wondered how you were. Keeping on the old water wagon, right? Good stuff. Maybe see you in Sneck when you get back from your travels. Okay? Give me a ring. Bye.'

Yeah, sure.

The other message was from Celia: 'Hi, Zander . . . just to say there's a party at Atherton's place, a real media do, but anyway, I thought you might . . . maybe not. Anyway, meet at the Albatross beforehand, Sunday night. If you're back.' There was a pause. 'I . . . miss you.' Then nothing but a bleep.

In a twenty-four-hour garage just outside Inverness I finally obtained some food. It was six in the morning, and the town was waking up. It looked like rain. More water. Three packets of salt-and-vinegar crisps, all of which tasted of fish; a can of real, sugary Coca-Cola, non-diet and red of tin – the real Real Thing, two Mars Bars. The carbohydrate dumping began almost immediately, and by the time I reached The Tub, all the adrenaline and energy and crazed, mindless reacting had vanished, replaced by a desire to sleep the sleep of the very unconscious. Somehow, I managed to get across the gangplank and inside the old barge without falling into the canal.

As I flaked out on the sofa, I heard the flubbering, strangely reassuring sound of heavy rain begin on the roof of The Tub.

It never rains but it pours.

What she felt, saw, knew, heard: an unbearable pressure, a red darkness, and then a blinding pink light, pain, choking. I am being born, she thought, and suddenly she could feel the piercing chill suddenly eased by scratchy swaddling, the separation and the presence of another, bigger body, a host, rocking and shushing. Oh, Christ, not all this again. Not the whole bloody thing, the whole of life from the off. It was bad enough the first time.

Eyes. She had eyes now. Sticky, stiff. She opened them, screwing them immediately shut in the striplight glare. Figures moving around her. She was suddenly back in that huddle behind the Mr Whizz club, and Bobby was off talking to that figure out by the bins, caught in the light. His face was somehow clearer now, in higher resolution, like one of those enhanced computer images. She knew who that was. How could she ever not have known? It was obvious.

She opened her eyes again. She couldn't move or speak for tubes, which flowed like hideous worms from her mouth, nose, both arms.

A voice: 'Are you awake? How do you feel? Can you hear me?' A face now, a man. The same man Bobby had been talking to that night. No question. She knew.

Somehow, it seemed only natural for him to be here. A doctor in the house. Doctorin' the house. Doctor Feelgood. And suddenly she did. She felt better than she ever had in her life.

★ Seventeen

'Well, fuck me sideways with a pool cue!'

If this remark discomfited the backpacker whose pint of Old Cholera Sludge was pulling as I walked into the Albatross, it did not show. But, then, she was probably Australian.

Sludge shoved the too-foamy pint towards the tourist, and ran a wet hand through what was left of his Elvis quiff. There was nothing sadder, I often thought, than a balding Presley fan, one with long sideburns and half a ton of Flora Margarine on their pate. And there was no doubt about the sadness of being Sludge or indeed the badness. That would be illustrated if you ever dared patronise him, or asserted that the late Presley was crap. I well remembered this being suggested by some goatee-bearded rockster of about fifteen in a long black leather coat. 'Fuck you, smegbrain,' Sludge had said, vaulting the bar and grabbing the unwise rock critic by the nostrils. 'The Las Vegas era! James Burton on guitar! The great ballads! Can't help Fucking Falling in Fucking Love! Take your Mystery Train and your plinky-plonky Scotty Moore and use it as a suppository, you pant-pisser!' No wonder the Albatross tended to attract a fairly select bunch of customers.

'Flaws, you bastard! What libation can I provide for your delectation? A little decaffeinated coffee, perhaps? A Virgin Mary with all the trimmings?'

'That mean with the ring-pull in the glass?' I inquired. 'No, just a poncy mineral water, that Welsh stuff if you've got it.'

'One glass of bluebottle piss coming up,' replied Sludge, a dreadful grin revealing the Shane McGowanesque suppuration which was the inside of his mouth. Imagine kissing that . . . But, amazingly, women did. That study in saliva, brown gums and purple tooth stumps, all reeking of the Samson roll-ups he smoked incessantly: something in the combination was an aphrodisiac. Mind you, he only slept with really drunk women.

Celia and the White Settler were waving at me from the corner of the bar, the Noxious Section, as it was sometimes called, near the men's toilet. Things had improved since the environmental health inspectors had insisted that the yellow river running under the toilet door, through the bar and out into the street, was unacceptably niffy. Sludge had asked them where the fuck he was going to play with his plastic ducks now.

'How was Loch Salvation, then?' Celia was smoking with her usual intensity and enthusiasm, like a kid sucking the last dregs of lemonade from a can. Her face, as ever, betrayed no sign of any current emotion. Everything that had happened to her in the past was in that face, though, in the chiselled outlines, the little wrinkles, the depth to which her eyes had sunk, their ever-increasing blackness.

'Okay,' I said, 'for the five minutes or so I spent there. Actually, I've just come from Ullapool.' There was a moment's impressed silence, or what passed for it in a pub.

'Christ, you certainly know how to pick newsworthy destinations, you bastard. Sinking klondikers? I'd have pinned it on you, but you're really not the James Bond type, are you? Thought not. Even if there is a cauliflower ear coming up there.'

'All over the *M&C*,' said the Settler, proferring a rolled-up and partly papier-mâché version of the latest Highland edition. 'Divers going down today. Can't get any sense out of the crew. Some of them did a runner, apparently, rather than talk to the police or even get fucking rescued properly. Thing is, they just vanished. Unless they went into the hills, there must have been someone there to get them, or someone they could call.'

'Wisnae me, officer.' I opened the rumpled paper as Sludge thumped down a glass of fizzy water and a bottle which looked like it contained perfume. For a moment I smelt Meljo Thiebault, and then she was gone. 'Put it on the slate, old chap, there's a good fellow, me lad.'

Sludge hesitated, then smiled. Not a pretty sight. But you got used to it. I was feeling quite at home. And no pangs. No liquid longings. So far.

The report was sketchy, agency copy from the Westerly Press crowd in Lochinver, beefed up with some round-the-houses calls by the staff guys in Sneck, and, by the looks of it, some fictional crap from Clingfilm McCorquodale. Suspected fire in the canning area, volatile liquids, sunflower oil, terrorist connection not ruled out, rumours of on-board religious cult . . . blah blah blah. Sunflower, eh? Smelt more like rancid rapeseed to me. Some of the crew had panicked, left the scene having managed to get ashore using the lifeboats. One body so far (that would be last night), drowned. No notion of how many might be trapped in the wreck. No mention of a missing mysterious 'quality inspector', either. Padraig and Big Donnie must have kept their mouths shut. I'd have to remember that pair of replacement wellies.

The klondiker sinking had pushed to the bottom of the page a report about the discovery of a young man's body in a disused salmon netter's bothy on the Black Isle. It had been identified as belonging to one

Robert Lacey, also known as Bobby the Busker. The terse item pointed out that police had been seeking Mr Lacey in connection with the recent spate of drug-linked deaths in the Inverness area, but that there were 'no suspicious circumstances' in his demise. Which sounded oddly conclusive. Disturbingly pat. But, then, there so much going on at Ullapool.

'Galician boat,' puffed Celia, banging her Doc Martens, patent fake crocodile skin in red, against the bar. Black biker jacket, long pencil skirt, she looked great. 'Word is there might be some sort of drugs involvement. Any connection with that Spanish boat you were chasing, Zander? Did you plant a bomb on it out of spite, or something? Anyway, I was going to come out there. Even left a message on that godless fucking answering service of yours. Maybe I spoke to you. Did I? Can't remember. But Clingfilm made me stay and do the fucking football while the big men did the sinking ship. Rats jumping on board a fucking story. Feminism? I fucking ask you. Like the bruises, by the way. Suits you.' Her eyes were glittering and, by the looks of things and the speed of her conversation, Celia was in the grip of the great god sulphate.

Rats. I thought of poor Rupert, drowned now, unless he had found a way to squirm out and swim for Alltnaharrie or Ullapool. Suddenly I felt shaky, sweaty.

'You smell funny,' said the Settler.

'The scent of honest sobriety,' I said, pompously. 'Since I stopped drinking, all these strange poisons have sweated their way out through my skin. I'll be sitting there, and I swear it's gin oozing out my pores. One day it's dark rum, one day whisky.'

'Lick your arm and get pissed. I like that,' said the Settler. 'Cheap, recycled booze.'

'Probably not alcoholic,' Celia exhaled the words along with bits of burnt lung tissue. 'Just the toxins, the shite that goes in with the alcohol to make it taste of whatever it tastes of.'

'Fuck me, that's pointless, then,' said Sludge, who was leaning towards us, pretending to make some of his already dirty glasses dirtier with a rank old bit of towel. 'It took me years to get to like beer when I was a kid, and then it was only worth while because of the effect. Fucking hell, imagine having the taste and no compensation.'

'Well, that's what those alcopops are about,' McGrooch sipped, lip-smackingly, from his pint of Gruntfarter. 'Alcohol without punishment. No price to pay save a hangover which tastes of fucking blackcurrant or lemonade.' Then he had the grace to look slightly embarrassed. There was a pause in which various forms of displacement activity were engaged in: inhaling, sipping, coughing, shuffling. They were all remembering Zander's Problem. Wondering how to deal with it, how I was coping with the loss of what made life good. The big fucking A. As for me, I'd forgotten to worry about it.

'Look, guys,' I began awkwardly, 'don't be so fucking sensitive. I'm not bothered being in here, so don't think I'm upset thinking or talking about drinking or not drinking. You know all reformed pissheads love to talk about it.'

'Hernia said –'

'Never mind what Hernia said. Treat me normal, for Christ's sake. I'm not saying I've cracked this, but I'm more than capable of getting through the evening without falling off the wagon. I've been taking that Antabuse stuff, and there's nothing like the fear of being sick in public to stop you from drinking. At least when you're sober enough to be embarrassed. And the smell is just fish, if you want to know. I got a fry from some boat in Ullapool, stuck it in the boot and forgot about it. Next thing it's everywhere, all over my clothes. And me.' I almost convinced myself I sounded convincing.

Actually, I'd spent some considerable time that afternoon trying to scrub the curious aroma of death, mackerel, oil, Meljo Thiebault's vengeful perfume and Loch Broom off myself. The resultant mixture with Davidoff Cool Water body shampoo – Prince Charles's favourite, so they said – was what I now carried with me. Not the gun, though. Not that nice wee Guardian. That was hidden away back at The Tub, in the secret compartment its Belgian owners had once used to transport PoWs and refugees along the great rivers of Axis-occupied Europe. It seemed somehow apt.

No doubt my new smell would wear off in time, just like the strange lack of regret, the emotional aloofness I felt towards the events of the previous night. I was relieved to be here, amongst my worn, slightly tattered drinking pals, but oddly, calmly, surprised at how well I was coping.

'Jukebox,' said the Settler suddenly, sliding jerkily off his stool. 'Any requests?'

'Plimsouls!' Celia was an obscurantist of the first water. I had sat through her collection of Peter Case records dutifully enough in the past, but her rare Plimsouls single – an early Case pop group – was not favoured by the inhabitants of the Albatross. Sludge allowed his little band of hardbitten regulars to stock the ancient Rock-Ola jukebox with their own singles, assuming the advent of CDs had left them with any, and so there was indeed this early offering available by the band which gave the world Mr Case. Even Celia hadn't managed to track down his earlier musical manifestation, as lead singer with The Nerves.

I ordered a round of drinks. Double gin and tonic, Old Fartworthy, and for Sludge, a large Longmorn. A twinge. Definitely a twinge in my gut, fluttering for a taste, a nippy sweetie, a hit. But I ordered my blue water and tried to stop my mind racing ahead, round the houses and back again, tried to prevent myself observing, feeling superior, doing all those fucking sober things.

Intimacy, dogmatism, certainty, and an inability to stand. By the time Sludge had closed up, everybody was having what they thought was a good time. And I'd almost succeeded in making myself drunk by just listening to all the crap that was being talked.

'Party . . . party,' Celia was singing, doing a curious little hopping dance while lying flat on her back on the floor.

'Elvis Costello. Wrote it for some dreadful British thug teen movie,' I said. 'Bombed.'

'You're so fucking sensible, you prick,' she said. 'Come over here and shag me senseless. I've got no knickers on.' She began to wriggle her skirt up, revealing those calf-length pretend tights and bare flesh beyond. Oh shit. Does sobriety make your cock shrink? I suddenly felt mine contract, as if I'd been motorcycling in an ice storm.

'Later, Celia.' Then I uttered the words that endear any sober person to a bunch of drunks. 'Atherton's party, then – anyone need a lift?' A ragged cheer indicated that they did.

The Settler had, in a calmer and less pished moment, rolled some cigarettes with prime Tain grass. One of these now filled Riefenstahl with that sweet pungency which, for whatever reason, always smelt exactly the same to me as Honeyrose herbal fags. At least it helped kill the aroma of oil and sea creatures which still clung to the seats. I'd tried to persuade the assembled bunch of reprobates that smoking dope in the back of a severely battered Mercedes on a Sunday night in Inverness was an easy way to get busted, but I was generally lambasted for having become a boring bastard. 'Fucking pish smell in here, anyway,' rumbled Sludge, who was wearing a godawful John Lennon hat to hide his baldness. He looked like a tug-boat captain with sideburns. 'Bit of waccy baccy'll purify the car.'

I could see in the mirror that Celia was interspersing tokes with occasional sniffs at her secret little silver inhaler, supposedly packed with mentholated crystals for her beleaguered sinuses. Mentholated crystals of something approximating sulph. Whizz. Mister Whizz. Just at that moment we passed the club with that same, arch name. And I thought of Victor.

'Only on special occasions,' Celia had told me, when she'd calmly offered me some speed in the midst of a sloppy, slobbering bout of half-conscious sex-making. 'Alleviates the drunkenness. Tightens up your loose accoutrements of pleasure.' I had avoided sulph since a dreadful business in an Aberdeen disco toilet, when I'd thought the heart palpitations were going to tear my chest apart and a headache like Trotsky's final one made me think my cranium was about to explode. Never trust a drug that makes you thin.

Jimmy Atherton was one of the producers on Radio Fuckwank's morning news programme, and rather too self-consciously strange to be taken seriously. An albino, his trademark long white hair tied back in a pigtail, and the word was apt. From the pinkness of his eyes, to his hairless, podgy face, he was pure Babe – except that he was six foot five inches tall and built like an emaciated racehorse. Women seemed to be hypnotised by him, despite fraudulent upper-class manners and a tendency to discard girlfriends like the condoms he ostentatiously carried in a silver cigarette case, engraved with the initials BC. Which he claimed stood for Big Cock. Maybe that was his secret.

He lived in a four-storey town-house in Ardconnel Street, the last ridge of Inverness's residential Crown district before it tumbled down the hill into the town's commercial heart. It was a kind of seedy corridor lined with guest-houses, the Blindcraft bed factory and a host of horrible bedsitter buildings, ready at any moment to slide into Woolworth's and Millet's. And indeed Mr Whizz. It was a place where women walked carefully after dark, and preferably not at all, as drunks used the street as both a gigantic toilet and a route home which could handle wide, inebriated wobbles from one pavement to the other. Cheap big houses, perfect for a wild party, running a brothel, or both. If Atherton was doing the latter, it was on a strictly amateur basis.

I parked Riefenstahl in a residents-only bay, got out and opened the back door, which allowed the giggling mass of humanity inside to tumble in a heap onto the pavement. In a swaying, clinging mass, shouting and screeching, they careered across the road, shouting at any car which dared threaten their progress, while I herded them; a sheepdog, laughing, trying to keep up, or a Coca-Cola-ed teenager at some adult do for the first time. And inside feeling utterly cold, irritated, with the beginnings of a vicious contempt for this . . . this complete and utter waste of fucking time.

Atherton himself opened the door, his pink features disguised behind a Chinese dragon mask. He was wearing knee-length black vinyl boots and tight red lurex shorts, his ghastly white midriff exposed by a cut-off green fluffy halter top. His belly button had been pierced, and flaunted a Celtic cross. I flinched, despite myself. It was partly the sight of our host and partly the force of the music coming hammering out. It was hard, furious drum'n'bass and jungle or whatever you called it, calculated to work with cynically sociable drugs like Ecstasy and bludgeon you into a kind of goofed-out mindless companionship. Not an opiate of the people. Not that good.

'FUCK me!' shouted the mask, battling the beat. 'It's supposed to be fucking fancy-dress, you assholes! Though I suppose in your befuddled little heads, you are indeed wearing all kinds of strange –'

But Celia, shrieking with laughter, had already attacked him, sinking her teeth, none too gently I surmised, into his exposed belly. There was a mêlée as Atherton staggered back, and everyone piled in behind Celia; one way or another, we were in.

There was little light. All the main illumination had been removed, and small spotlights in corners were all that you had to see by. It was like being in a Brueghel video, with all kinds of strange shapes, shadows and bizarre costumes, most of them torn, partially removed and involving some sexual depravity, half-lit, half-darkened. It was all somewhat familiar, and I remembered that I'd been to one of Atherton's Decadence Nights before. Only not in my current state.

Someone was screaming in my ear, over the music. It was Atherton. 'THAT BITCH has been speeding, hasn't she? Or something?' He, in the true spirit of the magus he longed to be, drank little, getting off on the antics he could encourage others to get up to.

I said nothing. It would have involved getting closer than I felt was healthy to Atherton's ear.

He kept shouting. 'Fine shag in a shit storm, my boy. But only if you share the territory. Word is you're lighting out for somewheres different these days . . .'

I just smiled and nodded, in best deaf disco fashion.

'Chill out in the basement, bonkerama in the bedrooms upstairs, booze out back. Your choice. If you're looking for your bestest pals, Val Crawford and Fergie Evelyn, you just missed them. They're heading to the Gurn Hedonists Society for a bit of slap and tickle.' Gurn, seventeen miles along the coast, was a hotbed of weird sex and dodgy get-togethers, mostly focused on the bus station. It occasionally caused Lucy's parents some spiritual pain. They had gone there for the golf, not the heavy transvestite scene and the arse-banditry in douce doorways.

'By the way, Zandy,' Atherton pinched my cheek, 'great costume. Man at C&A. I love it.'

That's what you get for wearing Gap when everyone else is wearing House of Psychosis. I guess.

I decided to work the house, check out what was happening, who was there. I supposed Hernia might be. Once upon a time it would have been unthinkable for him not to be there, not to have been among the crowd of fumbling, bumbling refugees from the Albatross. But things change.

In the upstairs lounge there was some form of drunken sex game in progress, involving most of the off-air employees of Radio Fuckwank, obviously enacting the hidden sexual tensions of their day-to-day office lives. It was clearly some office. They were dancing to an old Tamla compilation which combined weirdly with the muffled carpet clump of the ferocious techno club stuff foaming up from downstairs. Every time a song ended, whenever Marvin gave way to Smokey, they had to change partners and exchange one item of clothing with the person in whose arms they found themselves. There was a lot of teenage snogging and fondling going on as bits of fancy-dress made their way from leg to arm to head to torso. A rubber diving mask atop a tutu. On a large, fifty-something woman who looked kind of earnest. That sort of thing. By the time I arrived, and had spent a good half an hour watching, unheeded, it had turned into a kind of ritualised melding of identity. It would end, no doubt, in an ill-advised clump of naked bodies writhing in an aesthetically displeasing manner on the floor. My coldness and sense of dislocation grew. I left them to it as The Supremes tanked out *Nathan Jones*, and descended through the maelstrom of electronic beats on the ground floor, catching a glimpse of Celia dancing dervish-like with Sludge, his hat lost, his head gleaming in the occasional light, and continued down to the basement.

Chilling-out was right. It was cold here, beneath the level of the street, in a kind of murky blue light which was meant to be restful, made opaque by the smoke of several joints.

He was in a corner, slumped securely into a sofa like he was part of the fabric.

'Hi, Hernia,' I said. There was no need to shout. The music here was some kind of ambient house, but quiet. 'How are you? Climbed every mountain? Forded every stream? Followed every fucking rainbow? Discovered a hidden hoard of old *Beano* books? Found Hugh Grant was at the Cally and shagged him?'

His body stiffened in sections, as if an electric current had been passed through it. 'Zand . . . Zander?'

'The same. Your patient. Under the care of your sweet self, you signatory to the Hippocratic oath. Or should that be hypocritical?'

'What the . . . fuck? Zander, I've been doing a bit of partying tonight. You know, letting the old hair down. Did Ben Wyvis earlier just for the hell of it. Quick yomp up and down, and then ended up here. Must have missed you at the Albatross . . .'

'Must've, right enough.' I sat next to him in the soft, suffocating sofa, and spoke without looking at him, staring at a couple opposite who were involved in some complex oral and ambidextrous sexual activity, all fingers and tongues. 'Thought you might've been down An Teallach way. Way out west.'

'No. No, wanted to stay local. All day, as well, wet and dreich, didn't feel like travelling. Up to Strathpeffer was enough. Hard week as well at the surgery.'

'Heard from Victor?'

There was a pause, filled with the whine and bleep of muted synths and the small gasps and moans coming from across the floor. She was Wonderwoman, he was a Roman Centurion. At that moment, his head had vanished under Wonderwoman's silky pleated miniskirt. Previously, his toga had half-covered the pair of them. Unfortunately for the propriety of the moment, it had come completely adrift, revealing on and off a spotty back of great ampleness.

'Victor?'

'Yeah, Victor. My brother Victor. The brother you asked for when you phoned me on my mobile three days ago. The brother I never, as far as I know, told you about. Certainly never told you I was going to see.'

'Celia. Celia told me.'

'No, she fucking didn't. She didn't know anything about my trip except that I was going to Lochcarron. The only person who knew I was going to see him was Victor, because I'd phoned him first and left a message on his voicemail. And I never told you about him in the first place. There's no reason you should know him at all.'

Hernia shook his head, turned to look at me. And then he smiled. 'Fuck, Zander: all this paranoia. After everything we've been through together. All I've . . . we. Never mind that. And here you are. You're still sober, aren't you? You bastard, you're on the water wagon. Of course you are.' He shook his head. 'I wish I was. Thing is, when you're sober, you don't remember the things you do or say when you're pissed. Like you telling me about Victor. Lots of times. Lots. Fucking loads.' He smiled, a big, old-fashioned, friendly Hernia grin. 'You know, Zander, you could probably have one drink. Just the one. I mean, you're probably strong enough now. Ready to cope with it. Why don't you have a wee drop of Oban? I think Atherton's got a secret stash over in the corner.' Still the big smile.

And I knew. Even as I racked my brains to confirm or deny what he'd said about me telling him all about Victor, I knew. I fucking knew. 'So what did you do? Strike up a friendship?'

'Well, yeah, that's about it. I was concerned about you, over the past year or so. So, I phoned him, got his number out of the book, and we sort of kept in touch. Kept it from you, of course. Victor thought . . . I mean, Zander . . .' He leant forward, rubbed his face and turned back to me with a kind of medical solicitude. 'We both have your best interests at heart. Your brother cares about you. He really cares. And Celia, too, of course. Victor thought she . . . Now, listen, why don't I get that whisky, and we'll have a toast. To friendship. And absent brothers.'

I felt the burn of that malt, the light, classic smokiness of Oban, a wondrous collision between land and sea. Something in me longed for that, for the glow, the release and escape the inevitable next one, and the ten after that, would offer. Why not? Forget all the grief, the hassle, the guilt and hatred and betrayal. Dissolve it all in the only substance strong enough to do the business.

Get thee behind me, Hernia . . .

Satan was suddenly the man who had moved heaven and earth to get me to stop boozing. I looked at him, into his eyes, trying to see the reality behind the crap. My friend, my trusted medical friend. He wasn't that pissed. I drew my head back, slowly, then brought every piece of mental and spiritual shit to bear on the acceleration forward, carefully and viciously nutting him on the bridge of his nose, as hard as I could manage. It was a move I hadn't made since I was at school. The music changed. Someone had slotted on U2's *Numb*, from the *Zooropa* album and it sounded oppressively sinister after all the meaningless, wispy electronic doodling. I dabbed at my forehead, which stung, and watched Hernia pinch the bridge of his nose between two fingers, then lean forward. I stood up, and spoke into his ear, over The Edge's tuneless monologue. 'There's one you can heal your fucking self, physician. Now where's Victor? I phoned him earlier today, on one of the several unlisted numbers he doubtless possesses, and which it took the shit several months to give to me. And there's only the voicemail. Not even a mobile number. So where the fuck is he? Don't arse about with me. I know. I *know* . . .'

Hernia was scrabbling in his pocket. I suppose all doctors carry handkerchiefs in case of this sort of eventuality. He pulled out a white cotton square and placed it over his smashed proboscis, then looked up at me. 'I'm sorry, Zander. It shouldn't have happened like this.'

'Where is he?'

Hernia suddenly caved in, shrank, disintegrated, like someone had just turned his entire skeleton to jelly. The effect of my fist having thumped down on his already bloodied nose might have had something to do with it. I was only slightly concerned about the sharp twang of enjoyment I felt. 'Home . . . he went home . . .'

Home. Of course he had.

★ Eighteen

I was unlocking Riefenstahl's door when I noticed a figure slumped inside the privet hedge of the garden opposite. I say slumped: but it was more drooped, actually, and sunken into the hedge, like it had been jettisoned from a passing plane. The compressed air of the aged central locking had given its emphysemic hiss when I caught a flash of red leather from the object's feet. A closer look told me it was Celia. *Ah, Celia, you inconvenient bitch, what a pain in the arse* . . . but deep inside the new icy sobriety, with its sore forehead and scraped knuckles, something moved in sorrow and even love. Not the love which envelops and swaddles and sweeps you away to an ill-advised marriage on a beach in Hawaii, but a hard little glint of emotional zirconium nevertheless. Diamonds? I don't think so. Love doesn't have to be forever, or even lead to any kind of long-term relationship. Even cheap, pocket-money-at-Woolies love does, however, insist on extracting a person from a hedge and seeing them safely home. At the very least. Call it pity if you like.

Her slack body, reeking of booze and stale smoke, surprised me as ever with its heaviness, and its warmth. She was alive enough to groan loudly as I pulled her out of the privet, the strap of her leather mini-rucksack still firmly clasped in one bony hand. And when I sat her on the pavement, prior to the difficult manoeuvre of getting her into the car, she was copiously sick, but not on her clothes. A good sign. It could have been all over my attractively worn leather upholstery.

'Don't . . . don't hurt me,' she said, in an impression of her voice. Tears pricked at the back of my eyes. Could she feel the blood on my hands, smell the killing in the sour scent I'd been unable entirely to shower away, which the party's belched aromas hadn't hidden? Why didn't I care about it? Would I be haunted, pinioned by the memories in dreams to come? I shrugged it off, easily, worryingly.

I drove by the all-night filling station at Raigmore, and picked up some essentials: Beecham's Resolve, crisps, Mars Bars, Irn Bru, Silk Cut and mineral water. Celia remained slumped against the door, breathing like a ventilator. She lived, thank God, in a ground-floor flat, a modern development out in Hilton, which aways surprised me with its rigid

172

compartmentalisation; its precise cleanliness and organisation. It was the antithesis of Celia's ragged, blurred public persona. And maybe the key to it. I scrabbled through her rucksack for keys, unlocked the door and woke her enough to stagger us both inside. We stumbled through the cool, spotlit starkness of the tiny hall, with its single black-and-white photograph of the 1938 Empire Exhibition's Tate Tower, and into the raging, flowery femininity of the bedroom, all valances and flounces and onto the double bed, with its heartbreaking collection of teddy bears, its dried flowers on the bedside table, its Marks and Spencer's quilt cover. Once, I'd wondered aloud if this was all meant to be ironic, and she'd smiled woozily: 'Only if you want it to be.'

Everything smelt of fabric conditioner and breathed a cartoony, women's magazine peace. Bearing the unconscious Celia in, I recognised the place for what it was: a charmed, magical shrine to what might one day be, the deepest longings of her heart. Childhood simplicities. Cool sheets in a centrally heated house, a Dyson cleaner in the cupboard, fresh coffee, cut flowers and orange juice in the morning from a steel-and-oak ultra-chic kitchen. And I thought of Lucy, and how it had all begun for us in a womb-like state of comfort. Except the messiness and business of our lives had gradually bled all over our house, books and notebooks and newspapers and phones in the bathroom, bedroom, lounge, kitchen, a melding of borders, a submergence in work. There were no books apparent in Celia's house, until you checked, or were allowed to check, the big double cupboard crammed from top to bottom in alphabetical order with paperbacks. Amis, Bukowski, Conrad, Nancy Friday, Rimbaud all fitted neatly in with a built-in computer desk, on which an Apple Powerbook sat in solid, sleek, ineffably grey splendour. Taped to it was a small signed photograph of that Irish intellectual thug, some kind of poet, who sits in judgement on all forms of creative endeavour on that BBC2 wank review programme. Some kind of thinking woman's fantasy shag, no doubt. I couldn't see it myself.

Neat neat neat. Damned neat. The lounge was a tiny space which fooled you into thinking it was bigger by the use of rock-hard Japanese futons, walls in three different shades of white and clever lighting. No clutter of wires and amplifiers, but a tiny stereo hidden in a fake Shaker cupboard, along with a substantial, and uncompromisingly unfeminine CD collection: the complete works of Neil Young, including the crap country albums and that dire '50s pop pastiche *Everybody's Rockin'*. Sometimes we had fucked to the white noise bleeping of *Trans*, to oddly good effect. And of course nearly everything ever done by the obscure Peter Case, including a dreadful album called *Six Pack of Love*, which Celia liked, perversely. It contained one song which was breathtakingly, movingly good: *Beyond the Blues*. Would that I were.

Here in fluffiness central, things looked a little different after Celia had been sick again – no blood, thank fuck – over her lovely baby bed, and I had stripped it, put the soiled linen in the washing machine, and lifted her onto the bare mattress. It was free of dried semen stains. That was the condom effect. Once, pre-AIDS, mattresses of breeding age had been faded maps of a thousand couplings, in shades of sepia. Now they remained apparently pure and lying in their virginity. All I had to do now was leave her, go home.

But I didn't. I wanted her to wake up feeling as though there was some hope of recovery, not like some discarded Tennent's can, half full of fag ends and spit and flat lager, ripped and crushed by careless hands. So I got some cotton-wool from the bathroom and cleaned off the already Alice Cooper-like make-up. She was half awake, slipping in and out of sleep and sorrow.

'Don't hurt me.' Christ. Could I take off her clothes without getting an erection? No, but fuck me, big boys have got to get beyond that sort of thing. 'Don't hurt me. I'm sorry . . . I'm so . . . sorry.'

'Come on, Celia, let's get you undressed.' What was I, a nurse or something? What about the great seduction scenarios, all the painful paying for the tentative right to snap a brassière, finger a nipple, check if thighs had been shaved?

'Oh . . . Okay. I'm sorry.'

'I won't hurt you. I promise. I'm not going to have sex with you. No date-rape diggling, no nothing. I'm not going to . . . to take advantage of you . . .'

'Don't hurt me.'

I did, a bit. She was sluggish in her movements, and bits and pieces of clothing caught and snapped and stung. I tried not to let her warmth and nakedness stir me. The aroma of vomit was not inducing much flaccidity, to my surprise. Sickness is the great flaccidiser, after all. I was disgusted with myself. I felt oddly reassured by that.

I wrapped an old satin dressing-gown around her, then a coverless duvet, by which time she was drifting on the borders of consciousness. 'Can I have . . . a drink of something. Not . . . not alco . . . alcohol.' I gave her the small bottle of Evian. It stayed down. Her eyes closed, and I carefully positioned her on her side, though there couldn't have been anything much left to do that old Jimi Hendrix boke'n'choke thing with. I left the bag of goodies, the fizzy drinks and the sweeties, beside her on the floor, kissed her on the eyelids, and left, feeling as honourable as the Pope – well, one of the more recent Popes – only so aroused I could barely walk.

Maybe if I'd been able to perambulate more easily I would have gone straight past the cupboard containing Celia's Mac, not opened the doors, pressed the on-button at the back of the laptop. I did it without thinking, knowing what I would find, somewhere on that diminutive hard disk. It was an old 150, with a trackball and the feel of a Tonka Toy. *Welcome to Macintosh*: the desktop had two locked files on it, with their little Mac images of belts and padlocks. One was called Zander; the other Victor. I wondered what was in them. A comparison of sexual techniques? Performance statistics? A bitter shrivelling removed any need, or hope, of masturbation. The pity, love or whatever fell away. I felt ... alone. It was just as well I had no idea of the passwords needed to access the files. Maybe. Anyway, I knew enough. Too much. I went to the Special menu, dragged and dropped to shutdown. The computer whined into silence. A light, guttural snoring came from the bedroom.

It was a Sneck Sunday night, with all kinds of crawling constabulary to be concerned with, so I checked Riefenstahl's back seat for roaches, and found one small remnant of my earlier passengers on the floor. No doubt some sniffing spaniel would find enough to convict me of possessing 0.0008 grammes, sending Nicky Shearer, upholder of the law, into paroxysms of ecstasy with a small 'e', but fuck it. I would have my day in court. Vacuuming could wait. I drove back to The Tub, thinking about Celia, about Victor, and the nature of love and chance.

If I'd stayed, allowed my emotions and loins to be swayed by her weakness, Celia and I might have woken in the morning and played some skin games. It was the Kingsley Amis cure for a hangover, and Celia would not only be looking for emotional succour, she would want to distract herself physically from the horrors of post-party existence. And she was good at games. In fact, buying the Mars Bar had, perhaps subconsciously, not just been out of a desire to replenish her depleted blood sugar. We had gone the Marianne Faithfull route before, with conspicuous success, although the sheets had needed a full boil wash with Ariel to sort out the resultant mess. That had been a hangover fuck, otherwise I doubt if I'd have remembered it. I wondered if it was in that locked file on the Mac. And what else might be there.

There were toys lurking about that sweet and innocent bedroom, too. I recalled waking from a slobberingly drunken stupor to find myself blindfolded and tied to the bedposts by both hands, with silk scarfs no less. There had followed an episode involving ice-cream, neat gin and golden syrup, salt and sugar, lit candles, dripping wax – oh yes, all that Madonnaesque stuff. Which was fine until after I came, all too quickly, I'm afraid, and panicked myself into ripping the scarves, fighting my way out of the fantasy in a sweating, palpitating panic attack. Celia had just laughed. I asked if she would like something similar done to herself and she said no, she hated to feel out of control. And I said, don't you realise how much this sort of thing is really about male control? It's a symbol, really, of your weakness, a sort of pathetic playtime revenge . . . and she said, you like it, though, don't you? Which I didn't deny.

I woke to the telephone's hysterical shriek. Light was streaming in through the skylights, and a glance at the old Rolex showed that it was 11 a.m. I would have to get going.

'Hello?' I was expecting a female voice.

'Zander?' But not this one. A different life came rushing back. It was Lucy. Time stood still, then went into tyre-smoking, rubber-howling, tarmac-melting reverse. Of all people, it was Lucy. Lucy, my former wife; my former life, leaver of vicious messages on my answer machine. 'Are you okay? Are you sober?' Welcome home, honey.

'Course I'm fuckin' sober. On the wagon for . . . weeks now.' I smelt my armpit. Fish and oil, still, mixed with sweat and smoke from last night. Could it be an aphrodisiac? Doubtful. Not over the phone, anyway. From nowhere, the aroma that was Lucy: Armani Giò, a sharp tang of clean sweat. Sex. Oh no, not now. An erection tangled with the sheets distracted me. Being male can be such a pain in the ass. 'How are you, anyway? How's the young Robert Maxwell? Buoyant? Still forging ahead on the road to being a media monopolist?'

'Oh . . . yes, fine. Working hard. We're moving into a new flat in Hyndland soon. Four bedrooms, and a drawing-room for entertaining. I'm freelancing the PR stuff, getting one or two wee contracts, you know . . .'

'Lucy?'

'Yes?' An edginess. Something more.

'Why the hell are you phoning me on a Monday morning?'

'Why? Oh, just . . . I was wondering . . . well. Victor said . . .'

'Victor? My brother?'

'Well, not the manufacturer of electric fucking razors, you twerp.' Ah yes, the cut-throat blade that was the Lucy tongue, unsheathed at last. Vague mumbling had never suited Lucy. 'He said you weren't well. That you were drinking too . . . in fact he said you were a hopeless alcoholic, which was hardly news to me. That he was worried about you. Worried about what you might do. Seemed to think that would bother me. Frankly, I'd have happily seen you dead.'

'When was this?'

'Saturday. I mean, I obviously wasn't . . . I mean, to be honest I couldn't have cared less. But then, what the hell, I thought I'd better check if you were at least alive. There might still be some insurance policies in our joint names, after all.' She laughed. So did I. There weren't.

'And did he want to know if I'd been in touch, anything like that?'

'Well, he wondered if I thought I could do anything. I said any concern I had for you had been deep-frozen the night you threw me and Frederick out into the snow, you bastard. Christ I . . . oh, never mind.'

'So, it's still Frederick, is it? Not Fred? Or Freddy? Maybe you two should get on familiar terms . . . Anyway, what can I tell you? I was pissed, and pissed off. It was just a gesture. I fell asleep. You know that . . .'

'He said . . . Victor said . . . now what was it exactly? Yes. He said you needed protection from yourself. That you always had done. And of course, I agreed.'

'So.'

'So.' There was period of crackling phone-breathing. 'Not that you should get concerned that I'm about to jump back into your sordid and doubtless pathetic little life. I mean, private detective, for God's sake. I know you always had a fantasy about it, but sniffing around some poor adulterer's underwear . . .'

'You should know all about adulterous underwear, my dear.'

'Aw, fuck you, then. I was just . . . Jesus, I almost said concerned . . . curious about your well-being. For old times' sake. I should have known better.'

'Do you miss me?'

'Only the good bits. There was a pleasant enough five minutes in total, I'd say. I'm pregnant, by the way.'

Cold dark nothingness. 'Congratulations.' Ah yes. Here was the reason for phoning. The best revenge. And Victor had probably put her up to it. 'Did you . . . listen, just tell me this: did you tell Victor about your imminent . . . being with child, before he told you about me?'

A crackling silence.

'Well, yes. He just phoned because he'd heard we might be moving . . . I think.'

Ah yes. Victor, who knew everything. Information was power, communication its enforcement.

Still, the nagging hollowness was hard to fill with jaggy wee words. There was a bit of verbal to-ing and fro-ing, some niceties, some nastinesses, whens, marriage, was it, will you, a few inquiries about my parents, had I seen them. No, of course not. But the conversation had run out of fuel. Victor and the dregs of whatever had fired our love had provoked the call; and hatred, of course, revenge. Frederick gave me what you wouldn't. Couldn't. Think of his cock, think of how good it is compared to yours, his sperm so much better, stronger . . . No thanks. Not in the mood for a jizz competition, thank you. And Victor. Forcing, pushing me, all the time in one direction. Well, there was no point in avoiding him, in resisting. It was time to settle the whole business.

Only the good bits, she'd said. That was a woman for you. Pragmatism. Reality. Truth. Only the good bits. Suddenly I wondered if big brother was tapping into this line, checking up on me electronically. Could he do that? Oh yes. But it didn't matter. I was beyond paranoia.

I phoned Celia, and after about a dozen rings, during which I imagined all kinds of suffocations and chokings, the personification of privet-hedge gorgeousness picked up.

'This is your morning alarm call,' I said. 'Confirm, please, that there is life after hedgerow penetration.'

There was a long pause, and then a faraway, phlegm-ridden voice said: 'Don't hurt me,' and I said I would do my best not to, bright and breezy and feeling a dead, lead weight in my chest. 'I'm sorry, Zander. I thought it was . . . I was trying to help . . . and protect myself.'

'I don't know what you mean,' I said, gently, ashes forming in my throat. I swallowed them. 'I'll be away for a few days.'

I resolutely ignored the black hole of emotion on the end of the line. I couldn't be drawn into that. I wouldn't. It was a mess, she was a mess, and while some spark of cheap love lurked amid the past lust, I couldn't be brought down by it. Not now. Not again. No looking back. Don't look down. I was on my way to begin or end something which went way, way back, further than sex, beyond betrayal. I was equipped, just maybe, to cope. Something steely had emerged in me, and I was determined not to lose it. The hardness, the ruthlessness. I liked it.

'Wh . . . where?'

I paused. Was Victor listening? Fuck it. Fuck him.

'Home,' I said. 'Tell Victor that. I'm coming home.'

'Don't . . . don't hurt . . . me.'

But I already had. She had hurt me, too, but I didn't feel it. I was beyond that now.

I called Hernia at his surgery, but a puzzled and flustered receptionist told me he hadn't turned up for that morning's clinic. Did I know where he was? I said I didn't, and tried his home. The fucking answer machine was on. I didn't leave a message. I hoped he was all right. Or did I? No. Not really.

I showered for half an hour, until I couldn't smell my Ullapool self. The radio was warbling about divers finding several bodies in the sunken hulk of the Spanish-owned klondiker *Margarita*, but it was well down the news priorities, after some stuff about one of the Foreign Secretary's old affairs, some footballer beating up his wife and a pop star's suicide. The usual. I was packed and ready to leave when I remembered the Guardian, my little avenging angel. I opened the Anne Frank secret anti-Nazi cupboard and retrieved it, clumsily checking the magazine, removing the bullet which was in the breech, ready for instant firing, and slotted it back into the magazine. Good to go. Four shots left. I dropped it into my trusty Adidas bag, and then noticed the mobile phone lying dead and discharged on the coffee table. I'd had enough of being a communicable person. I left it where it was. Fuck communication. Look where it had got me.

It was a beautiful day, one of those days at the very cusp of summer, when everything has ripened to the utmost, is on the edge of turning to decay, beginning the slow slide into autumn, just a whiff of its golden chill lurking behind every too-green bush, every perfect flower. The canal was alive. Thomas Telford must have been smiling down from heaven as two Bewick swans and three eiders paddled sedately along, and a wee boy fished in crazed and useless hope on the opposite bank. Two big ocean-going yachts passed me, their inboard diesels chugging throatily, heading for the locks at Muirtown, and eventually the open sea. I felt my spirits lift as I watched them, and wished I was on board, moving inexorably towards the pure joy and risk of the open sea. Then I thought of the wankers who could afford such big boys' toys, and junked the thought. Canoeing. That was what I should do. Kayaking, not that stupid slalom stuff down sewage-ridden rivers, but out in the pure, salt ocean, half-submerged in it, journeying alone. Fighting the big breakers, getting fit, communing with myself.

My, but wouldn't that be an ugly conversation, I thought, doing it. Eichmann and Goebbels together in the one canoe. Saddam and Qaddafi, Thatcher and Joseph, Benn and Blair, Mandelson and Skinner, Woodward and Colson . . . Still, there was something appealing about a canoe. Like paragliding, it was a fantasy. In one you were a bird, in the other a, well . . . a duck or a swan. Or a big fat human in a stupid little boat. Meanwhile, I had a bigger ship to catch.

I retraced the route of my ill-fated escape from the Granite City, stopping in Keith for a dismal lunch among the cooperage reek of old brandy barrels, broken up for remaking into whisky casks. I breathed deeply, ate my bad bacon roll, drank the fake cappuccino served by the grimy café which had an Italian name and no pride whatsoever. Nescafé with aerosol whipped cream on top.

Doom gathered in my heart the closer to Aberdeen I got along the snaking, juggernaut-cursed A96. The smell of pigs came and went most of the way between Sneck and Elgin, with thousands of the porkfuckers free-ranged cynically in tin huts on both sides of the road. Then chemically fertilised fertility through Moray, the aroma of phosphate and soil baking in the sun. Up over the Grampians, feeling as if the road was running gingerly atop shifting rock strata, then down, down towards the sea, into an enveloping fog, the North Sea's chilling haar, merging with more and more industry and housing and the sure oily reek of money. Reaching the shadowy glimpse of warehouses and blue water, the metallic shriek of invisible gulls said, as ever, 'Fuck off unless you can afford me.' Aberdeen.

I parked Riefenstahl in a multi-storey by the station, feeling the old kick of imminent departure, that sense of leaving. The waterfront fog was shifting, choking. A classic frontier port, Aberdeen, sliding down one edge of its jutting sea-ledge to the beach, on the other to the harbour, with all the self-important granite buildings marching determinedly away from the source of the place's income. Without thinking, I headed for Marks and Spencer's, and loaded up with pre-packed bourgeois boatfood. Salads and ciabatta, fresh strawberries, mineral water. Things you could never get on the ferry. A last taste of the mainland, and an ingrained islander's habits. Home. It wasn't my home, it fucking wasn't, not any more. But there was nowhere else.

I checked to see if the Canadian Muffin Company still existed, catering for transatlantic oil workers homesick for oat bran and industrial-strength caffeine. It did, and so I lost myself in the papers over a succession of espressos, until I could feel the blood pounding in my temples, and the print was jumping in front of my eyes. Five unidentified bodies had been recovered from the *Margarita*, and the authorities were certain that was the lot. No suspicious circumstances.

What? It didn't make sense. Assuming Manuel and Smith and the faux-Thiebaults had been . . . unless they were still . . . no. Involuntarily, I looked over my shoulder, half expecting some seaweed-encrusted zombie to come waddling up, smelling of rotten mackerel. *The Fog*, John Carpenter's slick, silly and still deliciously frightening film. I looked out of the window. The air was like milk out there.

I slowly wandered through the swirling streets, half-feeling that I should be swimming in the near-liquid murk, down to the P&O terminal, where I booked an open return, single-occupancy cabin to Lerwick for that night's sailing aboard the *St Sunniva*. The former Baltic ferry loomed above, indistinct in the mist. I hadn't been on board her since the last refit; longer. Now I was going home, not as I'd expected, for the death of a parent or in a sudden collapsing of pride, a search for forgiveness and family roots. Not in warmth and weakness, but in coldness and strength. Fear, yes, but a kind of solid, banked-up anger, too.

I felt strong, invulnerable. In the pocket of my lightweight Schoffel jacket I touched the cold weight of the Guardian. Being able to carry it with impunity was one reason for taking the boat.

No drink. No cigarettes. Leaving Aberdeen was a good time for both, but no. Even a whiff of fag reek was enough to take me right back to the strangely objective horrors of Ullapool and, more precisely, a disgust at the way I'd smelt. Smell and memory. The keys to consciousness, said Freud, a stogie-smoker. He must have stunk like an ashtray. Died of mouth cancer. Stick a phallic symbol in your mouth, see what happens to you.

For old times' sake I wandered over to the dismal leaving-of-land bar called the Shipmate, a 1970s mess of stained wood and buttoned plastic built in the bottom of a prefabricated office block. The smell of imminent departure hit me as soon as I entered. It was packed. Of course, the fog would have grounded every Shetland-bound plane, and this was the result. A hundred or so travellers who had paid hundreds of pounds for the hour-and-a-half hop by battered Advanced Turbo Prop crap-plane or rattling Shorts Flying Transit . . . aircraft which had been flying the route for decades. Now this would-be airfreight was faced with fourteen hours all at sea accompanied by dozens of freight-container lorries, cars, sheep, cows and a couple of hundred people, tourists and returning inhabitants, who had actually chosen to travel by boat. Mad bastards. I was one of them.

For me, there was no rush. I knew that now. I knew he'd be waiting for me, one way or the other. And besides, I hated to fly, particularly where propellers were involved. If I was to make the trip back home, I wanted to feel the distance, understand what I was doing, physically adjust to the sea-change I would be making in myself. To re-establish that Shetland was far from . . . anywhere. The fact that the Guardian would be undetected, due to the lack of security checks, was an added bonus. I had grown used to its comfort.

A few half-known faces from the deeply repressed memory which was now breaking up and open nodded at me. There were one or two 'Aye, boy – how's du?' remarks, and then I was at the bar, ordering ginger beer and lime in a world of dark rum and Tennent's Special. A hand closed on my upper arm, not painfully, but unignorably strong. I turned, with a sinking heart and ready to grin the 'Christ, how are you' grin which I'd been preparing for just such an eventuality. The prodigal returns. But the wiry man in the expensive suit was utterly unfamiliar. He spoke with an English accent, and had the rolling pleasant tones of a radio phone-in host on some Essex local station: 'Zander? Could we talk for five minutes? Please. Just a quick word.' Not once did he let go of my arm.

My soft drink arrived.

'Let me get that – want a small vodka to go with it? Here, I'll . . .'

'No thanks.' I picked up the green and grey fog-like drink and followed him to a corner near the door. 'Who the hell are you?'

He smiled, the corners of his eyes crinkling in an attractive, Paul Newmanesque way. Except the irises were a dead grey colour. Like my drink. Like the fog outside. He was of medium height, thin without being emaciated. Possibly very fit under the expensive cream linen-mix suit. 'I'm no one,' he said, the voice now more starkly revealed as flatly received pronunciation, featureless and characterless as a Docklands newly built apartment building. 'Just a message boy. A request service, I suppose. I'm to ask you please' – the 'please' was the wrong side of sarcasm – 'not to go to Shetland.'

I laughed. 'On whose behalf do you, em, make this request, oh messenger of the gods?'

'Oh, the people I represent have your best interests at heart, Mr Flaws. And our authority has official . . . roots. I believe you may have had contact with one of our representatives, already. Somewhat . . . intimately.' There was the suggestion of a leer. 'Rosie sends her . . . felicitations. We could ensure that your business flourishes, should you decide to continue in the world of investigative endeavour. Or we could . . . prevent you flourishing. We might even work together. Or we could terminate your faltering business altogether.'

'With extreme fucking prejudice, no doubt.' I could feel my throat closing and drying at the urban, urbane fear wielded by this lump of privileged Englishness. Racism kicked in, fuelled by the threat he represented. He just smiled blandly, rolling his empty vowels around his throat, ready to trundle them out when necessary. I would have liked to ram his nose through his frontal lobes, but I had a feeling he would have me in some nasty karate hold before I'd dropped my drink.

'I'm past caring, pal. If you want to stop me, you and your people will have to kill me now. Let's be precise and straightforward about this, shall we? That's what you're threatening, isn't it?'

'Oh, don't be so melodramatic, Mr Flaws . . . Zander. Tell me, have you ever heard of a man called Georgi Markov?' He was reaching for his pocket. Christ, it would have to be a very small umbrella he had in that suit of his. Or just a pointy thing, a pencil or a pen with poison in the tip. Oh, don't be stupid, Zander . . . and then some great slab of insight came slamming in: *This is why they succeed, these people. Because their victims don't believe it can possibly be happening to them . . .*

Just then I was grabbed around the neck by a forearm which felt like a particularly flexible crocodile tail, extra-large. '*Fuck!* It's peerie Zander, the lost bairn o' Vallataing! Faur's du been, boy?'

I twisted my head just enough to see the massive, sunrise-red face of Morris O' Da Grice, whose dad had kept pigs – *Grice* is the Shetland word for pigs – on the croft three miles from ours. He had always been a delightful giant, Morris; his real surname was Gillockson. Loyal, clever and with a kind of quicksilver violence when he or his cohorts were threatened.

'Thank fuck it's dee, Morris. Get me awa from dis bastart. He's a fuckin' bailiff trying to get me car aff me. Twa fuckin' missed payments and . . .'

And the face of the man in the nice suit exploded. Morris was like a nitro-fuelled juggernaut when roused, and the mere mention of bailiffs or debt-collectors had a bad effect on him. Very bad. His father, mother and indeed the young Morris had been turned out of their Brae council house for an unpaid debt, and it had left its mark on the boy. Handily, as it happened. Now leaving marks was something Morris did rather well.

I grabbed the massive, bloodied fist and led Morris out of the door. Those in our immediate vicinity had moved away quickly, but as most of them were self-sufficiently hard oil workers or transfer crew for oilfield standby boats, they showed only mild curiosity, if any. The neat man lay unconscious on the floor, covered in beer and blood.

'Onyway,' said Morris, a huge Viking Beefeater smile splitting his face, 'how's du?'

We went aboard the *Sunniva*. Nobody chased us, and we drank appalling machine coffee on the soft seats next to the little shop, where that week's *Shetland Times* was on sale. I didn't buy one. We talked about the past, easily. No mention of Ruth. And then Morris said: 'Dy bridder? Doin' weel, eh? Weel for Vallataing, and Shetland, tae. And dy folks must be blyth aboot him settin' up by dem.'

I just made affirmative noises, the intakes of breath, clicks and 'aye' sounds which can pass for conversation in the Northern Isles.

'Aye, and Victor, I see him in da Lounge, occasionally, haein' a tune, wi' dat box o' his. He's no' bad. Strange instrument, da squeezebox. Soonds lik' he's been practisin'.'

I had an ear cocked for the sound of an ambulance or police siren, but none came. Eventually I walked out on deck as six o'clock and departure loomed. If they were going to come for me, it would have to be now. A Range Rover was parked on the cobbled quay, and I could just see a slumped figure in the passenger seat, dressed in what looked very like cream linen soiled with something dark. Leaning on the bonnet was Rosie. Her eyes tracked the upper decks of the ship, and eventually locked on to mine. She was wearing a business suit, and her hair was pinned back formally. Slowly, she raised one hand, the palm open. It looked like a signal giving permission to leave, rather than farewell. I hoped it meant there was no ruthlessly efficient representative of her superiors on board. She climbed into the big green car and drove off. Her legs looked fantastic in the short skirt she was wearing. The formal power of sexuality.

The *St Sunniva* set sail with a mournful howl from her siren and a series of announcements which attempted to convince everyone on board that the great tank of the car deck was safe from water penetration – at least it was now that the ship's bow door had been welded shut, as was the case for all ships on this, the most dangerous and longest of any ferry service in British waters. Aberdeen slowly slipped past, and then away, with the rest of Britain.

And the bar opened. I rejoined Morris, sketched in a few lines of my life, drank Pepsi, and watched Morris drink, his repetitiveness growing, inevitably, with can after can of McEwan's Export and nips of Stewart's Rum. 'Aye,' he said, 'dy brother has done a grat thing for Vallataing, what with the cages and the hatchery. Some isnae dayin' sae weel wi' da salmon, but he's fuckin' thrivin'. Ah'm on a salmon farm mesel, oot by Unst. Can't work oot hoo Victor's dayin' it. Anywa', he cam back and plooed his cash into the community. Fine ting, dat. Cam back. Fine ting, dat.'

I clapped Morris on the back and smiled. 'Du's right dere,' I said. 'A fine thing.'

My cabin was already assigned, but I went to the purser's office and bought another, very expensive single-occupancy top-deck cabin with an outside window. In the name of Wendell Gee. I doubted that characters from old REM songs would be recognised or considered suspicious, should anyone on board be after me. I had seen no sidelong glances from out-of-place strangers in this mêlée of smoking, drinking, falling-over returnees and befuddled, aged holidaymakers, their colostomy bags lumpily visible beneath their nylon leisure suits. I dumped my bags in the new cabin, then went back to Morris in the bar, where a truly mind-shatteringly awful band had begun to play, a duo with a drum machine and pre-programmed synth lines. It was like New York's Suicide doing karaoke covers of *Ruby, Don't Take Your Love to Town*, and *Ten Guitars*. The singer looked like Tony Blair's father-in-law, the one who used to be on *Till Death Us Do Part*, and sang like the guy out of Spandau Ballet. Yes, that bad. I bagged myself up with mineral water and enjoyed the inventive brutality of the insults suffered by the hapless, hopeless group, which was called Diamond Delight. ('Fuck off! Du's fit for nithin but da slurry pit!' 'Na na, da slurry reek's better as yon!')

Morris had been absorbed into a party of similarly large men, circling a central table and happily criticising the band with the epithets of crofting and fish-farming. But Morris had won the Shetland Young Fiddler of the Year competition at the age of eleven, and still, he told me, played every weekend he could in a country band 'wi' a peerie bit Grappelli and Coltrane for da fun o' it'. He had a perfect right to be aesthetically offended.

Avoiding any semblance of open deck, rails for the pushing over, I went to my cabin and locked the door. It was a calm night and the ship creaked slightly, but didn't pitch or roll much. I slipped into the familiarity of the movement, the kind of slow shiver as we voyaged north, two hundred nautical miles north, halfway to Norway. I felt the pull of it, the delight of distance. And the nagging, gnawing terror was a kind of pleasure, too.

My Marks and Spencer's spoils lay around me uneaten. I had no appetite for them. I kept my clothes on, pulled out the Guardian, ratcheted a round into the breech, and put the safety catch off, then on again. I was staring at the door, listening for footfalls, amid the muffled echoes of *Billy Don't Be A Hero* from a distant Diamond Delight, when I fell asleep. I dreamed of canoes with ducks paddling them.

★ Nineteen

Wakening into childhood. That first trip away, aged . . . I don't know. Five? Victor, sullen, smartass, superior, lurking in the top bunk, E deck in the old *St Clair*, stinking of oil and cattle. The voice crackling through the Tannoy seemed unchanged: 'Good morning, ladeez and genteelmentt. The time is 6.30. Six . . . thirty . . . ay . . . emm. Hot meals and snacks will be served in the Pentland Grill from seven ay emm. Our estimated time of arrival in Lerwick is seven forty-five ay emm.'

A wild excitement, a kind of bubbling breathlessness at the impending homecoming. Out on the deck to see Lerwick, sleeping and grey, slip past. Jumping convulsively in terror as the great, world-shoogling blast of the ship's hooter echoed off the stone faces of the houses, shaking every membrane in my body. Home. Wanting to be there, being drawn to it like a migrating bird, an eel to the same old spawning stream.

Now I stood on the deck as the familiar huddled town passed by, braced for the honking howl of the ship's hooter, but getting a fright nevertheless. And crying my fucking eyes out.

It was raining. That was one good thing. The precipitation hid the tears, as it did for several dozen other returnees. I looked at the low morning shape of Shetland and wondered what the hell I was doing, why I felt like this. And I knew that the connection was blood deep, soil deep, rock deep, ocean deep into the low land and the sea surrounding. I still hated the place, had never wanted to be there again, admitting the relationship. But the truth of it poured down my face with the drizzle.

I made my way through the crowd of haggard, drawn, hungover victims waiting to disembark, picked up my bag from the cabin, and headed for dry land myself. On the way I looked into the bar. There sprawled Morris in one of the booths, snoozing with apparent comfort in the company of two other equally large men I didn't recognise. In front of them were about thirty empty Export cans, the original red ones, neatly piled in a tower, balanced on top of one another. Clearly it had been a calm night. On the pier, I felt my body momentarily lurch, then regain its equilibrium. It didn't matter that it had been a quiet crossing. Boat balance for me took time to wear off. By the time I reached the terminal building, I was walking in a straight line. At least I hadn't fallen off Shetland yet.

The girl at the hire-car desk had been at school with me. I hadn't seen her for a quarter of a century, and her first words were classic: 'Aye aye, Zander – hamefarin' fir lang? How is du ee noo?'

I tried to smile, mumbled non-committal answers without enquiring about her own life, basically because I couldn't remember her name. I thanked her for the keys, and she said, 'Dy bridder's doin' affy weel wi da salmon. Fine boost for Vallataing.'

I nodded, smiled. I was getting more than sick of how well my brother was doing. No mention of Ruth, at least. Maybe Victor had been right. Maybe the forgiveness or at least the forgetting of a small community was a healing process.

Maybe if I went to Whalsay, knocked at the door of her no doubt beautifully appointed fisher-family superhouse, I would be welcomed by sunny smiles from Ruth and her mackerel-millionaire husband, asked to sit down, be given a cup of tea and invited to chat about the new abortion laws. Sure.

The hire car was a Mondeo, soulless efficiency with power steering so light you could drive the thing with one pinky. I spun around Lerwick, which seemed much the same, apart from a new supermarket on the southern outskirts, and the Clickimin Sports Centre which seemed to have quadrupled in size. Oil cash, I supposed. Now my brother was coming with his salmon cash, or whatever it was.

The plastic coiling tubes called flumes indicated a new swimming-pool. Maybe fishermen were taught to swim nowadays; I remembered two or three of the boys in my class refusing to learn, just before they went off as crew on their dads' boats, because the lore was that knowing how to swim was unlucky. That it was better to sink, to die quickly than let the salt cold get you. Me, I always thought it as well to have a breaststroke at your command, plus plenty of body fat and the prospect of a helicopter hovering near by if at all possible.

The café at the Co-op was open, so I breakfasted there, surprisingly well, on one of those £2.99-for-eight-very-greasy-things offers, plus unlimited tea. The *Shetland Times* was available to read, crumpled and stained by thousands of fingers, so I skimmed through it. 'New Atlantic field comes on-stream' was the splash. A killer whale had been seen off Sumburgh, down in the south of the main island where the airport was. A dozen two-paragraph court reports all contained somewhere the word 'drunk'. I passed an hour or so reacquainting myself with the delights of classified adverts for sheepdogs, quad bikes and 'wedding and matching bridesmaids dresses, never used', until the store opened. Then I bought some flowers, a box of chocolates and an aerosol can of oven cleaner, and headed out of town. I was partial to a spot of oven cleaner.

Going north you climb out of Lerwick, through an unashamed shambles of industrial buildings, pipeyards, and muddy side roads which lead to straggly docklands. Nothing is prettified. It is a functional town, with its own special beauty only if you look for it. I never had. I wound down past the golf course, where I could see one or two distant figures, bent like hunchbacks, gathering something from the dewy grass. Christ, it was that time of year, right enough. The end of the summer. Magic mushrooms, the best in the world, they said. I grinned. I'd never tried them. They said older Shetlanders would take them when they ran out of drink. Maybe I could substitute them for the Big Ethyl.

Then up again and down into the Tingwall valley, a kind of oasis in the peat desert which is the rest of the mainland. About thirty miles north was the oil terminal, Sullom Voe, with its eternal flarestack looking like either an Olympic torch or a permanent tactical nuclear explosion, depending on your point of view and the cloud cover. I turned off, past the little airstrip which served the outer isles, and headed west.

The road to Vallataing had been widened and resurfaced. There was a sharp tang of new tar, and the straggly sun which had broken through the cloud picked out thin wisps of steam from the smooth blue-black surface. Shaven summer sheep wandered in scrawny supremacy, fine-tuning my skills at braking and mutton-avoidance. As I wound around the coast, the wide bay called Ranwick appeared, the flawless golden sand running in a perfect crescent until the sharp black volcanic rock which jutted suddenly up, then curved deeply into a small natural harbour. Vallataing.

The house, perhaps half a mile from the shore, at the top of a rise which was mostly rough grazing land, but partly pockmarked with cultivation, was the same as it had always been. A big traditional croft house, extended approximately in character, to the side and back, painted white, smoking from the Rayburn chimney at the ben end.

I felt calm, but suddenly awfully sad. Before the road reached the house, where it stopped, a new track had been built down to the water's edge, where a raw concrete pier now fingered out into the sea, towards the four round salmon cages in the middle of Ran Voe. A large gouge had been taken out of the slope behind the pier, and from it a big white extruded metal shed protruded. Four tank-like structures, round and open, adjoined it. I stopped at the beginning of the track at the sign which read 'Vallataing Salmon', and looked at the boat anchored out in the voe, near the cages. She was a trawler, old but apparently well maintained, and not of typical Scottish design. Big drift-netter was my guess, no longer commercially viable, and probably with her fish holds converted for hauling salmon smolts. She could have been Spanish or French. My bet was Spanish.

I drove down the pier and parked the car. It was about half past ten in the morning and, as was typical, the sun had swept away the morning's bad weather with an easy contempt. Suddenly, the Arctic had become the Mediterranean, unless you were foolish enough to try the temperature of the water, which would be penis-shrivellingly icy. With the engine off, I savoured the silence. A seal popped its head out of the water and observed me like a small submarine with whiskers. I wondered if there were still otters around, or if they'd been frightened away by all the building work. Or shot because of the salmon.

There was the distant sound of a two-stroke engine, louder and louder until the smell of burnt oil grew overpowering, and a motorcycle appeared. The figure on it, dressed in orange oilskins, dismounted and heaved the small bike onto a centre stand. It was a beautifully restored Yamaha RD400, one of the highest performance air-cooled two-strokes ever made, and a real 1970s hooligan bike for teenagers. I'd always dreamed of owning one, when I was young, hormonal and brave.

'Nice bike,' I said.

'Yeah,' came an American voice, young, full of the morning's good cheer and all his nation's infuriating bigness and confidence. 'Some folks swear by Harleys, but I hate that goddamned thumping tractor engine. This is one of the most efficient engines ever designed. Still wheelie it in third, man. Whooo-hoo!' He removed the helmet. Dark hair, friendly eyes, about twenty-four or twenty-five.

I cleared my throat. 'Roger?'

He said nothing, but his eyes shifted a little to one side. Then from behind me, came a voice. 'Welcome home, Zander.'

Victor was cradling a rifle, and not a rabbit-removing .22; he was wearing a blue boilersuit and white wellies, topped with a camouflage jacket. He looked like a cross between a fishworker and a mercenary, aptly enough.

'Hi,' I said. 'You never told me you were the king of Vallataing.'

'You never asked. You never asked Mum and Dad, so they never told you. Besides. I asked them not to. Supposing you ever saw fit to get in touch with them. Call it . . . a surprise.'

'See them a lot, do you?'

'When I'm here, yes. Thinking of moving the whole Glendruin operation up here, actually. I've got planning permission for a house just along from the croft. Combine the two businesses. You know. Efficiency.'

'And what two businesses might those be, Victor?' A sudden screaming desire for a fag hit me, as fear and a kind of condensation of everything that had happened at Ullapool swept over me. I fought it, and the tremor in my voice, down.

Victor grinned at me, all fraternal. I wondered if he was mad. How mad he was. How mad we both were. It's good to have you here, Zander.

At last. It's all worked out. Of course, there have been one or two wee –'

I interrupted his bullshit: 'So, you and Mum and Dad, best of pals, is it? The wanderer returned, all forgiven?'

He looked past me at Roger, who was watching, sardonically amused, his arms folded. 'Okay, Rog – better get inside, get to work.' The black-haired boy, still grinning, turned away and went inside the shed.

'I hear you're doing lots of good things for Shetland,' I said. I was determined not to hear what he'd said to me, about things working out. Because I knew, I already knew. But I didn't want to admit it. I couldn't. 'But where are the local employees? That there boy ain't from around here, is he?'

'Well, you know how it is. Hatcheries don't need too much maintenance, and Roger can look after it on his own. Got two guys from round and about to look after the cages, and casual labour when we harvest the fish. But most of it's automated. We've got a computerised feeding system, the lot. Now you're here, you can –'

'And deliveries? All by sea?' I motioned towards the old trawler.

'By sea, yes. More direct. Less . . . hassle.' He motioned with the rifle. 'Want to come shoot some seals?'

'That's fucking illegal.'

'Not for salmon farmers threatened by depredations of stock. I've got a licence. To deal with, emm, natural predators. A pretty wide classification, don't you agree? And, peerie bridder, this is loaded.' He twitched the gun at me. 'Come on. Mind your . . . hand. We don't want any accidents.'

Another day, another boat. This one was aluminium, flat-bottomed and broad-beamed, powered by a massive Evinrude outboard. I was sent scrabbling along the bottom as Victor twisted the throttle and we surged almost upright in the water towards the nearest salmon cage, with its wooden walkway and silver threshing of crammed fish trapped with their pellets of rancid pilchard, organo-phosphates and pink dye to make their flesh look healthy.

Once he had tied up to it, we both climbed onto the wooden gang-plank, and stood about a metre apart, watching the teeming fish.

'Quarter of a million quid's worth here,' said Victor. 'Same in each of the other cages. But the bottom's dropping out of salmon. Need to move onto something more profitable. Halibut, maybe, if we can make it work.'

'Halibut,' I said. 'What about red herring?'

'Christ, you even talk like an imitation private dick. Red herring, is it? I would have thought you might've had enough of that. Like in Ullapool. Terrible business. I'm sorry you had that fucker Smith to deal with. I thought I'd paid him enough to negate any . . . personal animosity. It seems not.' He wheeled about suddenly, pulled back the rifle bolt, aimed and fired at a seal which had been watching us quizzically from about twenty yards away. He missed. The black rubber head disappeared.

'That was mackerel. Wrong time of year for herring,' I sighed. 'Pelagic species, though.'

A dreadful darkness was forming in my mind, just like in childhood, a sensation of utter helplessness compared to big brother, who had always known everything. I made a huge effort, got the words out, even though I could feel the edifice I'd built up over the past weeks falling apart, knew that sure and anything-but-steadfast inner collapse which came like an evil old friend, or relative. Which needed instant alcohol for running repairs.

'Can I . . . can I run something past you, Victor? As you've made patently clear, I'm just a Johnny-come-lately at this deductive stuff. You're the information specialist, the collator, the analyst. Tell me how it pans out to you. I mean . . . you know everything. Don't you?'

'Not everything, but a lot. Sure. In this instance.'

The sea was light, and while the cages were designed to be flexible, moving up and down with the swell, we were able to stand upright without the risk of being pitched into the silvery flicker of salmon. He was carrying the gun casually, in a huntin', shootin' and fishin' style. I suppose he was in a position to do all three if he could find a salmon big enough to shoot. In fact all he had to do was pull the trigger and something would die. I hoped it wouldn't be me. I put my hand in my jacket pocket, felt the tiny comfort of the Guardian, and the hidden cargo of its four remaining bullets. That was the thing about wee brothers. They didn't have the wherewithal to carry such weaponry. They were weak. Easy meat.

'Right. So let's see. We start with you leaving Shetland, I suppose,' I said.

'Leaving.'

'Yeah, that's right. You shoot me in the hand, and you leave. I never quite worked that out.'

'Easy. I'd had enough of you being the doted-on boy wonder, and then all the shit I had to put up with over The Accident' – pronounced with withering sarcasm – 'from Dad and Mum made me just want to . . . get out. So I did, and there was the army, waiting for me like a great big warm, louse-infested blanket. And it was good and it was lousy and of course it was everything Mum and Dad hated so much with their poxy radical big-fish-local-small-time bullshit.'

'But now they love you.'

'Oh, now they think I'm you and the best of me combined, recovered, repented, redeeming their precious little Shetland with renewable industry, just as the oil's running out. Your own departure nearly destroyed them, you know. It wasn't even as if they did you any harm, or hated you, ignored you like they did me. That's one of the reasons I decided to bring you back.'

'Bring me back?'

'Yeah. Set you a few tasks, send you off on a trail, get you to do a few things for me. And bring you back here. Here, to Mum, and Dad, and me.'

'You?'

'Yes, me. We can help you, Zander. I've told Mum and Dad about your . . . wee problems. And they feel sorry for you, like I do. It's time to come home. To the ones who love you.'

Christ, it was almost as if he meant it. I was speaking to myself then, not to him. Half-whispering to myself and the sea and the green and brown land, to the sky and the entire goddamned place. 'That was the problem, though. The smothering. And then Ruth, all the shit which seeped out about that, and marrying somebody they didn't like, and even worse, splitting up from her. And it was just . . . Shetland. Island life. I loved it, and then . . . I fucking hated it so much. I must have said some terrible things. And then I just stopped caring. Seemed to, anyway. Cut this place out of my life, out of my heart. And now I can't wait to get away. Yeah, maybe there's a bit of sentiment, some old stirrings. But this place isn't mine any more. It's yours. And I won't be part of your playpark, Victor.'

'Fucking hell, you can't think Inverness is paradise on earth. It's a fucking shit hole.'

I had to agree there. 'I've been working it all out, Victor, your plan for my ultimate welfare, if you want to call it that. And it all goes back to you and me, wee boys then, wee boys now. Doesn't it?'

'Does it?' He was gazing out to sea, where a small lobster boat was making its lumpy way in from the creels out past the headland.

'Oh, yes. You leave, and this is the big return, isn't it? In glory and triumph. With me in tow, ready to be saved? Did you think about it, all through that glitteringly dodgy army career, all the murky bits of economic and electronic spying, all your cyberspace business affairs at Glendruin? Did you imagine yourself as some kind of . . . emotional laird? I mean, how long have you been watching me, monitoring me? When did you start actually trying to play me like a Monopoly man? Was it the day I woke up at Flora Macdonald's feet?'

'Don't forget her dog. It has feet, too, and actually you can't see her feet for the dog's.'

'At the fucking dog's feet, then. And nearly got killed by a petty criminal psychopath called Jeremiah Gideon Smith.'

He said nothing.

'Amazingly, I escape. Then, amazingly, I escape again, in hospital. Amazingly, because I am at the time a useless fucking drunk with an amazing lack of motor functions, brainpower, ability or will to defend myself. Yet Smith, who has supposedly sworn absolute and utter enmity over an article I once wrote, fails.'

'Amazing.'

'So I sober up, a bit jangly, taking a few happy pills, but sober. Hernia, whom I believe you know, possibly under the name Holdsworth, or prick, is helping me out, looking after me. Then this couple turn up, from America, wanting me to find their supposed son, one Roger Thiebault, who vanished two years ago from Aberdeen. Again it was my story, and a local dickhead policeman, and maybe the fact that I am the only fucking private detective in the Highlands and Islands Yellow fucking Pages. They give me loads of money, some shit about an e-mail which has turned up connecting Roger to a trawler very similar to the one anchored just over there, and I head for the last known sighting of the guy, only to be subjected to yet another amazingly poor attempt at, ostensibly, terminating my hide.'

'So?'

'So. I turn up at your house, shag the convenient Rosie, woo-arr, fun fun fun, head to Ullapool, pointed in which direction by you, where Smith turns up, takes me aboard a klondiker . . .'

Victor stifled a yawn.

I sighed. 'Yeah, you're right. Tedious. Anyway, here's my point. And for fuck's sake, I'm so brainless, so fucked, I didn't see it, maybe didn't allow myself to see it until now. You set this up. All of it. All of the tedious crap I've been through. Therapy, maybe. Big brother trying to bring me back from the abyss of addiction. That's the bullshit line you're coming out with now. But then . . . I'm thinking, no . . .'

'Ah well, I've already told you that Smith sort of . . . lost it. I don't think anyone expected you to become quite such a . . . hardass so quickly. What happened on Loch Broom was, frankly, a mistake. Though I have to admit that the demise of the so-called Thiebaults was not inconvenient. Rosie, though . . .' He shook his head. 'Has her own agenda.'

But I hardly heard him. 'You never gave the impression of caring about anything in the past. What is it? Guilt coming home to roost? Age? Anyway, I can see how you set up all of it, but then there's the drugs. Hernia, Mr Whizz – which came first, you or the club? All this shite in Sneck, kids dying. Is that you? Is it me, for fuck's sake? What have you got me into? And maybe even the delightful Rosie with her own fucking . . . agenda. This place, the *Chuleta de Cordero*, bobbing about there, pleased as fucking punch to see me. A disappearing boy called Roger Thiebault, and here he is, hale and hearty, hanging out quite the thing, posing on a Yamaha RD400. I'd put my money on cocaine smuggling, if it wasn't such a cliché. Still, it's an expensive one, and setting me up as a kind of fall-guy, drunken old Zander, yeah. I could go with that. But no.' I was lost. What did I know? What was going on? Fuck it, I was desperate for a drink. Antabuse ya bass.

'You're just rambling,' said Victor. 'And it's because you're a stupid dick, drunk or sober.' He raised the rifle. Another seal, or the same one, had bobbed up about ten feet away. His whiskers glinted.

Inside my pocket, I had a finger on the oven cleaner's aerosol valve, and with an automaton accuracy, I crouched down, pulled out the tin of Tufkleen, and let loose a blast straight at Victor's eyes. The effect was immensely satisfying. He screamed, and dropped the rifle, which promptly went off, discharging itself harmlessly into the thrashing mass of salmon. Something pink and silver floated to the surface in bits. The other fish were already gathering greedily around it. Sushi to sushi, salmon to salmon.

'Wipe them with seawater, you prick, and you'll be all right. Probably. Go on, wipe it out. It's only caustic fucking soda in some kind of gel. Do it quickly. Go on!'

He knelt down and began scooping water onto his burnt face. I read the warning message on the tin. *Caustic soda. If in contact with skin wash with water. Seek medical advice.* The advice would have to wait.

'You might have blurry vision for a week or two, but all being well it shouldn't be permanent. Ish. Feeling better?'

He dipped his head towards the sea like some salt-water worshipper. 'You . . . fuck . . .' he said hoarsely. 'This was all for you, just to get you here, get you involved, clean up your shitty little life. Mum and Dad don't know, but I know they were hoping . . . Fuck. You're pissed off about Smith. None of this was meant to be about killing you. It was all just . . . you were fucked up. Big time. I was just trying to help. Get you interested in life. And of course, there were the Thiebaults. Okay, I admit you were . . . useful. In drawing them out.'

'Setting them up, more like.'

'Ah well. Think of it as . . . patriotism.' He laughed, choking, tears running down his face. It wasn't emotion. It was oven cleaner. I could feel nothing but constricting anger, building in me like wind from a particularly noxious curry.

'You prick, Victor. This was always about you, not me. Your power, your fraternal fucking authority. You were going to sort me out, salvage me. And use me. It was always that way, Victor. Revenge for all that favouritism, so called. You've always enjoyed making me feel pain. Always wanted some kind of stupid revenge, but for what? What the fuck was it? Nothing I could do anything about. Favouritism? Christ. Grow up.'

'You were so stupid . . . and so weak. Always so weak and soft and stupid, and yet they loved you. I've done my best to replace you, and maybe I'm on my way there, but even then I had to be you, become you, to do it. And it's not just them. Oh no. Ruth, picked up and shunted aside, Ruth who . . . who never bothered about me for a minute. Lucy, thrown aside and then all that fucking evil with her and her boyfriend . . . yet I bet the stupid cow still loves you.'

'I don't . . .'

'And then even fucking Rosie. I mean, she's harder than flint, that woman . . . But there she blows, all starry-fucking-eyed over little Zand. She did try to stop you coming up here. Thought I'd lost it completely, and I think the whole Ullapool business threw her and her superiors somewhat. The thing is, Zand, we're all shit. We all have to wallow in it, and then climb out, or we never become strong. I just helped you along the way. And now you are strong. Or stronger. Strong enough for me to underestimate you.' He shook his head, sending a shower of glittering salt tears into the light-dappled air. 'And besides, as I said, you were handy. Okay, you were a kind of Judas goat for the so-called Thiebaults –'

'A what?'

'Oh, fuck it, surely you guessed that? Then that psychopath Smith gets carried away in Ullapool with them and nearly with you. Of course, he wasn't listening to me, but by that time I knew you were at last, after all these fucking years, slightly dangerous. Put the two of you together and the balloon really goes up, doesn't it? Or the ship goes down.' He laughed, jerked his head in sudden agony. 'Who'd've thought it, eh, Zander boy? You surprised me. And now here you are, armed and dangerous with a can of oven cleaner.'

'Your idea, Victor.'

He turned his unseeing eyes towards me. 'What?'

'Your bright notion, that. Don't you remember taking a tin of Tufkleen to school, threatening Old Samuelson with it, because he confiscated your Uriah Heep album? I took it out of your bag before you could do any harm. Threw it in the voe.'

'Crap. That's fucking crap, Zander. If I'd wanted to sort out Samuelson, the prick, I would have.' He shook his head, driving away the past he didn't want to remember. 'Anyway, the thing is, you know now. You fucking ken noo. And here you are and anyway you'll know that Mum and Dad love me now, *me*. Because of what I've done. What I've become. And they'll love you, too. And we'll all live happily ever after.'

Jesus Christ.

I reached for his hand, held it gently, stroked it, said nothing. His eyes were full of tears.

'I'll say this, though.' His voice was low, whispering amid the lapping waves. 'That Celia's a good shag when she's conscious. But when she's truly out of it, she takes it up the arse, and that's really fucking good. That's what I really like. And she does, too.' His streaming eyes, blind eyes, met mine. 'All working together for the good of wee Zander, peerie Zand, all his pals, his lovers. It's good to have a personal knowledge of those who do work for you, I always say. Intimate . . . I mean, Hernia's always been more than just a pal to me. An employee, you might say. It's always handy to have a doctor in the, so to speak, house.'

I held his hand tighter, squeezed, then moved my grip to his wrist, held it tight against the railing, took out the Guardian and shot him through the palm. It didn't feel good. Or bad. It felt right, though. Celia. Hernia. How many others? He fell down onto the wooden walkway, groaning. There was a lot of blood. It would bruise, swell, ache too, I knew, for a long time. But it would heal eventually. I kicked him in the balls for good measure, but I don't think I made much contact. My legs were stiff with all the standing about.

'Thanks,' I said, 'for everything. I love you too.'

I left him there, and took the boat back to the pier. A new Isuzu four-wheel-drive had pulled up, immaculate in metallic red and mud, and as I came up to the landing ladder, I could see Rosie, slim and perfectly attired in jeans and a Berghaus top which was a considerable improvement over the Barbour with the ashtray pockets, but not over the business suit I'd last seen her wearing on the quayside at Aberdeen. Not in that class.

She caught the rope I threw, pulled me in. But then she was good at that.

I scrambled ashore, looking around for substantial, threatening company. But there was only the ever-smiling Roger, arms folded, eyes wide and friendly. He didn't look in the least like his dad. No hole in the middle of the head, going slightly blue at the edges.

'What have you done to him?' Rosie was calm, almost indifferent. 'I can see something moving out there. He's not dead, is he?'

'No,' I shook my head, 'just seeing things my way for a change, courtesy of some oven cleaner in the eyes and a sore hand. Payback for all the misery he made me suffer when we were kids. And more recently. The funny thing is, he thinks I was the one who did him down . . .' I laughed. I was determined not to see his point. 'Just deserts, at least between me and him. As for justice in the wider sense – and the bigger picture –'

'Oh, you should forget about that. There is no justice. And the picture is better seen . . . in just the visible details.'

'Spoken like a true servant of the Crown.'

She gazed at me, unblinkingly.

'Did you get your uncles' stuff sold, by the way?'

She blinked, shook her head slightly. 'Uncles? Oh you mean . . .'

'Or was that just another asset your, ah, company picked up, courtesy of Victor's little surveillance set-up? Did you get Victor to run some sort of blackmail operation on the so-called Nuncs? The Nunky-wunkies? What sort of corporate coercion do you engage in, anyway? What's your speciality?'

'I don't know what you mean.'

'Yes, you fucking do. What is it, your firm? MI5? The new post-glasnost, security service, scrabbling around trying to find some sort of role, one which makes money? Even if it's slightly off-colour? Or maybe your mob is one of those amorphous lumps of slippery, clever human poison which no one acknowledges still exist? Reporting directly to some Whitehall mandarin. Oh, forgive me. I forgot things like that have been got rid of under the auspices of our thoroughly open fucking teeth-and-smiles British democracy.'

But all she did was look slightly over my shoulder, towards the figure out on the salmon cage, as if receiving signals from Victor telepathically. Her gaze swivelled onto me, and she gestured with her head. 'Come with me.'

We walked into the big white shed, followed by the smiling Roger, ever jolly. Inside, the apparatus of the hatchery – a series of small tanks, a lot smaller than you'd expect – looked unused. The tanks were dry. Not the right time of year.

She turned to look at me. 'You're right – they weren't my uncles. But they were both . . . assets. And for some twisted reason, they left all their assets to the . . . to my company. Damned awkward, actually. But, in a limited way, fun going through their, ah, stuff.' She gestured to the lurking Roger. 'You know who he is?'

'Well. Let me guess. How about Roger Thiebault, citizen of the United States of America, last seen in the flesh walking out of an Aberdeen B&B two years ago?'

'Correct. Roger Thiebault, or The Chef as he was known in the States, or particularly on the Internet, where he was prone to publish his recipes for a whole series of brilliant new designer drugs, all mixed and matched with arcane medicines like tiger claw and rhino horn. Potent mix, eh? High-tech meets traditional myth, in powdered form. Spent a lot of time analysing stuff like elephant tusk powder to see exactly what's in it, what makes it do what the Chinese herbalists say it does. If it does. Obsessive. Bit weird. In fact, bonkers. Twenty-one years old, a research student at the University of Southern Louisiana, possibly the most brilliant chemist anyone there had ever seen. But an artist, with intuition, effortless memory and number-crunching ability. All that and a propensity for strangeness and mischief, probably because he was bored. It was the Internet which brought him to Victor's attention.'

'Of course it was. What did he do? Press *Search drugs, designer?*'

'Something like that. Anyway, Victor had money sloshing around, a lot, and he had to do something with it, he thought. Maybe he was bored, too. And this is the result.' She opened a steel door in a partition wall, and we entered a laboratory of academic status, last word, state-of-the-art stuff, where even the pipettes looked as if they'd been designed by Philippe Starck, and the Bunsen burners were piezo-electrically ignited. 'Your brother repays an eye being kept on him. And he saw the benefits of funding and, well, protection from people in our . . . position. Legitimacy. Semi. Ish.'

'Hey, you guys.' Roger still smiled, and looked like a man who was extremely happy in his work. What had he found here that had taken him from the cut and thrust and competition of an American university? Why was Shetland not boring? He had a kind of strange aura about him, a kind of glow. 'Don't touch anything. You could end up eight miles high and never ever wanna come down.'

'So, Roger. Your mum and dad said hello, by the way.' The smile never wavered; perhaps grew wider. I waited a moment, and then said: 'What are you making then? Ecstasy?' Always with a finger on the pulse of youth culture, me.

'Ecstasy? MDMA?' He crinkled his forehead into a pitying smile. 'Where have you been, man?' he said. And, shaking his head, he turned away.

'Ecstasy is old hat, Zander,' said Rosie quietly, 'as is Ketamine, all that dancehall shit. The new stuff makes them look like Junior Disprin. Roger . . . has a product which he thinks the user will eventually be able to control. The first absolutely user-friendly drug. It does what you tell it to. Except it doesn't, yet. Hence our little problem.'

'What do you mean?'

'What I say. It does what you tell it. You take it, and it reacts to your emotional and mental, call it spiritual if you want to, needs at that time. And to context. You can think yourself sober, say, or speeding if you need that, or you can have religious hallucinations . . . call them reality if you want. It could give religions something serious to chew on. Most of all, it taps into memory. You can remember everything. Like the salmon going back to its spawning ground, homing in . . .'

'It's seriously cool,' interjected Roger, that slight hazy glow in his eyes, his head, his hair. 'I mean, the bodymind – I don't, uh, separate the two, if you understand that – has the capacity to do loads of goodies for itself; like under meditation, you get these chemical releases into the bloodstream. And then there's the salmon, man, the fucking salmon . . . The Japanese, that sushi thing? I found this traditional recipe in Tokyo for a medicine to improve the memory and it's fucking powdered salmon brains, man. Like . . . what! Fuckin' brilliant! So a bit of messing around, a bit of analysis, and we're looking at not very convincing scientific proof of effectiveness. Like fuck all, actually, but, still, the concept!'

I turned to Rosie. 'What's this guy been taking?'

'Oh, everything,' she replied. 'I think that's the point.'

Roger was still vibing along. 'Yeah, so we're looking at what we can do to actually deliver the goods . . . You know about LSD?'

I nodded. He didn't seem to notice.

'Albert Hoffman, 1943, Switzerland, puts 250 millionths of a gramme in a glass of water and drinks it. Feels sorta weird, spacy. Cycles home, the stupid jerk, and spends twelve hours in domestic hell brought to jungle life. Fan-fucking-tastic! So anyway, I think, let's look at the natural equivalent, right? What grows like crazy up here, that all-night light this time of year? Hey, you should know!'

My mind was blank. Then I remembered the stooped figures in the morning mist on the way out here. 'Mushrooms.'

'Fuckin' A, man. Psilocybin mushrooms. Not far to look for psycho-active components there. So I already got some cannabinols isolated, controllable, mood-swing alteration like with good dope. Bang, in with some Norwegian powdered salmon brains for luck, maybe it works, whatever − and off we go. You got the perfect delivery vehicle for, ah, total mood enhancement and control.'

'Except not quite,' said Rosie. 'Tune didn't quite play as well as we hoped it would. That's what they started calling it on the streets, you know. Tune. Great name. Take a marketing department years to come up with a name like that.'

'What was it?' My head felt like a mushroom in the process of being digested by a sheep. 'What did the damage in Inverness? Overdoses?'

'No, man, no, that's not what we were lookin' for.' Roger was almost dancing. 'What would be the fucking point? Controllability was what we wanted. The ability to fuckin' remember. Enough is enough, you can make yourself feel how you want to feel. Less is more. What happened is we got some contamination. And I blame myself, I do. Honestly. Stupid. Looking for the groove, like with that tiger claw shit. The salmon powder was a mistake.'

I gaped. 'Are you telling me that those kids in Sneck died because they were allergic to fish?'

Rosie was smiling slightly. 'Not all of them died, Zander. Or not from Tune. Do you know what organo-phosphates are?'

Funnily enough, I did, from constant stories years ago about anti-fouling paint on yachts. And salmon farms. 'Chemical compounds invented by the Germans in World War One as nerve gas. Later used as anti-fouling paint on boats, banned for health reasons. It kills everything on the seabed if it gets spilt. But . . . still used by salmon farmers.'

'Common sea louse,' said Roger helpfully. 'Fucks the bastards up good. Fucked up my fucking salmon powder. Fucking Norwegians. Should have used these salmon here, then everything would have been fine. Purest water in the world.'

'Anyway,' said Rosie, 'the salmon thing was just a conceit of Roger's, a little . . . eccentricity. The bottom line is that we have a small manufacturing plant through that door.' She signalled. 'The Galicians are the biggest drug dealers in Europe. Ever been there? The coastline makes the west of Scotland look like Holland. Ragged and with a smuggling tradition that makes the whole place clam up tight at the approach of anything resembling authority. Victor's been getting them to bring in raw materials, like cannabis resin, basically, and whatever mushrooms we can't get locally. Then shipping out the finished product via the *Chuleta de Cordero* there. And before you came along there was the *Margarita*, too. Which of course handily brought young Roger here too. All he had to do was get to Aberdeen. Victor had some good Galicians. Controllable, civilised ones – or he did have until you so spectacularly fucked everything up off Ullapool. However you did it. If you did, and it wasn't some sort of freak accident. He seriously didn't think you had it in you. I warned him that he might be underestimating your . . . capabilities. But blood is thicker than sex, isn't it? It was all pretty personal from there on in.'

'What about Roger's parents? Meljo and Gareth Thiebault, deceased, severely, and not my fault, either.'

She smiled again. Roger had never stopped. 'Now that was clever. You're the only private detective registered in the Highlands, in Yellow Pages and everything, known to the police . . . plus you did the story on Roger back in Aberdeen. Those two suckers stumble in, looking for the poor missing boy, and all Victor has to do is wait until they show up in your vicinity, whet your appetite with some minor assaults, and watch from afar as you fucked yourself up. And them. Meanwhile, he gets Jeremiah Gideon Smith, or the late Jeremiah Gideon Smith, and his Galicians to remove the gruesome twosome from his somewhat complex equation.

'Fuck me! They were his parents! Roger, don't you fucking care?' But as I said it, I wondered how much I felt for my own parents; unknowing, up in the neat house above us, unaware that one son had returned and another was lying partially blinded out on the salmon cages, a bullet through his hand.

Roger shook his head. 'Don't look at me, man, I'm your original freaked-out orphan, with second-generation punk-hippy parents who just fucked off and left me in a box outside an Oregon police station. I never traced them and I don't wanna.'

'The people you know as the Thiebaults were working for a Swiss drug company called Guralnick Enterprises, SA,' said Rosie. 'Very big in the States. One of the biggest anywhere. They had Roger here under some sort of informal contract, they thought, doing moonlight stuff for them, along similar lines to this, actually, and not very legally. Built him a private lab, gave him a Porsche, everything. But when he got Victor's message on the net he skipped out, leaving them in the lurch. Just like that.'

'What the fuck did Victor say?' What on earth could Shetland have that drug-company millions could not provide? Why did a Yamaha RD400 outweigh a Porsche?

Roger had gone solemn. He folded his arms again. An insecure gesture. 'Four words, which is good on e-mail. Short and to the point.'

'Okay, so why don't you follow his example?'

'Blank cheque. Good birdwatching.'

'Birdwatching?' Surely the boy wasn't a twitcher? Yes, that level of obsessiveness would explain the move. They were all fucking mad.

'Yeah,' Roger's eyes danced like whirling skuas, 'this is one of the premier sites in the world for sea birds and migrants. *Birds.* Christ, man, didn't you used to live here? Victor told me so much about you. He really loves you, man.'

'And the Thiebaults, or whoever they were?'

'Victor can be quite ruthless when necessary. He used you to flush them out, and then . . . well. Then everything went pear-shaped in Ullapool.'

I looked around for a telephone. 'Enough,' I said. 'It's time for the police to have a look at this. I'm all through with detecting.'

Rosie put her hand on mine. 'I don't think so.'

I looked into her calm eyes, the certainty in them.

'I think you'll find that if any officers of the law turn up here, they will bow to the authority vested in me by my . . . company. You see Victor is, and in a sense always has been, working for us here. The Galicians' distribution network is limited, basically, to one subculture in about five cutting-edge clubs on the Ibiza dance scene at the moment, and we've got medical monitoring in place to see what . . . the outcome might be. But Victor could feed it out in a controlled and relatively scientific fashion nearer home. He's really been conducting a kind of experiment with Roger's new . . . substance . . . with a little help.'

'I like the name Tune,' said Roger dreamily. 'Turn on, tune in, drop in or out anywhere you want, as much as you want.'

'Yes, well,' Rosie was looking a tad twitchy. I guessed she fancied a cigarette, and knew that a dirty drug like tobacco would not be welcome in this pristine laboratory situation. 'An experiment to see what sort of effects we can expect. Whether any psychosis, or dependence or . . . anything else evolves. Because something like this could be useful in all kinds of areas. For treating depression. For . . .

'. . . Interrogation. Spying. Remembering things.'

A pause.

'Yes, maybe. And that's only scratching the surface.'

I felt suddenly sick. 'But how can you expect to get away with all this . . . all the deaths in Ullapool . . . all this stuff? You might be able to patch Victor up and get the Gilbert Bain Hospital not to blab to the *Shetland Times*, but –'

'Show him the freezer, Roger.'

Grinning, Roger got up and slid open a panel in the far wall of the lab. The inside was opaque with fog. At last it cleared and I could see boxes of what purported at any rate to be fish, stacked up neatly. And something lying on the floor, glitteringly white, like a fairytale princess, or prince. I stepped closer. It was Hernia.

'Our medical advisor,' said Roger.

'And the Inverness end for Victor's operation,' added Rosie, 'along with Mr Whizz, which belongs to Victor, of course. You probably guessed that. Overall, all that was involved was a small experimental release of, umm . . . Tune, there as well on the club scene. Small, compact, conservative. Controllable. Interesting to see the results.'

I sat down on a plastic chair as Roger slammed the sliding freezer door shut.

'I'm afraid Dr Holdsworth grew a trifle . . . emotional about the whole thing, and about you, Zander. An easy thing to do. You are quite . . . lovable, despite yourself. It was upsetting for Victor because he cared about . . . felt so strongly about you, too. Dr Holdsworth arrived here last night. I believe he got a plane from Inverness. I didn't arrive until this morning, or I might have been able to persuade Victor not to . . .'

I put my head in my hands. My new ruthlessness was failing to cope. 'Is there no fucking way I can stop this?'

'No fucking way,' said Roger. 'I mean, we are the future, man. Bound to be a few hiccups on the way, but what's the alternative? Drugs have been shit for so long – impure, uncontrolled, illegal. Gotta move to the new chemical culture, babe. I mean, alcohol is the only legal high, right?'

'Right,' I agreed, wearily.

'Well, what shit that is. Destroys the liver, shrinks the brain, fucks up the heart, the muscles . . . everything. Okay, a few mistakes, maybe, but in the future, I could give you the best high you ever thought possible, man, again and again, controlled by you. Add some tiger claw and salmon powder, and who knows? Eternal fucking life!' Roger laughed.

He was still laughing when I pulled out the Guardian and shot him through the head. That seemed to quieten him down a bit.

Out of a pocket in her breatheable weatherproof top, Rosie pulled a squat automatic pistol, much bigger than the Guardian, much more serious-looking. The guns faced each other, phallically. Hers was much bigger than mine. 'It was quite a good shag,' she said.

'Three, actually.'

'And despite . . . all this, it is in no way my remit to kill you, Zander.'

'Why not? Your jerk-off pal at Aberdeen was going to do something like that, to stop me getting on the *St Sunniva*.'

She smiled tightly. 'You have an overactive imagination. He was merely trying to persuade you of our point of view. The thing is, what can we do?' She sighed. 'You're hardly going to be tried in public for the death of the long-disappeared Roger Thiebault. It would all be too, too tedious and awkward for my . . . for us. What can you do? The police will not intervene, I'm afraid. Roger may not be around, but much of his thinking and his formulae are stored safely on computer disks throughout the country, not just here. You can go to the press with scare stories about a new drug, but that won't stop youngsters taking it. In fact, it might make the experiment bigger; more easily controlled. More effective surveillance of participants, and the after-effects. And would you succeed in exposing, manage to convince some newspaper editor, about all this?' She swept her gun arm around the shed, the pier, the salmon cages, my parents' house. Vallataing. Home. 'You could have killed Victor out there, Zander. Instead you destroyed his main asset. And there's the question of your parents.'

I put the Guardian away. Rosie, after some hesitation, shoved her automatic in a pocket, and we both walked outside. On the salmon cages I could see Victor trying to wave, holding one arm with the other. I looked up at my parents' house. Peat smoke wisped from the chimney. Nothing was moving there. Nothing at all.

★ Twenty

As I drove up the hill and away, I watched Rosie start the big Honda outboard and take the boat out slowly towards Victor, who was standing, hunched, one hand under the other armpit, the classic wounded wee boy.

I thought of Hernia, stretched out stiff and frost-dappled, and wondered what Rosie would do with him, and with Roger. There was an RAF base at Saxa Vord on the island of Unst, some thirty miles or so away. It was, supposedly, a top-secret surveillance station, one of the few left in the aftermath of the Cold War, and equipped with a small selection of spooks and SAS thugs. I imagined a helicopter from there would be making its way to Vallataing in the near future.

I searched myself for some sorrow, some emotion. Some regret. Hernia had led me out of one morass, when he was, for his own reasons – money, or a desire to impress Victor, and I knew all about that particular impulse – leading others into one which held terrible, unknown dangers. But people choose. That's the thing about addictions. At some point you decide to take that step towards dependence, be it booze, fags, crack cocaine or the alleged music of Michael Bolton. Maybe Hernia had simply been widening the range of choices available. Paid the price for being a pioneer of chemical capitalism.

He had been my friend. *Had been*. I shrugged the memory away. Maybe there was something wrong with me. Perhaps it would all catch up with me. But Ullapool hadn't. Not yet. Lucy hadn't. Victor . . . well. Maybe I'd caught up with him at last.

Up at the croft house, I saw two figures, tiny, unidentifiable unless you knew their movements, their frailties, move out into the garden. In the back of the car was the box of chocolates and the flowers I'd bought earlier. I picked them up, opened the door and threw them off the road, into a peat bog. They floated in the black sludgy water. The Guardian was out there in the voe. Rosie had made it clear that no one would be bothering to look for it, or the fingerprints on the grip. I took the oven cleaner can and threw it after the flowers and chocolates. Domesticity lay there, abandoned. Victor and I had cut peats here, so long ago.

He had once hit me with a tuskar, the sharp spade-cum-knife used to slide the muddy turf bricks out of the earth. It had just been a slip of the hand, he'd told Mum and Dad. An accident. He was punished for that. I couldn't remember how. Had I provoked him? Did it matter, after all this time? I wondered if he'd be able to play the accordion again, what with a hole in his hand. Probably.

I looked at my watch. There was an Inverness plane out of Sumburgh in an hour and a half. If I hurried, I could make it. I wondered if Rosie and her not-so-mysterious people would really let me live. It didn't really matter. But, well, one must make an effort, mustn't one?

The ATP – *Advanced Turbo Prop, Another Terrible Plane, Arrgh! Technical Problems*, call it what you will – was full, crammed with oil suits and twitchers heading south with binoculars strapped to their chests, desperate for one last addition to the life-lists. I got the last seat, an on-aisle emergency exit one, thank God. Quick escape and more leg room. I prepared for terror, but funnily enough I had too much else on my mind to worry about the flight much. A Loudon Wainwright song came into my head: *I'm not afraid of flying . . . I'm just afraid of crashing . . . I'm just afraid of burning . . .*

After the swift lurch airborne, the stewardess began her frenetic attempt to issue free alcohol to everyone in lieu of service or pleasantries. 'Now, sir,' she said, grinning that stretchy stewardess smile. Her make-up creaked and crinkled under the strain. 'What can I get you?'

I thought for a moment. I thought of Jim Baxter, his new liver screaming for alcohol, facing just this kind of temptation. How the old reprobate had always said no, had kept that liver pristine. I felt vaguely hungry. Were there black puddings on board? Chips? It seemed unlikely. 'Two of those wee bottles of whisky and a can of lager,' I told her, feeling a great sense of relief and relaxation spread through my body, from the tips of my toes to what was left of my hair. Suddenly, life seemed worth . . . living again. 'And a dark rum for after. In case I get nervous.'

The family had been shepherded onto the apron at RAF Kinloss, huddling together against the sudden squall which had come hurtling in from the Moray Firth, heading towards the small passenger jet, no bigger than one of the fighters standing near by in sinister, malevolent grey.

The jet had civil markings and was flown by men uneasily out of uniform. But the two women who accompanied them were clearly military in origin. One, the nurse, wore a plain white overall, but it seemed as if Karen hardly needed any real medical help now. She could walk unaided. It was just that she didn't speak, seemed always to be elsewhere, remote. As if she was remembering something endlessly fascinating, something she felt no need to share with anyone else. She seemed happy, anyway. Often she would smile, even laugh silently, at some secret joke. And she knew them, knew what was happening around her. Knew when and how to eat, drink, walk, shit, urinate. It just seemed as if her inner world was much, much more interesting. And pleasant. Sometimes he felt a kind of jealousy.

It had been made plain to him, by the woman and the two older, more clearly establishment men who had visited them at the military hospital in nearby RAF Lossiemouth, that a trip 'away' would be a good idea. Wherever 'away' was. That hadn't been clear at first. Intensive medical supervision for Karen was needed, and they had a location in mind, where, with help from some American specialists, proper physiological, neurological and psychological treatments could be administered. And, for various reasons involving national security, it would be valuable if this could be done away from the prying eyes of the press, or even the curious concern of neighbours. Out of the country, in fact. A day or two later, one of them had returned. There was an American air force base, it seemed, in Spain. To be exact, in Galicia.

It had seemed an unlikely story, the one he had been told. About a drug developed in strict secrecy for purely military purposes, purposes he should not know, for his own good, but which related to soldiers' ability to withstand interrogation and torture. How could a formula be stolen and then adapted for the illegal street market? How could that be allowed to happen? It seemed so . . . careless. And what had it done to his daughter?

And yet he was, technically, a government servant. It had been pointed out to him, when he made some irritated, emotional noises, that he was in fact a signatory of the Official Secrets Act in his role as a development agency head, had been necessarily party to military plans for the run-down of bases such as Kinloss. There was an irony there, he thought, flying out from an airfield soon to be shut down. And no one here, not the squaddies anyway, had been told. Maybe he should shout it out just before getting on the plane.

His wife had not wanted to come, but he had persuaded her they should both go, for the sake of Karen. Thank God she was relatively sober for once. Maybe this would save what was left between them, if he could keep her away from cheap Spanish plonk. That was ironic, too. Everything was.

He said nothing as he ducked his head to enter the aircraft. No one was there who could possibly care, anyway. Karen was still smiling as they strapped her into the luxurious seat opposite his own. His wife sat next to him. The door was shut and clamped behind them, and the engines began to whine, building up to a muted roar. Then, suddenly they were cut.

One of the pilots came into the cabin and smiled apologetically. His haircut gave away his military background, along with razor-sharp ironing of the short-sleeved shirt. 'Sorry about the delay,' he said, in a clipped, Home-Countified Scottish accent. 'Bit of a diversion, it seems. Civil flight from Shetland, some sort of engine trouble, so they're bringing her in here. Have to wait for it to land, then we're off. Just, ah, hold your horses.'

And Karen kept on smiling.

The plane, one of the British Regional Airways turboprops that were always breaking down, landed safely. He could see it taxiing towards them, and as it stopped, so did the rain. A group of four men in black boilersuits without any visible insignia marched to the foot of the steps leading up the forward door, just as a man fell down them. He appeared to be extremely drunk. Guttered. Blootered. Steamboats. Three sheets to the proverbial wind. The four uniformed men picked him up, apparently unhurt, and he was dragged, stumbling, towards a waiting Range Rover. Only once he had been taken away were the other passengers allowed off.

Their own engines started up once more. Briefly, he wondered who the poor drunk was, and what they would do with him. Then he put the thought from his mind. He had troubles enough of his own. What did one drunk, more or less, matter? He wondered if there was any in-flight booze on board, and if he could keep his wife away from it. And maybe sneak a snifter himself. He could have murdered a large Highland Park.